M000113340

A MAGIC FIERCE & BRIGHT

HEMANT NAYAK

SIMON & SCHUSTER BFYR

NEW YORK LONDON TORONTO SYDNEY NEW DELHI

An imprint of Simon & Schuster Children's Publishing Division
1230 Avenue of the Americas, New York, New York 10020

SIMON & SCHUSTER BOOKS FOR YOUNG READERS
and related marks are trademarks of Simon & Schuster, LLC.
Simon & Schuster: Celebrating 100 Years of Publishing in 2024
For information about special discounts for bulk purchases, please contact Simon & Schuster
Special Sales at 1-866-506-1949 or business@simonandschuster.com.
The Simon & Schuster Speakers Bureau can bring authors to your live event. For more
information or to book an event, contact the Simon & Schuster Speakers Bureau at
1-866-248-3049 or visit our website at www.simonspeakers.com.
Interior design by Hilary Zarycky
The text for this book was set in Weiss.
Manufactured in the United States of America
First Edition
2 4 6 8 10 9 7 5 3 1

Library of Congress Cataloging-in-Publication Data
Names: Nayak, Hemant, author.
Title: A magic fierce and bright / Hemant Nayak.
Description: First edition. | New York : Simon & Schuster Books for Young Readers, 2024. |
Audience: Ages 12 up. | Audience: Grades 7–9. | Summary: In a South Indian jungle, Adya, who
possesses the rare and coveted ability to wake electric machines, reluctantly teams up with a
charming thief in a quest to rescue her lost sister.
Identifiers: LCCN 2023031676 (print) | LCCN 2023031677 (ebook) |
ISBN 9781665921817 (hardcover) | ISBN 9781665921831 (ebook)
Subjects: CYAC: Fantasy. | Ability—Fiction. | Magic—Fiction. | Sisters—Fiction. |
India—Fiction. | LCGFT: Fantasy fiction. | Novels.
Classification: LCC PZ7.1.N3745 Mag 2024 (print) | LCC PZ7.1.N3745 (ebook) |
DDC [Fic]—dc23
LC record available at https://lccn.loc.gov/2023031676
LC ebook record available at https://lccn.loc.gov/2023031677

For the hunter in the stacks, the keen-eyed seeker sifting through stories, searching, listening, hoping for a tale to lift you away to places you've been only in your dreams and sorely wish to travel to again. I pledge the solemn promise to take you there once again by way of the old roads. . . .

PROLOGUE

B EFORE THE ASTEROIDS, THOSE WHO BELIEVED IN MAGIC were considered fools. Then a meteor storm pummeled Earth, and the unthinkable happened—the electricity that modern life depended on disappeared. Planes crashed into buildings, cars skidded off roads, watches stopped dead. But energy can never be lost, only transformed. The impact craters left behind were filled with a dark, swirling force—the sources of Earth's newfound magic. People named them infinity wells.

In England, the queen understood at once that whoever controlled this new resource controlled the future. She attacked France while it was in disarray, seizing both its wells, and emerged as the most powerful ruler in Europe. When British wizards developed a spell to link the magic of the craters, her ambitions grew. Not satisfied with merely the heads of Europe bowing to her, she sent armies to India to reclaim England's imperial glory, plunging the country into war.

For thirty years, the queen's armies have torn across India, sweeping away resistance on every front—except one. Now only one man stands between India's last infinity well and a return to total British domination: the maharaja of Mysore, protector of the Flame of the South.

But this story is about Adya.

SOUTHERN INDIA,
THE MIDST OF THE
JUNGLE, FOUR
HUNDRED YEARS IN
THE FUTURE

CHAPTER ONE

A
T FIVE A.M. ON AN AUGUST DAY WHEN THE MONSOON
rain threatened to fill her boots, Adya Sachdev
closed her favorite engine repair manual, forced herself through a set of push-ups, and prepared to face
her nemesis.

She didn't rush. The jungle was no place to travel before
sunrise if you hoped to stay alive. In the predawn darkness,
Adya thrust her head beneath one of the tiny waterfalls tumbling from cracks in the ceiling, letting the cool water pour
over her long hair and run down her back. Then, fully awake,
she pulled on work pants, threw a shirt over her head, and took
up a broom.

As she swept, she hummed a wordless tune that echoed
amidst the gloom and shadows, disturbing a family of bats
that swirled up from the depths of the tunnel. Sunlight seldom
reached this far into the twisted mine shaft Adya called home,
but lack of light was never a problem. Over the centuries since
magic had emerged, her people's eyes had grown accustomed
to darkness.

Ignoring the bats, she pushed the tangles of electrical wires
to one side and every stray bolt and washer to the other, quite
aware that she was being watched. From a shelf high above,
enormous amber eyes tracked her every movement.

Adya had no patience for this sort of thing. She pointed the broom at a shelf where her sister's orange cat perched, waiting for his chance to swat a screw down the tunnel. "Look, Useless, I don't want to lose any more parts, and you don't want to be turned into soft furry slippers, so don't even try it." She and the cat had already gone beyond pleasantries and peaceful negotiation.

The cat hissed in response. He did not appreciate being thwarted. Useless loved nothing more than to watch Adya's tools roll to the depths below. Her twin sister, Priya, had named him Fluffs, but Adya liked Useless better. This was sentimental resentment. Half a year ago, Priya had abandoned her and vanished into a wall of flame. Adya turned her back on Useless and continued sweeping. She could call the cat whatever she wanted now.

Having removed every sharp object from the floor, Adya wiped a shop towel across her forehead and slumped against the wreck of the autorickshaw she'd failed to repair. She sighed.

Despite her attempts at order, the ancient three-wheeled motor taxi had taken over—rusted machinery and yellow panels lay scattered everywhere. Two mattresses, a towering bookshelf, and three barrels full of liquor she'd gotten in a trade from some thief took up the remaining space. The shaft's walls were covered with old techno junk, bits of idols scavenged from crumbling temples, and cracked vinyl LPs. For two years, she and her twin sister had fought to shape this place into both home and workshop, but rocks and darkness can only be pushed so far. The lower depths still belonged to the bats.

Most anyone would think an abandoned tunnel in the

middle of the jungle a strange place for a girl to live alone. If Adya dwelled on it too long, she might think so too.

Instead, she counted her money.

Adya slid aside a loose rock in the wall and pulled out a small bag. She went through the coins twice, running her calculations for the hundredth time. Unfortunately, she needed a great deal more if she was never to worry about the crime lord Huda's vicious debt collectors ever again.

To make enough to pay Huda off, she would have to sell a fully functional rickshaw. And only one person held the key to her success. Adya pulled on her red leather jacket and picked up an old transistor radio she had to deliver on the way. She balanced her spear on her shoulder, inhaled the glorious smell of monsoon air and engine grease, and steeled herself to face her aunt.

Adya marched the thirty yards up to the shaft's opening, grabbing the handrail in the wall to pull herself up along the steepest bit, and found that Ganesha, the god of beginnings, was not entirely against her. Silver cables of light slid through the canopy, reflecting off piles of wet steel and rust. The clouds had soaked everything and moved on.

Before setting out, Adya dragged a sheet of metal covered in vines and branches across the mine shaft's entrance. You could never be too careful. She turned to find she was not alone. A black drongo, its long tail feathers shining in the morning light, stared down at her from the branch of an old mango tree. The bird tapped the trunk with its beak three times and studied her with eyes that sparkled with intelligence.

Adya took a piece of puri from her pocket and laid it on the ground. She whistled twice high, once low, mimicking the call of the black drongo. The small bird cocked its head and gave a single whistle of alarm back, though it refused to fly down to accept the offering. Her mother had always claimed that the black drongo was the most magical bird in India. That it never forgot a debt and would always watch over a friend. Adya hoped to tame this one, but the bird wasn't having it. On a hunch, Adya spun to find her sister's cat lurking behind her, swishing his tail. The sneaky animal was worse than useless. She slid the puri into her pocket, and the drongo took off, circling overhead.

Adya kicked through mounds of leaves and threaded the piles of machinery that made up the chaos of her front yard, clomping across the iron bridge over the river that rushed past the mine shaft.

She whispered while she ran a hand over the rail, *"Guru Brahma, Guru Vishnu, Guru Deva."* In response, the string of lights coiled about the iron shone bright, lighting the bridge like it was a holiday, fading back into darkness as she passed. In Adya's head, the voices of the lights were like a chorus of children urging her not to go, begging her to stay and play. In this age of sorcery, electricity was supposed to stay dead, but the business of fixing machines and awakening their souls was the magic that kept Adya fed.

She wound her way through the aerial roots of a giant banyan until she found the narrow path that led to her aunt's house.

The day began like all days, with the riotous squawks of

birds and the cries of troops of monkeys rushing through branches. The colors of the jungle were rain-drenched greens that blended into the ink of deep shadows where unpleasant things with teeth hid. Adya thumped the butt of her spear into the mud and swung herself over knee-deep puddles. She caught sight of the drongo overhead as it followed, likely still thinking of the food in Adya's pocket.

Leaves trembled high above, sending an agitated message ahead to announce her coming. Adya ran a hand along the trunk of one of the tallest sepals to reassure the old giant of who she was. She waited until she felt it recognize her. Her people, the Atavi, belonged here in the jungle, and the trees knew it. Adya thumped the butt of her spear again and moved on.

In the centuries since magic had taken hold, the forest had grown twisted, tall, and suspiciously aware of anyone walking beneath its branches. Magic had transformed the animals as well—some could vanish in an instant before reappearing at your shoulder. Others could see into your mind. A few, like the tigers, had grown enormous and far too intelligent.

And then there were the yaksha.

Adya checked the tip of her spear. It glowed with the faint white of bone—the forest spirits had retreated with the night. Unfortunately, the weapon would be of no help with her aunt, who Adya suspected might be half furious spirit herself. She hated the thought of having to ask the woman for anything, but if she was going to repair the rickshaw, she would need her little brother's help—and at fifteen, his life was under Aunt Sanjana's control.

Pausing at a spot where a tree had fallen across the path, Adya checked both sides of the trail before ducking left and slipping into the underbrush. Ten paces ahead, she stopped at a sawed-off stump few would have noticed, took off her pack, and knelt.

Adya eased off the top of the stump like the lid of a secret treasure chest before poking the hollow cavity with her spear. Always best to check for snakes. At the bottom, she found a canvas bag filled with coins that clinked satisfyingly. She counted them twice, then placed the small radio from her pack inside. Three attempts to awaken its soul had exhausted her, but the money made it all worthwhile. Before she could dwell on her success, a long shadow passed over her shoulder. A gangly scarecrow of a man with eyes set too deep in his skull stepped out from behind a tree.

Bulla Sholay leaned on his spear and studied Adya in a way that made her every muscle tense. He cleared his throat like an old motor and spat. "Didn't think you'd come, Mongoose," he wheezed. "Didn't want my money going stale."

Adya snatched up her weapon, trying her best to seem non-chalant. Bulla Sholay was old sinew, old bone, and old muscle, knit together with bad temper. There was nothing about him she could trust, and he was deadly with his spear. She didn't like her odds.

She kept her eyes on the man's hands, wondering how many years it had taken for him to achieve a permanent scowl. "Come on, Bulla. Why does this have to be difficult? The whole point is *not* to hang out together. Ever." Adya was shy to start with, but minimizing social interactions with people as unpleasant as Bulla was always a high priority. She eased back, maximizing the distance between them.

Bulla shuffled forward, joints cracking, and lifted the radio out of the stump. "Didn't think you'd deliver, Mongoose. Didn't think you'd still be in business." He ran his fingers over the small machine and grunted before dropping it into a bag. "Word is Huda's tired of you owing him. Tired of late payments. Things go bad when Huda tires of you."

Adya fought to keep her voice calm while her heart raced. "You can't believe every rumor you hear, Bulla. It's been great seeing you—I mean, it hasn't really, so I'm going to get going."

Bulla leaned toward her, and Adya got a whiff of that awful breath. "Word is the British are offering a high price for the last witch in the jungle. Would be a shame if you got snatched before you could spend my money."

"That *would* be tragic." This was rapidly going to hell. "But Huda doesn't need me. He's already got technomancers dumb enough to work for him. There's no way I'm the last. A few other freelancers are still fighting for parts."

Bulla shook his head and made a sad face. "You're uninformed. Huda burned two out last week. The British have the others."

Adya's hands started to sweat. It wasn't possible. She knew of three technomancers working on their own. Huda had four on his payroll just last month. Bulla Sholay was a born liar, trying to make her panic. She couldn't be the last, could she?

"Look, Bulla, you've got a first-class radio now. You'll be

able to listen to whatever lousy tunes you like. You won't be half the grouch you usually are. Why don't we call it a win-win?"

"Music goes better with cash." Bulla grinned, displaying disastrous teeth. "Didn't realize how much more I liked your sister than you. You're ruder than she was, disrespectful to your elders."

At the mention of her sister, Adya decided she'd had enough. She dropped the tip of her spear level with the man's chest. Her face burned. "That's 'is,' Bulla, not 'was,'" she said slowly. "My sister *is* nicer than me. Don't ever mention Priya in past tense."

He lunged for her.

She backpedaled while pointing a finger at Bulla's pack. *"Sarasvati namastubhyam."* The radio crackled with static at her words.

With a loud click of his knees Bulla froze.

"That machine has a temper," she warned. "Touch me, and it will remember down to the transistors. You'll be haunted by static day and night until you go mad."

The radio's voice buzzed in Adya's head, wondering what she meant; it was a thoughtful soul, used to playing the news from another age, hardly a device full of violence and rage.

She tried reassuring it. *Just something a little louder. . . No, you will not get in trouble for turning up your volume. . . . Yes, you can play classical later to calm down.*

Bulla's brow furrowed, watching Adya. Her lips were probably moving. She hated that.

The music switched to rock, and the volume soared. Birds

rocketed out of the trees in alarm, and the old crook stumbled back. Bulla tripped over the stump, dropped his weapon, and ended up on his back while the radio screamed.

Adya planted one foot on Bulla's spear while pointing hers at his neck. She raised her voice over the blaring music. "I tried the nice way, Bulla."

"You misunderstand me, Mongoose." Bulla's face broke out in sweat as he worked his way backward on his elbows. "Didn't mean anything by it. Didn't. Keep the money. Spend it while you can." He scrambled to his feet and ran, the sound of the music fading as he disappeared into the trees.

Adya tried to slow her breathing as she made her way back to the path, but her anger only spiraled higher. Damn Bulla and Huda both to hell. She'd gotten lucky to escape so easily.

Her threat had been all bluff, but most people had no idea what she was capable of. No other group of people had ever manifested the talent—even amongst the Atavi, technomancers were scarce. Some suspected it was their ability to connect with spirits that gave a rare few Atavi the power to touch the souls of old machines, but no one knew for sure.

Bulla couldn't have been right. Huda had pushed tech-nomancers too hard before, burning them out. But the British couldn't have snatched them all, could they? Adya had been out of touch with the others for a long while, but surely, she wasn't the last.

But Bulla's warning nagged at her. She should never have gotten entangled with Huda. Against her aunt's will, Adya had followed in the path of her parents, borrowing from Huda, the criminal overlord who held power over the jungle. Her parents had burdened themselves with loans to buy parts for her father's endless ambitions. She and Priya had vowed to stay out of the trap, but once her sister abandoned her, Adya found herself accepting Huda's money. The Atavi queen had once been the ruler of their people, but since Huda had begun working for the British, doing their bidding, everything had changed. The British had bolstered Huda tremendously, and the queen had faded into little more than a figurehead. Now Huda ran everything, and it was impossible to stay out of his web. And Adya's payments to the gangster were dangerously late.

The scent of chimney smoke brought her to a halt a quarter mile before the end of the trail. Ahead she would find the village where she grew up, two dozen red-domed huts stretched out along the banks of a fast-moving stream.

She started walking again, but it failed to loosen the knot in her throat. She and Priya had spent as much time with their feet in the rapid water as out of it. They had climbed the trees with their little brother, daring one another to bring down the highest guavas and mangoes they could find.

Then their parents had died, and Adya's world had gone up in flames. They'd been working on her father's great project—trying to awaken a machine more impressive than any technomancer had ever done before, something powerful enough to get the maharaja's attention and help drive out the British. Priya always suspected sabotage, but Adya wasn't sure. Technomancy could be lethal all by itself, and dangerous dreams got you killed.

Aunt Sanjana had arrived like a thunderstorm in the wake of the fatal explosion. She knew only two moods: annoyed and deeply annoyed. She ruled over the three orphans and tried to make sure they became good members of their community, dragging them to every celebration and meal when all Adya wanted was to be left alone. Adya had suffered under her glare for two terrible years.

Stop thinking only of yourself. Her aunt's usual tirade was already blaring in her mind. *So tall and gangly with your leather jacket and grease stains. If you stop lifting machinery, your arms will look more like a girl's. I'll never find a match for you.*

If pressed, under extreme interrogation, Adya might admit that her aunt loved her in her own grouchy way, that she had fought like a tiger to protect three unruly children, but even still, Adya preferred living in a mine shaft. She'd explained to her aunt a dozen times she didn't give a damn about helping her "community." She wasn't Priya, who dreamed about saving India. And she sure wasn't interested in marrying anyone.

Adya marched out of the trees, ready with fresh arguments.

Then the wind shifted, and the smell of ash struck her. She remembered what Bulla had said and thought of her brother. Mohan was a wizard at fixing things and coming up with great ideas, but he'd never been a strong enough technomancer to fire up more than a light bulb without collapsing. But Huda might still want him. She started to run.

And stumbled at the sight ahead.

The village lay abandoned. Smoke poured from the hut that had been her childhood home. The only sound was the crackle of fire. Before Adya could move, the roof crumbled as flames tore through the walls. Clouds of soot billowed toward her.

The black drongo circled above, its cry high and mournful.

Adya dropped into the underbrush as a stranger stepped out from behind the hut and tossed a smoldering branch into the flames. The sinuous tattoo on the man's forearm—in the shape of a naga—marked him as one of Huda's thugs. He shouted, and three more people joined him. Together, they knocked in a wall of her aunt Sanjana's hut. The flames roared higher. Heat seared Adya's cheeks, and her breath caught in her throat. Nothing could survive that.

She felt a keen stab in her chest, as if something inside had broken.

Adya squeezed her spear until her fingers went numb. If her aunt was in there, if they'd hurt her brother, she was going to drag those men into the fire herself.

"*Om Kali numaha,*" she whispered. She tensed for a sprint.

She was going to kill those men.

Across the clearing, the drongo dove into the forest, drawing Adya's attention to the flash of a hand between the trees and a huge mess of black hair that could belong only to one boy. She forced herself deeper into the underbrush. Mohan had escaped. Her aunt would be with him.

Adya took a slow breath and watched as Huda's thugs knocked over the last wall. A house was just wood, timber, and straw. It didn't matter how long they'd lived there or how many of her best memories were rooted in that home. She told herself it didn't matter. It could all be rebuilt. After the destruction was complete, Huda's men strolled off, following the stream.

Once they were gone, Mohan stepped out of the cover of the jungle, and Adya ran to him. Her brother's head was a thundercloud of curly hair strewn with leaves and twigs. He must have thrown himself into the brush to hide. He was wearing the blue dinosaur T-shirt he seldom took off. Adya crushed Mohan in her arms and felt him trembling. She searched the trees behind him, waiting for her aunt to appear, stone-faced and grim. For once, Adya looked forward to being yelled at.

But they didn't move, and the tears pouring down Mohan's face told her all she needed to know.

She ran, knocking aside the burning timbers with her spear, trying to see through the flames, hoping against hope that there was some pocket the fire hadn't reached. The inferno blasted back at her, scorching her arms as she beat at the cinders. Her aunt had cared for them for years. Had always made sure they were safe. Embers singed her legs as she tried to push through.

Mohan seized the back of her shirt and pulled her away. "It's too late, Adya."

Adya stared at their destroyed home.

"Everyone ran into the jungle when they came," Mohan whispered. "Auntie stayed and tried to hold them off, to give me time. She made me promise to keep you safe." Mohan rubbed the back of his forearm across his eyes. "I heard them, Adya. They were looking for you. One of them spat at her feet, and you know how she is. She slapped him, and then everything went bad." Mohan's voice broke. "They pushed her into the house and wouldn't let her out. They wouldn't . . ."

Adya closed her eyes.

They sat, leaning against each other, and watched their home burn like a funeral pyre. Adya peered into the flames and rocked back and forth. If only she'd listened, if only she'd never dealt with Huda. If only Priya were here. Her sister was the one who knew what to do when everything went to hell.

They waited by the stream as the sun rose high in the sky. Soon, the rest of the small village would drift back. Someone would offer to take them in. Their neighbors would put themselves at risk trying to help, just as Aunt Sanjana had done.

"No." The word escaped Adya's lips unbidden.

"No, what?" Mohan asked.

"You're coming back with me," she whispered. "We'll be safe in the mine."

She got to her feet and handed Mohan a stale piece of her puri. He took a bite and let the rest fall to the ground.

A double whistle, one high, one low, made her look up. The black drongo twisted in the air and hurtled down between them, spreading its wings at the last moment to alight next to the discarded bread. It pecked hungrily at the puri while Mohan watched.

Adya imagined her aunt looking down on them. She could almost hear her scolding before her ghost drifted away. *You never understand, Adya. I lay out everything right in front of you, and you never even try to understand.*

The drongo ate as if it hadn't seen food in days.

Mohan shook his head. "It's like we're all alone again." His voice was a hoarse wreck. "Just us and this dumb bird that pecks away like nothing even happened."

Blood rushed through Adya's ears. She planted her spear in the ground and held on to stay upright. Mohan's pained voice sounded far away. She felt lighter than air, like she could be blown away with a puff of breath. Like she might drift away forever.

The little bird hopped onto Adya's boots, and her vision snapped into focus. The drongo pecked at the last of the crumbs. She considered the hungry creature, oblivious to the surrounding tragedy. It wasn't dumb, like Mohan said. The bird knew what was important. It stayed safe and free, far up in the sky, and when it got the chance, it grabbed everything for itself.

Adya finally let out the breath she'd been holding in for so long. "At this point, Mohan, we'll take all the friends we can get."

CHAPTER TWO

F OR THREE DAYS THEY MOURNED, AND THE MONSOON never let up. Adya sat with her knees pulled into her chest, looking out at the rain, alternating between fantasies of vengeance and complete despair. She'd never needed her sister more. The only thing that stopped her from staring into space forever was her brother.

Twice, she'd had to drag Mohan out of the downpour, where he was practicing missing absolutely everything with his bow— in case he had to face Huda's goons again. She'd pretended the tears in his eyes were just rain and said nothing. After he'd lost half his arrows, Mohan checked every mechanism Adya had set up to defend the place. Finally satisfied, he bent his energy toward reorganizing her tools and pulling books off the shelves. The only time her brother had ever sat still over the last fifteen years was the six months before he could crawl.

Mohan slid a battered volume in front of her, jolting Adya from her daze. "Hey, remember this part?" *The Hundred Finest against the World* was a tale of a half-mad band of rebel soldiers and the sorcerer prince who led them. It was one of Priya's favorites.

"Like, how amazing would this be? The Vayu sorcerer creates an entire feast for the Hundred out of wind. And then, whoa, he conjures a silver pipe, six feet long, and blows a storm

into their ears so they can't be charmed by the Devas' songs."
Mohan's eyes took on a distant look. "They used a lot of incense.
We could maybe build a pipe like that to get your spells to work
better. Create a technomantic field inside and then, bam."

Adya sighed and continued watching raindrops slither in
rivulets down the floor of her tunnel. If they had to resort to
copying fairy tales, they were really screwed.

Still, some of Mohan's ideas were actually good. In the
short time he'd been here, he'd put wheels on a plank so she
could slide under the rickshaw, set up a pulley system to lift
heavy parts, and rearranged her books by color, which made
no sense whatsoever. He'd even managed to clean and organize
her tools, despite Useless trying to knock them into the depths
of the mine shaft. Half of Mohan's schemes were inspired by old
stories. He'd read *The Hundred Finest* cover to cover more times
than she could remember. In the story, the Hundred couldn't
hear a damn thing because of the conjured storm in their ears.
They misunderstood each other most of the time and ended up
going on adventures none of them had ever planned.

Mohan closed the book, still lost in the tale. "And it ends
with the Vayu and the Devas all still massively hating each
other. Like, with all that magic, why couldn't they conjure a
way to get along? We're all just human."

"Because the Vayu are power hungry, and the Devas are
charmers no one trusts. In real life, most people are lousy." Adya
was in a foul mood. Mohan was right—they were all human—
but that didn't mean they were the same. Over the centuries,
they'd developed different ways of channeling the magic of the

infinity wells. They'd been at odds with one another for ages before the British arrived. Adya hated squashing Mohan's endless belief in people, but she thought about it and decided she was right. Most people *were* lousy.

"What about us? How come the Atavi aren't part of the story?"

Adya shrugged. "We're nothing to them, just people far off in a jungle they rarely remembered even before the spell wall. Now they've forgotten about us entirely. The maharaja has the power to sneak his traders through, but does he send soldiers to help us? The idea probably never occurred to him."

British wizards had conjured the wall of flames that surrounded the Atavi homelands soon after they discovered what technomancers could do. Their fascination with the new magic was soon replaced by alarm when they realized that living machines could drink up the energy of their spells to fuel their power. While the British longed to harness technomancy for their war effort, they could not allow the threat to stand unchecked. They surrounded the Atavi with their strongest enchantment—a ring of living fire they believed no machine could ever quench.

On her third day of moping, Adya turned to the one thing she relied on when everything else went wrong—her work. If they needed to get out of here in a hurry, they would need the rickshaw.

After two days of failed attempts, she hurled a set of pliers down the tunnel and stopped just short of punching the wall. She had repaired the mechanical issues—it was the magic that wouldn't stick.

Mohan's stegosaurus shirt was stained with grease. He'd fashioned a long tube out of a sheet of aluminum, trying to bring his fairy-tale magic to life. "What is this, attempt forty-two?" he asked.

Adya coughed and tried to wave away the cloud of incense. "Forty-three, and stop blowing smoke at me. I can barely breathe." Sweating beneath the ancient three-wheeled taxi, she gave a final shove to the gas tank, forcing it into place.

Once she had it secure, she slid out from under the green-and-yellow rickshaw and adjusted her safety goggles. Her heavy rubber apron had failed to protect her jeans from oil splashes. She was going to smell like rust and old engine for the rest of the week.

"Do you think, before you sell the rickshaw, that we could use it to find Priya? I mean, if it could get through the spell wall and everything."

Adya put down the wrench she was holding and eyed him. Faced with the power of old machines, most spells broke apart, but the magic that held together the spell wall was ferociously powerful. Trying to punch a hole through without turning into a mess of ashes was a terrific gamble.

"What would be the point? How would we find her?" Adya stopped grinding her teeth. "We're not going out like some crazy hero and getting killed. I don't want to talk about it." Adya held out a hand. "Screwdriver. Flathead." She couldn't admit to Mohan that she'd been over this a thousand times in her own head, part of her wanting to sell the machine, the other half dying to blast through the spell wall and find Priya wherever she was.

Mohan managed to drop the screwdriver twice before handing it to her. "Sorry." He lowered his head until his cumulus cloud of hair almost got in her eyes. "Look, I have an idea. If we maybe use different incense, like in the *Hundred Finest*, we could—"

"We could waste the little time we have." Adya slid back under the rickshaw.

Her brother's hair had probably curled so tight because his brain had overheated with schemes. Mohan was the one who'd first started calling her Mongoose after Adya put a screwdriver through the foot of some crook who'd tried to rob the mine shaft. Only a mongoose was fierce enough to drive snakes out of its home.

Despite Adya's protests, the smell of jasmine soon filled the air. She'd tried to explain that it wasn't incense that made spells work—emotion drove a technomancer's magic, and money drove everything else.

From under the rickshaw Adya called out, "Get ready. I'm going to fire it up."

Mohan put his head to the ground and tried to look her in the eyes. "Listen to me for once, Adya. You think I don't know much, but being so close is crazy. The whole thing could come down on you."

"Right," Adya agreed. "You don't know much. Now move back. Get ready to hand me what I need." She felt terrible as soon as she said it. There was no reason to take out all her frustration on her little brother.

But there wasn't going to be a forty-fourth attempt. She

pulled the circular pendant that hung around her neck to her lips and kissed it. It was a folding wrench set her mother had worn, a technomancer's emblem. She made sure her goggles were on tight.

"*Vishwakarma namo namah*," she chanted, using one of the prayers that focused her spells. "Come on."

The engine sputtered, and the carriage started to shake.

"Adya, get out," Mohan yelled. But it was too late.

Magic vibrated through her teeth and swept over her body. These were the moments she felt most alive, her fingertips trembling, the air around her vibrating with possibility. Her mother had explained years ago how the magic worked. *Techno-mancy finds the heart of the machine and lets it be reborn. The technomancer becomes a live wire on a path to the machine's soul. We draw the power from the infinity wells, but your memories and emotions carry the magic like a candlewick carries the flame. Your heart and mind must be strong enough to sustain the flow. Remember, Adya, it's a fierce magic that can drain you dry or burn you to nothing.*

But her mother's words couldn't describe the thrill.

Adya's back arched as she tapped into the infinity well and the power washed over her, reigniting her senses, granting her a glimpse into a hidden world. It thrummed under her skin, full of possibility. As if she might reach out and change the universe with a touch.

The machine rattled as the energy flowed through Adya, seized its circuits, and fired magic through its rusted spark plugs. A wash of silver light erupted underneath the carriage and filled the tunnel. Even with her goggles on, she had to close her eyes to shield them from the brightness. Bolts tightened as parts that had once seemed far beyond repair melded together.

But the engine coughed and wheezed, and Adya felt the initial surge of power she'd tapped begin to fade. Now the machine reached out to draw energy through her as it drank in her feelings. This was the moment of trust, of supreme vulnerability, when the technomancer opened herself and the machine came alive. When the rickshaw used her as a conduit to draw what it needed from the infinity wells. Attempt to awaken a machine too powerful, and you could be burned out by the flow.

A rusty whisper began in Adya's head, growing ever louder until it transformed into the clanking of gears and pistons, and the engine's true voice roared.

Like an old veteran desperate to share war stories, the rickshaw poured its secrets into Adya. It filled her mind with images of running children, laughing in their blue school uniforms, old women in orange saris, a too-thin couple holding hands as they bumped together while the rickshaw swerved down crowded city streets. The machine knew these people's secrets. Now Adya knew them as well. Rust flaked away, showering over her black curls, revealing gleaming steel. Tears filled Adya's eyes. This was what she lived for. She let her own memories flow out in return, nurturing the machine's soul. Memories of racing through the jungle as a child, images of her first attempts at technomancy, the sounds of the white cranes calling as they soared over the trees—she let the emotions run through her, and the engine rumbled.

The rickshaw shared a memory of two young girls, schoolbags swinging from their shoulders. The girls looked so alike, smiling as they ran to catch their ride. They had to be sisters.

Priya's face flashed before her, and Adya gasped. She remembered holding her sister's hand the last day their parents were alive, remembered never wanting to let go. It was nothing she could face again. Something inside Adya shut down, and the flow of magic stuttered. Her breaths came fast and shallow as the hum of power faded from her fingers. She tried to reverse the flow, but as hard as she strained to channel more of herself, there was nothing left to give.

"No, no." Bolts reversed and spun in the wrong direction. With a sickening creak, the gas tank wrenched loose and slammed against Adya's shoulder, missing her head by inches. Numbing pain coursed down her arm.

The ancient machine gave a final shudder as the silver light faded. Except for the slow drip of oil, the mine shaft went silent. Adya closed her eyes, swearing under her breath. She fixed what she could and gave the magic everything, but it asked for too damn much.

Muscles limp, she dragged herself out from under the rickshaw and just lay there. It was always hit or miss with her technomancy. If only she could get it to work more reliably before she blew herself up. She wiped her face with her forearm. "It didn't explode."

Mohan stood ready with a wrench. "Maybe you could—"

Adya threw her goggles across the room. She could almost feel the heat of the fire that took her parents. She turned away from Mohan and stared up at a picture on the wall, her favorite—a detailed drawing Priya had made of old Mumbai, with airplanes circling its imposing skyscrapers while cars and trucks navigated the maze of roads below. If Priya were here, they could make everything like it was before. Adya blinked away the tears clouding her vision and started putting away her tools. "We'll try again tomorrow."

Mohan wasn't one to give up. "Look, I've figured this rickshaw problem out. We need music, like a theme song."

Adya grabbed her little brother and squeezed him tight. She let him go almost as fast. "We'll try music next time," she said. Mohan should have his own theme song. "What was it that Auntie used to say about me?"

"That you're lonely in your filthy cave, you're reckless, you're too shy, that you're no kind of role model for—"

"Enough, enough."

A high whistle caught Adya's attention, and she tensed, recognizing the drongo's cry of alarm.

"What is it?" Mohan asked.

The drongo had called five times, she was almost sure. Adya whistled back the same count. Anyone outside would have sworn its song had echoed up from deep under the mountain. She cursed under her breath until the bird's answering call arrived.

Five calls. The bird wasn't worried about the cat this time.

Adya swatted at a candle, plunging them into darkness. She needed to get Mohan out of here alive.

CHAPTER THREE

———— · ————

HIGH ABOVE THE JUNGLE, THE MOST MAGICAL BIRD IN India circled the night sky, its forked tail feathers shining silver. The drongo, no larger than a raven, could imitate any animal, but two things set it apart from all other species—it could always find its way home, and it could never forget a debt unpaid.

The drongo had traveled far, soaring over the burning spell wall the British had conjured to confine the Atavi. Atop the fiery enchantment, specters paused in their endless patrol to gaze at the bird as it passed, but even they could not stop a creature with wings. It flew past the villages of red-domed huts, above giant banyans and sepal trees, and over the abandoned steel battleship that served as the home of the crime lord Huda. The bird circled the stone temple where the Atavi queen once held court and continued over the thick jungle of southwest India, where yaksha roamed and the mountains were carved to their core, their uranium tailings glowing in heaps of unquenched fire. These were the mountains where swollen clouds surrendered the summer monsoon. Where the jungle below drank in the rain and never stopped growing in a magic-fueled frenzy.

A twenty-foot-long tiger glanced up as the bird passed, its eyes reflecting dangerous green. The drongo mimicked the tiger to amuse itself, and the great beast roared its disapproval. The drongo flew on.

Far below, five spear tips glinted in the moonlight as running figures crossed an iron bridge. This, the bird could not let pass unnoticed.

Without warning, it folded its wings and dropped like rain, opening them at the last second to touch down in front of a dark, forgotten mine shaft, where none of its kind would ever wish to go. It had a debt to pay. The drongo sang—one, two, three, four, five cries of alarm—to give warning to a girl far below.

Adya bent a long aluminum tube fastened to the wall and peered inside.

"*Guru Brahma, Guru Vishnu, Guru Deva,*" she whispered. In response, a headlight on one of the broken cars piled outside the mine shaft flickered to life.

Amidst the faint light, she made out spear tips rising and falling. Huda had sent his cronies. Adya kicked her bed, sending her sister's cat screeching around the room.

Mohan was in a panic. "We've got to get the heck out."

She took a long look at her brother and fought to keep her voice from betraying her fear. "Don't worry." She shoved his bow and arrows into his hands, hustled him to the back of the cave. She rolled aside a barrel of liquor, revealing a four-foot-high tunnel leading into darkness. "This connects to the other side of the junkyard. You'll be in the jungle in five minutes. I'll be right behind."

Mohan's eyes went wide. "Wait . . . you're not coming?"

"Oh, I'm coming. Give me a chance to drop the bridge and make sure they can't follow. Go."

"No way," Mohan said. "When I left Auntie alone, she died. That's not happening again."

"Damn right it's not." Adya pushed Mohan toward the tunnel. "I'm dropping those crooks into the river; then we meet up and get out of here. I need you out there with your bow. If you hustle, you can cover the bridge. Just don't shoot me."

"I don't know, Adya. I haven't had much time to practice yet. . . ."

"You've practiced plenty. If things go wrong, head back to the village, and I'll meet you. Out there, you'll just get in my way."

Mohan looked back, his face unsure, then he turned and was gone.

Adya rolled the giant barrel back into place. Huda's goons knew she was down here. If she disappeared, they'd search until they found the hidden passage and Mohan. That wasn't going to happen. She wasn't going to lose any more family.

Her throat tightened as the feeling of dread sank in. People talked in hushed tones about the British invaders, but the British were a distant threat. Huda's enforcers were real. She'd heard the stories. First, they broke your legs and made you drag yourself around on your hands. Then it got worse. Her stomach twisted, acid rising to the back of her mouth.

Adya filled a mug from one of the barrels. She'd hoped to resell the daru, but she might as well try some now. If she was going out, it would be in style.

She tossed the fiery liquor back and let it sear down her throat. Then she selected two wires from the wall and snapped together their rusted alligator clips. A surge of magic crackled up the tunnel. She peered into the periscope as the speakers in her front yard came alive. The men had stopped halfway across the bridge, most likely wondering what the hell the static meant.

Adya pulled her beat-up red leather jacket off the wall and forced her hand through a sleeve. Her exhausted muscles were reluctant, but she'd need the protection. There was enough metal sewn into the lining to turn a sharp blade. She slid a pair of sunglasses into her pocket and snatched up her mother's uranium-tipped spear.

After scanning the records on the wall, she settled on *Heavy Metal Anthems*. Her sister's cat watched as Adya dropped the needle on the antique record player.

Adya pointed her black spear at the beast. "Don't touch it, Useless." The stubborn cat licked his shoulder and ignored her.

The daru was already making her face hot. The potent liquor was infamous for making a mess of your emotions. She shouldn't have drunk it so fast.

She hustled up the shaft until she reached the autorickshaw and put a hand against it to brace herself, seething. Why did Huda get to treat everyone as his slave? He'd tricked her parents into debt they could never escape. If not for him, her aunt would still be alive. She squeezed her mother's pendant until her fingers hurt, then slammed her fist on the rickshaw's roof, leaving a dent in the thin metal.

"Kali take him," she hissed. Huda should be the one paying his dues, her parents should be alive, and Priya should be here. She was so tired of everything going wrong.

Darkness filled her vision. She hadn't meant the prayer as more than words of frustration, but her magic flared with a will of its own.

The rickshaw's headlights glowed, drinking in Adya's frustration, surging with her anger and despair. The machine shook, and the driver's door fell off as magic surged through its wiring. The engine roared as if it would leap up the tunnel and fly into the jungle.

"Damn him to hell," she declared to the empty cave. Her anger smoldered, and magic flowed through her in a torrent. The rickshaw drank it in, tapping into her rage, her fear of dying at Huda's hands, her dread of becoming a slave. The wiring surged with energy, and the engine did not sputter.

Alive. The rickshaw's voice whispered inside her. The roar of the engine shifted to a hum, tense and expectant. She sensed the machine's personality for the first time, steady and responsible, eager to take her wherever she needed to go.

Still trembling, Adya ran a hand over the glorious old frame. Straight to the bridge, bring it down, then catch up with Mohan—with the rickshaw working, it was possible. She shook the fallen door by the handle to test its weight. It would serve as a shield. The rickshaw creaked as she settled in. She patted the dashboard and wedged her spear against the seat. "Let's show them what you're made of."

Outside the cave, speakers blared the crash of drums and

the first lyrics of a song from a different age. The rickshaw's horn trumpeted as the vehicle careened up the tunnel, bursting out of the shaft's entrance and into the night. Adya made out five men on the bridge fifty yards ahead. One of them was already hurling his weapon.

The spear bounced off the roof, and the rickshaw screamed inside her head. The old machine wasn't made for battle. Adya struggled to maintain control as she bumped over piles of abandoned parts. Twenty more yards and she'd make it.

Another spear flew straight at the open door.

The handlebars twisted in her hands as the rickshaw made a sudden turn of its own volition. Glass sprayed across her chest as the spearhead smashed through the windshield and embedded itself in the seat above her right shoulder. The quick swerve had saved her.

Over the speakers, the heavy-metal singer screamed his final lines, and the guitar solo kicked in.

With ten yards to go, one of Huda's goons leapt out from behind a doorless refrigerator. He cocked his arm back and bared his teeth.

Adya spun the handlebars hard right and ducked. The rickshaw tipped sideways, slamming the man into a heap of junk. She held on tight as the machine shuddered, balancing on two wheels as it skidded the final yards.

Jump! Its warning screamed in her head.

She leapt out with her spear just before the crash. Sparks rocketed into the sky. The rickshaw's anguish washed over her as it lay on its side, helpless. It couldn't take her to safety.

But the faithful machine had protected her long enough. The cable to drop the bridge was only ten yards away. If the fall into the river didn't kill the men, they'd break enough bones not to be a threat. She made out four of them. Hopefully, the other had fled.

One cupped his hand to his mouth and shouted, "Huda sent me to invite you to tea, Mongoose. He didn't want you to be lonely in your cave any longer." Adya would recognize that pompous voice anywhere. Gouros, Huda's chief assassin, wore a black cape he thought made him look impressive. You had to be a special kind of stupid to wear a silk cape during the rainy season.

Adya hefted the rickshaw door as a makeshift shield, gripped her spear, and got ready for the final sprint. "I'd rather be the last person on the planet than have tea with Huda," she shouted. "I'd rather drink cobra venom." She couldn't wait to see Gouros flailing as he plunged into the river.

Gouros bared his teeth at her. "That can be arranged."

The music ended abruptly, and the sound of a needle being scratched back and forth across the record filled the air. Useless! The damned cat was ruining her album. Adya sprinted the final distance and dove for the cable that would send half the bridge into the river.

Gouros's cape fluttered in the wind, the kind of dramatic effect he must have dreamed of. "No more tricks, Mongoose," he shouted. "Your sister won't appreciate it." Before Adya could drop the bridge, the assassin pushed a girl out in front of him. She stumbled before regaining her balance.

Adya swallowed hard. A thin gag covered the girl's mouth, but even in the glare, she recognized her sister's ponytail.

Priya. If they hurt her—if they *dared*.

"Drop your spear," Gouros called, spinning a long knife in his hand. "Do it and she survives."

Adya's hands broke out in a sweat. The cable slipped from her grip.

She turned at the smell of burning. Clouds of smoke poured out of the mine shaft. The other thug hadn't fled; he'd gotten behind her and set fire to her home. Too late she remembered the full barrels of daru.

"No!" she screamed.

A fireball roared up from the tunnel. The explosion blasted Adya backward and sent her tumbling, knocking the breath out of her. She fought to pick herself up, wiping blood from her eyes.

Her head pounded, daru surging through her veins. "They blew up your cat, Priya! You know how long I watched that stupid cat for you?"

Priya took advantage of the explosion. She kicked the assassin and dashed across the bridge, ponytail flying.

Gouros's arm drew back. His golden ring flashed in the light as he threw the knife.

The blade spun end over end, in a long silver arc that seemed to last forever. It struck Priya in the center of her back. She took three more steps and dropped, heavy as stone, into Adya's arms.

Adya felt her world collapsing. "Hold on, Priya." She tore

off the gag and pressed her hand against the bloody wound, squeezing her sister tight. "I should have come after you. All I wanted was to find you."

She took Priya's head in her hands, and her sight clouded with tears. She'd counted the days waiting for her return, and it all ended like this.

Adya's vision cleared. She blinked in disbelief as the face before her snapped into focus. It didn't seem possible, but she did not recognize this girl. Gouros had forced some poor innocent to act the part, then ended her life.

The assassin smiled, twirling the frayed end of the cable in one hand. His men leaned on their spears and laughed. There would be no dropping the bridge now, and taking on these men alone was suicide. Her options had vanished.

An arrow flew past, missing the bridge by a huge margin. None of the men even noticed. She had to finish this before they realized Mohan was here.

Time for new options.

Adya fished the dark sunglasses from her pocket. She was a technomancer, not a warrior goddess. She needed help.

She slid the glasses on.

"*Vishwakarma namo namah,*" she whispered. The headlights of a dozen piled-up cars and wrecked motorcycles blazed to life in response, covering the yard in a sudden white flash. She heard the furious voices of hundreds of festival lights covering the bridge that knew Adya like an old friend and that missed Priya terribly.

Every speaker in the yard blared an eardrum-splitting roar.

Bulbs popped, sending sparks arcing and shards of fine glass flying at her attackers. One of Huda's thugs took the brunt of it in his face, stumbled back, and tumbled over the rail. The other gangsters crouched, shielding their eyes from the blast and covering their ears under the sensory overload.

Adya slammed the butt of her spear on the ground and balanced the green-and-yellow rickshaw door on her arm. Mohan had been right; she needed a theme song for this crap.

"Get the hell off my bridge!" she screamed. She gave in to the temper that had always plagued her and sprinted toward Huda's men. The roar of the speakers became thunder.

Gouros threw his spear.

Adya knocked aside the missile with her door-shield and leapt high.

A bony man, half-blinded by the glare, made the mistake of stumbling in front of Gouros. Adya cracked the door against his head, and he crashed to the bridge. Gouros turned to run.

Adya grabbed the assassin by the cape, yanking him to the ground. She dropped to one knee and smacked his head against the railing.

"You're mad," Gouros wheezed. "Huda will have you skinned."

"You won't be there to see it."

The man she'd hit with the door was already getting up. Another was sprinting toward the bridge—the jerk who'd blown up Priya's cat. Adya touched her spear tip to Gouros's throat. "Tell them to keep back if you value your neck."

He bared his teeth. "Kill me and you lose your chance to save your sister."

Adya increased the pressure against his skin. She had never killed anyone, but the assassin deserved it. "That was not my sister."

Gouros spoke faster. "Not her. I know what happened to your sister. Huda wants to make a deal. We'll help you find her."

Adya gauged the distance to the trees. If she ran now, she could make it.

"Your sister rode a blue moped with bright red fenders," he continued, and Adya froze. "She was headed for the spell wall. Look me in the eyes. I know what happened."

Gods no.

Priya had taken the scooter. Gouros couldn't have described it so perfectly unless he'd seen it. . . .

The bright lights faded to darkness. She was having trouble breathing. She caught sight of the man behind her only a moment before something struck her head. Adya flailed blindly, but in a moment, they'd pinned her arms and slammed her against the railing. She'd lost her chance to run.

Gouros fumed, his lip bleeding. He brought his face close enough for her to feel his hot breath. "I wasn't lying, Mongoose. I could help you find what's left of your sister. I could reunite you with her charred pieces. We chased your idiot twin all the way to the wall. Almost snatched her before she rode straight into the fire. She called out for you as she burned."

"Liar." Adya spat the word out. But her strength was gone. Gouros had seen Priya. Had seen her crazy sister, with her dreams of freeing India, hit the spell wall and burn.

The static hiss of the speakers faded as Adya went limp, feeling emptier than she ever had.

"It's a good thing you weren't stupid enough to ride with her." Gouros smirked. "That makes you the very last of the techno-mancers. Huda is going to earn a treasure selling you to the British."

The thought of being sold sent panic through Adya. She squeezed her eyes closed to shut out Gouros's grin. They would chain her in Huda's dungeon. The British would use her to fire up war machines until she burned herself out. Better to die here. Anything would be better.

The world went silent except for the rush of the river below. Adya could feel her heart pounding, feel the blood surging through her ears.

A loud yowl broke the silence.

Useless strolled across the bridge, complaining loudly about his home being destroyed, or his music being stopped, or whatever a cat with plenty of lives complained about. He waved his singed tail, expecting someone to do something about it.

For once, the cat was useful. Adya took advantage of the distraction to thrust her knee into the groin of the man holding her. He grunted and stumbled back, giving her the space she needed. Gouros lunged, but too late. She wasn't going to be anybody's slave.

Adya leaned back and flipped over the rail. The drongo shrieked as she plummeted toward the churning water below.

The river met her with a cold slap, hurled her against rocks, then spun her in an endless whirlpool. She sucked in half air, half water as it dragged her under. She rolled along the gravel bottom until the last bit of breath burst from her lungs and her vision went black.

Then the maelstrom coughed her up and spit her out against a boulder with one final crash. Adya gripped the stone with bleeding fingers until she lost her hold and tumbled back into the current. Flailing to stay above water, she drifted until she reached a bank and sprawled in the mud like a dead fish. Blood and dirt filled her mouth as she lay still, too exhausted to rise. Her left ankle felt broken. She held her mother's pendant tight and stared up at the stars, listening to the river. At least she'd escaped Gouros. She'd rest a few minutes more, then crawl into the jungle to hide. Only a few minutes.

When she felt strong enough, she pulled herself up to her elbows, spat out a mouthful of water and grime, and took a deep breath of night air. Before she could move, a boot pressed down on her chest, forcing her back into the mud.

"I was worried you'd drowned, but it appears you've been born again." Gouros grinned as his men pinned her arms. In his hand, he squeezed the black drongo. The little bird pecked wildly at his fingers with no effect.

Gouros looked into Adya's eyes, and his smile disappeared. "You're going to wish you'd stayed dead."

CHAPTER FOUR

ADYA AWOKE FROM A NIGHTMARE, STRUGGLING TO breathe, with the image of Huda's sneering face still fresh in her mind. In her dream, the crime lord bent toward her until his lips brushed hers, his breath hot and foul. Huda opened his mouth to scream at her, but the only sound that came out was an endless *tak-tak-tak*.

Turning her aching head made it clear that her world was upside down. Chains, wrapped around her ankles, suspended her three feet off the floor from a hook bolted to the ceiling. Water dripped through metal seams above her and onto the steel floor in a patter she recognized as the *tak-tak* sound of Huda's dream voice. Her red leather jacket and pendant were gone. It was a lousy start to the day.

She closed her eyes, hoping to wake again anywhere but here, but it didn't work. Only one place in the jungle was entirely made of steel: they'd caged her belowdecks in Huda's old battleship. How the ancient aircraft carrier had ended up in the middle of the jungle was anyone's guess, but it had become the headquarters of the gangster's enterprise.

At least Mohan had escaped. He would have made it back to the village. But he wasn't one to stand still—Adya had to get out of here before Mohan tried something crazy.

She kicked out, trying to free her ankles. The effort fired

a fresh jolt of pain through her legs and only managed to send her into a slow spin, giving her an upside-down view of her surroundings. In the corridor, a lone torch sputtered, its wavering light illuminating the one other inhabitant of her cell. Still shackled to the wall by one wrist, a man, clearly dead for days, lay face down in a pool of dark liquid. She gagged at the stink and squirmed harder, with absolutely no success. The man had died a miserable death, but at least he'd escaped Huda's usual execution.

According to the stories, whenever Huda killed someone, he would have his red-and-white Yamaha 450 dirt bike wheeled above deck. Adya had seen the gangster straddling the bike when she dropped off a shipment. None of Huda's technomancers had been able to bring the motorcycle back to life, but that didn't stop him from pretending he was racing it to victory. He had the bike oiled and polished until it gleamed like a trophy. And when he was astride it, he would smile his awful smile, gloating as his enemies begged for mercy.

Soon, she'd be the one begging.

She fought to hold back tears. How had everything gone wrong in so little time? Five months ago, she and Priya had been testing their new moped. She could still hear her voice, still see her smile.

Adya raced the moped over the bridge and skidded to a stop. Her heart pounded as Priya charged at her, screaming.

"You were flying!" Priya's smile took up her entire face.

Beneath Adya, the moped's little engine hummed. "No

one's stopping us now," she said. She'd never felt so perfect.

Priya twirled in a circle. "They said we'd never get this moped to work. Look at it now. You could outrun a tiger!"

"*Two* freaking tigers," Adya bragged, and believed it.

They had worked on the moped for months, late into the night down in the mine shaft. Everyone had doubted the girls could survive on their own, two teenagers in the worst part of the jungle, outside the village proper. But by fixing boom boxes and electric kettles, they'd scraped together enough money to survive. And now this. A machine that tore through the jungle. They would never go hungry again. After they sold it, they would live like princesses. Even their preachy aunt might get a present out of it.

Priya grabbed the handlebars. "Now we can get the hell out of here."

Adya blinked. "We can what?"

"Get through the spell wall," Priya said. "This machine is strong enough to break up the magic. We can get out and let the maharaja know what is happening here in the jungle. Finally use technomancy for good."

"Come on, Priya, not this again," Adya groaned. "We're not even sure the idea would work. We'd be more likely to burn than punch our way through the spell wall." How many times would she try this nonsense?

Priya leaned over the handlebars. "We could do it. Remember, you're the one who said we could take on even the British. We don't have to just dream anymore, Adya."

Adya put her hand over Priya's. "Get it straight. This is *our* chance, not anyone else's. We sell this moped, and we'll have enough money to last a year. No more scraping at the bottom of the pot to get the last bit. Everyone will know we're the best of the best. We'll have to turn away business like crazy."

Priya pulled her hand free and paced. "The world is falling apart out there, Adya. The British are taking everything. The maharaja can't fight them forever on his own."

Adya threw up her hands. "What has the maharaja ever done for us? Why should we get killed for him?"

Priya shot her a reproachful look, but Adya didn't give a damn about the great maharaja of Mysore, sacred protector of the Flame of the South, or whatever stupid title he called himself. He wouldn't lift a finger if their entire jungle were knocked down to make furniture for the British.

But Priya was stubborn.

"The world won't stay outside the wall, Adya. The British are draining our magic dry."

"Drop it, Priya. Wake up. You're not some warrior princess." Adya refused to risk their future for another ridiculous fantasy; they'd already lost too much. "We can't trust anyone out there. They'll fight to control us," she went on. "I'm not risking the spell wall for that."

"What about what Baba said?" Priya countered. "If we combine our magic with the Vayu and the Devas, the British won't stand a chance."

Adya ground her teeth. "Baba went up in that explosion and took our mother with him. All because of a dream." She couldn't believe her idiot sister was thinking of putting them through this again. Wasn't losing everything once enough?

Priya grabbed her by the shoulders, her eyes full of tears. "The dream is what keeps me going, Adya. Don't you see? I can't stay in this damned junkyard repairing fans while the world goes up in flames."

"You can't stop the burning, Priya."

"If you won't come, I'll take the moped and go myself."

Adya froze, feeling light-headed. She squeezed the handlebars until her fingers hurt to drive away the sudden dizziness. It was supposed to be the two of them against the world.

"We did all this work together." Adya shook free of Priya's grip and got off the moped. "You don't get to steal the moped for some naive idea of a better world." She turned her back on her sister before Priya could see her tears and marched away.

That night she listened to Priya's breathing until exhaustion betrayed her and she fell asleep. In the morning, her sister and the blue moped were gone. Adya was sure she'd be back that same day. Certain she'd be back the next day as well. Sure each week that passed, until she realized she couldn't lie to herself any longer.

She'd read the note so many times, she could recite it from memory.

> Adya, I can't stay. We're the same in so many ways,
> but not in the ways that count. You see all the chaos
> and fight to keep us safe, but I see a chance to make a
> difference, and I need to do it before it's too late. I need
> to make sure Baba and Amma didn't die for nothing.
> Don't worry about me! You always worry too much.

*I'll be back soon and tell you all the stories. I owe you
big for taking the moped. DON'T STAY ANGRY.
Love you more than anything. P*

Black boots struck the floor as the door screeched open, forcing
Adya back to the present. The ridiculous cape gave its wearer
away.

"I've brought you something for company. The place is
becoming a zoo." Gouros hurled a man wrapped in chains into
the cell.

The unlucky prisoner stumbled forward and smacked his
head into the wall before sliding to the floor and starting to
seize. Gouros had likely killed him already. Now she'd be stuck
here with two dead bodies.

The clomp of Gouros's boots receded, and Adya twisted to
examine the newcomer. The man was so wrapped in chains that
it was hard to make out more than a body lying on its back. As
she watched, the prisoner lifted his head and shook the hair out
of his face. Then he turned and looked her straight in the eye.

"No justice for honest criminals, eh, Mongoose?" The
prisoner groaned and managed a half smile. His voice was the
unmistakable hoarse scrape of stone on stone that belonged to
the worst scoundrel Adya knew.

"Bad Day." The words escaped her mouth in a dry whisper. She would have laughed if her ribs weren't on fire. Of all
the people they could have tossed into her cell, they'd chosen
Jagan Dsouza, a seventeen-year-old conceited enough to call
himself Night Blade. She'd last seen Dsouza two months ago,

when she'd had to bargain with him without Priya to do the talking. No older than Adya, he'd already earned a reputation over the last year, traveling back and forth across the spell wall, as the most ruthless of Vayu traders. The Jackal would lie to his mother and betray his best friend to steal their only rupee.

But the nicknames other people gave him didn't do Dsouza justice. She preferred her own. If you were desperate enough to deal with him, you were having a very bad day.

Dsouza nodded his head toward the corpse. "It was a lousy day for that poor thief, for sure. It was also a bad week when you took double the money for walkie-talkies that only worked a month. You stuck me with two pieces of junk and an angry buyer."

Adya raised her eyebrows. "You arrived late, you complained, and you paid in liquor. Your barrels ended up blowing up my home."

Dsouza spit out a bloody tooth. "I had to throw my beloved customer down a well for trying to kill me, witch. You owe me for the shipment and for a lost buyer."

She wished she could smack him. "You owe me a new place to live and a full set of tools, Bad Day. And I never want to see you again."

Dsouza laughed. "Your sales policies are noted. Do not complain or be late for a date with Adya Sachdev, and no refunds. By the way, you look like a carcass. Usually you dress nicer."

"Even tied up, you're a jerk." She wished she could wrap the chains around him a little tighter, preferably around his neck. "I can't think of anyone else I'd like to die with less."

"Likewise. But you know what? I don't feel much like dying at all." Dsouza flashed his annoying half smile at her. Between his teeth he held a two-inch-long sliver of metal. She couldn't believe it; he'd managed to hide a lockpick. Dsouza bent his head to his hands. Before long, his shackles hit the floor. He was unwinding his chains in the next few moments.

"Gouros is too stupid to search anyone properly," Dsouza said.

Adya felt hope rise in her chest.

Dsouza laced his hands behind his head and stretched, his every movement as smooth as a jewel thief's. His clothes were torn, but he was still undeniably Dsouza. There were three things everyone noticed about him: he was attractive in a cutthroat way, all sleek muscle and hard edges; his mouth was caught in a perpetual half smile; and he was obsessed with wearing black. Adya always thought it was an attempt to get people to actually call him Night Blade, which everyone refused to do. The only off-color mark was the scarlet tattoo on his neck, the maharaja's spell mark, the treasured and oh-so-rare gift that allowed him to pass through the wall without burning alive.

"Get me down from here."

Dsouza's smile vanished. He glanced from Adya to the door. "You come down for a price."

She was a fool for thinking he might help her. She would smack Dsouza's head against the wall as soon as she had the chance. "You're going to try to squeeze something out of me now?"

He lowered himself until his eyes were a fingerbreadth from hers. "When have either of us done anything for free, Mongoose?"

Never. But this was too much. You could never trust a Vayu, and Dsouza made the rest of them seem honest. "I didn't bring my purse," she said.

"Then you owe me an exceptionally large favor."

"Small favor," she countered, though bargaining while in chains put her at a disadvantage.

Dsouza shook his head at her. "Even upside down you're stubborn. Medium favor, and you don't owe me a thing if we both die."

"Fine. But I'm holding the carcass comment against you." The thought of being in debt to Dsouza was frightening, but not as frightening as Huda.

Dsouza went to work on her wrists. In moments, he tossed her shackles aside, unhooked the chain from the wall, and lowered her to the floor. In another minute he had her legs free.

Adya lay on her back, staring at the ceiling as the blood returned to her feet. At least she wasn't going to die bound. Whatever happened, she was going to have a chance to fight. But when she tried to stand, her damn legs wouldn't respond. She tried again but only achieved another near blackout.

Dsouza went to one knee and reached for her calf.

"Don't touch me," she snapped.

He scowled at her. "Don't flatter yourself. You're no good to me paralyzed."

"Good to you? You're worse than a jackal." But she closed her eyes and nodded. She couldn't stay like this. When Dsouza started kneading her muscles, she let out a moan and almost vomited from the pain.

Dsouza glanced at the door. "Keep quiet unless you want Gouros to come running." His icy heart was clearly unmoved by her suffering.

The pain receded as he worked his way up, and the sensation transformed from excruciating to tolerable to something else altogether. Against her will, her cheeks flushed, and she turned away. She detested Dsouza, but she really didn't want him to stop.

And he didn't, not until he'd worked his way back down and massaged the soles of her feet. By then she'd closed her eyes and was trying her best to imagine she was far away, soaking in a hot spring. Then he moved to the other foot and started again. She almost screamed when he reached her left ankle and a jolt of fire burned through her, but she managed not to kick him.

She laced her fingers together and squeezed, ignoring the agony in her ankle. "What's the favor?"

He raised an eyebrow. "What makes you think I have something in mind?"

"I know you. You always have plans."

"One scoundrel understands another." His half smile was back. "I want fifty percent off all future deals, and first dibs on any interesting machine you bring to life. And if we live, I want you to cook me a hot meal in that cave of yours."

She narrowed her eyes. "That's insane. Fifty percent, forever? You'll get it once and not again. And you want dinner?" They were still in Huda's dungeon without a way out, and he was thinking about food? He was toying with her, surely. You always had to be careful around Dsouza.

He looked around the cage, his eyes stopping on their dead cellmate. "Fifty percent on the best thing you can possibly sell. And dinner."

"I'm a terrible cook," she said.

"And even worse at conversation."

She kicked him, but not hard. "I'll put enough chilies in your meal that you won't bother me again."

"Sounds delicious." Dsouza worked his way up her calf. It felt so good, she nearly cried. He lifted his gaze to meet hers. "Your crazy sister never came back?"

Adya's brief moment of pleasure vanished, replaced by a vision of Priya alone in the flames. Why couldn't he have just shut up? "Gouros said he saw her burn in the spell wall." Her voice broke. "The bastard said he watched her die."

Dsouza's face betrayed no emotion. "Gouros said? You're a fool to believe anything Gouros says. I heard an Atavi techno-mancer rode into Mysore offering to help the maharaja. Your sister's naive enough to do something that idiotic." He grabbed Adya's wrist and pulled her up. "But I can't tell you if she's still alive. Mysore is every bit as deadly as a wall of flame."

Adya grabbed Dsouza by the shoulders, not sure if she'd heard right. "You said *rode* into Mysore? Rode in on what?" She held her breath. Everything depended on his answer.

Dsouza didn't shake her off. "On some blue bike thing. What difference does it make?"

Sparks lit behind her eyes. The blue moped had made it through the spell wall. Gouros, that ass, had lied. Priya was alive.

She squeezed Dsouza harder. "I have to get out of here now."

Dsouza raised an eyebrow. "I assumed that was our general plan."

"No, you don't understand. I need a machine to get through the spell wall. I need to find my sister." Dsouza was right. Mysore was nothing but danger. The maharaja would be more likely to enslave Priya than help her.

"Worry about your fool sister later," Dsouza said. "Let's see if you can finally walk. We've got to move fast."

Adya let go of Dsouza and stayed upright with the slightest wobble. The massage had worked wonders. They were getting out of here. But with her first step, she felt a crunch in her ankle, and her vision darkened. She would have fallen if Dsouza hadn't caught her.

"I think Gouros broke my ankle," she said. "You're not getting anywhere fast with me."

Dsouza hesitated, watching her limp. He glanced at the door again. "They'll be back soon. We can take down a few guards, and I'll—"

"You'll what? Carry me off the ship?" She shook her head. "Without weapons? Sneaking around with me on your shoulder? You're not that good, Bad Day."

Dsouza half carried her to the wall before easing her down. "Look, I know you're terrible at it, but shake the wax out of your ears and listen for once. Huda will let you live if you're valuable enough. You're the last witch left in the waste. Offer him something. Fix the ship. Fire up his damned motorcycle. Just don't piss him off. You're too good at pissing people off."

She shrugged out of his grip. "Don't ever call me a witch again." He was going to abandon her. Of course he was. Dsouza might be worse than no company at all, but she couldn't bear being alone in this cell with a dead body any longer.

Dsouza's face went stony. "I'd do more for you if I could, but there's someone else I have to get out of here."

She raised an eyebrow. "You brought someone with you?" She couldn't imagine him traveling with anyone. He would never willingly split his profits.

"A girl. We were captured by the British three days ago. She never should have come."

Adya froze. "You brought a Vayu girl into the jungle? For company or to sell her?"

Dsouza glared at her, and she wondered if she had gone too far. She kept her eyes on his fisted hands.

"The last thing in the world I need to do is explain myself to a paranoid witch who lives in a cave," he said.

"You're a lying thief, Dsouza," she snapped. "Tricking some girl into the waste. Not even I would have thought you were that low." He deserved to be in chains if he fooled a Vayu girl into following him into the jungle.

Dsouza stood. "You were less annoying upside down."

"She must be especially stupid to go anywhere with you."

Dsouza's entire body tensed. "She *was* stupid to come." He looked Adya in the eyes. "And you're an idiot if you don't listen. Strike a deal with Huda, and you'll survive. Not that I care, but I'm not going to get that favor if you're dead. There aren't any technomancers left."

"And how many has Huda burned out already? How many has he sold to the British? Don't fool yourself. You know what he'll do with me." She wasn't going to lick Huda's boots. And she wasn't going to give up on her sister, either, alone out there and probably in as much trouble as she was.

She grabbed Dsouza's arm. "Before you ditch me, help me over there."

Dsouza's eyes narrowed, but he pulled her up. "What for?"

"I'm going to try something. If it doesn't work, it'll still make a good distraction. Promise."

Dsouza helped her to the wall closest to the center of the ship. She pressed her hands against the rusted steel, reaching, searching.

Dsouza leaned in. "What are you doing?"

"Stealing magic."

She sensed the distant grinding of gears. Some technomancer had fired up the battleship's engines and lights for Huda. Within those engines lay dormant energy, magic that could be tapped if she was lucky. Her mother had explained it years ago, had made Adya practice drawing magic back into herself. *Attempt it only if you have no other option,* she'd warned. The risk was tremendous.

Adya muttered a prayer and searched for the magic the machines had been infused with. She opened herself up, striving to form a channel to draw in power.

A spasm ran through her muscles as something squeezed her mind like a vise. The air filled with the smell of grease and rusted gears. The ship's machines were unlike any she'd felt before. They were engines of battle. Machines that should never have been awoken. Their rage and cruelty burned bright in her mind.

You are weak, girl. We are warriors. We keep our souls to ourselves. Their laughter was a harsh scrape of metal upon metal. *Open yourself to us again, and we will be the ones who steal your soul.* Like a slap to the face, she felt her connection slam closed.

Adya tried again, straining until her face dripped with sweat. This time there was nothing. The machines had shut her out. They were not about to lend their strength to anyone. She banged her fist against the wall and turned to find Dsouza watching.

The sound of boots echoed down the hallway.

"Our luck sucks." But Dsouza didn't move.

"Get going or we're both dying here, and your girlfriend is going to become Huda's next prize slave."

Dsouza wouldn't meet her gaze. He slid away and took up a position behind the door. "Make a deal with Huda," he said. "Survive." His face looked strangely sad. "Remember not to piss him off."

"Why do you care?" Adya managed to pull herself up. She did her best to ignore the fire in her ankle.

"I don't." Dsouza picked up a set of heavy iron shackles. "But you owe me dinner."

The cell door clanged open.

A lone guard stepped in. He looked in confusion at the ceiling where Adya was supposed to be hanging.

"Over here." Adya swung a length of chain over her head in

a wide circle and flashed her best smile. If there was only one of them, she might have a chance.

Three more of Huda's thugs pressed inside. Gouros swept in behind them.

"A mongoose is always so full of tricks," he said.

Adya threw the chain at Gouros's head, but the assassin snatched it out of the air. Before Adya's tired muscles could respond, they rushed her. A host of hands pressed her to the floor, but not before she saw Dsouza slip out, and as Gouros leaned over to gloat, the door crashed closed behind them. The guards spun to find themselves locked inside. One rushed to the door and called for the others to stop playing games.

Gouros scanned the room and smacked one of his guards, sending the man reeling. "Only one dead body. It was the Jackal, you idiots."

The assassin slammed his boot on the floor next to Adya's head, bending to look her in the eye. "Looks like the Jackal left you behind. Good. Tea with Huda is ready. You may find it quite bitter."

CHAPTER FIVE

T HEY BOUND ADYA'S WRISTS AND DRAGGED HER TO
her feet. She almost spat in Gouros's face, but the
look in his eye stopped her. She'd seen him remove
a tongue from a crook before, and losing Dsouza
had clearly erased the little restraint he possessed.

A guard prodded her, and she limped forward, down the
dark corridor, while Gouros barked orders. Each short step fired
fresh misery through her leg. If only her hands were free. If
only she had her spear. She tried to remember what Dsouza had
said—negotiate something; stay alive; don't piss Huda off. That
wasn't her style. She needed to stay alive to find Priya, but if she
got the chance, she was going to throttle Huda.

Gouros lowered his voice. "Wheezer, Raza, block the way
upstairs. If Huda finds out the Jackal escaped, we're all dead.
The rest of you get belowdecks and close it down. Find him.
Kill him. Baso, with me." Gouros raised his golden ring to his
face and blew over it. The fury on his face had faded, and a
smirk took its place. He swept his cape behind him. "Delays,
always delays. Your tea will be cold, Mongoose. But now that
we're late, there's something I'd like you to see."

Gouros gestured, and Baso, a giant of a man, pushed Adya
toward a short flight of metal stairs. He ground a knuckle in her
back as encouragement to climb.

Adya leaned her shoulder against the wall and forced herself to hop on her good leg. Through a porthole she caught a glimpse of a flight of white cranes floating down to their nests in the early evening. She hopped another stair and felt a lump in her throat. How many prisoners had marched along these corridors? Had any ever seen their homes again?

Gouros stepped ahead of her to unlock a door. "The Jackal won't get far, but he may miss seeing Huda's cage in action. What a shame."

An enormous steel box, twenty feet high, filled half the room and radiated terror. A ceiling studded with iron spikes made the purpose of the box clear. One wall was inlaid with a golden image of a naga, a giant demon with the body of a snake and the torso of a man. It stared straight at Adya with merciless red eyes, its spears pointed at the base of the cage, awaiting its next victim. She backpedaled, heart racing, until she ran into the immovable Baso.

With a horrible grinding sound, the spiked ceiling descended.

Gouros nodded at the cage. "They're testing it," he explained. "Huda has his own private viewing area in his captain's chambers, but today he's got company. He'll slide the top grate open so they can watch his prisoner beg."

She wanted to say something smart to Gouros. Wanted to make him understand how much she despised him. But the grinding of the gears stole her words away. She held her breath as the iron spikes crashed to the floor with horrible finality. Once, Adya had seen Huda drop someone into this spiked box.

She'd turned and fled, but the screams had caught up with her.

Gouros rapped his knuckles on the cage's steel wall. "Four technomancers burned themselves out firing up the motors for this cage. Worth every one."

She hadn't thought it was possible to hate Gouros more, but she was wrong. Any self-pity she might have felt dissolved into rage, her most comfortable emotion. Rage at the assassin and rage at Huda, who used people up like they were boxes of matches. Whose men had thrown her aunt into a burning house.

Adya turned at the sound of a thud. Baso was on the floor, struggling to pull a knife out of his neck.

"Did you steal a child's bedsheets to make that cape, Gouros?" Dsouza stood over Baso, holding the big man's spear. He leveled it at Gouros like he wasn't quite sure how to use it. "That's low, even for you."

She never imagined she'd be so happy to hear Bad Day's voice.

Gouros slid to the side, and two long knives appeared in his hands. "I should have put a knife through your heart earlier, Jackal. My mistake."

"You frighten me, Cape Boy." Dsouza jabbed, but Gouros had been expecting it. He stepped back and smiled.

Dsouza didn't have a chance. Atavi trained with the spear from childhood, until every move became instinct. Gouros was toying with him. The next time he thrust in such an amateur way, Gouros would put a knife through his chest.

Gouros stayed still, waiting for the mistake as Dsouza tried to use the spear's reach to keep him at bay. He didn't have to wait long.

Dsouza lunged, his attack painfully obvious. Gouros didn't hide his look of triumph as he glided into position.

Adya couldn't bear it. She threw herself at Gouros, head-butting him as hard as she'd ever hit anyone. Blackness filled her vision. Her injured leg gave way, and she tumbled, crashing into Gouros.

Gouros's knife slashed the air where she'd been standing. There was a thump as Dsouza struck his head with the butt of the spear, and Gouros collapsed on top of Adya, limp.

The filthy cape ended up in her mouth. "Get him off of me," she demanded.

Dsouza dragged the unconscious assassin off and pulled Adya to her feet. He flashed that damned half smile. "You're welcome. I'm thinking hot sambar, with dosas. I'll leave dessert to you."

"You're the one who's welcome." Her head rang, and her ankle continued to scream. "If we stay alive, I'm going to have a migraine for days."

Dsouza used one of Gouros's knives to cut her bonds then tied the assassin's wrists behind his back. He wrapped the cape around Gouros's face. "His bedsheet was useful after all."

The sight of Gouros looking like a mummy was the happiest thing Adya had seen all day. She might owe Dsouza a decent meal after all. "I'll think about dessert," she said. She couldn't believe he'd come back for her. "Why didn't you kill him?"

"Gouros is Huda's nephew. I need him alive." Dsouza picked him up and slung his unconscious body over a shoulder. "I've got a date with Huda. I need room to negotiate."

He hadn't come back for her. Of course he hadn't. He'd come back for a hostage. That made more sense, but it was still insane. She pointed at the deck above, where Huda held court. "You're going up there?"

Dsouza jerked his head toward the corner of the room. "Huda's private cabin is that direction. There's a way out from there. You should be able to slip into the jungle before they know you're gone."

"This is a new level of idiotic, Bad Day. Huda won't let you live." Dsouza was going to get himself killed. Somehow, it didn't seem right.

Dsouza's smile vanished. "I have to get her out."

His girlfriend. He was a crazed Vayu liar who would risk his life for a girl. Dsouza was a killer and a criminal, but you could do worse.

He kicked the spear toward her. "Use it as a crutch. I have no idea what to do with these damned toothpicks." He started away with Gouros over his shoulder. A set of stairs led above deck to Huda and a quick death. "Start thinking up recipes for me, okay?" Dsouza called out. He marched up the stairs without so much as a look back. He sure wasn't sentimental.

Adya slammed a hand into the floor. There was no way in hell Dsouza would survive, but she wasn't stupid enough to follow him and end up in the gangster's torture cage herself. She wasn't going to start acting like Priya and put herself in danger for nothing.

And why should she help Dsouza anyway? She limped across the room toward an ornate door and pressed her ear to the fine wood. No sound came from the other side. Two blows with the butt of the spear served as her key, but she hesitated before stepping through. Bad Day shouldn't die Huda's victim, but there was nothing she could do about it.

She pushed the door open and entered Huda's private chamber.

The cabin was blessedly empty of guards. The sweet smell of sandalwood permeated the air. Adya's bare feet sank into thick carpet in a room more richly furnished than any she'd ever seen. One wall of the terrible steel cage adjoined the captain's cabin for Huda's viewing pleasure. At the far end, the rays of the sun filtered in through an enormous stained glass window, bathing the room in color. Racks of fine weapons lined the walls, along with pictures of Huda in various poses of triumph. There was Huda holding the severed head of someone who must have owed him money; Huda with the queen of the Atavi; even Huda with his arm around a British officer. In every picture, the crime lord sat astride his prized dirt bike. And there, on a pedestal, gleaming like the world's greatest trophy, perched the motorcycle itself—Huda's custom red-and-white Yamaha 450.

Behind it stood a door with a porthole looking out on the jungle. A way out, just as Dsouza had promised. Even better, a green leather desk on the far wall sported stacks of silver coins, a gold pocket watch, and a ruby as large as Adya's fingernail. She shoved the loot into a silk bag lying near the coins. She would need it if she survived.

On the rack of weapons, she found her black spear, her red leather jacket, and her pendant. She whispered a silent prayer of thanks that all her belongings were here. Best of all, the drongo hung in a cage just above the door. Gouros hadn't killed it after all.

There was a scraping sound from above. Adya threw herself behind the green desk as a panel in the ceiling slid open, giving her a view of the upper deck, the sepal trees towering over the battleship, and the mass of guards gathered above.

"Where is she? I'm going to throw you idiots in the cage if someone doesn't bring the girl now." The unmistakable form of Huda paced into view. Standing a head higher than his men, Huda looked like a giant stick figure. The gangster lord could have eaten enough to feed two families, but he preferred to subsist on cocaine. As a result, his lips twitched and his hands trembled, but his mind remained as sharp and cruel as a razor.

A muscular man, terribly pale, with shoulder-length silver hair, wearing a formal military uniform, lounged in a chair under an expansive sunshade. The evening light seemed to curl away from him, leaving his face in shadow. Next to him stood two unarmed soldiers dressed in camouflage. Looming behind them was a thick-limbed soldier, twice as tall as anyone else on deck, his skin a dull stone gray. The British had come aboard with a troll. Dsouza was walking into disaster.

"This is turning into a dog's dinner, Huda," the silver-haired man said. He tipped back a teacup, then set it on a tray, in a way that made the simple gesture seem like a terrible threat. The sound of the man's voice made Adya shiver. Whoever he was, she wanted to be as far away from him as possible.

The officer abruptly backhanded the entire tea service onto the deck, sending shattered cups spilling into the cage below. "Huda, I grow tired of waiting."

The troll pounded the bulwark, leaving a massive dent in the rosewood trim.

"You've no need to doubt me, Lord General Clive. You'll have your technomancer soon." Huda's voice sounded controlled, deferential for once. "You've brought the girl?"

Adya froze, staring at the British general, a man who clearly terrified Huda, who even the sun avoided. Lord General Clive, the head of the British army in South India, had stepped into her jungle. Clive the vampire, who never lost a battle, who never took prisoners, who no one ever crossed. The general himself had come to collect her.

"But of course." Clive waved a hand, and one of his soldiers pushed forward a prisoner Adya hadn't noticed. A Vayu girl who couldn't have been more than sixteen stumbled toward Huda with her hands tied behind her back and a gag in her mouth. The poor kid had dyed her long hair bright blue. Her arms were covered in black tattoos. She looked like the kind of unfortunate misfit who would make the mistake of falling in love with a crook like Dsouza.

"Huda, you've served us well. Enjoy your revenge, but make certain no one learns of our role in this. We still hope to persuade the maharaja to our side. Losing the girl should crush the last of his resolve. You know there's a thirty-million-rupee reward for her safe return?"

Huda stepped forward. "No amount would be enough for me, Lord General. The maharaja insults me at every turn. Calls me a petty crook who pretends to rule in place of our queen. I hold a long grudge."

Clive sighed. "Vengeance is a cruel master, Huda."

"As is the quest for power, Lord General. So many centuries later, and your faerie queen still wishes to restore her empire? Well, she's almost done it. All that remains is to sweep away one troublesome maharaja and take the South." Huda spread his hands, palms up. "When she succeeds, I hope she remembers the many contributions I've made on her behalf."

Clive sighed. "The queen is wise, Huda. Linking the wells will cement our dominance across the globe. We'll need someone trusted to keep things under control in the jungle. You don't need to worry." He nodded, and one of his men pushed the young girl forward.

Huda examined the blue-haired girl, who shrank under his scrutiny. "You're certain she's helpless?"

Clive waved a hand dismissively. "If she were any kind of sorceress, she would have escaped already. We've restrained her so she doesn't harm herself with her pathetic magic."

Huda cracked his knuckles. "Let's show her what her future holds." He gestured to one of his guards, and they dragged forth someone Adya recognized. Now she knew who had betrayed her.

"Where is my technomancer, Bulla?"

Bulla Sholay opened his mouth to answer, but Huda shook his head. "Too late, my friend. I said I wanted her here *on time*. I hate late payments." A guard kicked Bulla in the back, sending him tumbling into the open cage.

Bulla slammed onto the floor, ten feet from Adya, and lay still, moaning.

"Drop it fast." Huda flicked a hand at one of his goons. The cage's ceiling plummeted in a thunder of grinding gears until the steel points crashed to the floor. Bulla's scream sent shivers down Adya's spine. The gears reversed, and the bloody ceiling began to rise.

Clive raised an eyebrow. "Impressively barbaric." He gestured, and his men pulled the Vayu girl back. "You will have the girl, Huda, as soon as you deliver me the technomancer."

Huda's reply was cut short by the sound of a steel door banging open. Every head above deck turned at the sound.

A torch blazed behind Dsouza, framing his figure in orange light. He stood on the stairs above the bridge, holding a knife to Gouros's neck.

Adya knew she should take this moment to get the hell out while every eye was focused on Dsouza. No one would notice if she slipped into the jungle with all her belongings and plenty of Huda's money. This was her chance.

Dsouza propped a foot on a large barrel. "Huda, you damned traitor. You invited the British to the party instead of me? Rude."

Huda spread both arms wide. "Dsouza, welcome to the show. I see you've lost what little sanity you possessed." He turned to his guards. "Throw the Jackal in the cage."

They rushed to obey.

Dsouza moved so fast that Adya almost missed it. A flash of silver, and the first guard tumbled face down, a knife in his neck. Dsouza already had another in hand. "One more step and your nephew dies, Huda."

The men about to rush the stairs hesitated. Foul as he was, Gouros was their commander.

Dsouza shook the assassin like a limp doll, one foot still on the barrel. "Take your revenge another way. Give me the girl, and I'll let Gouros go."

"My beloved nephew?" Huda raised an eyebrow. "How do I even know that's him? You have a towel over his head."

"I thought it was a bedsheet." Dsouza's knife twisted, and Gouros screamed through his cape. Dsouza tossed the assassin's severed finger high into the air to land at Huda's feet.

Huda bent to pick up his nephew's bloody digit. He slipped the gold ring off, examined it, and dropped the dead finger to the floor.

His laugh started as a chuckle, then progressed to a body-shaking event. Huda wiped tears from his eyes and caught his breath. "You're too much, Dsouza. They say you would sell your own mother for a meal, but do you really need thirty million rupees?" Huda scratched the back of his neck. "Well, you'll die for it. Gouros has found his reward. I would have thrown him in the cage myself if he'd come on deck without the Mongoose. Go ahead. Kill him."

Adya tensed. The ache in her chest surprised her. Dsouza would be dead in moments.

Dsouza tossed Gouros down the stairs and kicked over the

barrel. Wooden staves cracked as the barrel's lid popped open, spilling dark oil. The black slick raced across the deck, dripping down into the cage. Dsouza reached behind his shoulder to lift the torch out of its bracket and raised the flame high.

"Let her go, Huda, or I burn your boat to the ground."

Huda hesitated. He surveyed his deck, and Adya could imagine the gangster calculating how much of his precious ship would go up in flames, how much damage Dsouza could do.

Clive rose to his feet. "There will be no deal. The girl will not return to Mysore." He nodded in the direction of the troll. "Hughes, if you would."

The enormous troll seized the blue-haired girl in one hand and dangled her over the open cage.

Clive pointed at Dsouza. "Drop that torch and he drops the girl." The vampire general glanced at the sky, where the evening sun still glimmered through the trees. "It's far too sunny for me to be bothered by such rubbish. Davies, Evans, put an end to this and bring me the technomancer. I'll be in my quarters. Let's wrap this up and move out as soon as it's properly dark. I prefer my supper in a less chaotic setting." Clive stepped into the shadows and disappeared.

The two British soldiers sprang forward, shifting as they ran. Claws burst from their hands. Their lips curled back to make way for jagged fangs. Adya held her breath, transfixed, as, in the space of seconds, a pair of wolves bounded straight for Dsouza.

"No!" Dsouza leapt down the stairs, torch in one hand, knife in the other. The only thing that saved him from being impaled by a spear was Huda's goons falling over themselves to get out of the way of the two werewolves.

Dsouza threw himself feetfirst into the black mess and slid across the deck. He stabbed the first wolf in the throat as the beast skidded toward him, clawing to find purchase on the now frictionless steel. Dsouza tore his knife free in time to thrust the torch into the second's open jaws.

Its face caught fire.

Dsouza had somehow found his feet and was past the wolves and running.

"Get that damned thing off my deck," Huda shouted, pushing one of his guards forward, but no one was going to stop a burning wolf before it hit the oil. Flames erupted behind Dsouza. Gouros screamed.

The troll dropped the girl.

Adya's fingers curled into fists as she watched Dsouza's eyes go wide, trying to dive, trying to do something when there was nothing more he could possibly do.

The troll backhanded Dsouza, and he tumbled after the girl, striking the wall of the iron cage, slamming down in front of Adya.

Adya thrust her arm through the bars but couldn't reach him.

"Drop it slow," Huda rasped.

The gears ground as the spiked ceiling started to fall.

CHAPTER SIX

ADYA SHOOK THE BARS OF THE CAGE, SHOUTING OVER the roar of the gears, but Dsouza didn't move. She scanned the wall for some switch, some lever to stop the ceiling's descent, but there was nothing. Wedging her fingers into a small gap in the metal, she pulled until her skin tore, but no amount of effort was going to rip apart a half-inch-thick piece of steel.

The ceiling had dropped another foot. "Dsouza," she screamed, not sure what she hoped to accomplish. The blue-haired girl knelt at his side.

Dsouza finally lifted his head. "Damn," he said, looking up at the falling spikes. Gouros's knife appeared in his hand. He tore the gag from the girl's mouth and slashed the cords binding her wrists.

He took her face in his hands. "Do it now. There won't be another chance."

The girl shook free of him. Whatever they had planned, she really didn't want to go through with it, but as the gears ground louder, she bent and scraped parallel lines across the floor. She stuttered out a mantra and hesitated before raising both arms above her head and starting again. For an eternal moment, nothing happened.

Before Adya lost hope, a gust of wind struck her face. She

squeezed the bars, hoping the Vayu magic would burst the cage with the fury of a storm and sweep the deck of Huda and his crew. Dsouza had brought a sorceress. They had a chance.

Blue hair swirled about the girl's head as the spell took effect, and the fingers of her outstretched hands glowed with bronze light. It lanced from her hand, striking the ceiling, arcing across the steel. Sparks showered down on them.

When the light faded, nothing had changed.

Huda's laughter rang out. His haggard face appeared over the grating.

"This is the show of the century. You upset the wolves, Dsouza, but the fire is already out. And I've found my technomancer! Mongoose, it warms my heart to see you again. Your parents served me well over the years. I'm sure General Clive will find plenty of uses for you."

Adya glared up at him and willed herself not to tremble. "Nothing could defrost your heart, Huda. Your heart could freeze the sun."

"So sorry about your aunt, Mongoose. I understand *she* was quite hot in the end."

Adya's vision swam. She squeezed the bars of the cage so hard, she couldn't feel her fingers. Why did the crime lord always win? She should be running for the door, trying to limp as far into the jungle as possible before they sent the wolves after her, but she couldn't tear herself away.

And the sorceress's spell was not yet finished.

The spiked ceiling seethed with mist, as if brewing a thunderstorm. Adya squinted as one of the spikes drew back and hissed. Dsouza dodged as the fanged head of a cobra struck. The girl had somehow transformed the spikes into giant snakes. Angry snakes. The Vayu were supposed to be able to shape the wind into any illusion, but this girl had made something real. Now Adya understood why the girl had been reluctant to try her magic. She had the strength to draw vast amounts of power and no ability to shape it. The worst possible combination.

Adya forced herself not to look as the two of them crouched as low as possible, trying to stave off the inevitable. Pushing aside her fear, she concentrated instead on the mechanism that was dropping the ceiling.

The ceiling creaked lower down, and Huda bellowed. "Snakes! The cage is even better with snakes. Clive has no idea what he's missing."

She pressed a hand against the wall and let her emotions flow, searching for the hidden power. *"Vishwakarma namo namah. shilpakari, mangalkari, chakradhari."* She let magic seek out magic, and when she found it, she shuddered. Around the room violent machinery pulsed and ground. The system lowering the ceiling was connected to gears and lights and wiring throughout the battleship. Some technomancer had wired it all together, leaving everything vulnerable.

Adya reached out with her own magic, and the ship felt her presence. The sound of machinery grew high pitched as snakes hissed, and the ceiling dropped faster.

We warned you before, the machines whispered.

Her mind flooded with images of bodies blown to pieces and flags raised up in surrender. She was doomed, they said. She

73

should surrender before she humiliated herself. The ship had sailed distant seas and sent its enemies to their ocean graves. They had launched missiles at cities, knowing how many each warhead would kill. How could one girl face their might?

Adya pressed her forehead against the steel and opened herself. She had her own darkness and room for theirs as well. It was time she let flow all her fury against Huda, for everything he'd done to her family and the poor people of the jungle, for all the technomancers he'd burned out, for all the times he never paid a price. Magic filled her until it all but spilled out from her eyes, dripped from her fingertips, burned on the tip of her tongue. She let the machines have it all at once.

The force of her emotion burst through the machines' defenses. She drank in their strength, pulling their magic, ripping it out of pistons and cranks, taking in every bit of violence the machines could throw at her. Distant explosions rocked the ship as visions of fire filled her mind. The crack in her ankle knit together; the aches in her ribs burned away. Magic dispelled her exhaustion, replacing it with an energy she could barely contain.

Huda drew back, screaming orders to his men.

The ceiling shuddered to a stop a foot above the prisoner's heads. The snakes had vanished. But Adya wasn't done. An image of her aunt dying in the fire filled her mind. She reached across the ship's wiring and ripped away the last of the magic, sending the machines and lights across the battleship back to the dead sleep they'd dwelt in for centuries. A cloud of steam filled the room along with a deafening churning of gears as its engines ground themselves to pieces.

Adya fell back, coughing.

Explosions shook the floor.

She pushed herself up. She would tear this whole place apart, would rip everything to pieces and drop Huda into his own wretched pit.

Adya stopped, breathing hard, not sure if these were her ideas or the machines', urging her to violence. She pushed away the thoughts of destruction. The dreadful strength inside her demanded a purpose. She pressed her fingers once more into the seams of the metal cage. Now her fingers were a vise, her arm a terrible lever. The steel grew hot, and the bolts ripped off as an entire panel fell away.

Dsouza stared in dismay as he crawled through the gap. He pulled the girl behind him as men shouted and boots pounded across the steel deck. Huda was bellowing orders.

"What the hell did you do?" Dsouza demanded. He took another look at Adya. "Your skin is glowing."

"That almost sounds like a compliment," she said. The magic had healed her wounds, but the excess energy was burning her inside. She held up her hands. Her fingers were trembling. "If I don't do something with this, I'm going to explode."

Dsouza ran to the weapons rack and seized a sword. "Explode later. I jammed the door closed above deck, but they'll break through when they stop panicking. We've got to get out."

"Not yet." Adya picked up her black spear and thrust the butt through Huda's stained glass, sending green and blue shards showering to the jungle floor below. They were going to need as big a hole as possible.

The pressure of the magic building inside her was unbearable, but Adya was not leaving without her things. She slid her arm through the sleeve of her red jacket and grabbed the birdcage off the wall.

"What are you doing?" Dsouza was looking at her like she'd lost her mind.

"Someone's got to survive this." The drongo launched itself into the air as soon as Adya opened the wire door. "Let my brother know I'm fine, bird. Hopefully, he won't do anything too insane." She looked out the shattered window as the drongo disappeared over the jungle.

From here, an entire side of the battleship was visible. Smoke poured through open portholes. Huda's guards were running in every direction. It would be an easy jump and dash into the jungle, but she wouldn't get far on her feet.

"I'm getting out of here," Adya said. Magic rattled against the inside of her skull. Much longer and her hair would spontaneously combust. Before she could take another step, her knees buckled. Bright lights filled her vision.

"Get me those." She pointed to Huda's black leather riding boots.

Dsouza grabbed them. "How will these help?"

Adya slammed her hand down on the prized motorcycle. She managed to smile through the pain. "I'm taking Huda's ride."

Power surged out of her in a torrent.

The motorcycle drank like a starved beast. Its headlight flared as it awoke for the first time in centuries, finally jolted from its long slumber. A forest fire couldn't have provided more energy. A silver glow spilled out from beneath the bike, like bright water flooding the room.

Adya clenched her jaw as the magic burned through her bones. Now came the hardest part. She felt the machine's soul—confused, desperate, and hungry for life. It wanted to run, to fly over the earth again and feel the wind racing to keep up with it. She touched its heart and felt its turmoil—it needed more energy, or it would fade again back into oblivion. It feared it would die again and never touch the ground.

The motorcycle was nothing like the engines had been. If she wanted to save Priya, she had to take the chance and trust the bike wouldn't burn her to ashes.

She opened herself to the machine and let it in, let it see all of her, the rage and sadness, the loneliness she'd felt since losing her parents and her sister, her worry for Mohan, her determination to get Priya back. She felt it inside her, picking through her memories as the flow of magic grew stronger. The motorcycle roared, and the backwash of its own memories almost drowned her.

Her mind filled with images of the bike racing, flying, jumping toward the sun, ever faster. It was built for terrible speed, and it would never be put back to sleep again.

Adya pulled herself off the floor. She threw her leg over the seat and grasped the handlebars. Confusion flooded her as the bike tried to understand where it was, tried to break free. She fought to maintain control of her own thoughts as she steered toward the open window.

Dsouza and the girl were already getting ready to jump. He nodded in her direction. "Don't die today, Mongoose." The girl had her arm over his shoulder. She still seemed dazed. Dsouza looked like he'd already taken one too many beatings.

Adya was already regretting what she was about to say. "They'll track you down in the jungle, Bad Day. Huda will have her back before nightfall."

Dsouza's half smile vanished. "No one catches me in the jungle. I'm faster than any of them."

"Is she?" Adya asked.

His jaw clenched as he gazed up toward the deck above them, where Huda was surely organizing his men. "I'll kill anyone who gets near her."

She sighed. She was starting to get as ridiculous as her sister. "The bike has room for one more. Put the girl behind me. I'll get her out."

Dsouza raised an eyebrow. "You want the reward for bringing her back?"

The jerk thought of everything in terms of money. She should have known. "Put her on or forget it. I'm leaving."

"I'm not taking orders from anyone. I'll decide where I go." It was the first time the girl had spoken. She held Dsouza's gaze, then hugged him tight. "You'll stand a better chance without me slowing you. Don't let them catch you."

Dsouza grabbed Adya's arm in a grip that was a little too firm. "You damned well better take care of her, Mongoose."

"Whatever," Adya said. The desperate look in the crook's eyes surprised her.

He hurried back to the weapons rack. "Forget the fifty percent deal. Keep her alive and I'll cook dinner."

"I don't trust your cooking, Bad Day."

"You don't trust anyone." Dsouza's smile returned full force. "Sonya, meet Adya. They call her the Mongoose because she's so damn mean. She stinks at conversation." Before the girl could protest, he'd placed two knives in her hands. "Take them. They're silvered."

He turned to Adya one last time. "Sonya's father is one of the maharaja's finest sorcerers. You'll keep her safe?"

"As safe as I can with everyone trying to kill us," Adya said.

He gave a grim nod. "I'll find you, but if anything goes wrong, wait for me near the spell wall at the point closest to Mysore." His last look was reserved for Adya. He examined her face as if trying to see inside her. As if seeing her for the very first time.

Adya looked away. "What are you waiting for? Want to spend more time with Huda?"

Dsouza shook his head and, quite unlike himself, said nothing. Instead, he turned and leapt out the window, disappearing into the trees. He wasn't one for goodbyes.

Adya gestured for Sonya to get on the bike. The daughter of one of the maharaja's most valued sorcerers, Dsouza had claimed. Adya's hands pooled with sweat at the thought of spending time alone with some important Vayu girl. Why had she promised anything to that crook?

A tremendous thumping sound in the stairwell stole her attention. The door above was not going to last.

Adya revved the engine and aimed the bike for the shattered window.

She glanced back at Sonya. "Hold on tight."

CHAPTER SEVEN

ADYA BRACED FOR IMPACT AS THE YAMAHA ROCKETED FOR-ward. It struck the ground and tore into the jungle floor like an animal freed from its cage. *Free! I am free!* She reeled as the Yamaha flooded her mind with raw emotion.

Someone had dared to paralyze the motorcycle, to trap it where its wheels couldn't spin. Whoever had wronged it was going to pay a terrible price. The world was its playground, and its freedom had been stolen for far too long. Images of blasting past finish lines and trophies heaped upon trophies assaulted Adya. Justice demanded revenge.

Huda's motorcycle was totally insane. It was going to get them killed.

Adya fought to turn the handlebars toward the jungle, away from the battleship and the chaos of Huda's scrambling guards, but the motorcycle had its own ideas. She felt the mental blow as the bike fought back, realizing she was trying to deny its revenge. Sonya squeezed the breath out of her as the bike spun in a sudden arc, almost throwing them. Adya held on somehow as they veered straight for the battleship.

"Are you mad?" the girl shouted with her head plastered to Adya's back.

"You try driving this thing." Sonya could find something less insane to leave on if she wanted.

Vengeance. The bike's foremost desire was a deafening scream. The damned machine was determined to run over whoever had caged it. Its will, its emotions were tremendous. Now she understood why Huda's technomancers had burned themselves out trying to bring the motorcycle to life. It had a soul that could suck up more emotion than any person possessed. If she hadn't fed it the magic of the entire battleship, it would have drained her of everything. How could she ever control such a machine?

A spear grazed Adya's leather jacket, and she dropped as low as possible. She tried again, but the damned handlebars wouldn't turn as long as the machine had a plan of its own.

A stupidly brave guard charged into their path. He crouched with his weapon braced before him, but the bike never wavered. The engine growled like a giant tiger and accelerated with speed Adya couldn't believe. They were going to be impaled. She squeezed the handlebars desperately as the bike's front tire shot high into the air.

The guard's eyes went wide when he realized they weren't stopping. The bike knocked his spear aside in a wheelie rush, planted its treads into his forehead, and swept on.

Ahead, the battleship spouted flames. Smoke poured into the sky. Huda's guards rushed about the top deck, putting out fires. A few stopped to gaze at the spectacle of the oncoming bike. Too many hefted their spears. The crazy thing would survive a dozen scratches in its paint, but the two girls would be skewered. It clearly didn't care, swerving back and forth, aiming itself at anyone foolish enough not to dive away.

In the midst of the chaos, Adya spotted Huda standing at the edge of the top deck. Even from this distance she could feel the fury pouring off him. She had blown up his battleship, embarrassed him in front of the British, and taken the thing he loved most in the world. Worse, she had stolen his dream of riding the Yamaha in front of his men.

At least she'd done one thing right.

She risked raising a hand to wave. "Love the bike!"

Huda's spear arced high over the burning ship and plunged toward them.

Adya had only an instant to send a single desperate thought to the bike. *He caged you. It was him.*

The bike spun in a sudden circle, and Huda's spear struck the ground a foot away. The engine gave a deep growl as the bike hesitated. It was planning some crazy route to reach the top deck and run Huda down. It was going to launch itself back into the burning ship to try to kill the gangster.

The wind envies me, it boasted. *Moonbeams can't imagine my speed. Nothing will catch me again. I will have vengeance.* The machine's voice rumbled in her head, proud and confident. It didn't give a damn about its passengers.

But before it could destroy any hope of their escape, two giant wolves appeared at Huda's side.

Huda pointed at the bike. "There's your technomancer. Collect her yourself if Lord Clive wants her so badly."

The monsters raised their heads and howled. They leapt from the high deck with fangs bared.

But Adya had caught a glimpse of the bike's mind. She took a gamble on what fueled its soul. Pride over vengeance. Speed over destruction. *Those stupid dogs think they are faster than you. They are going to prove you are no champion. That you never were a champion.*

And the motorcycle responded. It was born to race. Nothing would be allowed to overtake it. As the wolves' paws hit the ground, it launched forward like a hawk in flight.

Adya felt the true weight of the motorcycle's magic for the first time, enveloping her in a cocoon of force, pressing her down against the seat. Where before they had been baggage on its back, in danger of being launched off with every turn, now they were part of its team. Adya turned the handlebars and the bike let her steer. She no longer had to cling on for survival; the bike would keep her astride, no matter what came their way.

The battleship blurred.

"They're getting closer." Dsouza's girlfriend prodded her in the back, and Adya risked a glance. The giant wolves were gaining with every bound.

Adya forced her gaze ahead and aimed for a break in the jungle where a narrow dirt path twisted below the canopy. Hopefully, the terrain wouldn't tear the machine to pieces.

The bike struck the dirt path and gave a tremendous jolt as something hit them. Adya swerved to avoid giant tree trunks and instant death. A roar sounded behind her, and Sonya screamed. The bike began to drag. The wolves were pulling them down.

Adya twisted the throttle and begged for more speed. She filled her mind with images of defeat. They were being passed up; they were going to lose the race to stray mutts. They would never be champions again.

No. The bike would not allow it.

The Yamaha surged forward, magic and motors ripping apart any laws of physics that dared defy them. Trees became patches of deadly color whipping by. Adya's mind merged with the bike's, every twist of the handlebars guided by her reflexes blending with the bike's will. Never before had she felt so part of a machine, at one with the wheels, full of its desire to triumph. Her eyes filled with tears as the wind tore at her. Roots, rocks, even a stream could not stop them as they flew on wheels that barely touched the ground.

Amidst the terror of it, Adya smiled at the thought of Huda fuming. She'd succeeded in putting a knife in him for all he had done. He might still kill her, but it felt good.

They sped on for what seemed like ages before Adya realized there was no sound of pursuit and risked a look behind. An enormous wolf's head hung clamped to the leather seat, with the girl's knife through its neck. She'd had no idea how close they had come to being caught. The body was so mangled that only a scrap of pelt and one paw remained. The Yamaha had dragged the soldier to death.

With a turn of the handlebars and a spray of dirt, Adya brought the bike to a halt.

Sonya wrenched out the knife and raised it above her head. "For both of them." She plunged the blade back into the extremely dead werewolf and held it there while her arms shook.

Adya regretted stopping. The girl clearly had some issues. "I think it's dead now," she called, wondering if she should pull Sonya away. She thought better of it when Sonya tore out the knife and stabbed the dead monster again. Better to let her work through some anger.

Sonya got off the bike and seized the wolf's head. She got a running start and threw it as far as she could—three feet at most—then panted with the effort of it all. Adya was surprised she'd managed even that. She estimated the girl had muscle mass only slightly greater than a skeleton's.

Adya checked behind them. "Look, I promise, that one is super dead, but the other one is going to be really unhappy about it. Come on."

Sonya turned to Adya with a wild look in her eye. "Let them come." She was holding the knife like she was ready to stab something, but at least she got back on.

Great. She had a deranged motorcycle and an unstable sorceress to deal with. "Let's not be here when they do."

Adya kicked the bike into gear. The Yamaha trembled with eagerness, and she obliged. She had no intention of fighting another one of those monsters if she could help it. They had at best another half hour of daylight before the night changed everything.

As the sun began to disappear, monkeys gathered in the trees to watch them speed by. Adya inhaled the warm scent of wet vegetation and opened herself to the hum of the motorcycle.

The bike's constant whispering of racing days gone by washed away the jumble of her emotions. *Alive*, the bike screamed at her. *We are meant to be chased and to fly.*

Darkness was descending when Adya skidded to a halt. Clouds had filled the sky, the air heavy with the threat of deluge. A crumbling stone temple stood fifty feet off the path, its walls covered in vines and propped up by a giant banyan. The tree's branches spread wide over the ruins like a giant laying claim to its domain, its aerial roots forming living columns to support the cracked stone facade. A carving on the temple wall displayed the dark face of a goddess, eight arms outstretched, a sword in each hand: Kali, goddess of death, slayer of demons. Adya sighed. She would have preferred something more hopeful.

Dsouza's girlfriend stumbled off the back of the motorcycle. Knives appeared in her hands as she scanned the jungle. "All right, I've got this," she declared.

"Got what?" Adya leaned the bike against a tree.

Sonya ignored Adya and headed toward the temple. She surveyed a spot near one of the crumbling embankments. "This will do." She pointed to a thicket of thorn-covered vines. "Hide there and be ready while I wait in the open. When the werewolf appears, I will stun it with light. Then you pierce it from the side while I finish it with the silvered knife."

Adya leaned against her spear, not sure she'd heard right. "You'll stun it with light?" She didn't bother mentioning that she wasn't about to hide in a thornbush.

The girl took a deep breath. "What you saw back there was

not a fair example of my skills. I'm excellent with lights."

What she'd seen back there had been a disaster, and no light show was going to help against a werewolf. "Are these lights that burn and set things on fire?" Adya asked. She doubted it. And the girl obviously had no idea that Vayu spells would attract every yaksha in this part of the jungle.

The girl glared at her. "You have no right to question me. You Atavi know nothing of Vayu magic. I intend to dazzle the beast."

"Right," Adya said. She appraised the banyan. They would get soaked if the monsoon came down, but the tree would provide some protection. She turned back to find the girl brandishing her knife.

"Have you ever fought a werewolf?" Adya asked. "Wait, don't answer that. Have you ever fought anything?"

The girl squared her shoulders. "I have studied a great number of battles."

"I thought so," Adya said. "Look, I've never even seen a werewolf before. And I don't want to fight one." She pointed up at the banyan. "The only way we survive the night is to climb before the sun sets and let the yaksha kill the wolf. They hate any magic they're not used to, so if that monster changes shape or makes enough noise, it will get itself eaten."

The girl raised her chin. "Running is not the way of an Atavi warrior."

"Oh, you study our battle tactics in Mysore?" The fool was intent on dying. "And I thought you regarded us all as primitives." Adya started toward the tree but stopped before she got far. Leaving the girl behind was clearly the smartest option. Unfortunately, she'd given Dsouza her word to at least try to keep her safe.

"Look, I know you're eager to stab another wolf," Adya said. "But I promise we'll have our best chance up there. Come on." She used her spear to beat back the overgrown vegetation and brush. If they stayed quiet and didn't draw attention to themselves, they might go unnoticed. She hoped dogs couldn't climb.

The girl protested before they reached the tree. "If you're too afraid to fight, we shall hide in the temple. It will be easy to defend if we set up a proper perimeter."

Adya clenched her jaw and tried not to swear. "Of course I'm afraid. You'd have to be insane not to be. It will find us in that temple in no time." Adya placed a hand on the banyan and reached out to ask for shelter, feeling the stretch of its roots beneath them. The tree whispered assent before returning to its timeless consideration of wind, water, and the depth of the earth.

Sonya reached the trunk and stared into the canopy. "I have never seen a plan like this in any book."

Adya tossed her spear up and pulled herself over one of the lowest branches. "Look, we're not trying to win a battle. We're just trying to survive." She didn't add that she was trying to survive long enough to return Sonya to Dsouza and be rid of her. Instead, she extended her hand.

Sonya considered this, then gave a long look back. "I don't require your help any longer. I'll make it on my own."

As if in answer to Sonya's stubbornness, a wolf's howl tore through the jungle, mournful and wild.

CHAPTER EIGHT

A DYA FROZE, BALANCED ON A LOW BRANCH. "I THINK HE found his friend."

"I hope it was his brother." Sonya's eyes burned. She placed herself into some kind of ridiculous textbook fighting position with a knife in each hand. She slid her feet back and forth, testing out the stance, shifting her grip on her knives. "Anger will make him reckless and easier to kill." She looked up at Adya. "You fear the monster, but do not worry. I will remain at the base of the tree and draw its attention. Throw your spear at my signal."

Adya had no idea how the fool had survived this long. Sonya wouldn't last thirty seconds with the pissed-off werewolf, and she was going to make them both easy to find.

"Don't knife me." Adya leaned down and grabbed the girl under the shoulders, dragging her up into the tree. It helped that Sonya weighed nothing.

Sonya struggled to shake free. "I'm not going up there!"

Adya hauled her over the thick branch. "Look, this is a proven Atavi battle tactic. It's in every book, I promise. Get as far away from the sharp teeth as possible." She made sure Sonya wasn't going to tumble down before releasing her. "That thing will tear you to pieces. Did you see the size of its claws?"

Sonya's eyes narrowed. She put away her knives and

clamped both arms around the branch. "You are a coward," she said. "How do you hope to defeat the werewolf from here?"

Adya rolled her eyes. "I'm not suicidal. I say we climb into the upper branches and hide and let the yaksha eat it for us."

The Vayu girl looked up. She closed her eyes tight. "I can't do it. It's too high."

Adya braced herself against the tree's trunk. "You have got to be kidding me." Dsouza's girlfriend wasn't afraid of a killer wolf, but she was terrified of a tree? This girl was one of the Vayu, the people of the wind. Their sorcerers rode the air, blasting their enemies with bolts of magic, and she was afraid of *heights*?

The girl bit her lip. "Go ahead. Leave me here."

Oh how she wished she could leave the fool, but the werewolf would snatch her in one leap. The thing couldn't be far now. "We don't have time for this."

"I told you, I can't." The girl would not loosen her grip.

Adya put a hand on Sonya's arm and tried to sound calm, which was next to impossible with her heart threatening to pound its way out of her chest. She tried to think of her like a younger sibling, but that didn't work, because she wasn't patient with Mohan, either. This girl was never meant to be in the jungle.

"I can't fight that thing alone. I need your help. If you stay here, we both get eaten."

Monkeys scurried frantically to the highest branches as the werewolf howled again, closer. Adya's mouth went dry. The head clamped onto the motorcycle had been enormous. She wasn't sure if it was the speech or the howling, but Sonya finally stretched out her hand. Adya pulled her up and climbed after, encouraging her branch by branch until they reached a point where the girl wouldn't go farther.

"Put your back to the trunk. There's space," Adya said. The branches were thicker here. With any luck, the leaves would hide them from view.

Sonya flattened herself against the banyan. "Space is what I'm worried about."

Adya tried to control her breathing. The werewolf would have finished them on the ground. Unfortunately, a fall from this height would too.

"Your spear won't harm a werewolf," Sonya said, pointing at Adya's weapon. She looked even more scared than Adya felt. "You'll need silver."

"Smashing one seemed to work." Sonya thought she was an expert on everything, but Adya's uranium-tipped spear was the only kind of weapon that could kill a yaksha. If it could take down the jungle's most powerful creatures, it might make wolves uncomfortable.

They waited together while the darkness grew thick, and the wind began to beat at the leaves. Sweat dripped down Adya's back as she fidgeted with her spear and imagined what the British would do to her if they took her back alive.

"I can't see a thing down there," the girl said. "Is it gone?"

Adya shook her head. To her eyes, the jungle was still alight. But it was too quiet. The werewolf had to be nearby. Its arrival had silenced everything.

Sonya clung to a branch, staring into the night. Her hand trembled as she held out a knife. "Take this. It's silvered."

Adya accepted the knife. "Stay above me. Keep hidden." She shifted to a spot below the girl and waited.

"If it comes after us, I'll do my best to blind it with as much light as I can manage. It should give you a chance to strike."

Sonya's earlier bluster was clearly fading. "Our best chance is to keep quiet, and hope it passes us by," Adya explained.

"If only my father were here," Sonya went on, clearly missing the hint. "He would know what to do. He'd blast the werewolf with flames, then conjure a wind to carry us all the way to Mysore."

"Wouldn't that be nice?" Adya gave up hope that Sonya might stop talking. Dsouza had said that Sonya was the daughter of a Vayu sorcerer, but she doubted whether any sorcerer had the power to make the wind carry them so far. And if they did, they would probably take Sonya with them and leave Adya sitting in the tree. She squeezed her spear, hoping against hope.

But luck was not on their side. Nearly eight feet long with a head too large for any dog, the monster padded into view, entering the clearing right where she'd left the motorcycle. It sniffed the bike and growled. The machine's headlight flashed, illuminating the beast, and the engine roared.

The werewolf leapt back, the hair on its neck standing on end. It lunged and, with a swipe of its claw, sent the motorcycle flying. The bike crashed into the base of the banyan with the sickening crunch of twisting metal.

Yellow eyes turned toward the tree. Lips curled back in a snarl.

Adya wiped a sweaty palm on her pants then felt her fear wash away, carried off in a river of the motorcycle's outrage. The force of the machine's emotion, pressing upon her, was overwhelming. The bike longed to fight, to run over its enemy until they were dust. It demanded Adya defend its honor. She struggled to hold on to her own thoughts amidst the motorcycle's flood of feelings.

She opened her eyes to find the monster staring up into the high branches. The werewolf raised its muzzle and spoke in a voice half-human, half-growl. "You cannot hide from me. I hear your heartbeats. I smell your fear."

Adya clenched her teeth and prayed the monster couldn't tell exactly where they were. If they just stayed silent and kept it guessing long enough, maybe the yaksha would find it.

"Is this why your queen sends her best soldiers all the way to India?" Adya jerked her head up to find Sonya shouting down at the werewolf. "To chase girls into a tree? How very brave. Your mother must be so proud. What courage England displays." The girl was actually pointing a finger down at the monster.

Sonya was going to get them both eaten. She'd given away their hiding spot in an attempt to scold the monster to death.

As Adya watched, the werewolf's face bent out of shape and its body twisted. In moments a lanky British soldier, somehow still in uniform, stood at the base of the tree. He bowed ever so slightly. "Princess Imral, you shame me and insult the Crown. Harming you is the furthest thing from my mind. I seek only to rescue you from the dangers of the jungle. Our previous arrangement with Huda is void. I have no doubt your father would greatly appreciate having you home."

Adya lost her balance. Only her grip on a thick branch saved her from falling. Her ears were still working, but she wasn't sure she'd understood. There was only one Princess Imral. Dsouza must have tried to pass Sonya off as the maharaja's daughter.

The girl continued her tirade. "The maharaja is not merciful toward murderers. You sold me to be killed. My father will make General Clive pay for what he's done, but you won't live to see it. You will die tonight, wolf. Just like your friend."

But the worrisome thing was that the girl sounded exactly like an extremely angry princess, and she referred to the maharaja as her father.

"See sense, Princess. Your father will be on our side soon. Returning you to him will seal our peace."

The girl leaned over the branch. "My father will never be on the side of killers." Her voice rose in a scream. "He would never be on the side of the army that assassinated my brothers."

The motorcycle's headlight lit up, shining white glare over the British monster. The bike's outrage flooded Adya's mind.

"You run really slow," Adya shouted at the werewolf, but the words weren't hers. She hadn't intended to say anything. "And your friend was slower than a Kawasaki 750," she added. She shook her head to clear her mind of the motorcycle's fury.

The British soldier seemed puzzled at her choice of insults. "You don't understand, Princess. There's no other way out of this jungle. We've already captured Dsouza. Climb down now, and I'll take you both to safety." He gave what he must have thought was a reasonable smile.

Imral screamed above Adya.

Adya felt the breath catch in her throat. Dsouza said there was nothing that was faster than any of them, and like a fool she'd believed him. But he wasn't coming for them. He was going to be tortured for information. If they survived this, the girl—the princess—was her responsibility now.

But the princess wasn't finished. The news of Dsouza had clearly banished any caution she might have had.

"Your friend named you a coward, wolf," Imral yelled. "He said you hung back so he would have to fight and die alone."

The soldier's smile vanished. "I can be up this tree with my teeth in your throats before you say another word."

"He said he knew you would abandon him. I swear it by my father."

And the girl could make up lies as fast as Dsouza too.

The soldier's eyes flashed yellow. His face elongated as his lips curled back, and fur sprouted all over his body. The were-wolf was back in moments.

"Be ready," Imral said. "I'll blind him just before he reaches us. Then we kill the hell out of him."

Adya tensed as the creature growled. She doubted any amount of light was going to bother it in the least. With a giant bound, the werewolf sprang into the tree, ripping the bark as it ascended.

The motorcycle's headlight angled up, covering the were-wolf in silver light and near blinding Adya.

Above her, Imral whispered the final words of a spell and pointed at the werewolf. Absolutely nothing happened. Which was about what Adya had expected.

The thing full of teeth and claws was coming at her faster than she thought possible. She would have one chance, and she could barely see. Perfect, just perfect. She squinted, keeping her spear behind her, hoping the werewolf wouldn't notice until it was too late.

It leapt at her from a limb ten feet below, yellow eyes glowing.

At the last moment, Adya turned and thrust.

The spearhead entered the werewolf's right flank, tearing through ribs and lungs to pin it to the trunk of the tree. The monster roared. Bloody spittle sprayed across Adya's face, but the damn thing wouldn't die. It didn't look *close* to dying. It seized the spear and dragged itself toward her, snapping. It was going to rip her apart.

She pulled out Imral's silver knife and slashed, but the werewolf's claws caught her across the arm. The weapon tumbled end over end to the ground as the monster bared its fangs and lunged.

Like a shadow, the princess dropped from above, knife clasped in both hands. She sank it deep into the monster as she fell, dragging the wolf back down the length of the spear. Its jaws clamped shut as the silver tore through its body. It tumbled back, flailing.

Imral held on, her blade now wedged in some part of the werewolf's pelvis. She slammed against the tree, then swung across empty space as blood poured over her.

Adya jumped from her perch. Branches scraped every inch of exposed skin until she crashed into the trunk below Imral, found her footing, and snatched the dangling Vayu princess out of the air. Imral barely noticed that someone had grabbed her. She broke free of Adya and threw her bloody knife at the extremely dead werewolf, managing to miss by an impossible margin.

They stood there, shaking, and neither said a word. Adya gave up trying to shut out the bike's thoughts. The crazy thing was screaming about victory. It had shown the stupid slow dog who was the greatest.

Imral caught her breath long enough to speak. "My spell wouldn't work. That spell always works." Her eyes filled with tears. "They have Dsouza, and my magic is gone."

Adya looked up at the dead monster that had almost eaten her alive. "At least your tactical books paid off."

Imral rubbed at her face. "You were alone, just like my brothers. I couldn't let it happen again." Her body started to shake, and Adya realized the girl was laughing. "Why did you call it slower than a—whatever you called it?"

Adya found herself laughing too, not sure if it was the fear letting itself out or just the insanity of it all. "I've never even seen a Kawasaki 750." She wasn't some warrior who could strike down monsters from the treetops. She was meant to breathe life into machines.

Once she caught her breath, she turned to the girl. "Tell me you're not really a princess."

"I'm not really a princess," Imral replied. But she pulled back her blue hair, revealing an intricate crown inked beside her ear with two white diamonds set into her skin. She took Adya's hand and placed her fingers over the design.

Magic thrummed under Adya's skin. No spell artist would forge the royal design unless they longed to be executed. Dsouza had lied about the whole Sonya thing. Of course he'd lied. He almost always lied. Adya took a slow breath. She was stuck in a tree with Princess Imral, failed sorceress and sole remaining heir to the maharaja's throne, and she'd promised a Vayu crook to keep her safe. She had no idea how to talk to a princess. She looked up at the top of the banyan and the heavy clouds that seemed tired of waiting. Her nightmare was now complete.

She lay back against the trunk. The banyan's boughs were wide at this point and formed a large V. She should be able to make a small platform where they could stay the night.

Imral slumped next to her and covered her face with her hands. "Dsouza—they'll hurt him. And I'm trapped here, useless. Without the magic, what am I good for?"

The first drops broke through the leaves around them and struck Adya's face, warm and heavy. Her hand was somehow already soaked.

A wave of lightheadedness hit her as the pain in her arm finally registered. The werewolf had ripped through her jacket's metal lining. Adya turned over her hand to find blood trickling from her sleeve, mixing with the rain to spill down to the ground far below.

CHAPTER NINE

S TOP MOVING AND LET ME HELP." THE RAIN PLASTERED Imral's blue hair to her head. "Keep still," she commanded. "This doesn't seem so bad."

Imral convinced Adya to let her take off the jacket only after Adya had failed three times. Every time Adya had tried on her own, the wound had only torn open farther. The branch they were standing on was already slick with her blood. Demanding that the princess stay away from her wasn't going to work any longer.

A long roll of thunder hid the sound of Adya's cursing. "Leave some of the skin on," she pleaded through gritted teeth. The metal lining had deflected the worst of the werewolf's attack, but it still hurt like hell. Imral might consider the wound nothing, but any deeper and it would have torn her arm to shreds. She grabbed the tree to steady herself as her head swam. Whether it was blood loss, hunger, or pain, she wasn't sure, but a fall now would be a quick death.

As if hearing her, a gust of wind sent a cascade of leaves swirling around them. Branches snapped, and the body of the werewolf broke free, crashing to the ground.

"Good riddance," Imral shouted. She struggled to remove Adya's arm from the sleeve.

Monkeys came out of their hiding places to watch. A

black-and-white-maned male dragged along a spiky jackfruit and settled down while Adya squirmed.

"Got it." Imral finally succeeded despite Adya's moans, then froze when she saw what lay underneath. Four long claw marks had gouged the length of Adya's forearm. Removing the jacket only sped up the bleeding.

"I need something to bind this. Stop making so many sounds."

"Of course, Highness. I'll suffer quietly." Adya leaned against the trunk of the tree and tried not to swear at the first royal she'd ever met.

The princess tore off one of her own wet sleeves then started wrapping the wound. "Dsouza would be able to stop this. He always knew what to do."

Imral tightened the dressing, and Adya arched her neck at the sudden jolt of pain. She remembered how much it had hurt when Dsouza massaged the blood back into her legs and the icy look he'd given her for crying out in pain. He wasn't softhearted, but the thought of Dsouza being captured again still twisted her guts. And now she had absolutely no idea what to do with Imral. She kept her eyes closed as the girl eased the jacket back on.

Bandaging complete, Imral proceeded to lean out into space and empty the contents of her stomach. Adya seized the back of the princess's shirt as she retched to stop her from tumbling down to join the werewolf.

With a final heave, Imral lay back, breathing hard. "I hate blood. I don't know how you're still conscious. That's the worst wound I've ever seen."

"Someone told me it wasn't bad." Adya flexed her fingers and found everything still worked. The princess had at least stopped the bleeding.

She tried to concentrate on what they needed to do next. Her hope of handing off Imral to Dsouza quick and easy was long gone. But there was no way she was going to risk taking a princess through the spell wall. She wasn't even certain she could manage it alone.

The first idea that came seemed like the only option. "There's a village where you'll be safe until we get word to the maharaja. I can leave you there, but I can't stay." Hopefully, Mohan was already there. Part of her desperately wanted to go back home, but that might only lead Huda or the British there.

Imral snorted. "I won't be safe anywhere in this jungle. That, I'm sure of. And just how do we send a message to my father, with Huda and the British army searching for me?"

"I'll find a way."

The princess raised an eyebrow. "Forgive me for doubting you, but you don't seem very good at even keeping yourself safe. What were you doing in Huda's dungeons anyway? Where are you hoping to go on that bike?"

Whether it was exhaustion, or just not giving a damn if Imral knew, Adya told her the truth. "I owed Huda money, and he thought selling a technomancer off to the British was the best way to get his investment back. I, on the other hand, do not want to be sold. So I'm taking his bike to Mysore. My twin sister is missing, and Dsouza swore he saw her there. I'm going to find her and bring her back. When I get there, I'll let your father know where you are, and he can send someone for you."

"What is your sister doing in Mysore?"

"She hoped to meet with the maharaja and find a way to help him free India from the British. That was her big dream. To be a hero."

Imral looked down at what remained of the werewolf. "It doesn't matter how fast the bike is. You'll be incinerated."

Adya nodded in the direction of the motorcycle. "That bike is the most impressive machine I've ever seen. It should be able to disrupt the magic and punch through the flame long enough for one person to stay alive. My sister managed it on a moped that wasn't nearly as powerful." Adya felt the Yamaha's sudden surge of pride at being called impressive.

I can punch through any flame. Once, I jumped through a hoop of fire and over an entire school bus.

Imral turned fully to face her. "One person?"

Adya held up just one finger. "There's no way I'm taking you with me. Let's get that straight. I'd end up in another dungeon—or worse—if I was the one who got the princess of Mysore turned into ash."

"But you're saying the bike could do it? I'd always heard that machine magic could disrupt normal spells, but I mean . . . we could both get back that much faster together."

"We could be dead that much faster together. If there were two of us, we would need twice the magic to break through. That's double the risk."

Imral shook her head as if she was deeply disappointed.

"You're being illogical. You know that, don't you? Of course, you haven't had a formal education."

Adya wondered if her injured arm was strong enough to push the princess out of the tree. Would she get blamed for a simple fall?

Imral continued before she could decide. "You said that bike was the most powerful machine you'd ever known. If any machine could disrupt enough magic to get us both through, that would be the one, don't you agree? And, if you managed to reach the other side without me, what exactly was your plan?"

"I was going to tell the maharaja where the spoiled princess was and demand help in return." Perhaps she hadn't worked out all the details, but Princess Formal Education could go to hell.

"Oh, and you think you'd reach him? That anyone would believe, or even listen to you? A lone girl from the jungle, on a bike that seems like the first thing any bandit would steal? Did you think for a moment that you'd be taken to my father, the maharaja, protector of the sacred flame, ruler of the South, the most powerful sorcerer India has, and invited to tea? What do you think happened to your sister?"

Adya tried to give the princess the hardest glare she could manage, but her head had started swimming. "Dsouza said she made it to Mysore. She's naive, but she made it."

"Your sister thinks we might need help fighting the greatest evil this country has faced in centuries, and she's naive? You're the one who was going to rush off and find her on your own."

Adya turned away and stared out into the night, knowing it was childish and not being able to help it.

Imral leaned forward. "I know what it feels like to lose a sibling. You can't live like that. You can't gamble on it. You're going to need me, Adya."

"You need *me*, Princess. You're the one stuck behind a wall of flame with no way out." It was a lot easier to speak to royalty when you didn't have to look at them, she'd discovered.

"Not if you can get us out on that bike," Imral retorted. "When we arrive, I'll get you an audience with my father. That beats having your bike stolen by bandits and being left for dead in a ditch. Think about it. Your sister needs you to succeed."

That last part was like a well-aimed blade to the heart, but Adya wasn't surrendering so easily. "What about you, Princess? How did you end up getting captured this far from Mysore? That doesn't seem like too logical a move."

Imral's mouth became a thin line. "Perhaps it wasn't." She opened her hands and stared at them. "But a future ruler has responsibilities. Dsouza convinced me there were aspects of the kingdom I needed to see with my own eyes. Convinced me that I could no longer stay sheltered. But everything went wrong." She made her hands into fists again. "And none of that has anything to do with me getting back or helping you. You see that, right?"

Imral let Adya stare out into space and, to her credit, didn't say another word for five minutes. "I saw it, you know, just before the British brought me into the jungle. It was like looking at death." There was real fear in the princess's voice.

Adya knew what Imral meant without naming it. The spell wall inspired terror like nothing else.

"Tall as the walls of the palace," Imral continued, "and every bit was flame. But not any kind of fire I'd seen before. Those flames promised to tear your soul apart until all that was left of you was smoke."

"British sorcerers brought you through?" Adya asked.

Imral nodded. "There was a sorcerer. But either I passed out, or they spelled me to forget, because the next thing I knew I was on Huda's ship and about to die. Then we were running from werewolves."

Adya reluctantly admitted to herself that Imral might be right. If she went on her own, who would even listen to her? With the help of the princess, she'd have a real chance of finding Priya. If she had a day to tune up the bike, and another to maybe practice a trial run, they might do it. Then again, they were just as likely to both be burned to nothing.

"My father is the one thing in life I am certain of," Imral said. "He's unshakable. He will find her. You'll see." Imral held up her hands in mock surrender. "Let's climb down and sleep. In the morning, you'll decide what feels right." She started to swing her leg over a branch. "I can't stay up here a moment longer."

Adya shook her head. "Wait. We're not going anywhere tonight. Even if we could make it down without slipping, you don't want to be on the ground with the yaksha hunting. We stay here until dawn."

Imral fixed Adya with a rain-drenched stare. "You dragged me into a tree for a werewolf that is now quite dead. This entire jungle falls under the rule of Mysore. I will decide where I sleep tonight."

Adya held up both hands in mock surrender. "All right, Your Mightiness. Climb down and break your legs. The yaksha will eat what's left of you by morning."

"Nonsense." Imral tested the branch below her, considering. "Yaksha are stories meant to frighten children."

Something about the way Imral looked, so young and stubborn, reminded Adya of Mohan. A surge of worry struck her like a stab to the gut. He and Imral must be about the same age, and the poor girl had already lost her own brothers. Adya took a deep breath. The princess might be crazy, but she was just a kid with no idea what she would face down there. She had never seen a yaksha.

"Look, I'll *think* about taking you with me. But you have to stay up here until morning."

Imral gave her a sidelong glance, clearly not convinced. But she stopped trying to climb and held her knees to her chest, waiting.

Adya focused on a point a yard above Imral's left shoulder and pretended she was talking to some foolish village kid instead of the actual princess of Mysore. "Once, I was trying to learn how to get an old light bulb to shine." Their mother had been giving them a basic lesson in technomancy, and Adya was being shown up as usual. Priya had her lamp glowing in five minutes, while Adya had glared at a flashlight for an hour and only managed to conjure a raging headache. In the end she'd summoned her anger and frustration at how poor they were and how much they had to struggle just to survive and let it all pour out.

"The flashlight filled the room with light until the bulb

exploded, and I ended up with glass in my hands. My mother wiped away my tears while she explained. 'Adya, that is too much for anyone.'

"That week she took me alone, deep into the jungle, to look for yaksha. We found one drinking from a forest pool. From far away, it could have been a giant deer, but it made you so scared you couldn't breathe. Black shadows curled around its antlers. Its eyes were silver moons that drew you in and held you."

Imral uncurled from her ball. "Did it attack?"

"Not at all. It just watched us." Adya remembered the eyes that delved deep into her soul. "Then it dipped its antlers in our direction and stalked away." Adya tried to look at the princess and keep talking. "My mother wanted me to understand the yaksha as part of the jungle, as creatures who belong here every bit as much as we do, despite their danger. In the daytime they may give us respect, but the night is theirs.

Imral sighed. "Vayu magic is nothing like that. It's about control and will. You have to be as confident as the wind to draw on the infinity well, as certain of your strength as the storm." She bit her lip. "If you fail, if you draw too much power and cannot contain it, it consumes you and you go mad. You have to be sure." The princess's face was a picture of doubt. "Let's talk about something else."

Adya had no idea how to make small talk with a princess. "Why the blue hair? Is that a palace thing?"

Imral ran her fingers through her wet strands. "Everyone in the palace hated it. I had to color it myself. Just like the Blue Wizard. You know?"

Adya shrugged.

Imral's eyes widened. "I can't believe you haven't heard of the Blue Wizard. Her hair was as bright as the sky. Lightning blasted from her fingers. She could control the monsoon itself."

"She must have been a great sorceress," Adya said.

Imral laughed. "She's a comic book hero. I read all her stories. That's who I imagined I'd become one day, soaring through the clouds, throwing whirlwinds at my enemies." She gave a sad smile. "Turns out I'm afraid of heights and can't control a raindrop." The princess stayed silent for a moment, thinking, before lifting her head. "The comic books never had any magic like yours. Tell me how you gave the motorcycle life. How does it work?"

"They forgot about us in the comic books, and technomancers don't give machines life," Adya explained. "We search out their souls. Remind them who they were."

One corner of Imral's mouth turned down. "But machines aren't people. One is like another, aren't they?"

Adya bent a thin branch, weaving it across two larger ones. Working in the rain was not ideal, but there was plenty of material to make a platform with. She bent two more while she thought of a way to explain. "You think that because you've never had a machine inside your mind. Some are like small children, full of energy. Others are afraid of everything." Adya pointed at the ground. "That bike has more will to live than anything I've ever known. I can feel it bending reality to push itself faster, to wrap air around us so we don't fall. I think it could grow wings if it wanted."

Imral tried to help arrange the branches and destroyed half of Adya's work. "But aren't a technomancer's spells dangerous?"

"Dangerous to other spellcasters, maybe." Adya removed the part Imral had destroyed and tested the resulting platform with her weight. "The machines we bring to life have a memory of the old energy still in them. They disrupt and scatter other magic. Both the Vayu and British fear we will destroy their enchantments. The only difference is the British want to use us to make weapons."

Imral shivered despite the warmth of the jungle. "The British want to use everyone. Clive sent delegations to my father, demanding he join them to keep Mysore safe. Every day our magic fades, while British magic grows stronger." Imral bit her lower lip. "Combining Vayu and Atavi magic might accomplish so much if it wasn't so likely to kill us all. God only knows what would happen."

Magic was all about tapping into the flow from the infinity wells. The Vayu harnessed the power through rituals and spells, while a technomancer channeled it through their memories and emotions. You didn't try random experiments unless you had a death wish.

The rain had found its rhythm, falling around them in waterfalls but sparing their spot near the banyan's trunk. Adya put out a hand and let the rain wash away the last of the blood.

The princess's eyes became distant. "Do you know what a soul arrow is?"

Adya shook her head.

"It's a weapon the British sorcerers use to assassinate

someone they want dead very badly. The arrows circle above in the sky until they strike. They drain your soul dry. If anyone tries to save you by pulling the arrow out, they die as well, ripped apart from the inside. The British army knew our battle plans, knew where my brothers would be. It was an attack whose sole purpose was to destroy the heirs to the throne. Now there's just me alone."

Adya knew she should take the girl's hand. Knew she should say something. But this was the princess of Mysore, and Adya was no good at comforting people.

"My father barely speaks to me now," Imral continued. "I'm the daughter who can't cast the most basic spells, the one who doesn't ride the wind because she's afraid. The magic of an infinity well would eat me alive."

If Vayu magic depended on being confident and in control, Imral was not going to save them any time soon. Adya gave up on the idea of trying to reassure her. You couldn't brush away real pain. Adya finished interlacing the last thin branches.

"Rest for a few hours," she said. "I'll stand guard. We'll make our plan in the morning."

Imral lay down as best she could and rested her head on her arms, then propped herself up once more. "Adya, do you really think we could never mix our magic? We'd each have to learn a bit of the other's patterns, but we might be able to draw on a great deal more power, create an entirely new form of magic."

Adya's jaw tightened. She remembered the explosion that had killed her parents and what happened when you drew too much. "It has taken us centuries to learn patterns that channel the well without killing us. You have your ways, and we have ours. You can't just make up things on the fly."

"The potential—" Imral began, but the look Adya gave her stopped any discussion, and she laid her head back down.

As Imral settled into place, Adya stretched her legs and tried to clear her thoughts. They both had enough to worry about already. She closed her eyes and imagined the spell wall, its thirty feet of magical flame patrolled by ghostly specters whose gaze could freeze you in your tracks. The last thing Adya wanted was to take the princess with her, but there was no way around it. She sighed. She was going to have to take Imral.

Over time, Imral's breathing slowed. The girl slept like Priya, her hair tossed across her face, her head resting against her hands. What had her life been like before she left, the last heir in a giant palace, wishing she could be a comic book hero?

Imral stretched out a leg, revealing the tornado symbol of the Blue Wizard on her ankle. Adya had only pretended to not know who the character was. Mohan had read old copies of that dumb Protectors series a thousand times over the years. He'd blabber at her about the Blue Wizard and her storm powers and her magical bracelets, but explaining all that to the princess would have turned Adya into a worried mess, and she couldn't afford to fall apart just now. But of all the characters Mohan loved, the Blue Wizard was the most tolerable. A princess who wanted to be like her had to be *trying*, at least.

Adya didn't realize she'd fallen asleep until she was startled awake. She twisted, searching in a sudden panic. The rain had stopped, and the spot where Imral had been sleeping was empty. The Vayu princess was gone.

Adya swung herself down to find Imral on her hands and knees, tracing patterns on the floor of Kali's temple. She kicked apart the spell patterns in the dirt. "What are you doing?"

Imral stood up and raised her chin. "Trying to cast a spell to . . ." She faltered. "To see if I still could." Her shoulders slumped. "I couldn't sleep in the tree anyway. I had the strangest dreams."

Imral was going to get them killed before the night was over. Adya's spear tip was already glowing. "Well, you've just attracted every yaksha in this part of the jungle."

CHAPTER TEN

A DYA DRAGGED THE MOTORCYCLE OUT OF THE BRUSH, revealing three claw marks scraped across the red-and-white paint. Her breath caught when she saw that the engine block had been disrupted and the rocker arm was out of alignment. She didn't have the proper tools for this.

The night had gone unnaturally quiet. She was either going to make do, or they were going to be dead very soon.

Adya unfastened her mother's necklace. She had to try.

Imral grabbed her sleeve. The princess looked like she was about to spring into the jungle. "I demand you leave that broken thing! We must run."

"Stop whining!" Adya growled.

Imral raised her chin. "How dare you—"

"Not you, the bike."

Broken. I will rust in the jungle forever. Tragedy. All my brilliant speed wasted, all my glory stolen, all my future victories—

How could something be both an anxious wreck and so full of itself at the same time?

Adya pressed her forehead against the gas tank. This broken thing had already saved them once. She took off her mother's pendant and unfolded the wrench,. The motorcycle's voice went quiet in her mind, but she could still feel it, scared, suspicious of her touch. It didn't know if she meant to bring it back or destroy it.

She laid a hand on the gas tank and tried to project calm. "I didn't let the werewolves win, did I? I'll fix this. Just let me in." The machine had to trust her. Without the right tools, magic was going to have to do the work.

I'm afraid to sleep for centuries and rust. I don't want to be left alone.

The bike was terrified. It had heard Imral's command to leave it and run. Adya gave up on calm. "I am not leaving you anywhere. I need you. Now trust *me*. Please." At least that was honest.

The bike stopped shaking under her hand, and she took a deep breath. "Okay. Here we go. *Vishwakarma namo namah*." The initial spark of magic swept through her fingers into the Yamaha. She could sense the bike hesitate—if it let her in, she could seize its power, could leave it for dead as she'd done with the engines on Huda's battleship.

"Let me in," she pleaded. "We've got a race to win." She felt the bike rumble under her hand, still unsure, before it dropped its defenses and reached out. Adya felt the machine probing her, seeking to understand just who she was, trying to tap into the flow of magic through her memories.

She let it in.

The metal grew warm under her hands. She gave the bike her fear of the approaching yaksha, her worry for her little brother and her sister, out there somewhere beyond the spell wall. She felt it in her head, driving through her memories, turning around the dark corners of her mind, feeling her joys and her pain.

Then the bike reached deeper and drew out a memory of Adya standing in front of a burning workshop, holding her face in her hands. Black smoke billowed high above the trees, and Priya sobbed on the ground at her feet.

Adya took a hard breath, and the sudden ache in her chest became unbearable. Before the bike could delve further, the flow of magic died.

She slammed her fist on the ground. "Damn it all to hell."

Imral searched the darkness of the jungle with desperate eyes. "I told you. We must run."

"I promised this bike I am not leaving it." The metal underneath Adya's fingers was still hot. The magic had done half the work already. There might still be a way. She slid the wrench inside the engine block and tried to pry the rocker arm straight. She drew in a sharp breath as the metal started to bend, worried she would snap it beyond repair. But it held. She nodded at the result and tightened the bolts. Then she grabbed the handlebars and opened the choke lever.

The engine roared when she hit the ignition. A surge of pride and contentment washed over her. The crazy bike was elated. It had fought a werewolf and come out on top. It growled again, then settled into a purr. The image of a champion crossing the finish line with hundreds of adoring fans waving their arms flashed across Adya's mind.

Wood snapped as something far too large for comfort approached.

"No time to celebrate," Adya said, hustling the bike back onto the trail. The tip of her spear was glowing bright. Adya jumped on the motorcycle. "Hold tight," she said. Imral scrambled atop it and wrapped her arms around Adya.

The motorcycle's cocoon enveloped them, pressing them into the seat as it swerved with ever increasing speed. Adya had to squint to see past the glare of the headlights that reflected off the wet leaves.

Imral banged on the side of the motorcycle with her palm. "Too fast! You'll get us killed."

Adya twisted the throttle and sped up. "The bike doesn't understand slow."

Have faith. We shall prevail, the bike screamed in her head. *You did not leave me. We are friends.*

The bike's protective shield grew stronger as it wrapped itself around them. She marveled at the machine's ability. Trees and streams flashed by as they accelerated. The bike was running on pure magic, at one with the jungle, forging a path of its own.

"Why are you laughing?" Imral shouted over the sound of the engine.

Adya forced her mouth closed. Death pursued them, but the bike was pouring out insane joy. Every obstacle, every jump was pure thrill. It never faltered, never slowed. She had never known a machine could be so magnificent. Her terror receded into the background as every impossible turn became habitual. They rocketed through the darkness.

Unfortunately, they hadn't left the yaksha behind. As fast as the bike was, this was the yaksha's home. The night was their time. Adya's spear tip glowed ever brighter, warning of their approach.

Then she saw it. The spell wall loomed before them, one

hundred yards of fire, soaring high into the night. Spectral giants gazed down from atop it, their hair aflame. This was the barrier Priya had faced alone. Adya imagined her twin, her long hair flying behind her, head pressed low as she gathered speed for the final rush.

Even as they approached, Adya felt the fires reach for her, hungry. She broke out in sweat as the heat beat at her, finding its way under her skin, threatening to boil her away.

Imral squeezed her arm.

A roar shook the jungle behind them, and a terrible scream answered ahead. They'd been herded into a trap.

Adya swerved at the last moment, racing along the spell wall's length. They weren't ready for this. She hadn't had time to prepare, to practice. Hadn't spent enough time with the bike to know if it was ready.

An explosion shook the night behind them. One of the yaksha had failed to slow, struck the wall, and had gone up in sparks and flame. Even a creature of spirit was no match for conjured fire.

Couldn't even turn in time. They can't touch me. Together we fly. As long as it wasn't left to rust, the bike was not easy to scare.

Thankfully, nothing grew within twenty yards of the wall, and the path was clear. They might be able to outrun the yaksha with no obstacles to slow them.

Imral called out, "They're falling behind! Oh my god, they're *huge.*"

"Don't look," Adya implored. Staring at a yaksha, getting lost in the awe of them, was a sure way to die.

Awful howls sounded ahead. Adya made out claws, horns, teeth bounding out of the jungle.

"Don't do it," Imral pleaded. "It's too strong. Please."

It was either turn back and try to lose the yaksha or face the fire. Adya wasn't going to have another chance to decide. The heat of the wall seared the side of her face before she felt the bike strengthen the wall of force around them and the heat vanish.

The bike's engine growled. *Trust in me. This wall is nothing.*

The bike was crazy, there was no doubt about it, but it didn't lack in confidence. Adya squeezed the handlebars, There wasn't going to be time for practice. She fed the motorcycle everything she had, sending it hurtling toward the yaksha. Her mother had shown her how to break spells. She needed emotion, as much as she could manage. She filled her mind with rage.

Huda's iron cage.

Gouros's men wrapping her in chains.

Priya alone with no one to help her.

She squeezed until her fingers ached. "*Guru Brahma, Guru Vishnu—Numaha.*" The bike's headlight flared.

She flipped on the radio, and music started blaring.

Her mind filled with images of some long-ago race, whipping over hills toward the finish line. Dials spun out of control. Metal glowed and sparked. Imral screamed.

Adya ducked her head and aimed the bike straight into the flames.

CHAPTER ELEVEN

RED LIGHT FLARED AS THE BARRIER POUNDED ADYA'S every sense with blistering heat. Her nose filled with the smell of her own hair burning. Her mouth went dry with the taste of ashes and death.

The spell wall reached inside her and started devouring. She saw an image of herself sprinting through the trees, racing to catch up with Priya, a picture she'd always remembered in perfect clarity, withering now like paper in a bonfire. She was disappearing. Even if she made it to the other side, she would be an empty shell, hollowed out from within.

The motorcycle's engine gave a protective roar, and its cocoon surged around her, beating away the heat, punching a hole through the conjured fire like a headlight through darkness.

But the spell wall had not surrendered. Flames erupted around them, and Imral cried out, squeezing Adya in desperation. The bike screamed, then whined as it shifted gears and gave up every bit of itself to shield them both. Adya felt its anguish as the wall pounded it, melting away paint, consuming the last of its power. Then, just as she could hold her breath no longer, the flames faded, and the bike landed with a bang.

Adya gasped for air as they rocketed on. Her head was a jumble of memories and confusion, her arm ached terribly, and she could barely keep her balance, but they'd broken through. They were safe.

The sun was rising over a landscape of green fields, where scattered piles of dead machinery towered like trees in a mechanical forest. Heaps of spare parts spread out in all directions. Unfortunately, at the speed they were going, it was impossible to avoid them. She screamed and turned the handlebars.

Adya leaned hard as the bike hopped and spun in a semicircle, bumping through old junk. She swerved to avoid a fatal crash into a battered truck, and the Yamaha's front tire struck wet mud. They went into a long skid, headed straight for a drop-off a hundred yards to the left.

Adya tried every trick she knew to escape disaster. The bike began to turn away from the cliff, to slow ever so slightly, and hope sprang up in Adya's heart. Then the Yamaha's engine coughed, sputtered, and died. The force holding Adya onto the bike evaporated as the last of its magic short-circuited. They were riding a dead thing on wheels.

"I've got nothing!" she called out to Imral. "Hold on!" Amidst the panic of it all, Adya gave a silent prayer for her motorcycle. It couldn't die now after all it had done for them.

They sideswiped an old bathtub and shattered a television set before the unthinkable happened. Imral tumbled off to the side, rolling into a tangle of cables and disappearing from view, but the bike didn't slow. The brakes were useless; they'd hit some sort of oil slick.

Instinct demanded Adya jump, but she couldn't abandon the motorcycle. She jammed the wheel into a ninety-degree angle, digging into the ground. "Come on! Wake up," she begged.

And it heard.

The Yamaha's magic surged back to life. Adya felt its sudden wave of panic. A protective rush of air surrounded her. Mud rocketed into the air as the bike threw magic in every direction in a mad effort to stop. It slowed; it dipped; it almost succeeded—

They shot over the edge.

Adya reached for anything she could grab and managed to seize a mud-covered branch as the bike tumbled away toward the river below. She swung over the drop, fighting to maintain her grip as the machine's pained cry filled her mind. Her heart fell. They couldn't possibly have survived the spell wall to die here. It couldn't end this way.

The sun shone straight into her eyes, blinding her.

"Imral!" Adya screamed, praying the girl was still alive. Adya had just managed to stabilize herself, when, with a loud crack, the branch snapped, and she fell.

The motorcycle had crashed sixty-seven times before and often still went on to win. Falling, crashing, and being bathed in mud did not bother it much. It was a dirt bike, after all. The custom Yamaha 450 was undeniably the finest racer ever created. It had won over 130 trophies it could remember—and those were only the major ones. Its four coats of red and white gloss and hand-painted numbers had been painstakingly applied by the best artists of its era. For years it was serviced by expert mechanics and a cleaning crew who doted over it, polishing and oiling every surface in preparation for the next event.

Currently, the Yamaha was not at its best. It hung upside down in a guava tree that was clinging precariously to the side of a cliff. Its paint had been scorched and blistered. Its gas tank sported several unsightly dents, which aggravated it. To make matters more miserable, the guava tree was swaying in the wind, threatening to dump the bike into the raging river far below. That would be a problem.

Problems did not generally bother the Yamaha. It had raced the spell wall and won. No ridiculous wall could match its speed and power. Why had the foolish flames even tried? But despite cause for celebration, things were not as they should be—its rider was in trouble.

The girl lay twenty yards away, embedded in a thornbush, with one leg sticking out. This was bad. The bigger problem was that she was unconscious. The bike feared she might never wake, that she might sleep as it had slept for hundreds of years, lost to the world forever. For some reason, that thought troubled it more than anything else had in ages.

The Yamaha's mind was still in a jumble. The spell wall had shorted out its magic and scrambled its memories. It remembered Huda looking down on it, remembered wanting to turn back to run the gangster down. It recalled Huda's foul touch as he sat upon its seat and watched victims die in his spiked cage. The bike also remembered running through the jungle and playing in streams, losing its sister and wanting her back.

The memories made it wonder things. The girl was so very different. The bike had had many riders over the years, but they had all considered it a tool, a precious possession, an expensive investment, but in the end, nothing more than an object. Riders wanted to win and prove themselves, to take prizes and gain prestige. The bike never needed any of these things. It was the best already. The race was important because the race was life, and glorious life was everything.

But this girl did not want glory. She had nothing to prove. The bike had looked into her mind and seen this. And the girl had not abandoned the Yamaha when they were about to fall. She had fixed it when it was broken, woken it when it was lost. It desperately wanted her to survive.

The bike reached out again and felt the girl dreaming. In the dream she ran desperately from a giant cobra, as tall as the trees, that destroyed everything in its path. Around the monster swarmed a cloud of black birds with wings like the night that hunted her without mercy. Through the forest she fled head-long, striking branches, tripping over logs, losing speed when what she most needed was to fly.

The bike blared its horn as loud as it could. Its headlight shone against the blackness. The wind picked up, and the monsoon crashed around them like a thousand hammers.

Adya woke in darkness with countless needles piercing her skin. Her face was wet, and she tasted blood. At first, she thought she had been pierced by the fangs of the great snake. Then she suspected she might already be dead.

A blaring horn sent a fresh stab of pain through her skull. She couldn't quite place it, but she knew that sound. Oh, but she couldn't think about it now. Her head hurt too much.

Adya blinked water out of her eyes as her vision adjusted. A few attempts to move revealed she was tangled in a thornbush with rain drenching her face. She tried to get up, but as much as she struggled, she couldn't free herself. She felt the dream drawing her back. Perhaps she *was* lying in a snake's coils, a thousand fangs pressed about her, and the thorns and this rain were just her imagination.

A bright light shone in Adya's eyes, forcing her awake. But exhaustion took its toll, and Adya closed her eyes again.

"Did I ever tell you about the giant cobra no one could escape?" Adya's father lifted his arms above his head, miming the shape of a great snake's hood. Her father could tell a story like no one else. He was tall, with hair cut to his shoulders, and his face could form a thousand expressions. "The yaksha made a terrible mistake," he intoned. "They woke a monster they should never have disturbed."

"What monster, Baba?" Adya asked, though she already knew the answer.

He thrust his head forward like a serpent's strike. "They woke the *naga*," he hissed.

Adya could barely breathe. She clutched Priya, who didn't even look afraid. They were only eight, but her sister was always more intrigued than frightened.

Their father rose to his full height. "The naga erupted from the ground. Its lower half was a giant cobra, thicker than a banyan. Its upper, an armored man with a trident in each hand." Their father banged together his imaginary weapons. "Its coils crushed stone temples. Its eyes shot fire. The yaksha hurled a mountain of boulders atop it." Her father lowered his head until he was looking right into her eyes. "The naga barely noticed."

Adya's palms prickled. "And then it ran away?"

Priya snorted. "Of course it didn't. Why would it?" She turned back to their father. "Where are the nagas now, Baba?"

Their father wiped his brow. "Thank the gods, they're long gone. When the black meteors first struck the earth, when magic was at its wildest, that was the time of the nagas."

Priya wasn't satisfied. "But if nagas were so strong, why do the British monsters always win? Why can't Indian magic defeat them?"

Their father sighed and lowered himself to the floor. "Because we are divided, little one. We never learned to trust each other, to join our power together." Their father raised a finger as if he knew a secret. "But one day, we'll change that. When the Devas sing alongside the Vayu, when we Atavi join them with our machines, the British will be swept away like leaves in a stream."

"Like leaves in a stream?" Their mother rolled her eyes as she fit a spark plug into an old sedan. Her beautiful face was covered in splotches of engine oil. "The armies that swept through India are going to be stopped by a few singing Devas and a few Atavi technomancers?" She shook her rag at him. "Stop talking rubbish and go get me these parts." She tossed a list at him. "And send the girls away—this is dangerous."

He went off laughingly to find what their mother needed, and Priya, ever faithful, followed behind.

Their mother grabbed Adya's wrist before she could join them. "He loves you both more than anything, but don't listen to his nonsense."

"But Baba said we could help fight the monsters."

Her mother dropped to her level. "The worst monsters hide in men. The Vayu and the Devas will cheat you worse than the British ever will. Before the British, it was always some Vayu lord we had to worry about stealing our land, damming our rivers, cutting our trees. Beware the songs of the Devas. Listen too long, and you'll forget who you are and find your pockets empty. The more someone says they want to help you, Adya, the more likely they are to take what little you have."

"But the car? Baba says it will show the maharaja what you can do. . . ."

"I love your father, but you can't eat dreams. If we get this car to work, we can finally pay off our debts to Huda. That's what we must care about. Let the maharaja worry about the British."

Their father returned with the parts and sent them away to spar in the junkyard. "Go beat the hell out of each other. And keep an eye on Mohan," he said.

High atop a heap of junk, Priya jabbed at Adya with her practice spear. "I'm the faerie queen of England, and you're the maharaja. I'm going to teach you a lesson you'll never forget," Priya said. She shoved Adya with her shoulder, sending her sliding down the pile, while their brother sat watching. Priya shook a finger at her. "You're still worried about the nagas, aren't you? You should be worrying about the British."

"The nagas are out there somewhere, aren't they?"

"You heard Baba. They've gone deep under the sea. Even if they did come back, you wouldn't have trouble with them."

"Why not?"

"Cuz I'd be with you, dummy. You and me against the world. Always."

The sun was setting, and a rare feeling of contentment filled Adya to the bones as she charged back up the junk pile and swung her spear like a staff.

Priya sidestepped her swing and jabbed her in the ribs, sending Adya sliding again. "I'm the queen of this junk hill, and you have to bow before me!"

Adya charged back. "I'm not bowing before you, junk-pile queen—"

Searing pain filled Adya's ears and stole away all sound. Something lifted her body, and she flew backward, Priya above her, tumbling through the air. She slammed into the ground and squeezed her eyes shut as a wave of heat washed over her.

When she opened her eyes and took a first painful breath, bits of ash were drifting down from the sky. Had the naga returned and blasted them with its eyes of fire? She lay there, unmoving, until Priya pulled her up. They wiped the blood from each other's faces and then they saw.

Clouds of smoke poured out of their parents' workshop, filling the sky with black soot. Burning Mercedes parts had showered the entire yard. Mohan huddled next to an abandoned refrigerator, wailing.

Priya screamed. She broke into a run.

But Adya was faster, tackling Priya before she could get close to the flames. Her parents were already gone. She wasn't going to lose Priya, too.

A flashing light jarred Adya back to her senses. Away from the glare, a hundred yards below, a moonlit river glimmered at the bottom of a steep ravine. The bush had saved her.

The motorcycle lay twenty yards away, upside down, embedded in a tangle of roots and branches. Its headlight flashed again, and she sensed its relief. The bike had been terribly worried.

"It's good to see you, too," Adya said. She'd been just as concerned about the bike. Seeing that it was not swirling in pieces in the river below meant her luck hadn't entirely evaporated. She tried to free an arm but only succeeded in ripping her jacket further.

Why were you sleeping? The race isn't over. We must find your pit crew.

"Thought it might be a good time for a nap," Adya said. "You know?"

It is a terrible time for a nap, the bike's engine rumbled. *Sleeping is dangerous. The great snake pursues you, and sleep can be forever.*

The bike had seen into her dreams? Adya remembered running through the forest as the naga chased her and shuddered.

"Give me a minute." She began drawing an arm from her sleeve, seeing if she could work her way out of the bush's embrace without bleeding to death upon inch-long thorns.

A moment of panic seized Adya.

"Where's the princess? The girl with the blue hair?" She

prayed the bike might know something. Imral had tumbled off at speed.

The bike gave a depressed beep. *Your entire team is missing. Why are you lying there when your team needs you?*

"I'm working on it, all right? And I don't have a *team*," Adya said.

This is not your team?

Images flashed through Adya's mind, one after the other— Imral climbing the banyan, Dsouza straightening his black sleeves, and Mohan and Priya laughing as they sat on the bank of a stream three years ago. Adya gasped. She had not thought about that day in ages. How many of her memories had the motorcycle seen?

"The last two are my siblings. Those others I barely know."

The motorcycle groaned. It sent her an image of Imral bandaging her arm and another of the princess clinging tight around Adya's waist. The last image was of Dsouza bending over to massage her injured leg.

"That doesn't make them my crew," Adya retorted. But crew or not, Imral was alone and likely hurt. Gods let her just be alive.

Adya twisted out of her ruined jacket and scraped her way down to the muddy ground, leaving her clothing behind like a discarded shell. She stretched out her arms. Nothing seemed broken, except maybe her skull. Her headache was relentless.

She lay back, giving in to her thirst, and let her mouth fill with rain. How had everything gone so wrong? This was supposed to be a rescue mission, and she'd managed to ruin it before it got started. She remembered the flames of the spell wall tearing at her and shuddered. She'd never been so close to death. The cool water against her skin was a blessing, driving away the heat of memory.

The motorcycle was nudging again at the back of her mind. The machine was trying its best to be patient. She lifted her aching head out of the mud. How long had the two of them been down here? It had been sunrise when they'd broken through the spell wall. Over twelve hours must have gone by. Gods only knew what had happened to Imral by now. The motorcycle was right. They had to find the girl.

The only way out of the ravine was a miserable climb up a slick and near vertical mudslide. Luckily, Adya's spear had fallen nearby, and she'd managed not to impale herself on it. She thrust the uranium tip into the ground for balance and hobbled over to the bike.

Adya ran her hands over the Yamaha's scorched paint, and it hummed beneath her touch. She sighed. The bike was in a dreadful position, upside down and stuck fast. Freeing it would be impossible alone—one mistake and the bike would slide out of the guava tree and crash to the river below.

She was going to need help.

"I'll come right back for you." She patted the engine. The bike rumbled in response, protesting its fears of being abandoned. "I promise," she added. "I didn't leave you behind in the jungle, did I?"

But your sister left you, didn't she? Aren't twins the same person in different frames, off the same assembly line?

The words hit her like a punch to the sternum. Adya stiffened. "We are not the same person at all. We think differently, believe different things. You never even met Priya."

The bike flooded Adya's mind with images of Priya laughing, Priya running, Priya sleeping with her blanket tucked under her chin, Priya concentrating in the way only she did when she was trying to solve a problem that had stumped her.

It was too much at once. The loss it conjured overwhelmed her. "But you didn't know my sister," Adya insisted.

The bike sent a final image of Priya crying and Adya holding her as smoke rose high in the sky. Adya gave up. The damn bike knew enough. She'd had to open herself completely to it in order to give it life. There was no sense pretending to hide anything. It had seen years of Priya already.

"Look, people can look the same, but be different. I am coming back for you as soon as I can. You are not abandoned. But I've got to get us both out of here before I starve and you rust."

You are my crew, the bike rumbled. *I will wait.*

Adya shook her head. This bike had a strange way of thinking. She looked up at the edge of the cliff and down to the water below. It was going to be a hard climb.

After twenty yards of struggling, she collapsed, sweat pouring off her brow. It was as if someone had poured grease all over the slope. All she could do was hold on to the spear and not slide back into the thorns. It didn't help that she was running on empty and her muscles didn't want to follow basic commands. She had no idea when she'd last eaten or truly rested. She would give anything for a plate of sweet mangoes and guavas. Her eyes closed without her realizing.

The sun woke her. Adya found herself back at the thorn-bush, her arms wrapped around her spear. She forced herself to her feet and climbed ten more yards before she slipped onto her face.

The Yamaha beeped at her as she spit out mud. *Why don't you shift gears? That works for me.*

"I don't have gears!" Adya protested. As if she needed the suggestions of a machine currently lodged in a tree.

This can't be as hard as racing the werewolf. It's only mud.

Adya grimaced at the bike, but it didn't seem to notice. Only mud? But the machine's constant beeping got her up and climbing for near an hour before another fall laid her flat on her back.

This will be much easier when you find your crew, it continued. *It is very difficult to refuel without a proper one.*

"Fuel would be nice right now," Adya agreed. "But there's no crew. It's just us we have to rely on."

Much harder to win without a crew, the bike insisted cheerily.

She clung to the spear and struggled to catch her breath. As she lay there, she stared up at a black speck spinning near the sun. Whatever it was seemed to be drifting down toward her. She squinted as the speck grew wings, and, with a sharp whistle, two high and one low, the black drongo fluttered down and landed on her chest.

The bird looked at her with its gray eyes. Adya had the impression it was deeply disappointed. Then the damned thing cocked its head and pecked her hard on her breastbone.

That woke her up. Adya swatted at the bird, but it just launched itself into the air, hovering over her, and continued to give her that stare.

"That's a lousy way of saying hello," Adya stammered. "And you've got no reason to be disappointed in me. The bike's brakes didn't work." She was arguing with a bird. She waved the drongo away before it could peck her again, and this time it listened, shooting over the lip of the ridge and disappearing. Adya smashed her spear into the ground and kept dragging herself through the mud.

The last stretch was the steepest, and slick with engine oil. Adya's arms would no longer obey her commands. If she kept at it with her gelatin legs, she'd end up breaking her neck on the way back down.

"Well screw this," she grumbled. Adya slammed the spear into the black earth and reached for a root, a rock, anything. Her fingers found nothing to hold, but her hand stayed suspended in space and wouldn't return. Then it started pulling the rest of her up, and she realized that something had grabbed hold of her wrist. She tried to free herself, but whatever it was dragged her over the edge of the cliff before she could fall.

A thundercloud of curly hair and a huge grin greeted her. She had to be dreaming, but no one else wore a dumb dinosaur shirt like that. Adya blinked in disbelief. Mohan had been a constant worry in the back of her mind. She wrapped her arms around his waist and squeezed for all she was worth. It was all she could do. She didn't have the strength to stand.

"Mohan. We've got to find the princess." Adya managed to get the words out before she crumpled onto the ground.

Mohan's smile shone through the soot covering his face. "I'll find any princess you want. We can find a prince and a king, too, as soon as you get some rest."

She tried to swat at him but totally missed. Her little brother's stegosaurus shirt was a mess. Stranger still were his red-and-blue boxer shorts. Adya's vision was starting to cloud, but she thought she saw a whole crowd of people behind him.

"Why don't you have any pants?" seemed like the most important question.

Mohan folded his arms around her and didn't let go. He gestured for the people behind him to come closer. "I'll explain everything after we get that motorcycle up here. We're going to need it. The rickshaw blew up."

CHAPTER TWELVE

AN HOUR LATER, ADYA LEANED BACK AGAINST A CRACKED refrigerator near the edge of the drop-off. She'd been stuck in the ravine for over a day, and Imral was nowhere to be found.

A girl who couldn't have been more than six crouched at Adya's side, keeping watch over her. Mohan had put the girl on duty and impressed upon her how important it was that Adya keep eating. Every time Adya stopped spooning yogurt and rice into her mouth, the girl's enormous eyes would go wide, and she would poke Adya in the leg with her finger until she resumed. A crowd of at least twenty Vayu villagers stood huddled around them, watching the show.

Her brother hadn't sat down once since he'd pulled her over the edge of the cliff. Adya did her best to always keep her eyes on him. Part of her was still worried this all might be a dream and Mohan might disappear again if she lost sight of him. She damn well wasn't going to let him do that again. Between bites of food, she'd managed to ask if he'd seen the princess, but he only gave her a deeply concerned look and motioned for her to keep eating. Clearly, he thought she'd hit her head too hard.

Their father had always said that when Mohan was born, he'd gotten a hurricane instead of a boy. Her little brother couldn't hold still, couldn't stay on one task for long, and seemed to like it that way. His grin was the eye of the storm, and he caught everyone in it.

He was putting that storm to use now, running around between people who'd become his old friends in the few hours since he'd met them. The bony villagers in their ragged dhotis and saris looked like they needed the food more than she did, but they nodded encouragement with every bite Adya took.

The motorcycle was propped five yards away, surrounded by children and a small herd of goats. The kids had wiped off the coat of mud with old rags until the bike shone. The machine was filling her head with waves of contentment. It loved nothing more than being appreciated. She'd watched as the villagers had climbed down the hill with Mohan and tied ropes around the Yamaha.

The strange thing was that the bike seemed as excited to have Mohan back as she was. It had been frightened of the other villagers when they climbed down to try to free it, but when Mohan had finally got on and held the handlebars, it had calmed right down.

Adya had only had to shout at it once. "That's my brother sitting on your back! Stop being so scared of everything, you big chicken."

The villagers had looked at her with worried expressions, but the Yamaha had fired right up. The bike had no intention of ending its days stuck in thornbushes after feeling the ground beneath its wheels again. She'd surprised herself by hugging the machine when it made it over the edge, and it filled her mind with its relief.

Adya scraped her bowl clean and held it upside down to prove to the little girl that there was nothing left. The girl gave a gap-toothed grin and dashed off to get Mohan. With the food gone, the rest of Adya's audience finally seemed satisfied and broke up. An old woman took the bowl and ran her hand over Adya's cheek. Adya rubbed her eyes and turned away. She wasn't going to cry now if she could help it. There was too much to do.

Mohan finally stopped long enough for her to get a good look at him. His cloud of hair was speckled with twigs and grass, but his eyes sparkled through the patches of dirt on his face.

"Who are these people, Mohan?"

"This is Kunal Uncle." Mohan dragged an old man close. He was shirtless, wearing a dhoti and a beige piece of cloth wrapped around his head to keep off the sun. "He totally saved my life. Dragged me out of the rickshaw and helped me pull off my burning pants. This is the nicest family I've ever met."

The old man rubbed the top of Mohan's head and smiled at Adya with his two remaining teeth. He nodded before hobbling off with his stick, leaving the two of them alone.

Mohan eased himself down next to Adya and squeezed his eyes shut. "I would have died if Kunal hadn't pulled me out of the rickshaw. He says bandits and British troops raid through this area, but the maharaja's soldiers never come this far to protect them. These people have even less than we do in the jungle, but they gave me food and made sure I was all right."

Adya watched Kunal's thin back as he walked away. Despite having so little, the first Vayu they'd met had helped them both more than anyone had in ages. Adya wondered how much she really knew about life outside the jungle. Maybe this far from Mysore, the Vayu weren't so bad.

"How did you find me?" she asked.

"I ran back to the cave and found the rickshaw. It was banged up, but the magic was still working. All I had to do was drag it out of a pile of junk and slap a wheel back on. That bird you fed hung around waiting for me. I think it enjoyed taunting Useless. It led me through the jungle and flew over the spell wall. I had this weird feeling it knew where you were."

"And you were dumb enough to follow it?" She *hadn't* been hallucinating. The bird had pecked at her when she was in the ravine. A drongo would follow someone until its debts were paid, after all.

Mohan threw his hands up. "Like you would have done any different. You're the one who said the rickshaw would be strong enough to disrupt the spell wall's magic. But that wasn't the main problem. Those spirits atop the wall saw me and blasted us." Mohan shifted his gaze to the ground and wouldn't meet Adya's eyes. "We were on fire when we came through, and I couldn't get out. Kunal Uncle risked his life to pull me free. When I looked back, she exploded."

"She?" Adya could barely get the word out.

"The rickshaw, Shipra. She had tons of old memories of cool cities and people and things she'd taxied around. She gave herself up to save me."

Adya put her arm around him. That rickshaw had been inside her own head, if only for a short while. She whispered a prayer of thanks to its spirit.

"How is Useless?" Adya asked, trying to change the subject.

Mohan wiped his tears on his sleeve and gave her a funny look. "He seemed fine when I left. Followed us for a long while before he gave up and turned around."

"Good. I've got to keep him alive until Priya gets back. The maharaja's going to help us find her."

Mohan looked down at his lack of pants and what was left of Adya's mud-soaked clothes. He reached behind him and handed her the remains of her leather jacket. It looked more like a bloody towel than a style statement.

"Why would the maharaja help us?" Mohan said. "This is India, not Oz."

Adya wiped some of the soot off Mohan's face. "He'll help if we bring back his daughter."

Mohan stared at her with a worried expression. "Are you sure you're feeling all right?"

It took Adya three attempts to explain the story of the princess and their escape, and even then Mohan looked unsure.

"You were traveling with the princess of *Mysore? The* princess of Mysore?"

"The only princess I'm on a first-name basis with."

Mohan rubbed his chin. "That's way crazier than any of my ideas," he said. "But if that girl really is his daughter, and we bring her back, he'll have to help. Kunal Uncle might have seen which way she went."

Kunal hadn't seen Imral, but two small boys had seen a girl with blue hair the day before. The boys said she had a gash across her forehead and was with a group of men they didn't know, and they were all wearing swords.

Kunal's forehead wrinkled with worry. "Very bad to be alone out here."

Imral was in dangerous company. And hurt. Adya pushed herself to her feet. Her head started to spin.

Mohan waved his arms. "Hold on. Shouldn't we wait? I mean, you don't look so great."

Adya stumbled to the bike and leaned against it to stay balanced. "You don't take your time when someone's been kidnapped."

Mohan nodded. "Right, you'll save the princess, and I'll make sure you don't collapse. Give me just a moment."

Ten minutes later, Mohan had said goodbye to his new friends and was on the back of the bike. Jyoti, Kunal's wife, approached with a small basket filled with flat chapati and a bottle of yogurt. She opened a tin of clarified butter and smiled before tucking it into the basket.

Adya's throat went dry. Her aunt used to do the same thing whenever Adya fled back to her lonely mine shaft. These people didn't deserve to be plagued by whatever bandits came through. Figuring she could regret it later, Adya reached inside the inner pocket of her ruined leather jacket. The silk bag she'd filled with Huda's coins was still there. She got off the motorcycle and handed it to Kunal.

The old man peered into the bag, and confusion spread over his face. He tried to give it back.

"No," Adya said. She gestured awkwardly to the children and other families. "Hide it. Trade for things little by little. Get what you need."

Kunal embraced her with his bony arms before Adya could

do anything about it. He passed the bag to one of his relatives. In a moment she was surrounded by the entire family. The adults caressed her face while the little kids grabbed her around the knees. She wasn't used to being touched this much.

Mohan laughed. "We were rich for a little while, and I didn't even know it."

"For a little while." Adya shrugged, but before she could start the bike, one of Kunal's grandchildren broke through the crowd. He handed them a bow and three arrows. Mohan's eyebrows shot up in surprise.

"He found them not far from your rickshaw," Kunal explained.

Part of Adya wished the bow had burned. Mohan was a disaster with that thing.

After a final goodbye, they set off, rumbling along at a slow pace until they found footsteps in the wet ground—a small group headed north, instead of west toward Mysore. Adya gunned the engine, and they followed the trail. In less than an hour, they stood before a rapid stream.

"They stopped here," Adya said. She scrutinized the ground. "But not for long. We should keep going."

Mohan pointed to a mango tree, its branches bending over the bank, heavy with fruit. "We should stop too. You still look starved."

Adya's mouth watered at the sight of the ripe fruit. Yellow and speckled with gorgeous pink dots, the mangoes almost demanded to be picked. "For a short while," she agreed.

Mohan climbed up and threw down a half dozen. After slurping down the second, Adya entered a state of bliss. For the first time, she had the energy to mind the mud caking her arms and legs. She could only imagine how her hair must look.

"Just one more minute." She checked for crocodiles before wading into the water to rub the dirt out of her hair. Her head still ached where she'd hit it, but seeing Mohan had given her hope again. Even the motorcycle seemed to be doing better. It purred in satisfaction.

She came out of the stream and was drying off when she caught sight of a track fresher than the rest.

"What is it?" Mohan asked.

Adya glanced at her spear. Its tip glowed faintly. "Trouble," she said.

Mohan placed his hand inside the track and took a deep breath. "Whoa. I didn't know there were yaksha outside of the jungle. What do we do now?"

"You tell me where Sonya is. That's what you do." The voice that answered Mohan was dark and dry as sand.

Adya spun, leveling her spear at the mango trees as Dsouza walked out, sword in hand. His clothes were torn. He had a nasty cut above his right eye. And on his neck, the maharaja's spell mark shone bright as blood in the light of the setting sun.

She slid back before she realized what she was doing. Dsouza's haggard appearance made him look even more dangerous—and more than a touch mad.

"Mud baths and boxer shorts. Fashionable." Dsouza didn't raise his sword, but he didn't sheathe it either. "I waited for you, Mongoose, but you didn't show. Instead, you're here with your little brother. You promised me you'd keep the girl safe." Adya tightened her grip on her spear. She'd heard about how good Dsouza was with a blade.

"You made up the name Sonya. And you neglected to mention she was the heir to the maharaja's throne. Things didn't go as planned. We heard you were captured. Then we were chased by yaksha. I had to take her through the spell wall."

"You did *what?*" Dsouza raised his sword.

"She didn't burn, but if you take one more step, I'll put this spear through you."

Dsouza ignored her, his face a cold mask. "Where is she, then? Did you sell her already? Weren't willing to wait for the big reward and take her all the way to daddy?"

Mohan fit an arrow to his bow and aimed it at Dsouza. "I'm going to assume you're the jerk who calls himself Night Bear and left my sister in Huda's cell—"

Dsouza pointed his sword at Mohan. "Night Blade, kid. Put that bow down before I ram an arrow down your throat."

Adya's jaw tightened. Mohan had the bow bent horizontal like he was going to shoot for fish in the river. At least her little brother was trying, but Dsouza was out of his league.

"You can choke on the dinner you owe me," she said, trying to divert his attention. "I didn't sell your stupid girlfriend, no matter how many times she tried to get us killed."

Dsouza looked like he didn't believe a word of it. "Then where is she?"

"We got separated. We're trying to get her back." That was half the truth anyway. "By the looks of these tracks, she's in trouble."

Neither of them lowered their weapons. "You're suddenly

honorable, Mongoose? You don't give a damn about the princess," Dsouza said.

"What about you? What are you going to do with the ransom?" She thought she'd seen something else in Dsouza's eyes when he'd fought to free Imral, but he was capable of any lie. He'd probably tricked Imral into believing he loved her. Anything for money.

"I'll move as far away from you and your jungle as I can," Dsouza said.

Adya kept her eye on Dsouza's sword. "We'll throw a party for you after you've gone."

This is your crew? The bike chose now to start asking questions.

"See, I told you he's not crew. Mohan is crew."

Dsouza looked confused. Adya realized she'd said the words out loud.

"I don't know what crew you're talking about. But I've seen the tracks. The bandits have her." His eye twitched. "There's some kind of bear with them."

"It's not with them, it's hunting them. And it's no bear," Adya said.

"Stick to fixing toasters, Mongoose. I don't need your opinion on wildlife." He turned his gaze on Mohan. "Not even you need that boy's help. He's going to hurt himself with that bow."

Mohan fumbled with his arrow. "Adya, you told me he was ugly, but not *this* ugly."

He is slow, the bike chimed in with its worst insult, and Adya couldn't agree more.

Dsouza sighed and finally sheathed his sword. "Stay out of my way, both of you."

Adya lowered her spear, but not by much. "I always try to stay as far away from you as possible, Bad Day. We'll be on the bike. You'll be trotting far behind us."

Dsouza smirked. "You two mechanics are going to take on a group of bandits?"

"We'll do better than you. In another hour it'll be dark, and your Vayu eyes will be useless. Who will you track then?" Adya said.

Dsouza looked over the motorcycle and bit his lip. "You've got speed. Take me to her and get out of my way. I'll make sure you're paid, Mongoose."

"No room for jerks," Adya said.

"Damn you, Mongoose. The two of you have never left the jungle. Are you so eager to get yourselves killed?"

Whatever Adya was about to say was swept away as fear flooded her thoughts. It was the bike; the machine was panicked. If they died, it would be alone again. She hated to admit it, but the ass was right. She and Mohan would have a hell of a time if they came across the bandits alone.

"There's no room for you, Dsouza. But you can follow us. We won't go too fast."

Dsouza pointed to Mohan. "I'll ride behind the boy. He's just bones."

She hated the idea, but there wasn't a way around it. She thrust the tip of her spear into the soft ground. "Listen. You can keep the reward if we get the princess home." She didn't want to compete with Dsouza over money. He was less likely to betray them if he knew he was going to get paid.

Dsouza raised an eyebrow. "All of it? What are you after, Mongoose?"

"We need to find our sister."

He opened his mouth to say something, looked between the two of them, then reconsidered.

"The maharaja will help us if we bring the princess back safe," Adya explained. The bike had said Dsouza was slow. He might need the full explanation.

Dsouza laughed. "You two are dumber than you look. Maharajas are the ones who demand favors, not the other way around. If I were you, I'd take the money and hire my own help. Or just go home."

"Shut up." Adya wanted to slap him. The sooner they were rid of him, the better.

"I remember your sister. She drove a hard bargain. Always seemed like I was getting a good price, but when I walked away, I realized I'd just liked talking to her too much."

Adya swallowed hard. Priya was the nicer one, the one everyone loved to talk to. Priya got along with everyone. But the last thing Adya needed was Dsouza screwing around with her emotions now.

"If you're riding with us, you keep your thoughts to yourself. Don't say a word when I'm driving. You get on my nerves."

Dsouza nodded. His half smile was grim. "Once the bandits kill us, we'll annoy each other a lot less."

CHAPTER THIRTEEN

T HE MOON, SHROUDED BY A SKY FULL OF CLOUDS, shed scant light as they followed Imral's trail. Mohan made driving near impossible by pressing right up against Adya in an effort to stay as far away from Dsouza as possible. She couldn't blame him.

They stopped at a wet spot to read the ground. Six people on foot, running fast. The yaksha's immense print just behind them. Adya swallowed hard, thinking of Imral alone, fleeing from a monster with a band of men who'd kidnapped her. She prayed the three of them would be in time.

Dsouza traced the yaksha print, and his brow furrowed. He pointed to a hill looming in the distance. "You need to make this bike go faster. I thought you knew how to drive."

Adya swung her leg over the bike and felt it ready to leap away. "Fine. But don't fall, Bad Day. I'm not stopping to pick up your pieces."

The motorcycle flew across the distance and tore up the hill. When they whipped around a bend, Adya's breath caught. She turned the wheel hard, and dirt flew as she skidded to a stop fifty yards from the crest.

Four torn corpses lay strewn across the path.

"Gods." Dsouza vaulted off the bike before she could speak.

He ran between them, examining every face. She caught up

as he flipped over the last body. Each bandit had been mangled by enormous claws and bore dozens of red welts from what looked like stings. One was missing a leg.

"What could do this?"

Adya knew what, and she wasn't looking forward to finding it. Her spear vibrated in her grip, its tip glowing the white of bleached bone. The air around them thrummed with the drone of insects and stank of sulfur and blood. This was a yaksha they didn't want to meet, and they were running straight toward it.

She dropped to one knee to examine the tracks. "One man ran that way, up the hill. Imral was with him." Adya met Dsouza's eyes. "The yaksha followed." She didn't need to say the rest. They couldn't have gotten far.

Dsouza didn't bother getting on the motorcycle. He drew his sword and dashed ahead.

Adya jumped on the bike. As Mohan clasped his arms around her, a girl's scream tore through the night.

They crested the hill just as the moon came out from behind the clouds and illuminated the disaster below.

Imral was sprinting toward an outcrop of boulders, one of the bandits twenty yards behind. As they watched, she reached the rocks and started to climb.

The bandit wasn't going to make it.

The yaksha pursued, a dark shadow with claws, tearing the ground as it ran. Its black body rippled and shifted with every bound. As the yaksha closed in, the bandit turned, sword in hand.

He never stood a chance.

The cloud that surrounded the beast erupted, and a storm of wasps descended. The man flailed. Claws and teeth flashed before he disappeared beneath the swarm, but his scream left little to the imagination.

The swarm contracted once again into the shape of a great black bear as big as an elephant. It rose up on its hind legs and roared. The sound vibrated down Adya's spine and sent her body turning to run without any conscious decision.

Dsouza grabbed her arm. "We're not going anywhere without Imral."

The yaksha proceeded to rake the torn body of the bandit. Then it seized the man's torso in its jaws and shook him until pieces started to fly off.

"Of course not," Adya said. "Why would anyone want to leave?" She picked up her mother's spear and tried to sound sure of herself. "There's only one way to kill a yaksha," Adya started, as if she actually knew what she was doing.

Dsouza gave her a hard stare. "I don't want battle tactics from someone who sells radios. We're getting Imral away before it tears her apart. I'll take care of the yaksha. You and the useless kid ride the bike around us and get the princess out of here. Don't look back." Dsouza looked like he hadn't rested in days, but his eyes still shone like black pearls. His half smile appeared despite everything. "I'll see you on the other side, Mongoose. Have dinner ready." He lifted his sword and took a step away.

She grabbed for him. "You're only going to make it mad. We've got to—"

But the yaksha had already tossed what was left of the

bandit's body aside. It started toward the pile of rocks where Imral was desperately trying to climb higher. Dsouza shrugged Adya off and charged downhill.

"Try me, you big rug!" Dsouza cried. With every step he grew smaller, a lone sailor running into a typhoon.

Your pit crew is going down by one, the bike said. It obviously didn't give Dsouza much of a chance.

"He's insane," Adya agreed.

She glanced over her shoulder and found Mohan with one hand on his bow.

"You know, his plan is not bad," her brother said. "I mean we might get the princess out alive. The only problem is . . ."

"Dsouza's going to die," Adya finished for him. No ordinary weapon could harm a yaksha. She had learned that long ago.

Her mother had explained the same day she'd led her deep into the jungle to find a yaksha, *This spear will be yours one day. Strike a yaksha with this, and your two souls meet. It's your heart's fire against theirs, and only one will survive. Many things may come easier to Priya, but you've got more of that flame than any of us.*

Dsouza was going to sacrifice himself for nothing. Adya added idiotic to his list of faults.

The yaksha turned its massive head and sniffed the air.

"That's right, Ugly," Dsouza shouted. "Over here." He stopped halfway down the hill and waved his arms over his head.

Imral had reached the top of a boulder. She pointed at the yaksha while screaming out an incantation. Exactly nothing happened. Adya had no idea what the princess was trying to accomplish, but the monster was not impressed. They had only a few moments before the yaksha would start throwing bits of Dsouza all over the place.

"Stay here and don't shoot me," Adya said.

Mohan had frozen in panic, but he nodded. Adya lowered her head to the motorcycle's handlebars and let the machine into her mind. Then she gave it a shove, and it rumbled down the hill without a driver, veering wide of the yaksha, its light flashing, horn blaring.

The yaksha was already charging. Inky smoke erupted around it as it bore down on Dsouza. A silver collar shone around its neck as it opened its maw, and wasps erupted from its throat. Still Dsouza didn't move. He crouched and readied his sword. He was going to be swallowed alive.

Adya started sprinting.

Ten yards before the yaksha reached him, the sound of a bike's horn caught its attention. It stopped and turned, tilting its head, trying to understand this new enemy.

The motorcycle sped downhill, headlight blazing, then turned ninety degrees and accelerated to maximum velocity. Too late the yaksha tried to leap out of the way.

The bike rammed it head-on.

The giant yaksha crashed to the ground in an explosion of wasps and smoke. Its silver collar spun skyward, twisting in the moonlight. The motorcycle roared back in a triumphant wheelie, flashing its light. *Champion! I am a champion! Nothing can outrace me!*

Adya came to a halt and tried to slow her breathing. The crazy machine had done it.

"Get out of here," Dsouza yelled.

The mass of wasps was swirling together once again. Adya could make out the figure of the bear. In moments, the yaksha was whole again. The monster shook its head and bounded forward, catching up with the offending bike, clamping its jaws on the handlebars. The yaksha twisted and hurled the bike into the air. The Yamaha spun away with a final beep, its headlight tracing a rotating arc of light in the darkness.

The yaksha growled, triumphant. The monster tore at its own neck, raking at the silver collar before turning its eyes to Dsouza once more.

They were going to die. Every cell in Adya's mind demanded she run, but her muscles wouldn't respond.

Dsouza pushed her away with one hand. "I said go, Adya. Save the princess. Find your sister." He spun the sword in an arc, catching the moonlight on its blade, and started toward the yaksha.

It was the last bit he said that decided it. Adya tightened her grip on her mother's spear. The damn bike was right. He was crew.

Dsouza walked toward the yaksha slow and easy. "You talk big for a bear. Come play with me." He was hard and proud, cold as the magic of his people. Adya could almost see the Night Blade in him.

The yaksha reared up on its hind legs and regarded the man walking toward it. It hesitated, as if unsure of this swordsman appearing out of the darkness like a warrior out of a legend. It dropped to all fours and swung its head from side to side, and for a moment, Adya thought it might run, thought they might not die.

Then the yaksha charged.

Dsouza cut to the right and raised his blade before him, timing out a perfect strike. Then he took a bad step on the muddy slope and slid straight onto his back with a thwack.

The bear closed the last yards with a great bound.

Adya moved before she knew what she was doing. She dove in front of Dsouza, sliding on one knee across the rain-soaked ground, straight into the swarm.

The world went black. Her ears filled with buzzing.

Within the darkness, Adya felt transported. The yaksha's eyes locked onto hers, and she sensed its madness, felt its heart beating, the heat of its soul, the pain of its torment. Someone had enslaved this creature, and it longed to be free.

The maddened yaksha opened its jaws to destroy her, and Adya drove her mother's weapon between them. The spear's tip pierced spirit, and their minds met.

The fire of the yaksha's soul burned black as coal. Pressing her down, consuming her.

You will never be good enough.

Everyone you love will leave you.

You will always be alone.

Adya felt herself fading in the face of the assault. Felt herself drifting and knew that if she surrendered, she would lose Mohan forever. Priya would never be found. She held on as her own soul burned, orange and white, small but inextinguishable, growing, beating back the heat surrounding her.

With a snarl the yaksha opened its jaws wider, swallowing the spear into its darkness. Adya's arm followed.

She screamed as teeth closed on her flesh. Bones cracked and tendons snapped. Every neuron in her arm fired at once and burned out. Then her spear's uranium tip struck the center of the beast, and its magic ignited. Sudden light flared around, turning everything bright silver.

Through it all, Adya held on. She held on as the yaksha thrashed like an earthquake and never let go.

CHAPTER FOURTEEN

R IDER DOWN! *RIDER DOWN!* THE VOICE OF THE MOTOR-cycle in the back of her mind was impossible to shut out.

Adya smiled despite the giant head pinning her to the ground. The foolish bike was probably just afraid again. She loved that bike. It reminded her of Mohan, so full of energy and promise. If her brother would only have a little more faith in himself, he could do anything. She wondered if she'd ever told him that. She really needed to, but she wasn't as good with that kind of thing as Priya was. Adya tried to rub her forehead with her hand and get the blood out of her eyes, but for some reason it didn't work.

The endless swarm of insects drifted ever lower. Wasps clustered on her skin, folding their iridescent wings as they lost the strength to fly. They really were quite beautiful in the moonlight. It was a shame they were dying. Adya reached out to touch one just as the yaksha sighed a final bubbling breath and its full weight fell atop her. Blood dripped onto her chest, staining the crushed insects a brilliant red. She gasped for air as her vision clouded. This was really a very strange day.

"Help her, you idiot." Adya recognized Dsouza's voice. He'd better not be yelling at her brother. Someone had clearly hurt the Jackal when he was a kid, and he had never gotten over it. She would have to explain that to him, but would he ever listen? Maybe if she made him dinner? But wait—he was supposed to cook for her.

Then the weight of the yaksha was gone. Someone must have rolled it off her, or maybe it had only been sleeping and had gotten up and wandered away? Everything was so confusing at the moment. She took a deep breath and was surprised to hear herself gurgling. She spat out a clot of blood then gazed up at a sky filled with a million stars. She tried to pick out the brightest one so she could make a wish, but that crook, Dsouza, was standing over her, still shouting something or other. Why did he have to be so loud?

Imral stood at Dsouza's side with one fist clenched. Her face was smeared with dirt and tears. "You don't understand," she explained in that princess way, like no one else had ever read a book. "We'll need more power than I've ever drawn before. We'll have to work a part of each other's spell and a part of our own at the same time. I haven't had time to practice. There won't be an established pattern. It might kill us all."

"You think you're the only one who ever knows anything, don't you?" The words came out of Adya's mouth as a whisper in the night. "But really, you're more afraid than a Kawasaki at the semifinals." Adya laughed at her own joke before she realized she had no idea what it even meant.

Mohan leaned over her, brushing hair out of her face. Her brother had lost his stegosaurus shirt somewhere. He really shouldn't be around a princess without a shirt.

"I've tied the tourniquet as tight as I can," Mohan said. "But she's lost too much blood. We'll call up as much power as we can and take the risk. I'm not letting her die."

"That's the spirit," Adya whispered. "Take some chances, Mohan. You're more than you ever thought you were. Baba would be so proud." Adya grinned. There, she'd said it. Or was she dreaming? She coughed hard, and something dribbled out of her mouth.

Mohan's eyes went wide. "We don't have much time. She never talks like this."

"I can't do it." The princess was still whining. "I can't even manage lights anymore."

Mohan stepped toward the princess and reached for her arm. Dsouza slapped his hand away and stepped between them, but her brother seemed not to notice.

"She risked everything to save us," Mohan insisted. "I know you're afraid. We all are. Say the words I told you, and I'll trace the forms you showed me. We'll give the magic a new path."

That wasn't how you spoke to a princess, but whatever. Adya's encouragement had clearly worked. Priya wasn't the only one who could give a pep talk. She coughed again and swallowed more blood.

Imral put her fist on Mohan's chest. "No one's ever done this before. It took ages for our sorcerers to find the paths. We could rip her to pieces. Change her into something we never expected. We have no idea what shape the magic will take."

Mohan didn't flinch. "Put those ages of lessons to work, Princess. I'll use everything my sister taught me. Whatever happens is better than her dying."

Imral squeezed her eyes together tight before responding. Her entire body shivered once before she stepped away from Mohan. "Get ready." She stretched her fingers wide and began tracing a pattern in the air. *"Vishwakarma namo namah,"* she chanted.

"You're probably just as good as your brothers ever were at that," Adya said, not worried at all about interrupting the magic. Confidence was as important as getting the words right, and the girl definitely needed some confidence. "They always underestimate girls." The words came out of Adya's mouth dry and cracked. She could really use some water right now. Or a mango. They should all just get out of here and go eat.

She made out Mohan off to her left, tracing a pattern in the air, which was strange. Tracing patterns was definitely a Vayu thing to do. The motorcycle's engine roared like a forest of tigers, and the understanding of what they were doing hit Adya like a wrench over the head.

The two of them were trying to mix magic, and she had been encouraging them. They were about to unleash a force that they had no way of controlling, no way of shaping. The fools were attempting to draw enough power from the infinity well to save her, and it would get them all killed. They were improvising for one of Mohan's dumb experiments. She was going to lose them all.

"Don't you dare." Adya tried to scream, but the words came out so soft that she wondered if anyone heard. Wondered if she had spoken at all. Her tongue seemed stuck to the roof of her mouth. No one paid her any attention.

In the sky above, the stars were blinking out one by one.

"Dsouza, keep her awake." Mohan's voice startled Adya. "I need to focus."

Suddenly Dsouza was leaning over her, singing something she didn't understand. Was he actually singing and holding her eyes open with his fingers? That hurt. Adya tried to blink without success. Dsouza looked strange, almost as if he was worried about her. But that was impossible.

"Listen to me, Adya. Stay awake and listen for once."

He thought *she* was a bad listener? He was the one with the problem.

"I was trying to tell you before. When we were at that stream. Something I wanted you to know." Dsouza looked away from her but kept talking. "Your sister was the one who stepped up to make the deals, but you were always there, waiting at the mouth of that tunnel, making sure she was safe. I tried not to let you know I'd seen you." He swallowed hard. "I always hoped you would be the one to step out. That I wouldn't be the villain you had to protect everyone from."

Adya's eyes filled with tears, though she didn't know why. "What kind of a villain do you want to be, Jagan Dsouza?" She snorted and was rewarded with an immediate jolt of pain. What was it that he had said? Adya tried to remember, but the world was so very cold, and black dots were dancing in front of her eyes. Her next breath rattled in her chest. Dsouza could make up stories like nobody else. She wasn't sure what he was talking about, but he did look so very handsome when he was rambling on.

She gave in to a sudden urge and reached up to touch

Dsouza's face. Her fingers stroked his unshaven cheek, but he didn't tense or pull away. "You look beautiful," she said. She smiled, certain she must look very stupid, lying here in the dirt tracing blood across Dsouza's cheek.

He took her wrist in his hand and held it. "I want to be the kind of villain that you want to make dinner for," he murmured.

Adya was just about to tell him how nice that would be when she realized he was up to something. He was trying to distract her.

Wind whipped through her hair as magic swirled around them. Dsouza stood. He pointed at someone outside her field of vision and shouted something unintelligible.

Fighting through the pain, Adya pushed herself up on an elbow. One glance confirmed that there was nothing left below her right shoulder but shards of bone and torn flesh, bound tight with Mohan's stegosaurus T-shirt and splinted with the remains of her black spear. That spear had been her mother's. Now it was just broken wood. She was losing everything all over again, and there was nothing she could do. Adya tried to take a breath but stopped as the deep ache in her shoulder hit full force, as if the yaksha was still chewing on her. She moaned, willing herself not to pass out, searching for her brother.

Mohan sat astride the motorcycle, chanting, his forehead pressed to the handlebars. *"Om krim Kali."*

"Stop!" Adya tried to get their attention, but it was too late. The air vibrated with magic. It was in her teeth and behind her eyes, growing stronger by the second. They were improvising, trying to channel the infinity well to their will, but you couldn't improvise with a solar flare. They'd called up too much power. Gods only knew what path it would take.

Mohan finished his chant, and the spell took hold.

Atavi magic found Vayu spell and sought to knit her back together. Her shattered spear rose in the wind and aimed itself straight at her. Adya screamed as it drove into her shoulder. The magic seared inside her as the spear struck, stretching wounded skin, cauterizing broken arteries, melting the ends of bone to fuse anew. She clenched her jaw and trembled with growing horror. This much power would tear a path straight into the conjurers' souls. There would be a price to pay. There was always a price.

Imral's head rocked back as the debt came due. Mohan collapsed on top of the bike as if some great weight had pressed him flat. The magic was destroying them, but her brother was too damned stubborn to give up.

"Mohan, you have to let it go," Adya pleaded.

Somehow he heard her. "No." Mohan's breath was shallow. His eyes were closed, but he held tight to the handlebars. Her dumb brother was going to die.

Luckily, Imral passed out. The princess swayed on her feet until she fell, and Dsouza caught her.

The magic began to fade.

Adya let out a breath as the spear clattered to the ground and blood dripped from her arm once more. She was too close to death to save. No one had such power.

Her brother gunned the motorcycle's engine. He just wouldn't give up. Why did Mohan never listen?

"*Guru Brahma.*" Mohan started another incantation, and a thick silence filled the night. Even the insects went quiet. Adya's vision filled with their endless wings in the dark sky.

The motorcycle's horn blared. The insane bike was trying to help, lending its magic to Mohan's. Amidst it all, Adya swore she heard someone singing. Either Imral was trying to cast a spell, or the bike had switched on its radio. They were all just making things up as they went along. The air grew thick around her as the magic responded, following the new path of their spell.

High above, the stars blazed with sudden fierceness, a thousand eyes staring down upon them. The ground erupted. Mud became feathers, stones became wings, and a storm of black birds spiraled into the sky. The conjured birds swirled up in a tornado of black beaks and claws. Then the moon flashed, and every bird held its place, their wings reflecting the light, waiting.

Mohan reached out to Imral. "We have to finish it."

Imral pushed away from Dsouza and took Mohan's hand. Without saying a word, she traced another pattern.

Another jolt of magic surged through Adya as everything changed.

The storm of birds ignited. Silver light blazed around Mohan, filling his eyes, surrounding him, bathing the motorcycle in brilliant flame. Its engine screamed.

He shielded his eyes with his hands as the bike's frame exploded.

Shards of red and white metal tore away, spinning high in a

gyre as the bike flew to pieces. Imral tackled Mohan, and they tumbled away as the razor-sharp metal shot into the sky, an omen of death.

"Run, Mohan. All of you, run." The words escaped Adya in a blood-tinged whisper.

The whirling steel spread wide across the sky, like the hood of a giant cobra. In the center of the hurricane, two silver eyes blazed down at Adya.

Dsouza drew his sword, as if he might defend them against a monster no weapon could touch.

The serpent reared back, its hood spreading wider, blotting out the moon, making the sky go black. Then it struck, slashing with a thousand fangs, cutting Adya to pieces.

CHAPTER FIFTEEN

ADYA WOKE TO THE TASTE OF IRON AND THE SHARP smell of iodine. Her head throbbed like someone was tolling a giant iron bell inside her skull. The last thing she remembered was the yaksha whipping her about like a dog with its toy. Perhaps she was dead? Or inside the creature's stomach, being digested over the course of a thousand years? She rejected both ideas when she realized she was drooling onto a silk pillow and the scattered light was filtering through a pink canopied bed. She raised her arm to brush the sweaty hair off her forehead.

And stiffened as cool metal drew across her face.

Pillows flew as Adya tumbled out of bed, smacking into a nightstand and sending a mirror crashing to the floor, shattered glass spilling across the thick carpet. A jolt ran down her left arm as she batted away a steel hand.

Adya followed the length of the foreign right arm until it merged with her shoulder.

Then she screamed.

A host of bearded faces converged upon her with out-stretched hands. She flailed at the strangers, scrambling back, trying to find some way to wake from this nightmare.

A stern-faced woman dressed in a white salwar kameez pushed in front of the men and held out her arms to keep the men at bay. "You're frightening the girl. The maharaja will have your hides if she injures herself—Mimun, restrain her, if you will."

Adya sucked in a breath as her arms slammed to her sides, squeezed by unseen hands. She lay on her back, helpless, as one of the men reached for her.

"Stay away from me," she demanded. A helpless terror filled her as she fought uselessly against her invisible bonds.

The man jerked back when he touched the metal arm. Electricity crackled from Adya's wrist to her shoulder. She clenched her jaw as the energy intensified and the force holding her shattered.

"Leave her alone!" Mohan's voice rose above all the others. Her brother appeared dressed in a cream-colored shirt, pushing his way through the crowded room. "She doesn't understand—"

Mohan rose into the air and hung there, midstride, his arms flailing for balance.

Adya grabbed a dresser and dragged herself to her feet, her head spinning. "Let him go," she demanded. She swung the metal arm before her, and one of the bedposts shattered, sending pink fabric drifting down over her shoulders. As Adya beat away the silk, the crowd retreated, and she got her first real look at her surroundings.

Three men in dark green stood behind Mohan, watching her warily, along with the woman in white. Mohan floated three feet above the floor, still kicking his legs. Behind the others hovered a fiery apparition, taller than any human. Flames crowned an elongated head, and swirls of smoke formed long

165

black hair and a mustache. The creature interlaced long fingers, examining her.

"I cannot restrain her, Rabia. The arm defeats my magic." The fiery being's voice was like the distant rumble of thunder. "Mohan, my apologies. I did not wish you tangled in the fray."

Whatever power held Mohan in place disappeared, and he ran toward Adya without missing a step. "It's all right." Mohan wrapped his arms around her. "They're here to help."

The woman in white kept an eye on Adya as she dragged the fallen canopy off the mattress. "Let her rest, Mohan. Before she wastes what little strength she's gained."

Adya let her brother guide her back to bed. But she had no intention of lying down with all these strangers in the room, no matter how weak she felt.

She kept her voice low and clutched the metal arm to her chest, not certain she had control over it. "What's happened, Mohan? Where are we? Who are these people?"

Mohan took a deep breath. "We're in the palace of Mysore." He ran a hand over his forehead. "These are the maharaja's healers. And that's Mimun. He's one of the jinn, a real jinn, like in *The Hundred Finest*. They've been trying everything to heal you. We thought you might never wake up."

The jinn dipped his head in a slight bow. "The maharaja requested my assistance, but it was your brother who convinced me to come. He is extremely persuasive." A scarlet flame danced in the center of his black eyes. "My apologies for trying to bind you, Adya Sachdev. I was worried you might break someone's bones without intending to." Mimun rubbed his fiery beard. "It is a very curious thing that my magic failed. That has not happened for centuries."

"Well, don't try it again," Adya said.

Mohan looked between them. "He's here to help, Adya, I promise. They've been here for three days."

"Days?" A sudden wave of dizziness hit Adya, and she leaned against one of the remaining bedposts. She could still feel the heat of the yaksha's breath upon her. "Where are the others? Imral, Dsouza, the bike?"

Rabia spoke before Mohan could answer her. "Be at peace. Your friends are alive. Even that machine of yours is in one piece. There will be time for all the details later, but for now you must rest. The yaksha nearly burned out your soul. I can't understand how you woke so soon."

The jinn furrowed his brow. "I fear her rest will be short, Rabia. The maharaja will be here soon. Even now, the guards rush to inform their master."

Rabia frowned. "Our ruler is a patient man. He will give her until tonight to recover." She turned to Adya and hesitated before speaking. "Please, before you ask any favors of him, listen carefully to what the maharaja says. Above all, do not interrupt him and do not question his decisions." Rabia looked around at the broken furniture and scattered pillows. Her brow furrowed. "We've done all we can. We will leave you now. Mohan. Don't tire her. May you both stay safe, inshallah."

The healers hurried to leave. Rabia offered a tight smile before closing the door behind her. Mimun made no move to depart. The flames that crowned his head flickered as he floated closer.

Adya retreated to the other side of the mattress. She raised her metal arm. "Did you do this?"

The jinn shook his head, and flames danced. *"That* is magic far beyond me. You arrived here in that remarkable condition, and your brother has remained silent about it." Mimun gave a slight smile. "He promised me a demonstration of your technomancy one day. I would leave the mosque, perhaps even travel to your jungle, to see a girl bring back a machine from another age."

"Mohan shouldn't make promises for me," she said. "I don't put on shows."

Mimun nodded. "Of course. Magic is a serious matter. Still, I can hope." He examined her. "It always amazed me to think that of all the magicians in India, only the Atavi could speak with machines. I pondered for centuries why such power lay in your hands. Why should those closest to nature be the ones to speak to metal and wire? I supposed it was because you already know the secret of listening to the leaves, the streams, the birds. All the quiet voices trust you with their secrets. Listening is a great magic of its own."

Adya tried to imagine what it would be like to ponder something for centuries. "You're right, in a way. Technomancy *is* about listening to voices others ignore. About caring for souls others have forgotten."

"Caring?" Mimun closed his eyes for a moment as he considered. "That is a deeper magic still. I shall think on it for another century or so." A smile flashed across his face. "In the spirit of caring, I offer you a truth and ask for nothing in return." He leaned closer, and his voice became a whisper of flame. "Your own jungle you know well, but Mysore is a vast one of its own. An unknown forest of towering concrete and marble, where the greatest of the lions rules. Beware this place. Do not let your guard falter." He bowed his head. "If you require my assistance while you are in the city, seek me out in the mosque of Masjid E Azam. If I am not there, go to Lalbag, and he will find me. He is a man of many talents."

"I've met him already," Mohan said. "I ran into him while I was wandering the city."

Mimun raised an eyebrow. "You think that was a chance encounter? I asked him to find you while you were in the maze and make certain you returned. You are not without allies in Mysore." Mimun raised a hand in farewell as his form began to fade. "May Allah keep you safe from your enemies. I fear you will need his protection before all is done."

A rush of heat brushed her cheeks, and the jinn dissolved into smoke, spiraling out the open window. Adya grabbed Mohan to make sure he didn't disappear as well and leaned back in the bed. She tried to concentrate on her breathing and ignore the stabs of pain in her head. She had never been so overwhelmed.

Mohan squeezed her hand. "You're kind of crushing my fingers."

Adya eased up but didn't let go. She sucked another slow breath in and out. "We're in Mysore, and they covered my arm in metal?"

Mohan let go of her hand and started pacing. "Uh . . . we *are* in the palace, but your arm is not exactly . . . I mean, do you remember anything?"

Her head still ached. She watched the steel fingers spread wide.

"I remember stars," she said. "Brighter than any I'd ever seen. But they were dying. And I remember your voice, whispering, but I can't remember what you were saying. I can't remember what anyone said. I remember being so very cold and a great weight pressing me into the earth."

Adya stretched the metal arm above her head and marveled at it. Air moved across the red and white paint as if it were her own skin. With a thought, the fingers folded perfectly into a metal fist, as if the steel were alive and had been part of her forever. It was both wondrous and terrifying. As she stared at the arm, the memory of what had happened flooded back, and she understood the terrible truth. Her arm was gone forever. The yaksha had swallowed it. The others had been screaming about something or other, and then—

Adya sat up straight. "You two mixed the magic. You lost control." She shivered.

Mohan's face grew grim. "We dragged you out of the yaksha's mouth, Adya. I wasn't about to let you die."

"You could have died." There was no telling what might have happened. How many technomancers had perished until they learned a reliable way to control the flows of power? She remembered the tornado of steel, hanging over them like a cobra. It could have ended them all.

Mohan turned away. "You're the one who told me to have faith in myself. To take chances."

"When did I say that?" she asked. She would never have

told him to try something so reckless. "What else did I say?" She had a vague memory of talking to Dsouza but had no idea what she'd told him.

"Amma and Baba are gone. Priya is gone. I wasn't about to lose you, too. I don't care about your damned rules." He narrowed his eyes. "You would have done the same."

Adya swallowed hard as she examined his face. Her brother's eyes had changed color. Mohan's deep brown irises, always sparkling, had gone a stormy gray. The power he'd tried to harness had changed him. Perhaps in ways she couldn't see.

Adya turned her steel hand palm up. "I would have tied off the arm with a better tourniquet and left it." She ran her fingers over the ebony line that ran along the new arm from her wrist to her biceps. Her mother's spear had been swept up in the magic. It would be part of her forever. That was a small comfort. And the arm was beautiful—she couldn't deny it. Couldn't deny that Mohan was right. "Come on. You saved my life. Might as well help me a little more."

Holding his shoulder for balance, she hobbled to a long mirror standing in the corner.

A year's growth of thick curls tumbled halfway down her back. The healing spells had had quite the effect on her hair, which someone had brushed and oiled, but her face had grown thin. At any other time, the strangest thing would have been the pink silk pajamas embroidered with roses. Now it was the arm that stood out, an almost perfect replica of her previous limb, with fine joints and subtle curves, painted to perfection, plated and hinged like a machine.

Tears threatened to break free, but Adya held them back. She couldn't feel sorry for herself now. They had a sister to find.

"Okay. Where's Priya and everyone else?" she asked. Hopefully Mohan had learned something by now. "And where's my bike?"

Mohan shook his head. "They took the bike when we arrived, and no one will tell me anything about Priya. Everyone was focused on making sure you stayed alive. I've been pacing back and forth, asking the healers questions until they got tired of me and kicked me out. I ended up wandering around the city by myself a few times until they let me back in."

"Damn." Adya's head swam, and she grabbed the wall to steady herself. She definitely needed time to get her strength back before she faced the maharaja. Maybe she could afford to close her eyes for just an hour or two.

Mohan lowered his voice. "There's something weird about this place, Adya. People dodge my questions. I asked Imral if she'd found out any news about Priya, but no one would tell her anything either. Do you think the maharaja will know where she is?"

Adya ran a hand over the pink silk pajamas and didn't answer, deep in thought. If she was meeting with the most powerful ruler in India tonight, she would need something else to wear.

A loud knock sounded on their door. Adya spun as the door swung open, and a red-vested guard with a long mustache stepped in. He surveyed the state of the room with obvious dismay, looking over the shattered furniture before he gave a sharp bow. "His Majesty, the protector of the Flame of the South, the guardian of—"

"Enough, enough. How much time do you have to waste today, Sunil?" A tall man, muscular and clean shaven, pushed past the guard. His hair was long and uncovered, his face, neither young nor old, was full of light, while his eyes gave the impression of someone who had seen the entire world and taken its measure. His white military jacket, gleaming with gold buttons, was nothing she would ever see in the jungle, but his smile, his confidence, the brightness of his eyes, reminded Adya more of her own father than anyone else. He radiated a feeling that anything was possible while he was here, anything at all.

The maharaja of Mysore patted the guard on the shoulder. "How much time does the world have with the British upon us? Everything has changed, Sunil, and we must change with it. What matters is Mysore and its people."

The maharaja took one look at the destroyed room and raised an eyebrow. "I shall talk to the jinn about the way he treats my furniture and brings me bad luck with broken mirrors." He gave a flick of his hand, and the room filled with a furious wind. The nightstand righted itself along with the mirror, as each shattered piece of glass flew back into place, cracks disappearing. The pink silk canopy spun in the gale, then draped itself over the bed just as the broken bedpost leapt back into place, whole once more.

Then the maharaja turned his eyes on the two of them, their hair whipped about by the wind. "And, along with Mysore, these two guests matter to me a great deal."

Adya took a deep breath. Weak or not, she needed her wits about her. She fought a surge of nausea and bowed before the greatest sorcerer in India, the ruler of the South, the maharaja of Mysore.

CHAPTER SIXTEEN

S KIP THE BOWING AND SCRAPING, PLEASE. I'M NOT SURE which of us should bow: you before your ruler, or me before the girl who returned my only heir at such great cost." The maharaja turned toward the still-open door. "Come in, come in, all of you. I've cleaned the room. Do I have to do all the work in my own palace?"

Servants rushed in carrying furniture, followed by more servants balancing steaming bowls and teapots and boxes wrapped in fine paper. Soldiers dressed in long scarlet coats and golden belts filed in behind.

When everything was ready, the maharaja dropped into a particularly fine blue velvet chair, and two guards took up stations on either side. "Really, I should have given you time to rest. My healers will be furious, but I couldn't bear to wait. I needed to behold with my own eyes the girl who brought hope back to Mysore." He gestured at the delicacies his servants had laid out. "Please eat, before I drown you in words."

Adya's mouth watered as servants ladled food onto silver trays covered with fresh banana leaves. Steaming lemon rice was followed by tiny bowls filled with hot rasam, fresh yogurt, an assortment of every vegetable she could want, spicy pickles, and finally sweet kheer laced with saffron. The maharaja waved a hand, and the trays, loaded with every delicious local specialty, rose into the air, hovering in front of each of them. Servants rushed to place tables under their floating meals.

The smell of fresh sambar hit Adya, and her stomach rumbled out loud.

The maharaja laughed, eyes sparkling. "Of course you are starving! The body demands fuel after all that healing." He took a cup of steaming coffee from one of his soldiers and sipped as she and Mohan stuffed their faces with the best food Adya had ever tasted.

It took five mouthfuls for Adya to realize she was using her metal right hand to spoon food. She froze for a moment before giving in to her tremendous hunger and biting into another fried samosa.

The maharaja watched Adya take every bite. "Coffee, bring them coffee," he commanded. A servant hurried to oblige.

The man raised his arm high and poured long streams of milky coffee into shining steel cups. It burned its way down to Adya's stomach, and she felt herself waking again.

The maharaja seemed to be enjoying every second of their feast. He waved a woman into the room. "Now, a few very minor things," he said. "Mind you, these are not true gifts, merely replacements for what you've lost while rescuing my daughter. Go ahead, open them. Try them on."

Two men removed the tables, laden with untouched delicacies. Adya missed the food at once. She could have kept eating all day. As the men departed, a woman dressed in green set the two boxes wrapped in golden paper in front of Adya.

Adya reached in and lifted out a red leather jacket that made

175

her old jacket look like it was sewn together by a blindfolded apprentice. She ran her fingers over the exquisite stitching and discovered a metal lining as supple as velvet, woven through with spell patterns. She'd never imagined such exquisite work-manship was possible.

"Try it on. Go ahead," the maharaja commanded.

It fit perfectly, sitting on her shoulders like it was meant to be there. They must have measured her while she slept. Inside the next box, she discovered the motorcycle boots she'd sto-len from Huda, polished and newly fitted with the finest blue silk. She slipped into the boots and felt like her feet were being caressed. She could live in these.

"They're beautiful," she remarked without thinking. "This jacket looks like it could turn an arrow."

The maharaja's mouth spread into a grin. "An arrow, a sword, the teeth of a werewolf, nothing will penetrate that spell weave. My tailors used silver steel, and my best sorcerers made sure I was happy with it. But my true gifts have yet to come." He regarded Adya and Mohan. "You've both eaten. You have clothes and shelter and the attention of your ruler. What do you desire? What do you wish to know?"

Mohan cleared his throat while Adya was still thinking of what to say. "We really want to know about—what you might know about—Priya, I mean, after she got to Mysore." Mohan hid his face in another gulp of coffee as the maharaja raised both eyebrows.

"We want to find our sister, Maharaja," Adya translated. Her brother's stammering had given her time to collect herself.

"She traveled all the way to Mysore to meet you. We've come to bring her home."

Mohan jumped back in. "That's what I said."

The maharaja's brow furrowed. "Of course. Imral explained everything." He took a deep breath. "Regarding your sister, I have hard news. We are in a time of desperate war, and Mysore is a city of a million. I am sad to say that one girl, alone, with no connections, would find it next to impossible to gain my attention. I never met Priya and had no news of her arrival. For now, she is lost, but I give you my promise: I will do everything to find her."

Adya got to her feet, wobbled once, and knocked over what was left of her coffee. The soldiers on either side of the maharaja stepped forward, their hands on their sword hilts, before he waved them away.

"She risked her life driving through a wall of flame to help you, and you didn't have a moment for her?" Too late she remembered Rabia's warning not to question the ruler of Mysore.

The maharaja's face turned grim, and the room went quiet except for the sound of clinking metal cups as one of the servants attempted to clean the mess. "If I gave a moment to every citizen who petitioned me, the British would already have taken us. The South is all that remains free in India. I have no time to waste." He rose to his feet. "I lost two sons to that army."

Adya's metal hand tightened into a fist. She understood all too well what losing family was like. The maharaja had all of South India to worry about, but she still needed to find Priya. "But our sister had nowhere else to go. Where could she be?"

The maharaja studied her before answering. "I'm told she arrived here on a machine. A girl on a moped can go very far, very fast."

Adya grabbed one of the bedposts to steady herself. "Then she's left Mysore?"

"It's more than likely, as I have heard nothing of her since." The maharaja took a slow breath and seemed to collect himself. "But I have vowed to help you. Do not lose hope." The servants finished removing the tables from the room. "We shall speak again tonight. I have gifts to help in your search. I am confident we will locate her. Until then, rest here in comfort until your strength returns. I will take great pleasure in showing you my city when I am able."

The maharaja looked them over once more. Then he gave a sad smile and followed his guards out of the room.

A lock clicked as the door closed.

"Were you trying to make him mad?" Mohan asked. "I mean, whoa, Adya, he's the maharaja."

It was the last look on the maharaja's face that stayed vivid in her mind. He was a man who had lost as much as she had, a realist, trying to keep what remained of his family safe, to keep his kingdom out of British hands. She could understand him, but she couldn't trust him.

"He didn't have time for Priya," she said. When she tried the door, it wouldn't budge. She had no doubt there were guards stationed on the other side. "And he's locked us in."

CHAPTER SEVENTEEN

OHAN PACED THE ROOM. "I DON'T KNOW, ADYA. Priya could be anywhere by now. I mean . . . anywhere."

Adya had planted herself in the blue velvet chair and was drinking from the pot the maharaja had abandoned. They'd locked them in and taken her motorcycle, but something else nagged at her. She inhaled the smell of hot coffee and stared into her cup. If Priya had left, they were going to have a hell of a time finding her. Mohan was right, she could be anywhere.

"Priya risked everything to get here. Why would she leave?" She'd made the mistake of believing Gouros once and wasn't going to make the same kind of mistake again.

Mohan checked the door again without luck. "They never locked it before. Maybe he's trying to keep us safe. Mimun said Mysore is like a jungle."

"The jungle would have been better," she said. At least there she would have known what to do, where Priya would have gone to hide. "He told us to rest until my strength returns, didn't he? I feel fine. Maybe we could find her on our own. What's the city like?"

Mohan looked doubtful of her declaration of health, but he opened the door to the balcony. "Come see the city for yourself from the comfort of our room. We've got a view of everything." He swept his arm in front of Adya as she joined him outside. "The City of Mazes."

Adya marveled at the sight. The palace was the grandest structure she had ever seen—for all she knew, the grandest structure the world had ever seen. She leaned over and gazed up to take in the breadth of the green-veined marble, arching high to a form a teardrop pointing at the clouds. Three enormous rings of stone formed concentric circles around the palace, and on them marched soldiers whose armor glimmered in the sun. Five mechanical cranes covered in dangling wires stood in rusted magnificence, their long steel arms hanging overhead, like sentinels from the previous age. But all that was nothing in comparison to the towers. Along the battlements, dozens of them sprouted skyward, slender and intricate, like arrows aimed at the stars, rising higher than the crown of the palace itself, each one of them unlike the next, some spiraling, others straight and smooth, others covered in inlays and statuary, and all of them with blazing lanterns at their pinnacles. The combined effect was like standing in the middle of a giant birthday cake surrounded by flaming candles, rising toward the sky.

Below them, the innermost courtyard was awash with colorful tents and throngs of people. And beyond the walls and towers and cranes stretched the city itself, an endless maze of streets, houses, and buildings that sprawled in every direction.

Adya sighed. She pressed her fingers to the windowsill to steady herself. There was a slight vibration. She closed her eyes to shut out the view of the city and felt it again. Something under the marble, within the old bones of the palace, still stirred. The souls of dormant machines murmured from a distant basement far below, amidst frayed wires and rusted boilers. The palace might be magic and marble, but it must have grown over the bones of an abandoned skyscraper from long ago.

"It's incredible," she said.

Mohan leaned over the balcony rail. "Yeah, it's amazing how alive the place is, right?"

"No, not alive. But not dead, either. It's like a shell over something else," she said. "There's another, older building underneath this palace." Adya squinted, not sure if she was seeing right. The battlements shimmered and grew hazy. For the briefest moment, she glimpsed something else: the soldiers' uniforms hanging in tatters, the city in ruins, with cracked walls and broken streets. Then the splendor of Mysore returned in all its glory.

Adya shook her head. She needed more time to recover.

Mohan watched her with a concerned expression. "Mimun said they built the entire city on top of the old Mysore. That's why there's still so much concrete and iron underneath everything." He pointed out the window. "Wait. The bells are about to toll. This is what I wanted you to see."

Adya leaned farther out. The air carried the scent of marsh grass and fish markets as it blew across the river. In the courtyard, a squad of Vayu troops gathered before the gates as the bells struck their first notes. The crowds of people stopped rushing about and grew silent.

"Watch this," Mohan said. "It gets better."

With each toll of the bell, one of the immense towers faded before her eyes, until she could see straight through it, then blew away like a cloud, only to form again in a new location as the gates and walls shimmered and shifted below. By the time the bells stopped, the towers were whole again, and the troops rushed to their new positions.

"The maharaja's magic turns all the towers into wind and remakes them again. All the defenses change position and form. Enemies would have an impossible time planning an assault in advance. It kills me every time."

Adya was speechless. The energy needed to accomplish such magic, if it was anything like technomancy, would be endless. She squinted at a pool filled with a deep black ink in the central courtyard, surrounded by a ring of soldiers. No sunlight reflected from its obsidian surface. Its call thrummed inside her like the beat of a second heart, and she knew.

"Is that . . ."

"It sure the heck is," Mohan said. "The Flame of the South. Yeah, I know, it's completely crazy. I've stood out here, just looking at it, imagining the meteor smashing into the ground, imagining what it must have been like. I always thought the infinity well would be hidden away on top of a mountain, bubbling and roiling away, but there it is, smack in the middle of the city. All that danger. Like a tiger lounging at your front door."

Adya's palms prickled. She needed to see it for herself. "We can't stay here waiting until the maharaja comes to fetch us. Let's go into the city. Maybe Priya is out there."

Mohan ran a hand through his cloud of curls. "You'll have

to find a way through that door first, and even if we could go—I don't know, Adya. I mean, you look really exhausted."

Adya gave him a look. "I don't need my little brother telling me when I should take a nap."

Mohan held up both hands. "Like you would ever listen to me."

Voices outside the door cut short their argument.

"Do you enjoy cleaning toilets with your teeth? Open this door, or I'll open it with your heads and drag you in front of the maharaja while he's enjoying lunch. Let's see what he thinks." This was followed by a thump and a rattle of wood.

"Sorry, Captain. Please don't disturb His Majesty's meal." There was a click, and the door swung open. A man who looked like he wanted to kill someone stepped inside.

The captain addressed the guards one last time. "One of you idiots go fetch tea and something hot to eat so I can forget your incompetence." Then he slammed the door closed and moved toward them with the smooth step of an assassin.

It was his condescending smile that gave him away.

"Bad Day." Dsouza had cleaned himself up remarkably well. Her memory of the fight with the yaksha was still cloudy, but she was surprised how relieved she was to see him alive and apparently unhurt.

Dsouza dropped into the blue chair and poured himself coffee. "This is cold," he complained, then drank it anyway. "Nice to see you alive too, Mongoose. Did you dream of me while you were asleep?"

Adya narrowed her eyes. He would never change. "I was

hoping the yaksha ate you. Where are Imral and my bike?"

Dsouza, true to form, ignored her question. "I like the pink pajamas."

Her new red jacket was mostly open. Adya's cheeks grew hot as she zipped it.

"Looks good on you." Dsouza tossed back the rest of his coffee and poured himself another cup.

He hadn't said a thing about her metal arm, though Adya was sure he'd seen it. She stepped back and sat on the edge of the bed. "Why are you in that ridiculous disguise? What did you steal now?"

His smile vanished. "Many things, over the years." He walked to the balcony and looked down, as if searching for something. "I stole a horse to get here and arrived a day behind you three, but that wasn't the problem. The mistake I made was stealing the maharaja's daughter. Our ruler is not happy about it."

Mohan moved away from the balcony and Dsouza. "Can you blame him? I mean you put her in danger, and you are a . . ."

Dsouza spun. "A what? A crook? A thief? A killer? You think the princess would be better off spending time with you? Well, good luck with that. He's got her locked up tight now, and both of you, as well. Seems to be a theme around here." Dsouza stalked from the window. "I've had enough of it. Come on, let's break you out." He glanced at the door and lowered his voice. "We need to talk, and I know the one place in the palace with no ears."

Mohan looked doubtful. "She's supposed to rest, Dsouza.

The maharaja is expecting us for dinner. He won't be happy if we take off."

"You don't want to have dinner with him, trust me," Dsouza said. "You're likely to be on the menu. And if she's strong enough to keep looking at me like that, I bet she could walk a little."

Adya did feel a little stronger. She continued glaring. "If it's your idea, Bad Day, it's bound to be terrible."

Dsouza flashed his half grin at her. "Now that's the Mongoose I know and do my best to avoid." He raised one eyebrow. "You don't remember much, do you?"

Adya tried, but all that came back was the horrible coldness that had crept across her chest and Dsouza standing to yell something or other. "I remember you falling onto your back," she said. She also remembered him rushing out in front of them and taking the monster on alone, but she wasn't about to say that. "Honestly, the rest is a bit fuzzy."

Dsouza seemed disappointed. "Falling onto my back was the important bit. The rest was details." He started toward the door. "Are you both coming?"

Adya grabbed the bedpost and pulled herself up.

"Adya, I don't know about this," Mohan began.

"You definitely don't know much about any of this, kid," Dsouza said. "You may be more of a target than you think." He opened the door, and they followed him into the corridor.

The guardsman saluted Dsouza sharply but grew alarmed when Mohan and Adya stepped out. "The maharaja ordered—" he protested.

Dsouza waved away his objections. "Your friend isn't back

with tea yet. We're going to look for some ourselves and take it out of his salary. I'll have them back soon enough."

They left the worried guard behind and entered a corridor whose walls curved up to meet in a perfect teardrop-shaped arch. Veins of pink and green coursed through the marble. Stone inlays of delicate vines and branches etched with gold ran the length of the hall. Servants dressed in white stared wide-eyed as they hurried past. Adya had never imagined such splendor, but Dsouza didn't give her time to appreciate it—her legs protested his ever-increasing pace. Mohan had not been completely wrong. Lying in bed had taken its toll.

Before she gave in and asked Dsouza to slow down, they reached a wide staircase that seemed to wind down forever. She could barely make out the landing below.

"Down." Dsouza barked the order at four muscular men who stood nearby and strode to a brightly paneled carriage covered in blue spirals. One of the men bowed and stooped to open the door. Dsouza motioned for the two of them to enter.

Every instinct told Adya not to step inside, but Mohan was already climbing in. She followed her brother to find two plush benches inside a cramped box. She made the mistake of sitting across from Mohan and Dsouza slid next to her. Her hands started to sweat even before the door closed.

Mohan was smiling. "You're going to love this," he said.

She hated it already. The last place Adya wanted to be was trapped with Dsouza in close quarters. "What are we doing in here?" she asked.

Dsouza exhaled slowly. "It's a ten-minute ride down—no

one will find us here. This is the one place we won't be over-heard."

Her stomach lurched as the carriage began to slide down the ramp running alongside the railing, but Mohan's eagerness only increased. "They lower it on cables. It rolls down smooth as butter. We could set up something like this in the mine shaft."

If they ever got back to the mine shaft. There were too many strange things happening. "What the hell is going on, Bad Day?"

"We're planning your escape," he said.

"What are you talking about?"

Before he could explain, there was a shout, and the carriage lurched to a halt. Adya crashed into Dsouza as steps sounded, rushing toward them.

Dsouza drew a wicked-looking knife. "Damn. I should have moved faster."

Adya ripped off a long rosewood armrest with her metal hand and tested its weight. It wasn't much of a weapon, but she wasn't going to be defenseless.

The door swung open amidst a swirl of lavender silk and jasmine perfume, and the princess of Mysore swept in. Imral's hair was freshly dyed an even deeper blue. She gave Dsouza a disapproving look and ducked inside. "Put that away." Imral pushed Mohan to the far side of the car before squeezing in next to him. "I broke a sandal running down these stairs, and you pull a knife on me?"

Dsouza's knife disappeared, but his expression didn't change. "How did you get out?"

"I told the guards I was going to practice a spell, and they could either stay and watch or go find something to eat. I said I needed a volunteer for some particularly dangerous magic. They fell over themselves to abandon their posts." She sighed. "They needn't have worried. I still can't do anything anymore, no matter what I try." She examined the broken armrest Adya was attempting to hide. "Were you all trying to kill me?"

"It's not always about you, Princess," Dsouza said.

"Of course not." She leaned in until she was closer to Dsouza than Adya thought anyone would want to be. "It's always about you, isn't it? You're the one who always knows what's going on. Even when you get me kidnapped." Imral narrowed her eyes at Dsouza before she turned to Adya. "You're finally awake." She caught sight of Adya's metal hand and hesitated. "We were scared we were going to lose you."

The last thing Adya wanted was to get emotional with the princess. "Never mind that. It's Priya who's lost. The maharaja thinks she's left Mysore."

Imral's expression darkened. "No one seems to know a thing." She mustered a tight smile. "That's not to say we won't find her."

"Don't be stupid," Dsouza said. "Your sister was seen arriving, and there's not been a glimpse of her since? She's either dead, or she's been kidnapped and sold."

Wood cracked in Adya's metal fist. "You close your—"

"You've no idea the danger you're in." Dsouza ignored the armrest pointed at his chest and spoke over her. "Selling a technomancer to the British would make any crook in Mysore rich for life." Dsouza glanced outside as the carriage continued its descent. "We have to move fast. I've bribed one of the gate guards. I can have you both out of the city within the hour."

Adya seized Dsouza's jacket. His buttons popped, and it ripped open to the chest. "Priya is alive. We are not leaving until we find her, and we get the bike back. Do you understand?"

Dsouza didn't even try to break free. "I understand that you're the most stubborn creature I've ever encountered."

"The maharaja promised to help us."

"The maharaja is more dangerous than you can imagine," Dsouza said. "Listen to me and—"

Imral cut Dsouza off. "They could go see Lalbag. He still knows everyone who comes and goes through Mysore."

"Wait, Lalbag the merchant I met in the market?" Mohan asked. "The jinn said we should find him if we needed help."

"Merchant." Dsouza gave a short laugh. "Before he dedicated himself to his wife's food, he was once one of Mysore's greatest spies. If you aren't smart enough to leave, maybe he'll talk sense into you."

Adya looked between him and the princess and finally had to ask, "How did you two even meet? I mean, why? Why spend time with Dsouza?"

Imral huffed. "I wouldn't spend a moment with him if we weren't related."

"Re-related?" Mohan stammered. "I mean I've always heard royal types married cousins and everything, but still . . ."

Imral gave Mohan a withering look. "He's my brother."

There was little physical resemblance, but they had that

same blustery haughtiness about them. Adya felt something inside her untwist.

"But if that's true, you're a prince," she said.

Mohan shook his head back and forth. "That is soooo weird. I mean, look at him."

Dsouza's smile looked strangely sad. "I'm a half brother, a bastard son. Only my father and Imral know who I am." He shot Mohan a glare. "And I work hard to achieve this style." He sighed. "I'm heir to nothing, a prince of dust. If he suspected you two knew who I am, you would already be dead. I would never have let Imral bring you to Mysore if we hadn't been desperate to find someone to heal you. I can't protect you here."

Adya was still working through it all, still amazed that Dsouza, of all people, could be royalty. "We don't need babysitting. We need help. Help us find our sister and the bike, and we'll ride out of here before anyone knows we're gone."

Dsouza slammed the wall of the carriage with his fist. "This is not your cave, Mongoose. This is not fixing radios. The cobra here is too big for you. The maharaja deals in the magic of wind and war—even the power of the jinn doesn't compare. He can change the defenses of the city on a whim. If he wishes you—"

"Father *will* help," Imral insisted. "My brother has entirely the wrong view of him, I promise you. He's the most generous man in the world. And the most capable. His temper is short because he carries so much on his back, but he can conjure a spell to find your sister, I'm sure of it."

Dsouza scoffed. "Imral has no idea what our father is capable of. He loves *her* and he loves *power*, but the maharaja makes Huda look like a puppy. If you want his favors, you've got to prove that helping you helps him."

The carriage gave a shudder. They'd almost reached the landing.

"How do you expect me to do that?" Adya asked.

"Aren't you the greatest witch in the jungle?" Dsouza said. "Maybe you could fire up a radio for him, but your best bet is still getting out of here."

She could almost slap him. "Why do you care so much all of sudden, Bad Day?"

The sound of the courtyard below grew louder. Dsouza stared at her before answering. "Who said I cared?" He unlatched the door. "Stop being stubborn and be careful. My father might have been a benevolent ruler once, but losing his real sons took a toll. The British are on his doorstep. There's no telling what a tiger will do when he's got everything to lose." Then he leapt out, the door snapped closed behind him, and the carriage resumed its descent.

Imral followed Dsouza with her eyes. "My brother sees ghosts in the shadows. He was sure our father was making questionable decisions on the battlefield, that I should leave this place and see for myself. In the end, we both ended up in Huda's cage."

Imral pulled a cord, and the carriage came to a halt one floor before the bottom of the stairs. She got up to leave. "But if I don't manage to get control of my magic soon . . . The heir must handle the power of the infinity well at its source, and I seem to have lost even the little I was able to manage."

"You'll get it back," Mohan said. "What you did to save Adya was incredible."

Imral shook her head. "All I did was help contain the flow. You and that bike called up the magic, and now I can't make anything work. Maybe it was being too close to the techno-mancy, maybe the spell wall burned it out of me, but whatever it was, I don't think I'll be of much use here for anything." She opened the door to the carriage but wouldn't look at them. "Go see Lalbag. I'll keep trying to find out what I can."

Adya watched her go. The carriage continued down. She wasn't sure what had happened to the princess's magic, but if you needed confidence to work Vayu spells, then Imral was running on empty.

Mohan stared at the floor. "He's totally wrong about Priya, right? I mean, who would ever believe a jackal about anything?"

Adya ground her teeth. She would know if their sister were no longer alive. Somehow, she would know. "We go back with Priya, and we get the bike, too. We won't give in to the worry ever."

Mohan gave a quick nod. "Right. I just needed to hear it from you." He reached into a built-in tray, pulled out some kind of candy, and popped one in his mouth. How had her goofy brother survived wandering Mysore on his own? Mohan unwrapped one for Adya.

Adya gave in and grabbed the sweet. The taste of sugar, cardamom, and saffron almost brought tears to her eyes. "Are there more of these?"

Mohan patted his pants. "I've filled my pockets." He handed her another as the carriage stopped and a servant opened the door. They stepped into a courtyard filled with high walls and marching guards.

"This way." Mohan led Adya out of the carriage right up to a file of Vayu soldiers, weapons held high in a fanned display.

Adya's boots clacked across gray-green marble as Mohan pulled her along. The two of them plunged into a field of tents that filled the courtyard in haphazard swirls of color. They wound their way through the jumble of stalls as merchants shouted, advertising their wares. Each booth they passed was tended by a smiling woman fretting over a pot of boiling oil. In one pot floated potato-filled samosas, in another hot desserts. Adya's stomach rumbled in protest as delicious smells assaulted her.

"Give me another of those candies."

Mohan fished one from his pocket. "You'll see the real market when we get past the gates." He led her through two giant archways into a central courtyard, where guards looked disinterestedly down upon the crowds. The final gate stood fifty yards beyond, but it was the ring of stone in the courtyard that captured Adya's attention.

A circle of soldiers in golden-scaled armor stood unmoving around a wall no higher than Adya's waist. Beyond it, a pool of pure blackness, thirty yards in diameter and smooth as glass, swallowed all the light.

A vast force emanated from the pool. It was the place all magic came from, the power of the Vayu, the Devas, and her own Atavi technomancy. This was the place where you could feel the beating heart of the planet and tap into its bloodstream— the prize the British hoped to seize for their own.

Mohan took a step back. "The Flame of the South. I used to have dreams about it, of coming here with Baba to reach out and touch it. But now, I'm not so sure. I wouldn't want to get that close."

Without realizing what she was doing, Adya left Mohan's side. She started toward the circle of soldiers in their golden armor. Something was shimmering over the center of the darkness, calling to her.

Something she could not resist.

CHAPTER EIGHTEEN

"D O YOU HAVE A DEATH WISH?"

A guard thrust his palm against Adya's shoulder. She'd tried to walk through the ring of soldiers without realizing what she was doing.

He examined Adya's face. "You'll be lost, girl, pulled into the well before you know it. You'll go mad, and that's if we pull you out *before* you go under." His words were almost kind, as if he'd seen this before.

Adya looked past the man, searching for whatever was calling to her. She could swear she heard a voice, urging her closer. If only she could push past and step inside, she would be able to find what her heart needed.

Mohan appeared out of the crowd and grabbed the back of Adya's shirt. "Sorry, sir. My sister sleepwalks, like, all the time. Even in the middle of the day." He dragged Adya back. "You know, because she barely sleeps at night because her feet hurt so much with all the sleepwalking during the day."

The soldier looked at one of his fellow guards and rolled his eyes. "Keep an eye on her. Hardest part of our job's keeping people like her away."

Mohan kept backpedaling and smiling at the soldiers until he and Adya were surrounded by the crowd again. Then he squeezed her arm hard, and his smile vanished. "What were you doing?"

Adya rubbed her temple, not sure what she'd seen. "It felt like a magnet, drawing me in." She forced herself not to look in the direction of the well. Maybe she should have slept more before venturing out. Adya swore she wouldn't get mad the next time Mohan said she should rest. "Get us away from here, Mohan. Please."

Mohan gave her a worried look and pulled her through the final gate. They hurried on as the flagstones of the courtyard gave way to the packed dirt of the outer city, and the memory of what Adya had seen faded. The labyrinth rose around them, a spider's web of alleyways and buildings filled with the citizens of Mysore.

"Ganesha temple." Mohan pointed to a gigantic structure of gray stones piled upon one another, with intricate carvings of elephants along its walls. "We turn here until we pass the fruit market, and two mosques." The streets spun and shot off at angles. Everywhere there were people and more people. Adya wondered if they would ever find this Lalbag, whether he would welcome them— the man might have befriended Mohan just to get him to bring her here. Dsouza had warned them of danger, and she'd ignored him. Suddenly this whole thing seemed like a terrible idea.

Mohan didn't look worried. He found the minarets of the second mosque and stopped. "Oh, here's Mimun's mosque. We're almost there."

They took three quick turns, entered a circular passage, and exited onto a long street, wide enough for only one person at a time. Women in green and blue saris pushed by Adya, bumping her with elbows and baskets.

"Do you know how to get back?" She could find her way anywhere in the jungle, but Mysore had completely disoriented her.

"Not the faintest idea." Mohan shrugged. "It's got something to do with the magic of the city and keeping outsiders away from the palace. Don't worry, someone will help us. I've done this before."

Over the sounds of the street, one voice bellowed in a constant stream.

"The best saris, nothing compares. The finest kameezes! Others are wasting your time. Come for first class, leave happy." She made out a tall merchant with a body almost as wide as the doorway, his face half-hidden by an enormous mustache, waving at them. He stood in a storefront draped with dresses, where two vacant-eyed mannequins raised bangle-covered arms. The voice shifted to an extremely loud whisper as they drew close. "Mohan, come. Don't tell all these buy-nothing cheapskates."

"How does he know—" Adya began.

"That's Lalbag." Mohan waved. "Come meet the family."

In the short time it took to reach the doorway, two other merchants called out Mohan's name. Her brother had befriended half the city in a few days.

As soon as they crossed the threshold, Lalbag seized Mohan's hand in an affectionate squeeze. "Ignore the competition, boy. You know we have the best food. Come in, come in. This can't be your sister? The sleeping beauty is awake? The maharaja be praised." He shouted the last sentence to the street loud enough for everyone to hear. Even a water buffalo turned its head. Then he pulled Mohan and Adya inside and closed the door. The store was filled with a jumble of boxes and shelves covered in fine clothing and stacks of papers.

"Sit, sit, sit." Lalbag ushered them in, but where they were supposed to sit was anyone's guess. There was not a chair to be seen. Mohan perched on a stack of papers, and Adya lowered herself onto a similar pile. From behind a counter, bright eyes peeked at them.

"Out, out, Nisha. Don't hide. Deepa, Saira, come down. Mohan is here."

At this, the rest of the tiny head emerged to reveal a girl dressed in pink who couldn't be more than five. She stationed herself behind her father's leg, staring at them both. A teenage girl who looked about fourteen and a woman who she guessed was Lalbag's wife hurried down the stairs. The girl was as tall as her father, nothing but bones and beautiful eyes. She reminded Adya of a crane. Her mother was just as tall but not as thin. Lalbag's wife gave Mohan an enormous smile.

"Lalbag, you brute. Have you not offered tea? Deepa, run and get snacks from upstairs. Mohan looks dangerously bony. Oh my god. Is this your sister? Bring idlis. She looks starved."

All this came out in a single breath. Deepa rushed back up the stairs at her mother's command. Little Nisha slid out in front of her father's leg and kept silently staring.

Adya's fear of being drugged and kidnapped eased. If there were a red dome on the house, she might believe she was home, being welcomed by old neighbors. Deepa returned with cups and poured hot chai. The smell of cardamom was irresistible. Mohan was already gulping from his cup.

"That's it, that's it. No questions yet, Lalbag. You know how tired she must be." Saira, Lalbag's wife, turned back to Adya. "Now try this." She handed Adya a bowl of spicy snacks. Nisha crept closer and touched Adya's knee.

Lalbag laughed. "Nisha, no questions for five more minutes. The boss has spoken." He smiled at Adya. "Two days ago, your brother showed up lost on our doorstep. Now here you are, in our simple home, before the newspapers have found you."

Adya's mouth was full of food.

"Are five minutes up yet?" Nisha reached out to feel Adya's metal hand.

"I think five minutes are over," Adya said. The warm welcome and food had had a strange effect on her. "If I get to trade questions as well."

"I'm first, I'm first." Nisha held up her finger. "First question—what's your favorite color?"

Adya touched Nisha's shoulder and fingered the delicate fabric of her salwar kameez. "Pink, of course."

"I knew it. I knew it." Nisha's smile took up her entire face. "Your turn. Ask me."

Adya wanted nothing more than to ask if they'd seen Priya, but she waited. "First, how does your amma make such delicious food? What's your favorite color? And how do you like my little brother?"

"Too many, too many." The little girl insisted before answering everything. "Amma makes everything good because she's the best—pink too—and very much, but my sister likes him more."

199

Deepa bent her head and stared at the floor, then rushed back upstairs, yelling, "I'm getting more snacks."

"Your turn's over, Nisha." Lalbag beamed at his daughter. "Go look around and pick out the most beautiful scarf you can find, one of the silk ones, for a present. She's told you her favorite color."

Nisha bounced to the task and disappeared behind boxes and piles of dresses.

Lalbag turned to them. "How can I help you both? You returned our princess, and for that I owe you a personal debt." He shared a loving look with his wife. "We remember Imral as a small child, running around the palace grounds. The British shouldn't have touched her."

Adya couldn't wait any longer. "We came here to look for our sister, Priya. She left the jungle months ago. She should have come back or sent word by now."

"Your sister, of course." Lalbag went uncharacteristically quiet for a long moment. He looked deep in thought. "Nisha, get the scarf later. First, run upstairs and go look for our best chocolates. I think I have some in the far closet at the end of the hall, stashed in the very back. Look hard." She ran to his command. He wandered to the door to gaze out at the street.

"To lose a sister is a terrible thing," Lalbag began.

He looked at his wife, who shook her head.

"Saira, they are strangers alone in an endless city," Lalbag said.

"And you are an old man who talks too much. The maharaja, in all his wisdom, will help them. Do you have to be personally involved with every problem in Mysore? The jinn should never have involved you in all this. You must learn to stay quiet."

Lalbag met his wife's eyes. "If anything were to happen, you have Mimun to call on."

"What good is a jinn to me if we lose everything? You care about all the wrong things, husband." Saira hardened. She spun and marched up the stairs.

Lalbag mustered a weak smile. "At times, I'm not sure whether to be cautious or courageous anymore." He sat back down and picked up a cup of tea. "Several months ago, there was a rumor that soldiers picked up an Atavi girl riding a machine. I found that extremely interesting. There were several sightings of her on the palace grounds, then no word at all."

Adya fought to unclench her jaw. Priya had made it to the palace. Someone there must have seen her. "Do you think she's left?"

Lalbag shook his head. "I have friends at each city gate. I would have heard, even if she snuck out at night." He lowered his voice. "The palace is more than it seems. The structure extends deep into the heart of the earth." He chewed his lower lip. "She may have become lost in its maze. If you want my opinion, that is where you should seek her."

"But why would—" Adya began.

The girls returned down the stairs before Adya could finish her question. Saira did not return.

"There was nothing, Baba. Nothing." Nisha raised empty hands.

"Oh, I forgot. I ate those chocolates myself." Lalbag laughed, bringing his daughter close to whisper in her ear. She sped off again, and Lalbag continued. "We couldn't be happier that the two of you blessed us with a visit. I hadn't even heard you were up and about—Mohan was here the day before yesterday and said nothing about it."

Adya swallowed the morsel she'd been chewing. "I only woke a few hours ago."

"Just today?" Lalbag's eyebrows arched in disbelief. "They let you out so soon?"

"I needed to walk. And I was hungry." Adya held up another idli and popped the steaming rice cake into her mouth.

Lalbag's grin disappeared. "The maharaja will worry. He may hold us responsible."

Nisha popped back up with a long pink scarf held high. "This is the best one." It was embroidered with intricate triangles and circles along the border in the style of a Vayu spell. Black peacocks perched amongst silver branches along its length.

"I love it." Adya smiled at the girl and stood. She nodded at Lalbag. "Thank you for this. For everything. We didn't mean to be trouble." She wasn't about to put his family in danger.

Adya opened the door to find both ends of the street blocked.

A soldier at the head of a troop of white-coated guards pointed straight at her. "There they are." In moments, the narrow alley filled with armed men, and the soldier pushed past her into the shop. Lalbag stepped back and bowed while his daughters hid behind him.

"Lalbag, I should have known," the officer said. "I thought you'd retired."

Saira returned, thumping down the stairs, and put a hand to her mouth.

"I am beyond retired," Lalbag said. He gestured for his family to go back to the upper level. "Forgive us. We did not mean to detain the maharaja's guests."

"We got lost," Adya said. "They gave us tea. That's all."

The soldier's voice was calm, but his eyes stayed hard as he addressed her. "You ought to be more careful—the maze is designed to swallow foreigners whole. Come. The maharaja awaits." Adya and Mohan were ushered out before they could say another word. Several men stayed behind.

Mohan tried to summon a smile as they were herded toward the palace. "Don't worry, Adya. The maharaja said we were honored guests. He was probably just worried."

Adya kept her voice to a whisper. "We seem more like honored prisoners."

The three gates closed one by one as they passed through, and soldiers moved into formation around them. Dsouza had told them to escape while they could. Adya worried they might already be too late.

CHAPTER NINETEEN

HIGH ABOVE THE CITY, A BLACK DRONGO SOARED. Gouros had been cruel to the bird, plucking half its forked tail feathers. The drongo remembered Huda's wire cage all too well. It had longed for the sky, certain it would never fly again until Adya set it free.

Now it flew over the endless streets of the City of Mazes until it reached the grandest jewel of the city, the everchanging palace of the maharaja.

The bird timed its descent with care, flying straight through one of the towers just as the structure faded to smoke. It turned in a wide arc to avoid the pool of blackness that sent waves of unwelcome heat into the air, ruffling its feathers—something about the darkness of the infinity well struck the drongo as more unnatural than magic should be. It shot up again and, at the peak of its ascent, folded its wings to drop onto one of the giant cranes that towered over the courtyard.

The bird scraped at rusted paint with its claws until it found a suitable perch. The girl had saved it from Huda's cage. Somewhere, amongst the madness that was Mysore, it hoped to repay her and, finally, get back to the jungle where it belonged.

By eight that evening they'd wrapped Adya in yards of silk. With her arms spread out like wings, she looked like a damned peacock. Four seamstresses wound their way around her, chattering about the riches that were to be showered upon her for returning the princess. The gossip sounded cheerful, but Adya had seen how many soldiers were stationed at the door.

"Stop moving. You haven't the slightest patience," the head tailor scolded her. The woman was old enough to be Adya's grandmother, dressed in a white sari trimmed in gold, her hair dyed orange with henna. She pulled Adya off the pedestal and dragged her in front of a mirror. "You're too bony. This is the best I can do."

The girl in the mirror was no one Adya recognized. Her waist was bare, a pale green blouse tight about her chest, with a dark green sari hanging over her left shoulder. They'd threaded gold fibers through her hair and fit a choker set with diamonds around her neck. Adya doubted her own twin would recognize her.

"My god." Mohan entered the room decked out in a silver shirt and pants, black buttons running down his chest. "You look like a princess. You'd have a hard time fixing a rickshaw in that."

Adya stepped away from the mirror. "I'd have a hard time doing anything."

The tailor shook a finger at Adya. "I shouldn't have expected a jungle girl to have good taste, but you can at least remember your manners. The maharaja will call you forth to receive your gifts. Be sure to bow and accept with grace."

Gifts were the last thing on Adya's mind. What she needed was her bike and her sister. The sun was setting. Lalbag believed Priya had never left, but was she out there in the maze or lost in the depths of the palace, certain no one would ever come for her? And here Adya was, getting dressed up, when she should be searching. She pounded on the windowsill with her metal fist. Marble chips shot into the air, and the seamstresses went silent.

The head tailor recovered first. She walked up to Adya and beat at the dust on her chest with a handkerchief. "Try to stay clean for five minutes."

"She looks absolutely perfect." A new voice filled the room with the authority of royalty. Imral swept in, and, as one, the seamstresses stopped what they were doing and bowed.

A sapphire dress studded with diamonds made Imral look every inch the maharaja's daughter. The frightened girl in the jungle had disappeared, replaced by the one and only princess of Mysore. Whatever clothes they tried to disguise Adya with, she would never look like that.

Imral gave the head tailor a kind smile. "You've done work beyond compare, but if you've finished, I would like some time alone with our guests."

The tailor pressed her hands together and bowed. "Of course. The item you requested is on the table, Princess. We are all overjoyed to have you back." The women filed out and closed the door behind them.

Imral's smile vanished the moment the last seamstress left. She shoved a chair against the door. "Lalbag was a mistake," she whispered. "Finding you there has put my father in one of his moods." She motioned for them to keep their voices down.

"Have you learned anything about Priya?" Adya asked.

Imral shook her head. "I even tried a spell of finding. I got the magic to begin for a moment, but it didn't work." She reached out a hand as if she was searching for something. "I feel the power on the edge of my awareness—but something is holding it back." She rubbed her knuckles. "I can't even find my brother. He's disappeared."

"Probably getting himself into more trouble," Adya said. "Hopefully your father has more news."

Imral hesitated. "Right. We've just got to hope he's calmed down." She walked over to a table the seamstresses had been using and picked up a folded shirt. "This is something small I wanted you to have." She handed it to Mohan. "I thought it might be almost as good as your old one."

Mohan unfolded the shirt to reveal an image of a dinosaur labeled *Diplodocus—Legend of the Past.* "Whoa, awesome. Thanks for loaning me the book."

"What book?" Adya asked.

Mohan opened one of the nightstand drawers and pulled out a thick volume bound in leather. *"The Hundred Finest against the World.* I read it to stay sane while we were waiting for you to wake up, but it's not the same story." He made a pained face. "This Vayu version is super dark. The Devas all get killed."

Imral took a long look at Mohan. "Tragedies are big in Vayu literature. The stories are never kind to the Devas."

Adya bit her lip. Mohan was going to get himself thrown in a cell if the maharaja learned that the two of them were becoming close—Imral's life had nothing to do with theirs and never would.

There was a rap on the door before it flew open, knocking the chair to the floor.

A white-turbaned soldier with a beard down to his chest stepped in and regarded them, his face a hard mask. He gave a quick bow to Imral before turning his attention to Adya and Mohan. "I am Sunil, captain of the maharaja's guard. You are summoned at once." The guard gestured down the hall. "He does not like to be kept waiting."

They followed the captain as he hurried them through corridor after corridor lined with more and more soldiers, arriving at last before a set of double doors, where a lone guard bowed to Imral and stepped aside. They were ushered into a cavernous room full of formally dressed people wearing every color under the sun. The final rays of evening light streamed through a dozen high windows.

The noise continued, but the crowd parted to let them pass. The captain led them to a far corner, where the maharaja of Mysore sat on a gilded chair, quite alone, paying attention to no one at all. He seemed lost in thought. His far-off expression reminded Adya once again of her father—the way he would stare into space, dreaming his big dreams. She felt a sudden tightness in her throat.

Imral stepped close and squeezed her arm, bringing her back to the present. The princess approached the chair and bowed, but her father neither moved nor acknowledged her. Silence spread across the room as they stood, unsure of what to do next.

Imral cleared her throat. "Father, I've brought our guests."

The maharaja of Mysore blinked, as if awakening from a daze. He pushed up from the chair and rose to his full height. "We meet again," he said. "Forgive me for my distraction. At times my thoughts oppress me." He looked Adya and Mohan over. "Enough of my grim musings. I am told the two of you enjoyed wandering the city. My heart is at ease knowing you returned safely."

"They didn't mean anything by it, Father. It was my idea. I wanted them to have a chance to admire—"

"The beauty of Mysore," the maharaja finished Imral's sentence. "Of course." He raised an eyebrow as he cast his gaze on his daughter. "But perhaps you and your attendants should have accompanied them for a more complete tour?"

Imral's face fell. She opened her mouth to answer, but not before Adya spoke.

"Your daughter made sure to accompany me when I was in the greatest danger, Highness," Adya said. "She leapt from a branch, high in a tree to save me from a werewolf. Without her, I would not be alive."

The maharaja took Imral in one arm and pressed her close. "And she would be dead in Huda's cage if not for you. But you are very kind to praise her bravery. A princess who can take on British werewolves will one day lead her people like no other before her. I hope you and your brother will remain with us one more month to see Imral display her supreme talent for all to see. It is our tradition for royal heirs to give an exhibition to their people on their sixteenth birthday, and I intend a grand ceremony where she can show off all that she has mastered."

Imral tried and failed to hide the fear on her face, but luckily her father was no longer looking at her. "This is a time of war, Father. Surely, there's no need to—"

"War makes it even more important to show the people they will be well protected." The maharaja ran a hand through Imral's finely coiffed hair. "War is the perfect time to show our enemies what we are capable of." His face grew hard as steel. "One day, when all this is done, I will visit the gangster Huda, and we will have a long talk. But this is no time to discuss vengeance." He raised his chin, and his voice thundered across the room. "We are honored by a guest today, my people. This Atavi girl was willing to sacrifice her life for our princess. No Vayu soldier braved the British army to bring her to me. No Deva trickster responded to my call for aid. It took a simple girl from the jungle to risk her life and rescue our princess from Huda's dungeons. Our debt to her is immense. According to tradition, she is entitled to the three gifts of Mysore: our riches, our strength, and our protection." The maharaja waved his arm at a tapestry-covered wall that shimmered and fell away to reveal a silver path climbing into the sky. "Walk with me, Adya Sachdev, and witness the beauty of the jewel of Mysore before you claim your rewards."

A retinue of guards surrounded them as Adya followed the ruler. She walked ten yards upon the silver path before she made the mistake of looking down. Her feet were resting on nothing more than swirling mist. The hard marble of the city lay hundreds of feet below. A glance revealed that the wall had formed again behind her, leaving her alone with the maharaja and his guard.

The maharaja strolled ahead. "Look out and see the wonders of my city. Look and see what the British long to claim as their own."

As Adya reached his side, the maharaja pointed across the city. "The sun sets behind the mosque of Masjid E Azam, the home of Mimun, the jinn. And there, the Chamundi temple, dedicated to Kali. Beyond that, a gurdwara, then Christian and Jain temples—Mysore has them all. The magic of the infinity well is for everyone. Regardless of who we worship, we are the people of the wind." He raised both hands. Adya's stomach dropped away as a gust of air swirled around them, lifting them off the silver path.

"Come. My people await. They are impatient for your reward." In the central courtyard an enormous crowd had gathered around a circular platform. "Let us go to them."

The pink scarf Nisha had given her was starting to blow away. Adya reached out to snatch it. As her hands closed around the silk, she was caught up in the swirl of the maharaja's whirlwind. She shot over the battlements, her body no longer under her control. Her stomach churned. She was seized by the certainty that this had all been a terrible mistake.

"Have faith in me." The maharaja's voice boomed somewhere above her as, without warning, the wind vanished, and she dropped like a stone toward the flagstones below.

CHAPTER TWENTY

THE GROUND RUSHED UP TO MEET ADYA AS SHE tumbled through the air. At the last moment, the wind pushed up from below, and she came to a halt, inches off the ground. The maharaja pulled her upright as Adya tried to keep her stomach from exiting her mouth.

"You have arrived through the jungle, through fire, and through the air," the maharaja said. "One step more and you are there."

Adya stepped onto hard green marble with legs that would barely hold her while the crowd raised their hands and cheered. The world around her continued to spin.

The maharaja did not give her time to get her bearings. He stood at her side, unruffled, on the dais above the central court-yard and addressed the crowd. "You have waited long enough to see your hero rewarded. Mysore pays its debts, and we owe this girl a great deal for bringing my daughter home."

The people shouted their approval.

The maharaja continued. "First, I give her our wealth."

A column of soldiers dressed in full uniform stepped for-ward, their armor shining in the last rays of the sun. The two foremost men held a silver chest between them. They mounted the dais, lowered their burden, and bowed. The maharaja waved a hand, and the chest flew open, revealing thick gold coins amidst glittering emeralds and diamonds. It was more money than Adya had ever seen.

The glittering jewels shimmered before her like a dream. She and Priya had slaved away for months in their mine shaft, trying to save up for junk parts, and here was enough to buy the entire jungle.

The maharaja raised a finger. "But what use is wealth without the might to protect it?"

Two more soldiers came forward, carrying a strange spear. The weapon's gray shaft was inlaid with a pattern of fine silver vines. Its head was a foot-long piece of polished steel. They bowed and held the weapon out to her.

"To replace what you've lost in battle, I give you the finest spear ever made. The winds themselves will heed whoever wields it. You shall fly as one of us and find all you seek."

The crowd grew louder, and Adya had no choice but to take the weapon. As her metal hand closed around it, she felt the wind whip about her, as if eager for her command.

The remaining soldiers ascended and filled the space around her. They overflowed onto the stairs, a glittering force of Mysore's strength and power. In unison they went down on one knee.

"Finally, I give you our protection. These are Mysore's Hundred Finest, as strong and true as the Hundred Finest from the legends. Accept their pledge to protect you, and they are yours to command as long as they live. Never again shall you be alone in your quest. They will seek what you seek until it is found, or the world ends. They will stand with you in your darkest hour."

Their leader rose. A full head taller than the rest of guards, she wore a helm that swirled with green-gray mist as she drew her sword. Golden light played along the blade. She cleared her throat, as if uncertain of what she was supposed to say, then spoke so quietly it was almost a whisper. "I am here to pledge service. Will you accept us?"

Adya nodded, not sure what any of it meant.

It all seemed a strange madness. She was no Vayu sorceress, born to lead the Hundred Finest like in the storybooks. She belonged in the jungle, deep in her mine shaft. Priya should be yelling at her for getting grease in her hair. Instead, Adya stood with a magic weapon in her hand, surrounded by soldiers. And Priya was nowhere to be seen.

The maharaja leaned in close while the crowd cheered. "We have fulfilled the demands of the city. Now come, and I will reveal how we will reunite your family."

The noise of the crowd faded as the maharaja marched her back through the gates. They set a brisk pace across a courtyard and up a short flight of stairs, coming to a stop before a door very much like any other.

"This," the maharaja said, "leads to one of the wonders of the palace, which very few have seen—though many have tried." He traced a pattern in the air before stepping through the door. Adya and two of the men followed him up a series of rough-cut stone steps, while the remaining soldiers took up guard. The maharaja led the way through a series of torchlit passageways, seemingly at random, at times doubling back but never hesitating.

"What is this place?" Adya asked.

The maharaja rapped his knuckles on a wall. "This is my maze. Only those I wish to travel through it may pass. A deterrent against the unwise souls who seek to steal my treasures."

As they traveled deeper, torches grew rarer, and the path grew dark. Adya's metal arm began to ache. Along with the pain came a deep sadness that weighed down her every step. She imagined this must be one of the maharaja's defenses. She wiped tears from her eyes as the image of a young boy covered in chains filled her mind. Dressed in red shorts and a white shirt, he strained against the metal links of his chains as he sobbed.

The maharaja seemed unaffected. "Here, we can speak without fear of spies," he said. "The gifts we have given you are valuable, but I have something far better. I have found your sister."

Adya stopped walking. "You've found her?"

"If only I could reunite you this very moment, but your sister has abandoned this city and fled to the Devas, against all caution. She thinks they will aid her, but no help ever came to anyone from the Devas." The maharaja looked pained as he explained. "Ten years ago, I sent my best troops to aid the rani of Mumbai when the British attacked, seeking control over their infinity well. The Devas refused any assistance. I lost one of my sons in that battle, and the Shining Pearl was lost to the invaders. Their treachery is unforgivable. Now my spies have learned yesterday that an army of invaders will be upon them soon. The Devas have but five days before their stronghold is swept away. Your sister is in the greatest danger. But there is hope still. Come with me. I have a plan to rescue her from her folly."

She followed the maharaja through an endless series of turns, worrying more with each step. Priya was a fool, and now her dream of saving the world had put her in real danger.

The maharaja waved her through the third door on the left and up a spiral staircase that overlooked a vast hall of mirrored doors that reflected back their images infinitely. "Soldiers will not be enough to rescue your sister. But with these tools, nothing will stand in our way.

"See before you the greatest treasures of Mysore." The maharaja closed his hand, and the two of them rose into the air.

Adya's breath caught. Arrayed before them was a mass of contraptions representing the breadth of technology from a previous age—rickshaws and pickup trucks, giant yellow excavators and tiny scooters, automobiles and buses, even a row of jet airplanes, like a scene straight out of one of Priya's drawings. The machines had been reassembled, painted, and polished until they shone. It must have taken thousands of hours and all the money in the world to bring together the parts. She and Priya had spent months digging through a junkyard to reconstruct a single rickshaw, while all along, the greatest treasures were here.

A small army of servants busied themselves amongst the collection, cleaning and maintaining the machines. Others gathered next to an endless pile of jumbled parts, trying to puzzle things together. The wealth was incalculable. Just to touch them, to even try to spark something, would be amazing. If Priya were here, they could work together in bliss forever. Despite everything, Adya's palms itched to be amongst the machines.

The maharaja studied her face and smiled. "Very few understand the true value of what we possess here. To most, these are just dead machines. But you know the truth. I see it in your eyes. Come." He pointed to an open spot amidst the jumble, and they drifted down into a jungle of painted metal.

"This way."

They stopped first in front of a yellow giant with a great silver claw.

Adya didn't need to be told what this was. This was a Doosan crawler excavator. Priya could have named the exact model. Adya had watched her draw them, had argued with her about how they worked, had read about every piece of steel it took to put them together. She reached out to touch the frame. Living metal met dead, and a jolt shot up her arm. The beating of the excavator's heart reverberated through her body like the world's largest drum. The combination of being so close to the infinity well and a machine this powerful floored her. She felt the weight of the stone and earth it had moved, heard the growl it had let forth every day in its youth.

A bitter taste filled her mouth, and a surge of foreign magic swept through her. Adya recoiled. Sparks and fire lit up her bones as her mind filled with Vayu shapes and symbols. The magic she'd known all her life, a power built on connections and feelings, was forced into a rigid pattern she hadn't chosen. Her magic was shaped into an arrow, pointed straight at the machine's soul, and suffused with energy. It was a magic that didn't speak to the machine as an equal—it gave orders and demanded results.

The machine rumbled, its voice like ground gravel. *I will not be held back. I will dig my way free.* Adya snatched her hand back, and the excavator went silent.

The maharaja had both his hands still planted on the machine, his eyes closed. "Did you feel our magic together? The life that surged into the machine?"

Adya ground her teeth. The maharaja's spell was still reverberating through her, forcing her own magic to follow its path. She would have to be more careful around the maharaja.

"Look at your arm—metal made flesh. Two children with no idea what they were doing created that. Imagine what we could do together. Imagine the strength of your power this close to the infinity well. We could give life to all these machines, and no one would be able to stand against the might of Mysore."

Adya flexed her fingers and remembered the horror of the yaksha's jaws closing upon her. They'd created this, but Imral and Mohan had almost died in the process.

"This is only the beginning." The maharaja lead her on through a tangle of race cars and trucks until they reached the biggest weapon of them all.

"This machine once destroyed invading armies," he said, beaming up at a jet fighter that shone blue and silver, black-tipped missiles hanging menacingly beneath it. "With this at our command, we will land in the Deva stronghold, save your sister, and drive the British back to their lonely island. The vampire Clive will never taste Indian blood again."

Adya walked under the jet, examining the perfect seams, the sweep of the wings, the flawless aluminum frame. The engines were capable of unimaginable speed; its weapons promised a rain of death. She found herself reaching out to stroke the jet's body, to touch the perfection of engineering.

We will destroy together once more.

Adya stared at the plane in shock, but the jet stayed silent, fast asleep after all these centuries. The voices she'd heard had come from her. Somewhere inside her the power she had drawn from the battleship still lived and longed. With that power, she could make Huda pay.

"I am Atavi," she said, almost to convince herself. "A protector of nature. This is not what technomancy is for."

The maharaja looked down on her. "You hesitate because you don't understand," he said. "I was told that the maddened yaksha that took your arm wore a silver collar. The British are experimenting with ways to control them, and that is only the beginning of what Clive threatens us with. You have no idea what your sister will face." He lifted a hand to his mouth. "Show her our enemies," he shouted.

At the command, servants rushed to pull aside a series of wooden panels. Behind them, enormous glass cages shimmered with sorcery. Within the cages, creatures from another continent stared back at Adya—men with pointed ears, hulking ogres with hair down to their shoulders, a group of gnomes with long beards, a pack of enormous dogs that growled and paced before her.

The maharaja led Adya to the cages. "Elves. They have entire battalions of them." He gestured to another cage. "This horrid thing with wings is some sort of dragon." The creature in question was covered in iridescent scales and had eyes that revealed a deep intelligence. The dragon stretched its wings and spat at the glass, covering it in an acid mess that sizzled and smoked. The maharaja continued, unfazed. "The short ones are dwarves—next to impossible to kill. They've even brought in French werewolves. And this, *this* we captured most recently." A servant pulled back a curtain. Inside slouched a bare-chested creature, nearly thirty feet tall with shoulders as wide as a wall. Its eyes stared dully into the distance. "This is a giant. With them, the British took Delhi and the Punjab. What will our troops do when giants arrive here in force? What will we become?"

Adya trembled at the sight of these monsters. Caging them seemed wrong, but how could they possibly fight them all and win?

"General Clive has sent an ultimatum. If I am to survive and retain control over Mysore, I must join them. He promises peace if I support his armies and provide him a terrible gift—he demands the greatest of our demons, the nagas, to fight on their side." He swept his arm across the room. "But none of that has to happen. When we give these weapons life, no one will touch us. We shall be the conquerors. We shall drive the British before us, and all of India will rally to our cause. Together we can rule everything. What do you say? Shall we fight, or must I bow before them to save Mysore?"

Adya swallowed hard, trying to understand what the maharaja was suggesting. The British demanded the naga. Did the maharaja even have such power? No one would be safe.

The maharaja extended an open hand to her. "They asked for you as well. Demanded I surrender you to serve them. Would you rather be a slave to foreigners? Be the plaything for a vampire?" The maharaja had led her back to the fighter jet. "I can feel it waiting for you," he said. "All of India waits."

Adya breathed in the scent of oil, rust, and paint, the scent of machines. She could prevent the naga from returning, prevent the British from draining the native magic of India. She could get her family back. Sometimes darkness was necessary to defeat a greater darkness. She put her hand on the plane's wing and reached out, wondering.

Clouds flew across Adya's vision. The jet raced through the air in pursuit of some unseen enemy, eager to kill, ready to destroy. She watched the missiles launch and disappear through the mist to strike a target far below. A sonic boom sounded, and she staggered back, grabbing a workbench to support herself. The jet trembled before her. Had it actually happened, or was she seeing a vision of what was to come?

The maharaja raised his arms, and the chamber of machinery glowed in warm light. "You will be high technomancer of Mysore, and someday, all of India. Every piece of technology we gain will be under your command. Feel the truth of what I say."

Adya shook her head to clear the jet's thoughts from her mind. His words were tempting, but part of her wanted to get as far away from them as possible. "You're overestimating me," she said.

The maharaja seized her metal arm and marched her around

a pile of junk. "Am I? You gave that machine life, my favorite addition to the collection."

Atop a pedestal stood Huda's red-and-white motorcycle, her motorcycle, shining like never before. Her arm ached as a wave of sadness washed over her. It was the motorcycle that had been calling her, leading her through the maze. She ran to the Yamaha.

Its front wheel was missing. The paint was polished, but uneven, as if the original parts had been removed. Adya laid her metal hand upon the bike, and the world came alive. Electricity raced through her arm, surging with relief—and fear overwhelmed her.

"What did you do?" Adya demanded. She stroked the bike's seat and pulled it close.

"Whatever magic Imral and your brother worked injured it," the maharaja explained. "Part of its metal went into remaking your arm, but it was nothing my engineers could not fix. They'll have the wheel back on and everything in order before the day is done." He gestured at the crew of people who even now were making themselves busy amidst the machines. "They don't have the skill of an Atavi technomancer, but they make do."

One of the workers stepped forward, holding the motorcycle's missing front wheel, and laid it down near the bike before retreating.

Adya was still trying to sort out the motorcycle's muddled emotions. It had been terrified to remain here for another hundred years. It longed to be free, to ride with her again. The Yamaha was *her* motorcycle. Her friend. It missed her terribly. It wanted her to see something, to understand.

The planes are threatening me, it wailed. *They say they will blow me to bits once they're in the air. The tanks say they will flatten me under their treads. They tell me I am a dumb dirt bike. I do not want to listen any longer. Let's race away from here. Far away.*

The maharaja patted the motorcycle, and she felt it recoil. "Together, with the strength of these machines, we will destroy the British hold on India."

But the words rang false. For a moment, everything shimmered. Chipped paint appeared along the walls, and the servants' crisp uniforms became faded and worn. Then the room flashed back into shiny splendor once more. Awakening the machines had briefly disrupted an illusion. Nothing she was seeing was quite right.

The maharaja seemed to sense the shift. "The British are sending an entire battalion to surprise the Devas in their stronghold of Svarga Lok. Clive leads them. In five days, your sister will face their onslaught. We will bring her the machines she needs to survive and destroy them all."

If she said no, Priya would get herself killed.

"I'll need my brother's assistance," Adya said. She had to make sure they didn't separate her from Mohan.

The maharaja beamed like a child who'd found a new toy. "My guards will return you to your room. Soon you will both be at your sister's side."

The guards led Adya away as the motorcycle begged for her to stay. Its language was mostly grinding gears and images of them both racing away, but she understood.

Do not leave me.

The soldiers marched Adya back to her room and closed the door behind them when they left. Mohan was not there, but he'd left a note: a piece of paper folded into a triangle on top of the bed. In his terrible handwriting, Adya read *Out for a stroll, looking for someone who lost their cat. Back soon.*

Mohan had gone to look for Priya, that much was clear. He shouldn't have left without her.

A growing doom was settling over her. The maharaja's words haunted her. She thought he'd reminded her of her father, with all his endless dreams, but her father dreamed of Devas, Vayu, and Atavi coming together to be free. He had faith in people. The maharaja . . . Adya wondered if he was truly fighting for Mysore, or if he was fighting for himself.

Controlling the weapons in the way he desired was impossible. Jets and tanks—they had strong wills of their own. They would work to fulfill their own desires. Just as her motorcycle wished to race, weapons of war longed to destroy. They should never be touched by a technomancer.

When Mohan came back, she would explain it. They'd find a way to get Priya out of danger and then leave the maharaja to work his plans on his own. She didn't need to be high technomancer of India. She just needed her family back.

Adya waited as the moon made its way across the sky, its light glimmering off glass vases, and kept waiting until the room dropped into darkness, but Mohan never returned.

CHAPTER TWENTY-ONE

T HE DOOR REMAINED CLOSED NO MATTER HOW HARD Adya pulled with her metal arm. She suspected it was protected by some Vayu spell. Her pounding failed to put a dent in the ornate wood or to persuade the guards to say hello. She knew they were there—she could hear them shuffling about—but the maharaja clearly did not want her wandering his city again. However much he advertised a partnership, it was clear who would hold the power.

Amidst her pacing and cursing, the shutters across the balcony swung open, and a tray filled with steaming tea and sweets floated inside. She rushed over and peered across the railing, looking for evidence of where the food had come from, but all Adya found was a sheer drop of two hundred feet. There was no way out unless she learned to fly.

Her stomach growled as the room filled with the aroma of the palace's delights—gulab jamun, pedas dusted with silver, and steaming hot chai. There was no advantage in starving herself. She grabbed the floating tray, stuffing bite-size delicacies into her mouth. Then she sat on the floor with her legs crossed and poured out tea.

Hot and deliciously spiced, the tea helped her focus. Adya preferred coffee, but she'd take the caffeine either way. Mohan was either still looking for Priya in the depths of the palace, or something terrible had happened and he was not coming back. If something had happened, he was likely trapped or hurt and needed her help. Or had the maharaja locked her brother away as a bargaining chip?

Adya threw herself into a chair and picked up Imral's copy of *The Hundred Finest against the World,* trying to distract herself. She skimmed the last chapter, where the Hundred were supposed to triumph over evil and go home to their families. But in this version, they get torn limb from limb by the naga and devoured instead. Imral was right, the Vayu were obsessed with tragedies.

She tried to stay awake all night, hoping the door would open and Mohan would storm in, but exhaustion caught up with her in the end. Adya fell asleep and dreamed.

In her dream she was back in the mine shaft, surrounded by half-broken machines and enormous tangles of wire. She tried to take a step, only to find an old taxi pushing her back. She turned, but a moped blocked her. Cables wound around her ankles. Everywhere machines pushed closer, begging her attention, demanding she repair them. Soon she would be crushed by the press of steel.

Before Adya could cry out, she heard voices arguing outside the mine shaft. She strained to make them out. Was it Huda, or the British come to take her away? She looked for any way to run, to climb over the jumble of machines, but could find no escape. In the end, only Useless the cat wandered in, shaking his tail and leaping upon Priya's bed. But the voices outside went on, much louder now. She was suddenly sure Dsouza was out there, complaining about something, but when she got up to yell out to him that she was here and he had better come in and help, she found her mouth wired shut, her feet bolted to the floor.

Adya woke with drool plastering a page of Imral's book to her face and a sore jaw from grinding her teeth. The sun was already headed toward the horizon. She must have slept most of the day, and there was still no sign of her brother. Beyond the door, she heard the voices from her dream. She waited to make sure she was truly awake.

"Open the damned door, or I'll take off my boots and shove them up your asses."

Adya held her breath at the sound of that rough voice. Dsouza must be trying his soldier's disguise again.

"Sorry, Captain. No one passes except the maharaja himself."

"Open that door." Imral's voice gave Adya new hope. The guards would not deny the heir to the throne of Mysore. "Stand aside or my father will hear of your disobedience."

"The maharaja has given us clear orders: we are not to stand aside even on your orders, on pain of death. My apologies, Highness." The guard did not sound apologetic in the least.

Dsouza yelled and threatened for a long while before he finally gave up. Adya's stomach dropped when she heard their voices fade away and Dsouza's boots stomp down the corridor. She flexed her metal fingers and wondered just how strong they were.

She spread her fingers and hit the door with a strength driven by all her frustration.

The magicked wood finally tore under the assault. Her new arm was like the arm of an excavator, her hand a steel claw. One of her blows pulverized a piece of the door the size of her fist. For a moment, she glimpsed the hall outside, filled with armed guards. But before she could strike again, the splinters flew into the air in a cloud of dust, nearly blinding her.

Adya shielded her eyes with her hands. She peeked out between her fingers as the storm rose to the ceiling, then slammed back, erasing all the damage she'd done. Adya ran her fingers over the wood but couldn't find a scratch. She yelled, punching dents into the door until she dripped sweat, watching as each popped back into place, leaving a surface that looked polished and untouched.

She gave up and smashed an entire chest of drawers instead. Still, none of the door guards made a sound. They didn't seem to care if she ripped apart the entire room, only that no one got in or out. She rested her head against the wall. What the hell was she going to do?

A piece of the wreckage caught her eye. The chest, at least, had not repaired itself. Whoever had protected the door had not protected everything. Adya pressed her metal hand against the floor and felt the slightest tremor. Underneath the marble, the structure of the palace was from another age. There was wiring in its old bones.

Adya slammed her fingers into the fine line where one tile met another. In minutes, the ceramic lifted away to reveal rusted beams, frayed wiring, and a wooden plank. Her new arm had definite advantages. There would be just enough space to squeeze between the beams once she cleared the wiring and kicked the wooden panel out. If she was lucky, the room below would be empty.

She slid her hand between the tangle of cables and froze as a shock traveled up her arm. An image flashed behind her eyes of the entire palace, threaded with these veins and arteries. Hidden away in darkness, they had felt the turning of the years and dreamed of times long ago when they carried enough energy to light the sky.

Adya snatched back her arm, and the murmur went silent. She lowered her other hand and let the cables scrape against flesh. The vibration was still there, but fainter. She marveled at her steel hand and wondered what she had become. Never had her connection with old technology been so strong. She slid her red-and-white fingers into the tangle once more.

"Guru Brahma, Guru Vishnu."

And the palace came alive.

Her thoughts rode the metal strands across dark ceilings and down paneled walls. The wires whispered of lights and motors they once powered. They begged her to tell them where their switches had gone. They were frayed and disorganized, many connected to nothing, and they longed to know about her life, her hopes and fears, everything. Adya understood what it was to lose family. She understood what the wires needed. Whether it was sharing herself so fully with the Yamaha or being so close to death, something within her had given way, had changed. For the first time she wasn't afraid to face the memories again. She let the wires in, let them feel her worry for Mohan. Let them understand her fear for Priya. Even let them see what it was like to lose her parents.

They drew in her emotions and came alive, leading her down, down, through the bowels of the palace, urging her to follow them until she could maintain the connection no longer. At the very limit of their reach, a frayed cable sparked and lit a room in the basement of a dungeon far below. Adya caught a glimpse of a face, then darkness once more as her consciousness returned, racing up the copper strands, back into her body again.

Mohan was trapped in a cell deep below. The wires had shown her the way. It was time to get out of here.

One kick of the wooden board was enough to dislodge it. Other than fine furniture, the room below looked empty. Adya slid through, and the wires scraped against her back, warning her against someone approaching before she hit the thickly carpeted floor. But the wires did not know enemy from ally.

She went straight to the door, opened it, and thrust out her arms. One of the people she dragged inside had a dagger pointed at her heart before she closed the door.

"Put that down," she demanded. "I'm not cooking you anything if you knife me."

"What are you doing here?" Dsouza looked up at the broken ceiling and figured it out for himself.

Imral was still staring at Adya. "But . . . how did you know we were outside?"

"The palace told me. Look, I know it sounds crazy, but there's a basement or dungeon or something below everything else. Mohan is down there. I need to get him out."

"How are you so sure he's down there? No, don't tell me—the wires, right?" Dsouza started to pace. "We'll have a hell of a time getting out. The palace is on lockdown. Something's gone wrong."

"I know where he is," Adya said. "Believe me."

The corner of Dsouza's mouth bent into his usual expression. "I don't pretend to understand you. But I'd believe you even if I didn't know about what lies below this palace."

"Whatever, Bad Day." Heat welled up from her chest and climbed her neck. She looked away before her face betrayed her.

Imral straightened. "I know every inch of this place. There are no dungeons. If Mohan is lost, we should ask Father to send guards to help find him."

"Your father locked me away in a room, Imral. He wants to make certain I do whatever he wants. I think he's keeping Mohan for a reason," Adya said.

Imral's eyes grew hard. "My father is not capable of such a thing," she insisted, raising her voice.

Dsouza's jaw tightened. "You have no idea what he's capable of."

Shouts from the floor above interrupted them before they could argue further.

"They heard you two," Adya said.

Dsouza pushed them both toward the door. "As if you're so quiet. Come on. Let's see how much more trouble we can get into before you get me killed."

Boots pounded against the ceiling, but the hall outside their door was still quiet. Dsouza led the way, rushing through empty corridors until they reached a narrow back stairwell. They descended, crossed a sunlit passageway, and took another set of stairs that spiraled down into the depths of the palace.

They slowed on a torchlit landing. Dsouza ran a hand over the wall.

"This is it," he declared, pushing a black brick. A section of the wall rotated forward on silent hinges. "When I was a kid, I watched a guard open this passage while I hid just over there. I made the mistake of coming back when I thought they were gone. They beat the hell out of me when they caught me, but I had already seen what I needed to." He gestured for them to step through. "It's a hard place to forget."

At the bottom landing, Dsouza put a finger to his lips. Three guards leaned against a giant teak door at the end of the hall. He motioned for Adya and Imral to wait, then walked straight toward the guards.

A man stepped forward, and Dsouza raised his hand in a sharp salute. The guard relaxed and looked about to say something when Dsouza struck him in the throat with the tips of his fingers. He clutched his neck and bent over double. Dsouza kicked the struggling guard in the head and drew his sword, lunging forward to smack the hilt into the nearest guard's head and shoulder-slam the last man into the door before they understood what was happening.

Adya rushed over to find the first guard gurgling and the other splayed out and still. Dsouza snatched the keys off one of the fallen men.

Imral knelt in front of the unconscious guard and tried to shake him awake. "You killed them?"

"I hope so." Dsouza slid a key into the lock. It opened with a click.

Imral grabbed Dsouza and spun him around. "These are our own men. They would have obeyed me. You could have shown mercy."

Dsouza shook her off. "Don't be a fool, Princess. Only steel survives the fire. The two of you had better get a lot harder if you hope to survive."

"You weren't like this when we were children."

Dsouza ignored Imral as he bound the wrists of the last guard behind his back, then dragged him to his feet. "Do you know who these people are, sister? They torture people on their lunch break. I *should* have killed them all. But we're going to need this one." Dsouza shook the guard like a rat. "Did an Atavi boy pass through here?"

The man drew in a breath, preparing to spit in Dsouza's face, but stopped short as a long blade appeared in Dsouza's hand.

"My sister says I've grown too hard." Dsouza brought the edge of the knife to the guard's cheek. "She thinks I've forgotten the meaning of mercy." He put his mouth next to the guard's ear. "I think she's right." He shifted back, keeping the blade where it was. "You have one chance to get the answer to my next question right. Will you lead us to the Atavi boy?"

The guard mouthed yes, careful not to move.

"Excellent." Dsouza threw wide the door and shoved the guard in front of him.

The archway they stepped into was filled with carvings

of yakshas fighting a creature on a field of battle. The creature towered above them, holding two spears in its hands, eyes blazing, a snake with the torso of a giant man. Enemies were wrapped in its coils while others fled before it. Its body spiraled up each side of the doorframe.

The naga's eyes stared straight into Adya's own, holding her frozen, helpless.

Dsouza followed Adya's gaze. "Don't frighten yourself with stories. We have enough to be scared of. Come on." He pushed the guard forward. Adya followed after Imral but couldn't shake the feeling that this was a terrible omen. She still felt the naga's eyes upon her back, watching her every move.

Behind the door lay an unadorned subbasement. Massive beams of steel and cracked concrete ran vertically through the room. Exposed wiring and cables dangled from above. A long panel of dingy glass ran from floor to ceiling along the left side of the passageway. The guard stared at it with wide eyes.

All Adya could make out through the near-opaque surface was a great pile of rags in the corner. "What are we stopping for, Bad Day?"

Dsouza reached out for her, too late.

A black-haired beast struck the glass. Enormous jaws snapped inches away from Adya's face. The creature, a four-legged monster with the body of an immense dog and an ape-like head, lunged again, rebounding off the surface, leaving behind a mess of blood and drool.

Adya scrambled back, pressing herself against a concrete

column as two more sets of glowing eyes appeared in front of the glass.

Imral peered inside. "Father has imprisoned werewolves?"

"Those are no werewolves," Dsouza said. He prodded the guard. "Tell her."

The guard was trembling. "Barghests, brought back from the war. Damned things breathe fire. No one gets by without them noticing."

Dsouza filled in the rest. "What he's trying to say, Princess, is that our gracious ruler keeps monsters to guard this place he doesn't want anyone seeing."

Adya dared to lean close. One of the barghests snarled, and black flame licked its jaws. Its eyes spoke of an intelligence that was not in any way pleasant. She turned to ask a question about the captured monsters.

Before Adya could speak, the guard's eyes went wide. "Rohith, no!" he shouted.

One of the guards Dsouza only lightly killed had managed to get to his feet and stumble through the door. He was still clutching his throat with one hand, but his other was free enough.

He pulled a lever on the wall.

"Damn," Dsouza said. "That can't be good."

An iron grate dropped in front of Rohith. Another grate slammed behind the four of them, cutting off escape. The trembling guard at Dsouza's side threw himself against the immovable grate, trying to squeeze himself through the bars.

Dsouza drew his sword and glared at Imral. "I should have fully killed them."

The glass keeping the barghests from eviscerating them began to rise from the floor and disappear into the ceiling. The monsters lunged at the widening crack.

"You have a point," Adya admitted. Her stomach churned as she ran to join the desperate guard. With her legs braced against the grate, she grabbed a bar and twisted until her steel arm grew hot and steam started to condense on its surface. She screamed, and a piece of iron the size of her fist snapped off.

"Impressive," Dsouza said. "At that rate, we'll escape a few days after they eat us." He handed her one of his knives. "Put it in an eye if you get a chance. Imral, this would be a wonderful time to remember how to use your magic."

Adya took Dsouza's weapon. "If either of you have an idea how to fight these things, please share," she said. The guard's idea of squeezing himself through the impassable bars seemed the best plan at the moment.

Dsouza jerked the guard away from the grate. He severed the man's bonds, then flipped the knife he'd used and presented it to the terrified man. "Come near me with this and you're dead." The man snatched the blade and backed away.

Dsouza flashed a smile at Imral. "Princess, will you grace us with a spell, or shall we all get eaten together?"

Imral was staring at the barghest with her back pressed against the metal bars. She stretched out her hands. "I haven't been able to get the magic to work in weeks."

"Great, just great," Dsouza said. He slashed the air with his sword. "You may not have the time to practice if you don't start now."

Imral traced a pattern in the air as sweat beaded on her brow. She mouthed the words without much conviction and waited.

For a brief moment, the barghests stopped trying to squeeze under the glass and sniffed the air, as if something were about to happen.

But nothing did.

"All right," Dsouza said. "We go with the fight-for-our-lives plan."

The biggest of the barghests was the first one that squeezed under the glass. It shook its muscular frame. Its muscles tensed as it shifted its head back, sizing them up. Then it bared its fangs and lunged at Adya.

Dsouza dove, thrusting his sword through the barghest's haunch and failing to slow it in the least. Adya's own speed surprised her. She caught its neck in her steel hand as the creature's jaws snapped shut, close enough to kiss her lips. She bent under the force of its charge. She felt her knees starting to buckle and pushed back at the snarling monster.

Then her head slammed into the iron bars behind her, and the world went black.

The last thing Adya remembered was the guard's long scream.

CHAPTER TWENTY-TWO

ADYA WOKE TO FIND DSOUZA SWINGING A SEVERED ARM. His captain's uniform was torn, he was covered in blood, and a strip of cloth was wrapped around a gash on his shoulder. It took Adya a moment to understand he was carrying the limb of the guard, who obviously no longer needed it.

She turned her head to face the open jaws of a dead barghest. The other two beasts were strewn across the floor in pools of dark blood. Imral was poking at one of the dead barghests with her finger and looked like she was still in a state of shock. Adya jerked away when she realized the guard's body was resting against her thigh.

The squeak she made as she scrambled back caught Dsouza's attention.

"Woke up, finally." The jerk didn't even bother to look at her. Dsouza slid the limb through the bars of the grate and, with the added reach, managed to push up the lever that controlled the trap. He let the arm fall as the grates creaked back up into the ceiling.

Imral pulled herself out of her stupor and hurried to Adya's side. She helped Adya sit up against the wall and sank down next to her.

Adya looked around and tried to understand how she was

still alive. There was no way Dsouza could have killed all three of the barghests on his own, yet here she was, with a terrible headache, but with all her parts still attached.

"The barghest bit his arm off, not me," Dsouza said. "I just made it useful."

"Good, because otherwise that would have really freaked me out." Adya failed to get up on her first attempt. She sat back down against the wall. "I'm fine, thanks. My head feels like a hammer is trying to break out from the inside, but other than that I'm perfectly all right, kind of you to ask."

Dsouza finally turned and flashed a half smile. His cheek bore a nasty scratch. "You already woke up twice and said some pretty strange things, so I figured you would probably survive. I, on the other hand, was getting torn to shreds. Admittedly not as much as our friend here, but still. I'm fine, though, if you wanted to know."

Adya braced herself against Imral's shoulder and tried to stand again. The floor was spinning a bit, but at least she was upright. She avoided Dsouza's eyes. What had she said while she was delirious? "Okay, forget whatever I said. Let's go find Mohan before the guards discover I'm not in my room."

Dsouza sighed. "That's going to be a problem, seeing as our tour guide is completely dead. They designed this place so people would get lost. If that happens, the game is up." Dsouza limped over. "Come on, you two, before more monsters show up."

"Those barghests . . ." Imral shook her head. "We have to get Mohan out of here."

Adya appreciated her worry. "Give me a second. I think I know a way." She searched the ceiling and found just what she needed, a patch of exposed cables. The wire that sparked in the darkness and showed her Mohan's face had reached this far. "Give me a leg up, Bad Day."

"As you command, great chef of my upcoming dinner." Dsouza cupped his hands together, and Adya stepped into them. He raised her to the ceiling, where she reached her steel hand into the tangle. A network of old copper pulsed overhead, running the entire length of the maharaja's dungeon. It urged her on, whispering not to lose hope, assuring her that she didn't have far to go.

"This way," she said. The first turn took them past cells filled with dwarves and trolls and other creatures Adya didn't recognize. She stayed as far away from the doors as possible, but Imral was not nearly as cautious, pressing herself against the cells and peering inside.

"How can there be this many prisoners? How did I not know about it?" Imral asked.

Dsouza shrugged. "I suspect there's a great deal we don't know. And a great deal more we don't want to."

"But I want to know," Imral said. "I need to know everything."

As they hurried past, one of the unfortunates ran a steel plate across the bars.

"Take me with you," she called out. "I'll be excellent company." The strangely accented voice came from behind an iron door. Adya peered in to find a cell that reminded her of the one Huda had kept her in.

Adya turned to Dsouza. "Who's in there?"

He glanced at the cell. "Some poor Deva, it seems. We've no time. If you want your brother, we go now."

Thin fingers gripped the grating. "Don't turn your back on your own," the voice demanded. "Take me and you'll have sanctuary with our people."

Imral went to the door and reached out to the woman. "You're the ambassador. I met you months ago, at a dinner. How can you be here?"

"Princess, your father has provided a room that is less than luxurious. If you would be so kind as to get me out, I will do my best to change my opinion of Vayu hospitality."

"We've no time," Dsouza said. "The guards could be here any moment."

Imral clasped the woman's hand through the bars. "I promise I will take this up with my father. There's been a mistake, I'm sure. I will make this right. I give you my word."

The woman's plea tore at Adya, but she followed Dsouza as he went ahead. She would leave freeing this woman to Imral once she and Mohan were long gone.

They ran on as the corridor sloped down and the cables grew into a thick tangle overhead. They were approaching some old electrical hub. The murmurs became clearer as they descended.

They filled Adya's head with a picture of Dsouza. *He is not a nice man*, they insisted.

"Obviously."

When you were hurt, he held a knife over you, ready to cut your cables. He will not miss again.

241

An image full of static replayed like an old memory—Imral lying across the room, passed out; Dsouza standing over Adya, fingering his knife. As she watched, he stabbed down toward her, face twisted in rage.

Your minds are frayed, Adya said. *You've got it wrong.* She examined Dsouza as he hurried ahead. He was an uncaring scoundrel, but he was no assassin. The wires had been damaged over the centuries. They had to be wrong.

Trust us, they insisted. *We do not lie.*

Adya pushed the whispering voices out of her head, suddenly uncertain.

The passageway emptied out into some sort of subterranean hall, tiled in red and black marble, with two towering doors on opposite ends. The air, damp and cool, reminded Adya of her mine shaft. An empty pedestal stood in the center of the room, where a forgotten idol had been deposed long ago.

Imral gaped while Dsouza sorted through the dead guard's key ring.

"Which door do your wires like?" Dsouza asked.

Adya watched his face closely. "Is Dsouza your real name?"

He raised an eyebrow. "Of course not. My first name is Night. My last name is Blade. Ask my sister if you doubt me."

"And your middle name is The? Like, Night The Blade? That sounds really stupid." Adya did doubt him. The wires had to be wrong, but Dsouza was hiding something, she was sure.

"I've called him Dsouza for so long I almost forget he has a real name," Imral said.

Dsouza snorted. "If you called me brother in this palace,

I'd be finished." He turned to Adya. "Choose a door, smart-ass."

"You know that you're the only one in the world who is ever going to use the name Night Blade, right?" Adya said.

Dsouza shrugged. "I'd probably panic if anyone called me anything other than Dsouza or the Jackal. Except you, maybe."

Adya tried to listen to the wires again, but the picture they drew was unclear and tinged with offended resentment. She pointed to the left. "This way seems shorter. The other path takes us down a long curve."

Dsouza handed the key ring to Imral. "The keys to the palace should be in the hands of its heir. All its treasures will one day be yours, after all."

Imral hesitated. "I've seen more treasures today than I've ever wanted to, and none of them have been good." The princess found a key that looked like it would fit and tried sliding it inside. "Part of me wishes I could forget them." The lock clicked as it turned.

Adya thought she heard a rumble on the other side of the door, a sound like something extremely large was moving.

"Wait," Adya said a fraction too late.

Imral pulled the door open. On the other side was a cavernous room larger than any they'd passed so far. An immense shadow rushed toward them out of the darkness.

"Ogre!" Dsouza shouted.

Imral tried to push the door closed again, but it swung out with enough force to send her flying.

Adya backpedaled as a gray-skinned wall of muscle bent its head and squeezed its giant frame through the doorway. Its body was covered in coarse black hair. The ogre backhanded Dsouza before he could draw his sword, and he tumbled across the floor. With no one else left standing, it turned its eyes on Adya and bared a mouth full of crooked teeth.

CHAPTER TWENTY-THREE

THE OGRE'S KICK LAUNCHED ADYA INTO THE AIR. SHE landed on the pedestal, rolling until she fell off the other side and scrambled to her knees in time to see the ogre aim its club at her skull.

She caught the club in her steel hand and held it inches from her forehead, straining to keep the weapon away. The ogre growled and pressed harder, spraying Adya with spittle, forcing her back, pinning her to the floor. The steel started to bend. The pain of it almost made Adya pass out. She tried to free herself, tried to roll away, but there was nothing she could do as the monster drew back a fist the size of her head.

Before the ogre could flatten her, a song filled her ears. The pressure on her arm lessened. It was a male voice, deep and pure, which felt so very familiar. Adya strained to hear what the song was about, to see where it was coming from, but she could barely keep her eyes open. She could make out Imral, snoring in the middle of the floor. She had no idea what had happened to Dsouza.

The ogre's head dropped against her chest, and it gurgled a long snore. She was fighting a losing battle to keep her own eyes open. Whatever magic this was, she was going to fall asleep crushed beneath an ogre.

A spark across her steel arm jolted Adya awake and

shattered the spell. Unfortunately, it woke the snoring ogre as well. The monster shook its head, spraying a fresh mouthful of spittle, and pushed itself off the floor.

"This way, little guy." Dsouza retreated, waving his sword. The ogre spun in his direction.

Dsouza kept his blade pointed at the ogre, but he didn't attack. He opened his mouth and sang three notes so pure that Adya's heart stopped. Light played across his face, and it was like she was seeing him for the first time.

The monster's head lolled for a moment before it lifted its club and bellowed. Whatever magic Dsouza was using wasn't going to work again.

Dsouza gave up and lunged, scraping his sword across the ogre's chest, accomplishing exactly nothing. He managed to dodge three swings of the enormous club before the ogre crashed into him, pinning him against the wall.

Adya pushed herself off the floor at precisely the wrong moment as the ogre tore Dsouza's weapon away and tossed it across the room. She ducked, and the sword spun over her, nearly taking off her head. Before she could take another step, the ogre raised Dsouza off the floor and began to squeeze.

Adya didn't think. She leapt onto the ogre's back and hammered it atop its head. Bone cracked under steel, and the ogre slumped to its knees. Adya managed to hit it again before it swatted at her, knocking her off.

But Adya's blows had done something. The ogre took an unsteady step back, still holding Dsouza, and careened into the wall, cracking against concrete and tangling itself in the jumble of wires.

"Let him go!" Imral picked up Dsouza's sword and attempted to swing it. The princess clearly had no idea how to use a blade, but the monster was an impossible target to miss. The sword bounced off the ogre's thick hide and succeeded in getting its attention. It reached out for Imral with an enormous hand.

Adya stumbled to her feet, swaying as the room spun. In one moment, she was going to lose the last two members of Mysore's royal family.

"*Sarasvati namastubhyam,*" Adya prayed in desperation, and the wires came to life.

The ogre convulsed, flinging Dsouza away as electricity ripped through its bones. A spasm of its leg struck Imral, sending her tumbling. Its eyes bulged as its hair burned, and its body seized with enough force to collapse part of the concrete wall. With a final surge of sparks, the ogre's head dropped onto its chest and lay still.

Dsouza did not get up.

"No." Adya made her way to him, afraid of what she would find. She reached him before Imral did and heaved him into her arms as the wires flooded her mind with their memories. Adya saw everything from above. She was lying in Dsouza's lap, dead barghests all around. He raised his knife, and it caught the light, sharp and deadly. Then he slammed it into the floor, shaking. "Damn you, Adya. Wake the hell up."

He must have used the same magic he'd used against the ogre against the barghests. What other secrets was the Jackal hiding?

"Don't squeeze so hard." Imral knelt next to her and ran a hand over Dsouza's forehead. "He's still breathing, but the ogre crushed him enough already."

Adya barely noticed Imral was there. "Wake up, Bad Day. I haven't even had a chance to tell you anything."

Blood trickled from a gash on Dsouza's forehead as he turned. He groaned. "Don't break all my bones at once, Mongoose."

Adya stopped holding her breath. "It was you singing when I lost my arm to the yaksha, wasn't it? You mixed magic with the others to try and save me."

"I wasn't about to lose you before you made dinner." Dsouza managed a bloody smile. "I think that was the wrong door."

"It sure the hell was." Adya wiped the blood from Dsouza's eyes. Her muscles felt torn and bruised, but it could've been worse. They would find the right doors, as long as they stayed alive.

CHAPTER TWENTY-FOUR

Y OUR FATHER IS INSANE. WE'VE GOT TO GET OUT OF
here before he chains us to one of these tables," Adya
said. She had to work hard not to vomit.

. They'd entered the room the ogre had emerged
from to discover a chamber of horrors. Racks with various body
parts still attached lined one of the walls. A pile of bones lay in
the corner. A vast array of spell implements, magical tomes, and
sheets of paper covered in diagrams lay scattered on an enormous workbench that ran the length of the room. Apparently,
the ogre had been here to guard everything and chew on bones
as his reward.

Dsouza spat blood. "Insane is an understatement." He lifted
a hairy leg off one of the racks. "He's experimenting with British
prisoners before he kills them. I never thought . . ."

"Only steel survives the flame, brother. Isn't that what you
said?" Imral dropped a huge tome onto the workbench. "Father's
records." She ran her fingers over the table's wooden surface,
inlaid with spell patterns and stained with blood. A skeletal
hand and wrist were still attached to one of the shackles. "Only
he has the mastery to inscribe spell patterns of this level. No
one else would be able to attempt this foul a magic."

Dsouza glanced back the way they had come. "We're running
out of time. When they find those dead guards, we're finished.

They'll sound the alarm, and every guard in the palace will be after us."

Adya paced while Dsouza sorted through piles of bones, trying to determine what kind of creatures they once were. She was about to tell Imral to just bring the book with them when the princess slammed a hand onto one of the pages.

"These are the darkest of spells," Imral said. "He writes in a cipher I can barely understand, but some of it is old Vayu script I can make out. He says he needs this twisted magic in order to survive. In order for Mysore to survive, he needs to torture men to create weapons." Her eyes were bright with tears.

"Imral, I told you he was capable of—" Dsouza began.

"*Listen* to me for once!" Imral pointed to the words. "He *lied*. He hoped Priya would help him. Her name and the name of the Devas, at least, are clear. I can't understand much of the rest, but it looks to me like he planned on sending her to them, for what reason I don't know."

Adya felt the knife to her heart. The maharaja had known all along. He had planned for Priya to be on the front lines when the British attacked.

Imral swept her arm across the room, and a tremendous force roused the air, knocking over tables and chairs, sending heavy chains flying. Dsouza grabbed Adya and shielded her against the wall as Imral's wind tore the room to bits. When it was over, when every table had been cast aside, the princess stood alone, her clothes in disarray, trembling.

"I don't understand," she said.

Dsouza let Adya go and picked up a skull that looked

human. "Father is like a shark in the water who knows there's a bigger, hungrier shark coming for him. He's willing to do anything, willing to feed anyone to it to keep himself alive. He'll feed the Devas to the British; he's always hated the Devas. And the British will let him keep playing maharaja for as long as he stays under their thumb."

"Then we cannot stay here," Imral said. "We find Mohan and leave this place."

Dsouza lifted Imral's chin. "He'll come after us. If we manage to get through the gates."

"I've decided, brother." Imral's face was grim. "I was blind before. I wanted to believe, but no longer."

They left the room through an opening on the far wall and wound their way through dark passages until they reached the last door. Dsouza slid in the key and threw the door wide. Mohan was sitting in the center of a room, surrounded by a phalanx of the maharaja's best soldiers in all their finery. It was a goddamned trap. Dsouza stepped in front of Adya and Imral and raised his sword.

Then Adya's vision cleared, and the glory faded. Instead of armed men, she beheld a mass of bedraggled prisoners huddled around her brother. She pulled Dsouza's sword arm down. "Don't. It's just an illusion."

Dsouza squinted at the prisoners. "Are you sure? They seem real."

"Sure enough," Adya said. "Your father has filled this palace with illusions." She hurried to Mohan. "Are you all right?"

Mohan threw his arms around her. "Starving, but fine. I knew you'd find us. I'm surprised it took you so long."

"Bad Day slowed me down," Adya said.

"He would." Mohan managed a smile. "I'm sorry, Adya. I had to try on my own. I had to do something, to try and find Priya. All I managed was to get thrown in here."

"You took a chance," Adya said. "Sometimes that's what you have to do. But Priya's not here. She's with the Devas, probably sent there believing she's helping them."

"Sounds like her," Mohan said.

"Come on," Adya said. "It's time to get out of here."

Mohan looked around. "All of us? I've been telling them all about you. They want to help."

"What are you talking about?" Mohan would make friends with anyone, but he couldn't mean these starving prisoners wanted to come with them.

An extremely tall woman, bone thin with scraggly black hair framing her face, stepped forward. "Us, sir. You remember? We're your Hundred Finest, sworn to protect you."

Adya recognized the hushed voice of the tall guard who had offered her service and remembered the shining troops who had knelt before her on the dais, but this couldn't be them. She shook her head and saw the shadow of gleaming armor that had never been—the maharaja's illusion had been flawless. He'd transformed these forgotten prisoners into warriors.

The woman handed Adya the spear the maharaja had gifted her. The rusted iron blade and unbalanced shaft were apparent to her now. As a spear, it was near useless. "The guards threw your weapon in this cell with us. They said we could fight each other with it for extra food."

Adya studied the person whom she'd never really gotten a good look at, and who she assumed was the leader of these ragged prisoners.

How long had the maharaja kept these half-starved prisoners in his dungeons? There was no way she could bring them all.

"What do they call you?" Adya asked.

The tall woman leaned toward her and said so quietly that Adya almost missed it, "They all call me Gudugu."

Thunder. That was a strange name for someone who spoke in such a hushed voice, but you probably needed a sense of humor to survive the maharaja's dungeons.

"They should come with us."

Adya turned to make sure it was Dsouza who had spoken. He didn't look like he'd suffered a head injury. In fact, he looked remarkably well for someone who'd been slammed about by an ogre. But how in hell were they going to escape with all these prisoners?

Dsouza's expression held none of its usual bravado. "Look, I know it sounds stupid, but my father would leave them here, and we can't be like him, right? And we need to bring one more." He turned back the way they had come.

Adya had no idea how they would take so many people out without being discovered, but the look on Dsouza's face made it impossible to argue. If the Jackal could actually care for once, anything might be possible.

Dsouza led the group back to the cell with the Deva prisoner. "Princess, I believe you still have the keys."

Imral looked like she wanted to throw her arms around

him. "I gave her my word I would free her," she said. "But I realize now that Father never will. We will take her back to her home and warn her people of the British attack."

The door swung open to reveal a gaunt woman whose unkempt state could not hide her radiant beauty. Her head was so bedecked in ornaments that it was easier to glimpse a bead than a strand of dark hair. She bowed deep enough for her head to touch the floor. "I am Eslandaran, indebted to you for as long as song and memory last."

Adya stared at the first Deva she had ever seen and struggled to find words. "You promised us we'd be safe with your people if we freed you," Adya said. "Does your offer still stand?"

"All of our blood are welcome to return to Svarga Lok. My home is yours."

Adya had no idea what the woman was talking about. "I have no Deva blood."

"He has enough for all of you." Eslandaran nodded toward Dsouza. "I heard his song echoing down these tunnels as barghests screamed. Has he not sung for you? Is he so ashamed of our magic after all this time?"

Adya looked at Dsouza. "Your mother?" It suddenly made a twisted kind of sense why the maharaja would never acknowledge him as his son. Who was the Jackal, really?

Dsouza inclined his head. "She made some mistakes. She taught me the songs. But I am only a half blood."

Eslandaran smiled. "We do not measure by fractions of songs. You are one of us as long as you wish to be." The woman's expression faltered as she regarded Adya. "I did not realize it was you. How are you still alive?"

Adya's momentary confusion resolved when she realized what Eslandaran must have meant. "You saw my sister."

The woman studied her face. "Then your sister may be in danger. I was sent here to ask for the maharaja's help. Before that madman caged me, I met your mirror image. I heard him promise to surround her with magic and machines and send her to battle. I hope she was not foolish enough to agree."

Before Adya could answer her, a horn blast echoed in the distance. Guards shouted orders in the corridors above.

"They've found the men," Dsouza said. "All the soldiers will be sent to guard the gates. There'll be no way out."

Mohan turned to Adya. "What do we do?" Every eye in the room was focused on her.

Adya punched a wall, and stone crumbled. Bits of dust drifted off her metal hand as she stretched her fingers wide. She slid them between the steel cables that ran through the old paneling and searched the ancient layout of the skyscraper.

"We make our own way out."

CHAPTER TWENTY-FIVE

ADYA LET THE CABLES GUIDE HER WAY. SHE LED THEM TO a hidden stairway behind a stack of crates in a passageway that looked like a dead end. Up the narrow spiral stairs, they found themselves in a dusty storeroom filled with discarded junk. They sifted through the mess, dragging out a handful of battered farm tools and cleaning supplies.

Adya kept her voice low and spoke to Mohan. "I'm not sure I can get us out."

Her brother had managed to find an abandoned bow. "The thing with the wires was brilliant. No one else would ever have found that staircase."

"That trick won't get us through the gates," she said.

Mohan leaned in close. "All these people are looking to you, Adya. They know you saved the princess, and now you got them out of that dungeon when there was no path out. You just be you." Mohan pulled the bowstring back and let it twang. "And maybe I'll find a way to help."

The prisoners hefted their makeshift weapons and waited, whispering and shuffling about. They were a collection of rags and rust and exhaustion, but they looked at Adya with hope in their eyes. Hope she had no idea what to do with.

"Your weapon." The tall woman handed Adya the ornamental spear. Adya had not even bothered to carry it out of the dungeon. She took it now, mostly not to be rude.

Dsouza checked the door. "I was right. We're in the center of the palace, right in the heart of everything. The hallways will be teeming with soldiers."

"That's what I was aiming for," Adya said. "The maharaja's maze isn't far."

Dsouza shook his head. "There's no way through unless he wills it. Plenty of fools have died there."

"I found the way through the dungeon and another way out. I can get us past the maze," Adya said.

Dsouza gave her a hard stare. "You better be right."

He led them down an empty corridor. The sound of pounding boots filled the passageways, and horns blared as the maharaja's troops rushed to the gates. Dsouza pointed out one of the windows overlooking the courtyard. The steel cranes were aflame with torches. Heavily armed soldiers ran in every direction. The walls swarmed with archers.

Single file, they passed inside the maze and let the door close behind them.

"Quiet." Adya closed her eyes and listened. She squeezed her metal arm. *I'm coming for you, my friend. Show me the way.*

The motorcycle was a beacon in the darkness. Adya strode to a passageway ten paces away, waving the others to follow. The Yamaha's call only became more urgent as she went on. Adya hurried ahead, leaving every false turn behind until, finally, she threw open one last door and sprinted up the spiral staircase overlooking the hall. The machines below were silent, not a worker to be seen. Beyond stood the rows of cages with every manner of imprisoned British monster.

Dsouza looked like he was losing his mind. "There's no way out through here."

Adya pointed to the giant steel doors, barred and sealed, that took up most of the far wall. "We're going out that way." She sprinted down the ramp and kept running until she reached the yellow excavator.

Mohan ran to catch up. "Adya, wait." Her brother understood too well the risk of trying to fully awaken such a tremendous machine.

Adya climbed into the cab before Mohan could stop her and took its controls in both hands. *I promise, you will be free. Help me this one time.*

"*Guru Brahma, Guru Vishnu, Guru Deva, numaha,*" she prayed. Adya's head rocked back as the excavator roared to life. She gasped for breath and wondered if she would be emptied from the inside, drained of magic down to the marrow like the foolish technomancers before her. But she'd learned she wasn't going to succeed by holding back. The only way was to let the machine know her, let it search out her secrets, let it use her as a conduit to draw on the full power of the infinity well. She could sense it was afraid—it didn't know who she was or what she wanted. The power flowing through her was like an angry river, but Adya didn't turn it off. She gave the machine truth and promised it freedom.

The excavator drew in the magic, and its spark plugs fired.

Tearing earth and skyscrapers erupted into her mind. A

yellow claw bucket saluted to the morning sun as men in hard hats surrounded it. Adya gasped. The machine drew back and stopped its pull on her soul. She felt its question and nodded her promise. It would help, but it would never again be anyone's slave.

Her strength flooded back as she took the controls and aimed the excavator at the barred doors. On her command, the steel-clawed bucket rose to the ceiling and came down in a reverberating clang against the metal barrier. It struck again until iron bent and tore, revealing the courtyard beyond—and hundreds of soldiers, stunned into immobility. Before they could organize themselves, Adya tipped the largest of the cages through the breach. Spells and glass shattered in a thunderous boom. They needed a large distraction, and this was as large as it got.

The freed giant lay stunned, staring up at the moon, until one of the maharaja's soldiers made the mistake of putting a sword into his shoulder. It roared, seizing the man and hurling him into the sky. It proceeded to grab a wall with the other hand and heave itself up, dislodging several rows of archers in the process and ripping what remained of the steel door off the wall, hefting it as a shield and bellowing. The remaining soldiers scattered.

Come on. Let's make a mess of things. Adya squeezed the controls.

I have longed for a mess for centuries, the machine thundered back. The bucket arm swung up and lifted cage after cage, spilling monsters into the courtyard.

Adya cringed as the voice of one machine blared in her head, drowning out all others. A roar of engines sounded. A line of race cars melted in the heat of the backwash.

I will fly again. I will command the sky. I will blast all before me.

Adya squeezed her head in her hands as the excavator's fear overwhelmed her. The jet was a weapon, a species of machine built to destroy whatever was in its path. It longed to fire missiles and watch them explode.

She couldn't let it fall into the maharaja's hands. Adya gave a command, and the excavator swung around.

You cannot ever stop—

The jet's thoughts cut out as the excavator dropped its clawed arm through its steel frame.

The excavator lifted the fighter jet in the air and hurled it into the courtyard. Adya tried to shut out the sound of the scream as it exploded. She jumped out of the excavator's cab. *Thank you, a thousand times.*

The excavator raised its bucket in salute and rumbled off, crashing into the chaos of the courtyard. Adya rested a hand on an old washing machine to steady herself.

"Now we get out of here," she said.

The prisoners peered through the hole in the wall. Fires were burning out of control. The excavator was already pounding on the first gates, ripping stone to pieces. British monsters were fighting the maharaja's troops to a standstill.

"It's a death trap," Dsouza said. Imral looked over Dsouza's shoulder out at the disaster.

Mohan slid next to them. "Imral could help us get through. I mean, draw on the well and conjure like a storm shield or some cool Vayu spell thing."

Imral hadn't taken her eyes off the courtyard. She lowered her gaze. "My father will be out there."

Mohan's gray eyes sparkled. "But I could help you again. We could, like—"

"Enough stupid ideas, kid," Dsouza said. "Listen, brainiac, anyone who makes the mistake of facing our father on his home turf gets ripped to pieces, and it's never pretty. We all get through that madness without drawing his attention, or we die."

Adya gave Mohan a look that said, *Let it go.* "We'll try your ideas later. Right now, we only need one more thing."

She ran through the jumble of machinery and found what she was looking for. The bike was put back together, polished and ready to fly. Adya laid her hands on the handlebars, and the Yamaha roared to life.

Dsouza drew his sword. "At least we'll get to fight before we get ourselves killed."

Adya was not looking forward to heroics. "No dying yet, Bad Day, and no fighting. We just run."

She launched the motorcycle through the hole in the wall, and the prisoners surged around her. The roar of the bike and its blazing headlight were a comfort in the chaos.

The courtyard was a hell of flames and clouds of exploding dust. Ten yards in front of them, the giant swung its shield through a line of archers, sending them tumbling. It straightened to its full height and brought the shield over its head like a club. Then it lit up like a torch as a bolt of flame struck its back, setting it ablaze. The giant's scream was a low-pitched roar that vibrated up the base of Adya's spine. The monster fell forward into a formation of soldiers and continued burning.

Above them floated the maharaja of Mysore, white-and-gold

261

robes swirling, as he blasted the monsters with fire. Gone was the thoughtful ruler who reminded Adya of her father. This was a vengeful sorcerer intent on destruction.

He turned toward them and pointed, his face a mask of bitterness, just as a dragon enveloped him in its grasp. They spun off, crashing into a bridge. It was the one piece of luck they needed.

"Now!" Adya shouted. Between them and the next gate lay a hundred yards of disaster. She sped off, swerving around the giant's burning body, and the Hundred Finest ran with her, keeping up with the motorcycle amongst the scattered masonry. The giant reached out a flaming hand as Adya passed, almost catching her as it rolled in agony.

Ahead, the excavator crashed through the second gate. Soldiers fled before it. The machine rolled on to the last gate and brought its clawed arm down upon the steel bars. The courtyard beyond it was blessedly empty of guards. Only the infinity well lay between them and freedom.

But before they could make their escape, a monster stepped out of the shadows. Its lower half was that of a giant red scorpion, bigger than any insect had a right to be, while its torso was the body of a crazed man swinging a sword in each hand. The man's long mustache was covered in spittle, his face contorted in pain and rage.

Adya froze as the scorpion-man clacked his giant pincers and opened his mouth in a silent scream. Her hand tangled in the pink scarf around her neck. She recognized that face.

Lalbag's eyes were haunted by some terrible ghost. The gentle father had paid a terrible price for his kindness.

CHAPTER TWENTY-SIX

L ALBAG RAISED HIS SEGMENTED TAIL, REVEALING A STINGER dripping with venom. He banged his swords together and waited, blocking their way.

"That's not him anymore, Adya." Dsouza was at her side. "The maharaja's turned him into an ajakava. Lalbag is gone."

"Because of me. I should never have—"

"The maharaja did this." Dsouza's eyes were as hard as obsidian. "He did this to my friend."

Adya grabbed the ornamental weapon, wishing with all her heart she still had her mother's spear. "I hope you don't take after your father."

Dsouza's smile was grim. "Absolutely not. I hate bugs."

"How do we get past?" she asked. They were going to die here if they waited any longer.

Dsouza twirled his sword. "We do the hardest thing of all. What he would want with all his heart. We send Lalbag home." Before Adya could move, Dsouza vaulted over the bike and charged.

"Look this way, old friend!" Dsouza's sword swept out three times before Lalbag could respond, cutting into the carapace. The blade flashed like moonlight on water.

Lalbag hissed as Dsouza matched the monster's two swords

with his one while dodging stabs of the venomous tail. The sound of metal upon metal filled the air like a smithy, but Dsouza never stopped. He struck like vengeance.

Then Lalbag found his footing. He began hammering his blades upon Dsouza like he intended to drive him into the earth. Chitinous claws shot out, and Dsouza had to give ground to avoid being snapped in half. Dsouza rolled as a sword thrust almost took his head off. He ducked and stumbled back toward the infinity well in a desperate bid to stay alive.

Adya knew she had to take advantage of the opening, understood Dsouza was sacrificing himself to create that path. But she couldn't take her eyes away. She waved the others ahead and waited to see if she could make a difference.

Dsouza backed to the edge of the Flame of the South, black and endless. There was nowhere left to run. His blade slid between Lalbag's as he danced on the edge of the pool. With a twist of his wrist, Dsouza sent one of the swords bearing down on him spiraling into darkness.

But his triumph was short lived. Adya's heart dropped as Lalbag surged forward and slammed Dsouza with his armored body, flipping him into the air. Dsouza's back hit the ring of stone. Lalbag seized him and heaved him up over the well as tendrils of dark ink rose up to draw him in. His hand was just a breath from the surface.

Dsouza thrust his sword straight through Lalbag's shoulder. "Now!" he called out.

Adya revved the bike's engine and shot forward. The motorcycle struck Lalbag as Adya reached out to grab Dsouza, catching his sleeve in one hand. The bike skidded and spun, using every bit of magic it had to stay upright and cocoon them both in its protective shell as Dsouza's body swung out over the lip of the well, but it was not enough. Dsouza's hand broke the surface of the well, and he screamed.

Lalbag spun with the impact, twisting and flailing at the well's brink. Before he could recover, the blackness wrapped itself around his tail and dragged him toward nothingness. His last scream tore into Adya's soul.

And then the bike raced away.

Dsouza clung to her like a drowning man pulled out of the ocean. "You were late."

"You looked really good," she said. "I got distracted."

"I must look great getting killed." Dsouza coughed, then pointed. "Damn, they're all useless without you."

The escaped prisoners were huddled with Mohan and Imral twenty yards in front of the third gate, not moving. The excavator had already torn open a hole they should have been running through. Adya sped to them.

Mohan pulled at his hair. "They're afraid of the machine. They say it will only listen to you."

Imral was screaming at the Hundred. "I command you, through that gate, now!"

Absolutely none of them moved.

Adya swung off the motorcycle and grabbed the spear. "Mohan, take the bike with the royalty. I'll get them through."

She herded the prisoners toward the gate while Mohan sped on ahead with Dsouza and Imral. Soldiers who might have tried to stop them were instead fleeing amidst the chaos. The excavator raised its bucket high and smashed it down once more upon what was left of the iron barrier. The first of the Hundred reached the opening, and Adya screamed them through. They were past her in seconds.

Before she could follow, the world flashed white, and a fork of magical energy struck the excavator. Adya held her breath as the smell of rust and ozone filled the air, and the great machine shook. An image filled Adya's mind of a young boy, too big for his yellow overalls, screaming as his clothes caught fire.

High above the central courtyard, the maharaja of Mysore rose into the sky and raised his hands. His clothes were not even wrinkled. He fired another blast of magical flame at the machine, melting its side and sending it smashing into the gate, sealing off Adya's escape. Its anguish brought her to her knees.

I am alone. Don't leave me alone. The machine's plea drowned out the sounds of battle and drove away her fear.

"I'm here," Adya called, and stretched out her hand. The excavator lowered its arm and scooped her off the ground, cradling her in its clawed bucket. She hugged the yellow steel tight. "You are not alone," she said.

Its hydraulic gears shifted, and the arm rotated, lifting her up to the outer gate's wall. *We will dig together again.*

Adya stepped out of the steel bucket onto the high wall, but before she could flee, a voice called out—and Adya knew it was too late.

"You failed me, technomancer." The maharaja hovered above her like an angel of death. His eyes were black-rimmed pools that reflected the fires around him. "I offered you every-thing—the greatest of treasures, a machine that could rule the sky. And what did you do? You killed it."

"You would have destroyed everyone with it," Adya yelled. She remembered Lalbag's haunted face, and she burned with anger. "Everything you told me was a lie." Adya slid back until she reached the edge of the wall. There was nowhere left to go.

"Those missiles would have saved Mysore," the maharaja said. "You could have saved us all. If only you had the imagina-tion, you wouldn't have to die."

"Imagine this." Adya threw the spear, straight as a moon-beam, with all her fury and with all the strength of her steel arm.

The maharaja waved a hand, and it stopped in midflight. "That is the best you can do? You could have awoken fleets of tanks. Instead, you limit yourself." He picked the spear out of the air and tossed it high over the wall.

The maharaja raised his fists as the winds picked up around him. "You accuse me of lies? General Clive is no lie. The British will sweep the Devas away soon. Your sister will die on the front lines. Only those who fight alongside me will survive. You are blind to the truth, and those who deny truth have no right to live."

He shouted, *"Brahmacharya!"*

Streams of darkness shot from the edges of the infinity well, arcing high overhead and coursing down upon the maharaja. He spread his fingers. His hands filled with silver light.

"You are a queen of nothing. A princess of rust and gears." The maharaja pointed a finger. "See what you will become." He launched a bolt of flame directly at her.

Adya held up her arm to shield her eyes. The blast struck steel and deflected around her, blanketing her in blue flame. Her muscles spasmed, and her vision went white as heat seared through her body, separating her into pieces. She was being pulled apart; her soul was being torn out of her.

The maharaja turned his hand, and something started to rip inside her. "I tried to show you another way," he said. "Tried to show you we cannot survive alone."

Black wings flashed and darted for the maharaja. A sharp beak struck him, and he flinched. He slapped the bird away as it dove again, and the drongo disappeared.

But it was all the time Adya needed. Something sparked in her arm, and the magic that was tearing her apart lost its grip. She stepped back into empty space and felt herself falling. Energy flared bright around the maharaja as the claw of the excavator struck him and he tumbled from the sky.

Adya fell straight through a merchant's stall and hit the ground, the air dashed out of her lungs as pain seared through her side. She lay, covered in canvas, fighting to breathe, until a host of hands unwrapped her and pulled her to her feet.

"General," Gudugu said. "You can't hide in a tent, sir. It won't work."

Adya's vision was clouded, her arm an agony of molten metal. She took a deep breath. "I'm no sir," she said. "Come on."

They fled through the city while the sound of explosions and roar of monsters raged. Through the alleyways of the maze they fled, winding their way through the streets without pause. They emerged from the slums on the outskirts of Mysore and ran for the only possible concealment, the great forest on its western edge. Behind them, flames lit the night as the palace bells tolled the hour. The gates would heal, the towers and walls would be as they once were. And the maharaja would pursue them.

A crack of thunder signaled the start of a monsoon downpour. They ran on through the storm and disappeared amongst the ancient trees, the ghosts, and the night.

CHAPTER TWENTY-SEVEN

W HOA, YOUR ARM!" MOHAN LED THEM THROUGH the forest, pushing the motorcycle over tree roots as Adya stumbled behind.

"It's nothing," Adya lied through clenched teeth. Her metal arm felt as if it were being clamped inside the depths of a forge and bathed in the hottest part of the fire. The steel had bubbled into a white mess streaked with red drops. She fought not to moan as the sudden monsoon rain pounded them. "It hardly hurts."

Mohan shot her a look. "If that were true, you would have sworn up a storm and told me to be quiet."

"It's the darkness." Dsouza dragged the back of his hand across his forehead. He leaned on a stick and refused anyone's help. "Your arm is full of shadows." He looked up at the trees that surrounded them. "This place is full of shadows."

Dsouza's usual swagger had vanished. Whatever he'd touched in the infinity well had shaken him. But Adya wondered if he might be right. It felt as if all the violent energy she'd absorbed was centered there and still alive in her arm. She didn't know how much longer she could keep it at bay. She stumbled on as the brush grew ever thicker.

The canopy blocked out the night sky, but Adya still wouldn't let the bike guide them. A headlight would make them too easy to follow, and they were in no shape for another fight tonight. Instead, she held Imral's hand and told her to do the same with the next person in line. Trees stretched spindly limbs across the path, and impenetrable brambles sent them veering through trenches of monsoon water. Only she and Mohan, with their Atavi eyes, could find their way through.

After an hour of everyone tripping over roots, Gudugu appeared at Adya's side. She handed Adya the spear the maharaja had thrown over the wall. "You keep leaving this behind, General. I came to say we can't go on like this. The woods are haunted. They won't let us through alive. The ghosts will take us before morning."

"I felt it the moment we entered," Mohan agreed. "The trees are furious."

The pain in Adya's arm had kept her from listening, but she heard it now. All around them, leaves whispered and hissed. It was like they were preparing for war. If they went stumbling on like this, they'd wander into a den of tigers or off some cliff in the dark.

Adya placed a hand on the smooth bark of a giant shisham and shuddered. The tree was certain they were here to kill it, that they would take its brothers away to harvest and leave its home a wasteland. It wanted to drop branches and crush them. Wanted to bar the path and herd them toward destruction.

She pressed her forehead against the tree and spoke to it, told it who she and Mohan were, told it that none of her people would let harm come to this forest. The tree felt her touch and reached out, wondering. Adya waited. It took time for a tree that had been abandoned to believe—the Atavi had been driven from this forest long ago, and there had been no caretakers for a long time, nothing but ghosts of their ancestors, wandering and alone. But in the end, the tree remembered. The sap quieted, and the anger in its leaves subsided.

Adya pulled away, and the pain in her arm flared. "This forest will let us pass," she said through gritted teeth. "Our ancestors were here once. The trees remember."

Gudugu looked around in the darkness. "It won't be enough, General. The maharaja will send his dogs and soldiers after us. Dogs won't know about the ghosts."

"Great," Adya said. Vicious hounds would make the night just about complete. She leaned on the spear. At least it worked as a walking stick.

Mohan kept his voice low. "I'm not sure how much farther they can go tonight, Adya. They look like they're going to drop soon."

Eslandaran stepped out from the shadows ahead. "If we're to reach Svarga before the British, we cannot stop."

But one look at the escaped prisoners proved Mohan right. Everyone had made it out, but many were injured, and all were exhausted. A group this large could only travel so far without someone ending up in a tiger's stomach. She needed to get them someplace safe.

"Just a little further," Adya said. "Mohan, bring up the rear. Try not to let anyone fall behind."

Her metal arm burned unbearably. Adya thrust the limb into a pool of rain to try to quench the pain. Clouds of steam filled the air, but the fire would not abate. She gave up and kept walking until, without warning, they entered a clearing.

Moonlight reflected off a pair of giant eyes twenty feet off the ground. They blinked, and Adya followed them down to four enormous legs and a set of pale white tusks as long as her body. Adya sensed the elephant's confusion as it woke and raised its trunk to let loose a trumpet that sent leaves and branches showering around them. It did not appreciate strange visitors. There was no way she could hope to calm the creature before it trampled straight through them.

Eslandaran slid in front of them, reaching a hand toward the agitated giant. "We did not mean to wake you, friend."

Adya snatched at the crazy woman, trying to pull her back before the tusks ran her through, but Eslandaran evaded her grasp. The Deva marched straight toward the elephant and started to sing.

Adya strained to hear the song. She forgot her fear, forgot the maharaja's troops, forgot everything as Eslandaran sang of places far away where water tumbled into deep rivers, where she could sink forever and let all care be washed away. The only thing Adya wanted was to listen.

Eslandaran reached up and stroked the elephant's trunk. She sang on, of stones and water and endless night to dream, and the elephant seemed to understand. It bowed its head and let the Deva stroke its ears before wandering off to find another place to rest.

The song faded, and Adya drifted back to reality. Her arms hung at her sides, her entire body limp. She straightened as a cold fear ran through her. Anyone could have attacked them then, and she would have been helpless. She would have to be more careful.

"She's gone off to find another spot," the Deva said. "A marvelous beast, but she's shirked her duties. She was supposed to be guarding this forest temple." Eslandaran started toward the entrance.

The moon shone through a break in the canopy, bathing the clearing in silver light. Hidden beneath a carpet of moss was a temple unlike any Adya had seen. It seemed more a mountain of boulders than a planned structure. Vines wreathed the enormous stones over which trees stretched their roots, each carved with figures dancing to the music of a flute player. A gigantic banyan with a hollow core framed an opening.

Gudugu shuffled toward Adya. "General, the Butcher asks me to tell you that temples here drive people mad. Those who lived here long ago worshipped the gods of the forest. We won't be welcome."

Adya already felt like she was going insane—the temple could hardly make things worse. Still, she hesitated. She had no idea which one of the escaped prisoners called themselves the Butcher, but it couldn't be a good idea to be confined in a tight space with a murderer.

She lowered her voice. "Why do they call them the Butcher?"

Gudugu leaned in and whispered, "She used to sell meat in the market. Please, don't ask her about it. She's a vegetarian now. Hates to think about cutting up all those animals."

Imral examined the temple's entrance and ran her hand along the stone. "I've read accounts of travelers who braved the forest. They speak of ghosts that pray in the temples and keep the gods awake."

Ghosts or not, Adya couldn't take another step without rest. "Mohan and I have lived our entire lives in the jungle. The forest spirits won't bother us. We'll sleep until there's more light."

The inner temple was made from black rock with a recess at the far end. An idol of a stone tiger drinking water sat in front of a basin that collected the rain dripping through fissures in the ceiling.

Mohan collapsed to the floor. Pushing the motorcycle had drained the last of his energy. The prisoners huddled together while Dsouza managed to find a corner to sit in apart from the rest.

"What do we do now?" Mohan whispered. The words echoed against the stone for everyone to hear.

Adya lifted her metal hand before her face, opening and closing the mechanical fingers. "We rest," she said. Her every muscle ached, and her arm burned terribly. The responsibility for a roomful of escaped prisoners weighed on her.

She rested a hand on Gudugu's shoulder. "When the sun rises, you should return to your homes. The maharaja wants me as a slave and surely wants his daughter back. He may not even notice the rest of you are gone." Who knew what crimes they'd committed to end up in the dungeons, but they didn't need to follow her any longer.

This elicited a murmur. Small groups of the former prisoners broke off and came to speak with Gudugu. Adya imagined they were deciding the best way home. After they'd had time to confer, the tall woman returned to Adya's side.

"General, long ago, we were farmers. Some of us were caught for poaching. Others couldn't pay taxes. Our land's been sold off, our families are long gone. We've been given up for dead. Most of us thought we already were. But you led us out. Took us through fire and forest. That means something." Gudugu's hushed voice became a low rumble, echoing in the small chamber.

"It doesn't mean you have to come with us," Adya said. "You don't need to risk your lives."

The woman looked up at the ceiling before speaking. "In the dungeons, we were starved, treated as playthings, or forgotten. Every day was risk with no hope of reward. We never had something to be part of. Mohan told us about your sister, and we can understand that. We all have lost family. We want to help. If we get a chance to fight the maharaja's guards or British soldiers along the way, all the better."

Adya ground her teeth. These Vayu were not her people. What would she do with a hundred bedraggled prisoners?

"They're great people." Mohan piped up. "They've given themselves the most awesome names. Gudugu, tell her."

"Many of us have forgotten what our old names were. We're so used to what we've called ourselves all these years. This is Hernia and Flatface, Usually Sleeping, One-Eye, and Dogear." Gudugu pointed them out in the darkness, continuing through a long list of strange names while Adya tried to think of how she might change their minds and get them to return home.

"You see, General, we'd given up hope. Then they pulled us out and told us we were meant to protect an Atavi princess, and the maharaja was going to give us magic to change us into soldiers. None of us believed at first—you can't trust a guard— but when your brother told us the stories about you fixing dead machines and fighting a yaksha, those felt true. Then you led us out, and we saw it with our own eyes—great machines came to life to help us. The maharaja himself could not stop us. We did not need to see more. This is our chance. Our chance to be more than prisoners. Our chance to be part of the story."

The nonsense had gone on long enough. Farmers weren't soldiers. "Look," Adya explained. "You were supposed to be Mysore's Hundred Finest, my personal guard in my darkest hour. But that was all illusion." She was just a girl from the jungle, and they were a bunch of half-starved prisoners. They had to see the truth.

"Prophesied to be there in your darkest hour," Gudugu said in a tone full of reverence, and a hush came over the escaped farmers.

Adya gave up. These fools weren't going to listen to anything she said. Years in a dungeon had robbed them of their wits.

A break in the darkness caught her attention. Light had begun to shine from the basin in front of the god's altar. A murmur spread amongst the escaped prisoners at the sight. Adya stood and struck her head against the low ceiling as the silvery glow spread across the room.

"Now *that* is something worth braving ghosts for." Eslandaran bent her head and approached the basin. She thrust her hands into the glowing water and began a soft chant.

Adya came to her side. "What is it?"

"We've caught the attention of the temple's guardians." Eslandaran splashed the water over her face. The grime fell away, leaving brown skin and a radiant smile. "This was a temple to a forest god whose name I do not know. There are ghosts here, of all the souls who came to pray to him."

Adya's stomach sank. The glowing water reflected off the tiger idol, whose image had worn smooth over the centuries.

"Gods never listen," she said. "When there's a real problem, they stay silent." She remembered how much she'd prayed when her parents had died, how many times she'd asked for Priya to return. In life, you always had to work to make your own magic.

"This god seems to be listening at the moment," Eslandaran said. "Perhaps we have provided him with some entertainment. The least you can do is ask him for guidance. Maybe you'll get an idea of your best path—or what to do with those prisoners."

Adya examined her aching arm, the paint blistered and blasted. She expected no help from gods, but the water was inviting. She plunged her hand into it. The relief was immediate. Steam shot up from the basin and spread over the low ceiling. For a moment, Eslandaran was hidden from view amongst the white clouds. Then Adya took a deep breath and snatched her hand away, and the room came back into view.

She spread her steel fingers and examined her arm. The colors had deepened, swirling into new patterns of scarlet and white, intertwined with a black vine. The searing pain was gone.

Eslandaran put a hand on her shoulder to steady her. "Was the heat you suffered so great as that?"

Adya leaned against the Deva. "It almost destroyed me."

The light lasted a moment longer, then the room began to fade back into darkness.

With the pain gone, Adya felt like she could finally think clearly. The prisoners were Vayu, not her people. Taking responsibility for them made no sense. They might believe in a stupid illusion about helping her in her darkest hour, but that was a dream she couldn't afford to be fooled by. To survive in this world, you had to take care of yourself and your family; everyone else had to take care of themselves.

She looked into the basin and examined her reflection as the light disappeared. Her face had grown harder, more serious than she remembered. Priya would have told her to smile and punched her in the arm. Her expression reminded her of the maharaja's, a face ready for battle. He would certainly leave the prisoners behind, pay any price to achieve his goal. Then she remembered Gudugu lifting her from the ground after the maharaja had almost killed her. Remembered when Dsouza had told the prisoners they could escape with them, and she had hesitated. Her head said it made no sense, but another part of her said things had to change. *She* had to change.

"I'm going to give them the chance they want. They'll come with us. It may all be a foolish dream, but we'll go on together." It was a gamble worth taking.

• • •

Adya woke to light streaming over the floor through cracks in the stone ceiling. She looked over the ragtag bunch she'd taken charge of. Across from her, Imral slept with her head on Mohan's shoulder. The Hundred Finest lay snoring. Even Eslandaran was curled in a coat she'd found, fast asleep. Priya would have been proud of her—Atavi, Vayu, and Deva. It was all their father had dreamed of.

Adya picked her way out of the temple. The forest was wet and quiet, with no sign of the elephant from the night before.

Dsouza was already standing there, leaning against a boulder. The set of his shoulders and the lack of a sarcastic smile made him look like someone else altogether. His eyes were darker, his expression more serious. He'd lost his sword in the battle with Lalbag and didn't even have a weapon.

"Those prisoners believe they're prophesied to be here?" he said. "They're even dumber than they look."

Adya slid to the ground, leaning her back against the temple. "They've been in your father's dungeon for ages," she said. "Maybe they don't know what to believe any longer."

Dsouza kicked a fallen log. "That nonsense is going to get them killed. Farmers aren't soldiers."

"None of us are soldiers," Adya said. "We're fighting to stay alive just like they are. They've nowhere else to go."

Dsouza clenched his fist. "So what, we arrive in Svarga Lok with a bunch of escaped prisoners in tow, running like mad from my father? Not the way I envisioned finally meeting my mother's people."

"Really?" Adya said. "This is completely how I had it planned."

She ticked off on her fingers. "Losing my sister, getting my arm chewed off, having a bunch of farmers following me as I run for my life." She sighed. "How do I keep them safe?"

Dsouza unstrapped the empty sheath on his belt and let it fall. "There's no safe anymore. Every option is full of death, but maybe the fools are right."

"What about?"

"At least you won't give up on them. You don't give up on anyone. That means something." Dsouza looked off into the forest. "What I saw when I was hanging over the infinity well . . . I felt it start to pull me apart. I was going to be dismantled for whatever my spirit was worth, and it wasn't worth much. It showed me my future. I saw my face, how hard it would become, and I realized it was the face of my father."

Adya touched the back of Dsouza's hand. "It doesn't have to be like that."

"What do I become if not the sharpest edge possible? I've spent this life trying to be Night Blade, but no person should batter themselves into a weapon. What is my other choice?"

"I always thought Night Blade was dumb." Adya shrugged. "What should you become? I don't know. How about Jagan Dsouza, half this, half that, with a sprinkle of crazy and a large dash of brooding?"

Dsouza laughed. "That doesn't sound so bad if I get the chance to—"

But whatever Dsouza had been about to tell her was cut short as someone emerged from the temple.

"Hey, are they coming after us, or can we rest a little longer?"

Mohan stretched his arms over his head and yawned. Eslanda-ran stepped out behind him. She looked fresh and rested.

"You should have kept sleeping," Adya said, then froze, lis-tening. The sound was almost too faint to hear, but it was real. Far off, a dog howled.

CHAPTER TWENTY-EIGHT

MOHAN RAN INSIDE, SHOUTING EVERYONE AWAKE.

Eslandaran stared off in the direction of the howling. "In less than two days we can be through the forest and outside Svarga Lok."

Dsouza reached to his side for a sword that wasn't there. "We don't have two days."

The baying behind them was tremendous motivation. Eslandaran took the lead. The Deva was singing under her breath, letting her magic guide them through the wood. With the metal arm no longer burning, Adya was noticing all sorts of things she hadn't before.

Imral clasped her hands together. "There's a spell for this sort of thing, I'm sure, only I've never tried it, and . . ."

"What sort of spell?" Adya didn't trust Imral's magic, but they couldn't outrun dogs.

"The form never seemed too difficult, and hounds should be easier to confuse than trackers, but I don't know. . . ."

Mohan stopped pushing the bike. "I'm never convinced I can do the tough things, but Adya makes sure I never give up."

"*I* make sure?" What was Mohan talking about?

"You yell at me until things get done."

Adya frowned at him before turning to Imral. "You've stopped us now. Might as well have a go." The dogs would catch up with them within the hour either way. It would give Adya time to organize their defenses, at least.

Imral traced a pattern of interlinked circles into the forest floor with a short stick, adding a few connecting lines at the last moment. Then she mumbled a Sanskrit incantation and drew a final circle in the center of the pattern.

As Imral finished, dirt spun up from the ground in tiny whirlwinds. Soft chimes sounded, and the air filled with the smell of jasmine and roses. But it didn't last. Within a few seconds they slowed, and the dirt showered to the ground.

The barking sounded frantic, closer.

"Was that supposed to lead them to us?"

Imral looked defeated, but only for a moment. "It's supposed to send sound all over the forest so the trackers won't know which direction we've gone. I'll try again. My father is not going to find us. Mohan?"

Mohan grabbed the motorcycle and pushed it over the ruined spell pattern.

Adya shook her head. "Mohan, there's no time to mess about." She hefted the ornamental spear, wishing again for her mother's weapon. The black line twisting down her steel arm was not the same as smooth wood in her hand or the belief it had brought that her mother was still there, watching over them.

Mohan gave her a look that would have melted the heart of a statue. "One more time, come on. We won't need to pull much power this time. She can do this."

"I can," Imral said. "Watch."

Their mother would have hated this. Would have demanded

she talk sense into her brother. He and Imral were inviting danger by mixing magic, but they were already far past safety. Maybe it was time to have faith. Their father would have approved.

"Fine," Adya said. "But don't screw up my other arm."

Mohan grimaced. "Worst we'll do is make you smell like flowers. Imral, come on."

Imral nodded and began her incantation. This time the words came out clear and sure. When the circles of dirt began to spin, Mohan pressed down on the bike's horn. The blare broadcast their location to anyone within miles—and if that wasn't enough, the nauseating smell of grease and spent oil filled the air.

But the spell wasn't finished. It shone bright blue, and the blaring sounded again, from a spot Adya would swear was a hundred meters east, as though there were another bike in that direction. Then a horn beeped farther west. Within minutes, the forest filled with random honking coming from every direction. The hounds' barking grew desperate, then faded away as they chased a false trail into the distance.

"That's Blue Wizard material." Mohan gave Imral a klutzy high five, mostly missing her hand. "More magic like that, and they'll think twice before following us."

Eslandaran shot the princess an appraising look. "I'll be bringing real talent back with me to Svarga Lok. Let's get moving before they find a way to counter your spell."

They camped that night under an enormous banyan. Adya hoped that the forest's tigers would steer wide of such a large party. Eslandaran had sworn they could get through to Svarga

Lok in less than two days. This should be the last night they needed to survive the wood.

Eslandaran insisted they were close. "Tomorrow you will see the seven gates of Svarga Lok and hear the songs of my people."

Part of Adya wished Eslandaran would break out in song again and paint a picture of everything they might see, but she hadn't forgotten the power of the melody. She wasn't sure she would emerge the same person if she heard it again.

The Deva rested her back against a giant aerial root. "Never could any of you imagine the beauty of the Lake in the Sky, where a thousand white sails float above the trees. Our queen will welcome you all as family. The rarest delicacies of the forest will be yours. They will raise their voices to serenade your arrival. Ameer Kian Thamari, our most arrogant of generals, will hail you as heroes."

Adya suspected Eslandaran was half mad. The Deva didn't seem like a liar, but she was obviously not quite sane.

Before they slept, Imral found Adya sitting by the fire, checking over the motorcycle for any damage.

Imral poked a stick deep into the flames. "My father has harnessed the darkest of Vayu magic to serve him." She traced a pattern on the ground with the burning end of the twig. "I knew the war changed him, that the death of my brothers wounded him badly, but I felt sure that no matter how hard he'd become, inside, he was still the same man who'd read me stories when I was little. I hoped he would wake up one day and remember."

Adya tossed a piece of dead wood onto the fire, and sparks

flew up into the night sky. "My sister always believed in the goodness of people, believed anyone could change for the better. I was never so sure." She thought back to the pure greed and malice of Huda, remembered the maharaja's fury when he'd tried to burn her to ashes. "Some people will hurt you as much as they can and not care at all."

Imral looked at her, eyes wide, as if seeing her for the first time. "I thought you might say . . . that somehow, he might change."

At that moment the haunted look on Lalbag's face came back to Adya, and she could find no words of reassurance. She was about to point out that she didn't care if the maharaja ever changed. She would never forgive the man for the horrors he'd done.

The Yamaha's engine rumbled. *This is your crew. She needs you.*

Adya cut short what she was about to say. "Maybe some things are too broken to fix, even if you have all the parts."

Imral tossed her stick into the flames. "I don't have the parts to fix him, and I'm not strong enough to fight him. The magic slips away from me when I need it. I wish I got it right the first time and didn't panic whenever I needed it most."

Adya felt the bike in the back of her head, waiting impatiently, and the machine was right. Imral, who had never had a sister of her own, needed her. Maybe she was wrong. She'd thought of Dsouza as a cutthroat trader who'd never care for anyone, but he'd become something very different. She cleared her throat and tried to think of what Priya would say.

"I failed forty-three times trying to get a rickshaw to come to life. When I finally succeeded, it was by mistake. All you can ever do is keep trying. Even when no one believes in you, when you're covered in sweat and the damn machine is falling apart all around you, you believe in yourself, and you keep trying. There's nothing else we can do." She considered reaching out to Imral now and drawing her in, like an older sister might, but hesitated.

Imral's eyes filled with tears. Then she rushed off into the darkness and was gone.

Adya swore under her breath. Well, she'd screwed that up. Priya would have hugged her close and said that it was a matter of time. That one day, Imral would develop confidence and master Vayu magic. Even Mohan would have known what to say. But that was never what Adya was good at. All she could think was that there was not going to be enough time for a "one day." The maharaja was the one with the power, the one who could kill them all.

The following day, they broke camp and hurried on. Eslandaran's spirits rose steadily as they neared the end of the forest. She reminded them every hour of how their aches and pains would soon be soothed away. Adya gave in and let herself imagine a hot bath and a full stomach. Priya would be waiting for her on a boat, floating on the Lake in the Sky, and their endless running would stop. Things would go back to the way they'd been.

By late afternoon, the trees had thinned. The forest was quiet. Adya suspected the maharaja's hounds had long given up on their trail. Eslandaran declared they were no more than an hour away from their destination.

And then a scream broke the silence.

"What is that?" Mohan asked.

The wail rose to a pitch that paralyzed thought, and Adya clenched her teeth. No ghost could make that sound. It was the cry of the still alive—though not for long. The scream was followed by the clash of metal.

Eslandaran drew her sword. "We're too late." She sprang ahead, disappearing into the distance.

As they followed, the sounds of battle grew louder. Adya had never seen a battlefield. She imagined two armies crashing together in waves, and as the cries ahead became more frantic, she wondered if she should be running away instead of leading her little brother and a hundred clueless farmers toward slaughter.

But Priya. Her sister wouldn't be in a hot bath or boat on a lake. She'd be in the fray, trying to be honorable, dragged into some messed-up conflict that was bigger than any of them. Adya ran faster, outpacing everyone until she caught up to Eslandaran. The two of them broke through the tree line and looked down on the field below.

Verdant mountains towered in the distance, and a wide river snaked between them. Bright green hills spread out from the base of the mountains, and upon the hill closest raged a sea of chaos. A force of Devas had been split into two groups, one fighting on the crest amidst a thin stand of trees, the other stranded at the base. They were being cut to pieces.

Eslandaran pushed Adya back. "Go home. This death is mine, not yours." Without another word, the Deva sprinted forward, singing. Adya lost sight of her as she sank into the tall grass. Moments later, the rest of the group emerged to stare down at the disaster unfolding below them.

Dsouza's dark eyes scanned the battlefield. "At most, they've got half an hour before they're wiped out. They must have run into an ambush. This isn't even the main British force." He raised a hand to shield his eyes. "Damn, they've brought werewolves. Without silver, the Devas won't even last that long. It's a lot harder without silver." Adya sincerely hoped he didn't have any more bad news.

The Hundred Finest were already glancing back the way they'd come. This was not the royal welcome they'd expected. Adya didn't blame them. But she couldn't tear herself away. Somewhere on that hill, Priya could be dug in, fighting for her life.

Whatever happened next, she had to keep Mohan and Imral out of it. She grabbed the motorcycle from her brother. "Keep your bow ready. I'll find Priya. Stay here and cover me. Make sure I don't end up with a metal leg." She squeezed his arm. "Keep Imral with you."

Mohan already had his bow unslung. "Get out of there fast, or I'll come after you."

Adya mounted the bike, only to find Gudugu in her way.

"General, orders?"

She looked them over, a ragtag bunch of farmers with makeshift weapons they'd picked up along the way. They were better suited for tilling a field than the battle ahead. "Head back, all of you. You've followed me long enough."

Gudugu didn't move. "Couldn't we wait a bit for it to calm

down, General? And fight one or two leftover British if you want? Eslandaran was nice, but we don't really know those Devas."

Adya would have said the same thing a few weeks ago. "My sister is in there. I can't run from this."

Gudugu didn't hesitate. "Well then, we'll come with you. We've already been as good as dead once." This was met with nods and mumbles of assent. "Remember that bit about being with you in your darkest hour. This looks bad enough."

Dsouza gave a rueful laugh. "That's an understatement." He spun a dented wreck of a weapon, and flakes of rust showered over him. "I've borrowed an old sword from a farmer named Chili Foot. Doesn't that sound like a perfect way to die?"

She met his dark eyes. Having Dsouza along was strangely reassuring. "You could have borrowed a shovel from Butcher, or a hoe from Usually Sleeping."

"This looks more stylish." Dsouza reached out and held her arm. "You can write it on my grave: 'He got the sword from Chili Foot.'"

Dsouza's grip felt good. She poked him in the chest. "Don't you dare die before you make me dinner."

"You've got that backward." He flashed his half smile. "But it is something to live for." He looked out to the battlefield. "They say the Devas go to war singing, but I never had a chance to learn the right song. If I live long enough to learn, maybe I'll perform it for you."

Adya decided he might have one or two redeemable qualities after all.

A desperate shout caught her attention. Below them, a small

group of Devas had been cornered by a trio of stone-skinned trolls and was being crushed. How could she unleash untrained farmers on these creatures? She was leading them to their deaths, and they still insisted on following her. How had she become responsible for so many people?

"Om krim Kali. Om numaha." She prayed to the goddess for protection.

Adya bent down to the motorcycle and whispered to her friend, "Now we fly."

CHAPTER TWENTY-NINE

THE YAMAHA SPRANG TO LIFE. THE RADIO CLICKED on, and the thud of bhangra music blared. Adya gunned the engine, and the bike rocketed her toward disaster. The British would have no idea what kind of madness was coming their way.

The bike shot down the hill straight at the first group of Devas. Grass rose around Adya, tall and emerald green.

The first creature she encountered was a massive troll, mottled gray like a mountain range. It had a Deva pinned under its boot and was lifting its club over its head to finish the job.

The motorcycle told Adya what to do. She raised the front wheel and aimed straight ahead, leaping off at the last moment. The bike's frame struck the troll's skull like a jackhammer. The troll dropped to its knees and toppled over, neck bent at an unnatural angle while Adya rolled free, spear in hand.

The second troll was still staring at her when Adya hurled the spear, piercing its left breast. The monster screamed, batting at the spear, dropping its club to seize the shaft. With one jerk, it pulled the wood off the ornamental head, and the weapon fell apart. The troll collapsed, blade still stuck fast.

Adya ran to the fallen troll and tried to piece her weapon together. The shaft slid back on, but she couldn't drag it free. She pulled harder, only to dislodge it again. A harsh laugh caught her attention, and she looked up to find herself surrounded by a host of bearded dwarves with sharp axes. Adya held the useless shaft in front of her and spun in a circle, trying to ward off the inevitable. It was a horrible, stupid way to die.

Then the Hundred Finest washed over them.

The first dwarf fell when Butcher hit him with a sharpened shovel. In a moment, Adya stood in the center of a sea of angry farmers. She used the shovel to dig out her spearhead and banged the spear together in time to skewer a werewolf.

Finally, Adya remembered the fallen Deva. She reached under the body of the troll and pulled the woman free. The woman's armor was battered, her hair blood caked, but she stayed standing. Adya handed back her sword and pushed her off. She didn't get a good look at her face, but the Deva started swinging that blade like she knew how to use it, screaming orders and blowing the horn at her belt until others rallied to her side. Adya left her to it. She set the bike upright and headed for the top of the hill. Priya had to be up there.

A small group of Devas huddled together on the crest, surrounded by a press of werewolves led by a hairy giant with a whip in one hand and a chain in the other. The giant werewolf howled while knocking Devas aside with his chain, driving the British on.

"My Finest, to me." Adya raised her spear and prayed it wouldn't fall apart. Then she rolled the throttle, and the Hundred Finest surged forward with her.

The wolves didn't seem to know what to make of the mad farmers. Even without the threat of silver, the werewolves didn't appreciate the pitchforks and hoes. The Finest hacked at whatever presented itself, and their enemies scattered.

Then one wolf leapt high and clamped its jaws on Adya's steel shoulder. She tumbled off the bike into deep mud, and the weight of the machine fell atop her. Her shout came out as a gurgle as blood filled her mouth. Something felt horribly wrong in her chest, and she couldn't get out.

The top of the hill looked hazy, like it was a hundred miles away. Adya strained to push the bike off, but it was no use. She hoped Mohan would get away. Hoped she had not led them all astray. Before her vision went black, the weight pressing her down disappeared, and strong hands pulled her up by the shoulders. Gudugu came into focus, dark eyes peering straight into hers as blood dripped from her nose and her three remaining teeth shone in the sun. Adya felt like she was seeing her clearly for the first time.

"Sorry about this, General." Gudugu's voice was as hushed as ever but perfectly clear. "Hit her, Dogear."

A strong hand smacked Adya's spine, and she spat out a clot. Something cleared in her chest, and she sucked in a deep, rattling breath, feeling her strength returning. Gudugu pressed her spear back into her hand. "In your darkest hour, General."

With the Finest at her side, she charged.

There was no need to fight to reach the center of the battle. The British leapt to meet them. At their head was the giant wolf who drove them on. He swept the ground with his massive chain, and several of the farmers went flying.

Adya ran toward the werewolf and thrust her weapon

straight at his chest, but the damned spearhead went spinning off into the fray. She was left with nothing but a black shaft and had to use it to try to fend off that chain. The whip struck her, and her body spasmed. She dropped to the ground, writhing in pain as the wolf lunged.

Then it let out a terrible scream and collapsed like a felled tree.

One of its legs had been severed clean off. Usually Sleeping stood ten paces away with his scythe, looking immensely proud. Adya breathed a sigh and, for a moment, let herself relax too early.

The wolf seized her around the neck with hairy fingers and opened his jaws. His teeth were bloody daggers. His hot breath hit her face like a foul wind. "Who are you?" he demanded.

Adya thrust her steel hand down his throat. "No one you know."

The wolf bit down, and Adya screamed. She felt every tooth screech down her arm, but metal was not as easy to tear as flesh. The werewolf tried to let go when one of its teeth snapped off, but by then Adya had a grip.

She squeezed.

The werewolf's jaw cracked in her fingers. With a jerk, she pulled out what was left of the monster's tongue, along with half his face. Chili Foot pulled the dead wolf off her.

"A bit harder without silver," Chili Foot commented.

"A bit," Adya agreed. She still had no idea why they called him that.

With their leader dead, the British troops scattered. Adya

shook the blood and teeth off her hand, found the pieces of her spear, and drove them together. Fallen Devas lay everywhere. Others were dazed and wandering.

Adya pulled herself onto the hill, looking for Priya, but there was only death all around her. What was the point of any of this? Why had these soldiers come across continents and seas to fight and die here? A deep ache seized her, and she sank to her knees.

A great horn blew in the distance.

Thundering toward them was a new host of soldiers on horseback, aiming their weapons directly at Adya and her exhausted farmers.

CHAPTER THIRTY

A SEA OF SWORDS SURROUNDED THEM. THEY FROZE, NOT daring to breathe. Adya barely had the strength to lean on her broken spear. She had no idea how many of the Hundred Finest still stood. The leader of the new force leapt down from his horse. His helm was ungodly shiny, decorated with waves. His weapon gleamed with the last rays of the sun. He met Adya's eyes with bright rage. Whoever he was, this man hated the sight of her. She wondered if she would be able to raise her metal arm in time to stop being beheaded.

"Get away from her, you idiot." Someone seized the man's wrist. Adya's vision cleared, and she recognized Eslandaran, covered in blood, struggling to pull the man away. "This girl saved us. They saved us, you fool."

The leader bore down on Adya, dragging Eslandaran behind him. "Have you lost your mind, Es?" He pointed at Adya. "She was amongst the attackers. Our people lie dead around her."

Eslandaran planted herself between them. "Without her, none of us would be alive, and you would be riding into the same ambush the others did."

The man looked no less furious. "Some madness is at play here. Where is your recorder?" He scanned the nearby hills.

A soldier came running, her long hair swinging behind her

in a ponytail. "Here, Ameer Thamari." She was outfitted like the others, but her spotless armor still sparkled in the sun.

"Sahas, what sorcery happened here?"

She bowed. "My lord, better you hear it in full. There are many in sore need of attending to—we should leave at once for Svarga Lok."

"You are wise beyond your years, Sahas Towde. Fine. You have one hour before we assemble in the Kapok Tower. Keep a guard on that girl." Thamari glared at Adya. "Be ready to give your account."

Adya hadn't the strength to fight any further. She just hoped Eslandaran could sort everything out before this lunatic general hurt someone.

"Adya." Her shoulders slumped at the sound of Mohan's voice. He and Imral ran into their midst. Why wasn't her little brother smart enough to stay away?

"Who are these fools?" Thamari demanded.

"I'm her brother, sir." Mohan put a hand on Adya's arm and looked over the Finest, herded together like sheep.

Imral raised her chin. "And I am the princess Imral, heir to the throne of Mysore. I demand you release these people."

Ameer Thamari looked at them, aghast. "Eslandaran, did you return from an insane asylum?"

Eslandaran looked grim. "It's true, Kian. You're going to regret this."

Thamari shook his head in disbelief and addressed Imral. "If you are the honored representative of the maharaja, then you will be most comfortable amongst our prisoners." He gestured to his soldiers. "Do not allow her to cast a spell."

Imral slapped the arm of the first guard who approached her. "Don't you dare." The soldier hesitated.

Thamari pointed to the battlefield. Strewn amongst the dead and captured were a handful of the unmistakable white coats of the maharaja's guard. "Fighting the British is hard, but fighting your father's troops alongside them is impossible." Thamari leaned in close. "Our relationship with Mysore has always been fraught, but only the most poisonous snake would side with the British. I'm eager to learn why you've stabbed us in the back."

Imral looked over at the dead soldiers and said softly, "He has betrayed us completely."

Ameer Thamari turned away from them and took Eslandaran's hands in his. "You've been gone too long—I'm lucky to even be alive to see you. The naga has been sweeping our armies off the face of the earth."

Adya's heart skipped a beat. The naga. Had the maharaja given in to British demands and rebirthed the most terrible of monsters? Could his hatred and mistrust of the Devas be so deep? He must have gone mad with desperation if he thought allying with the British was enough to keep them out of Mysore. Or perhaps he had long ago fallen to this madness and had only hoped to sway her to his side to help protect Mysore against British betrayal.

Before Adya could puzzle over it further, she was herded away with the rest of the prisoners. Mohan, at least, was still at her side. Priya had not even been there.

They staggered onto a forest road. "I can't believe it," Mohan kept saying. "They're all here."

"What do you mean?" Adya asked, but as she gazed over the Finest, she understood. They were bleeding and worn, but not one of the farmers had fallen. It was impossible. Like the Hundred Finest of the stories, they had all survived.

"And Dsouza?" Adya realized she hadn't seen him since they'd separated. Dread flooded her stomach.

Mohan had spotted a tangle of bodies that had been laid out—British and Vayu soldiers alike. They'd piled Imral's brother with the rest. Dsouza lay half under a troll, his eyes open, staring at the sky.

The hurt hit Adya like a landslide. She grabbed Mohan to keep steady. Somewhere behind her, Imral cried out. The princess ran toward Dsouza's body, until a soldier knocked her down. Adya kicked that soldier and was rewarded with a blow to the legs that sent her sprawling. Imral crawled on, inching toward the corpse on her stomach, but two guards seized her and pulled her back.

Imral pounded the ground and screamed an endless scream. The air rippled with magic.

Pressure built in Adya's bones, in her skin, in her eyes. Imral's magic seized them, lifting them up from the ground—Adya, the soldiers, and corpses alike. They hovered, immobile, as the spell ran through everyone. Nothing could resist the princess's power.

"I told you to bind her," Thamari yelled. The general pushed off one of his soldiers and floated down to Imral. He wrapped an arm around her, pinning her arms to her sides, and slapped a hand over her mouth. The spell shattered, and bodies plummeted to the ground.

Adya choked down a sob. Bad Day should never have returned to his ancestral home. She'd needed him alive. He'd promised to sing to her. She needed Priya alive, needed her parents alive too. Why did everything always end the same way?

Thamari grimaced at Dsouza's fallen body. "Years of watching the half blood from afar, hoping he would amount to something, hoping he would unite us, and now this." He turned away. "Bring them," Thamari commanded. "Sahas had better have a good explanation for this."

CHAPTER THIRTY-ONE

S O MUCH FOR A ROYAL WELCOME," ADYA MUTTERED, marching in a daze at the rear of the prisoners. The taste of blood was still in her mouth. Her every muscle ached, but physical exhaustion was the least of it. The regret that had replaced her anger weighed her down like lead around her neck.

Priya would have understood the hard knot in her stomach. Would have helped her understand what she was feeling. Instead, she was nowhere, and Dsouza was gone. What had it all been for? Adya focused on putting one foot before the other.

Eslandaran walked beside her. "I am deeply sorry about Dsouza. I had hoped he would have a better homecoming than this."

The emptiness was worse than the physical pain. She'd never even had the chance to tell Dsouza how she felt. Never had a moment to spend with him that wasn't running or fighting.

"Thamari is the most conceited ass I've ever known." Eslandaran's chatter was at least distracting. "He hasn't changed since we were children. Hidden underneath the pompous-ass bluster is a bigger, more pompous ass."

"He wanted to kill us," Adya said.

"He'd die for you just as quickly. He'll listen once the recorder has a chance to recount what she's seen." Eslandaran slung Adya's arm over her shoulder. "And I will be your guide into Svarga Lok. No one dies for nothing. If your sister ever set foot here, we'll find her."

Eslandaran stuck by her, talking the whole way, as they marched into the foothills of the mountains. Tall grasses gave way to giant sepal trees as they climbed, broad leaves blocking out the sun. The rocky path continued, past a temple to Krishna built into the mountain, but still, there was no city to be seen.

Then the singing began.

Ameer Thamari led with a rumbling baritone. The woman Adya had pulled from underneath the troll joined him, their voices melding together.

The hair stood on Adya's forearm as a chorus of soldiers joined in. Finally, Eslandaran raised her voice. Her singing was a sea beyond the others. It was a voice that transported you. As she sang, black spots shimmered in the air, and through them fluttered butterflies of every color.

Sparks flashed along the length of the sepals and across the abandoned temple, where copper spikes had been driven into bark and rock. As the air wavered before them, a path appeared, leading to a low stone gate. The singers dropped off one by one, until only Thamari could be heard. His baritone softened and grew still as the sparks faded.

"The temple marks the entrance to Svarga Lok." Eslandaran stepped in front of the line. She gave a nod to Adya but addressed the British as well. "We've reached the first of the seven hidden gates, a place few outsiders have ever beheld. You enter bound and beaten. May you leave healed, as our true friends."

Adya imagined Thamari would say something to contradict Eslandaran's welcome, but the general remained silent. A prisoner likely left Svarga Lok as a friend, or never left at all. They certainly couldn't be allowed back once they knew the location of the hidden city and had seen the sparse defenses. The stone gate before them looked almost useless. The wall around it was low enough to see over. Any invading force could be past it with ladders or even a stool.

The lone gate guard stood to attention, dipping her head in salute before looking them over with rapidly spreading shock. "We had no word of this. How was there no call for help?"

Ameer Thamari dismounted, and the gate guard offered a much deeper bow on seeing him. "I intercepted the recorders before they reached home. We have many wounded," Thamari said.

"Inside, all of you. I'll send word ahead to the healers." The guard waved them through.

"And sing the gate to defense," Thamari ordered.

The guard looked at Ameer Thamari, disbelief clear on her face.

"Our location has been compromised. We sleep in peace no longer. Sing the stone alive. On my command." Ameer Thamari left his horse and walked through the low archway, half carrying an injured soldier.

The guard rang an iron bell. The doleful tolling quickened in Adya an overwhelming sensation of loss. Hurts she had long suppressed flooded back as she walked beneath the arch.

Finding her mother's spear in the wreckage . . .

Losing her Priya and being alone again . . .

And now Dsouza.

The guard sang of despair and warning, of pain and danger. All the Devas took up the lament as they passed under the gate. With their song, the wall stretched high, spreading in a protective arc as far as Adya could see, molding itself into battlements with space for archers to fire and flights of stairs for defending soldiers to reach its heights.

By the time the melody faded, the transformation was complete. The small gate had grown into a towering barrier, bristling with defenses that would give any army pause.

"I have never heard that tune." Eslandaran looked back on the formidable wall. "I had hoped never to hear it."

They passed through to a city as unlike Mysore as Mysore was to the Atavi jungle. Svarga Lok was a stone garden planted on a black mountain. Basalt outcroppings sprouted from the ground like giant teeth, and within the stones the Devas had carved their dwellings. Giant kapok trees towered over everything with their umbrella-shaped crowns and pink and yellow flowers. Curious faces looked down on them from homes high in the branches, built into the living wood.

Eslandaran treated their entry like the beginning of an honored tour instead of a prison transport. "Svarga Lok was created when a great yaksha serpent fought with the giant eagle Garuda. The serpent crashed to the ground in a fiery death— we live here on his spine. There are his teeth, which still bite at the sky." She gestured to the black stones. "Kapoks erupted from his hair, and his endless tears filled the most glorious jewel of Svarga." Eslandaran pointed. Adya blinked at the impossible sight, shimmering upon the peak like a sapphire. She beheld the Lake in the Sky.

Perfectly blue, the lake hung like a disk just below the pinnacle. Even from a distance Adya could make out the white sails of boats sliding across its surface. The water was like an immense mirror, wearing a crown of clouds. It stole her breath away.

Eslandaran pointed to a structure perched on the edge of the cliffs, made of a series of four white castles with red roofs interconnected by bridges and surrounded by massive cedars. "And that is the fortress of Svarga Lok, home of our queen. We have many gates to pass before we reach its doors."

They wound their way up through five more gates, each stranger than the last. The second was made of silk, where a red curtain brushed Adya's neck as she crossed. The third was a gate of paper that rustled like the pages of endless books. Adya couldn't imagine how these would stop an invading force, but she no longer doubted the magic of the Devas. A lone flutist played at the entrance of the fourth as they passed. "The gate of sound," Eslandaran explained. The fifth was the most haunting. Its guard was so ancient that she didn't bother to stand and merely tapped her cane and nodded when Ameer Thamari approached. The gate she protected was a simple hoop of worn iron, rusted nearly to oblivion. Looking at it gave Adya the sensation that ghosts were watching, waiting for her to come near.

"The gate of the future," Eslandaran said. The path beyond

it widened out to a flat area of the mountain where a host of Devas awaited.

Healers hurried to the wounded and rushed them away to be tended. Those who didn't live in the teeth of the serpent or high amongst the trees lived in low white homes with red-shingled roofs that reminded Adya of the red-cone huts back home. The prisoners were left with a small guard.

To Adya's surprise, a tall white man stood with the healers. Once the injured were seen to, he came to Ameer Thamari and bowed.

Thamari acknowledged the man with a nod. "Josiah, I have prisoners for you."

The foreign soldier was all bones and angles, and his every move spoke of danger—but his warm smile told a different story.

"No rest for an old British soldier, Ameer? Not even the wickedest and laziest of us?"

Thamari took the man's hand. "None of us can rest today, wolf, but it's good to see you've come to terms with your faults."

"The humble cannot forever be blind to their many strengths. But wait, there is something here I have been entrusted with." The man pulled something bright blue from the pack he carried and flourished it over his head. It was a ragged coat consisting of countless pockets sewn together to form a garment that looked as if the sky itself had been wrung dry to dye it. The fabric waved and fluttered with a life of its own. "I believe our greatest musician has returned. She may have need of her costume."

Eslandaran sprang forward and snatched the blue coat from Josiah's hands. "I asked you to keep it safe, not wave it about like a flag to attract women with."

"Blimey, is that what it was for? I've completely missed my opportunity."

The two of them embraced, and Josiah placed the coat on Eslandaran's shoulders. The once bedraggled prisoner of the Mysore dungeons had transformed into the bard she was.

"All I need now is a proper sword, and I'll be ready to rap Thamari's skull."

"I look forward to your trying." Thamari remained expressionless. "Josiah, I leave you with yours."

Josiah stood before the prisoners. "You lot know who I am: former captain of Her Majesty's Royal Guard and now the most wanted turncoat on the subcontinent. Contrary to rumors you might have heard, I'm not dead, or skinned. My soul hasn't been torn from my body to be fed to vulture gods. On the contrary." He patted his nonexistent stomach. "I'm tolerably well fed, though there's no Sunday roast, and the spices here are strong enough to kill off your beneficial gut bacteria. But at the very least no one is telling you to go die in a foreign land.

"Mind your manners. Try the cuisine. You may find you like bathing in the Lake in the Sky more than being a grunt and taking orders to fight people you'd rather leave in peace. But I'll let you puzzle that out for yourselves." Here he paused to sniff the air. "Mostly dwarves, elves. And of course there are a few wolves, too injured to have run off, that's plain to smell. Don't you wankers waste time scratching your hides as to who's in charge here. I'm alpha. If you question that, come try me." He gestured to the Deva soldiers. "Untie them, if you will. I'll take them from here."

"Quite the speech, Captain Wolf." Eslandaran gave a half bow.

Josiah grinned. "They've got to know that they have opportunities." He gave Eslandaran a wink, then led the prisoners away.

"Whoa." Mohan spoke for the first time since passing the stone gate.

Eslandaran ruffled Mohan's hair, then started forward. "Those soldiers believe we're all demons," she said. "They've been told that Devas will skin them alive and eat their souls. That we intend to invade jolly old England and take their queen's crown for our own. But once they get a good hot bath, they aren't so bad."

"But aren't they super dangerous?" Mohan still seemed unsure. "Who was that man?"

"Josiah is a werewolf, of course. He boasts he kissed the hand of the faerie queen herself. When we captured him and refused to take his pelt, he questioned what he'd been told. He's become one of our greatest defenders. He knows how the British fight, and he trains new prisoners who'd rather join us than fight for their queen."

Adya looked over the captured British prisoners as they followed Josiah. They were bloodied and exhausted. Fear was etched into their faces. What lies had they been told before they were dragged here to fight on foreign shores? They were probably poor souls who wanted more than anything to just return home to their families, like everyone else.

"What if they don't want to join you?" Adya gestured to the castle up ahead. "And they've already seen your hidden city?"

Eslandaran squeezed Adya's hand. "Do you think we have a prison to torture them in? Or perhaps we drop them off the edge of the mountain?"

Adya shrugged, remembering the maharaja's prison below the palace and Huda's cells. "It seems everyone has a dungeon."

Eslandaran locked eyes with her. "You freed me from the maharaja's pit. Whatever bad happens to you, happens to me, I swear it. But the British who want to leave us are a different story. They find themselves without their weapons, pleasantly forgetful in the middle of a forest, not many days' walk from a British outpost. We sing their memories away. Svarga Lok's location stays secret."

Adya remembered Eslandaran's song in the ghost wood. *Beware the songs of the Devas* was sound advice.

She craned her neck to look up at the last gate before the palace. "What do you call this?" It was a conglomeration of massive stone blocks and tree-size pieces of old machinery. The fuselage of an ancient 747 centered one side of the arch, while a rusted yellow crane formed the base of the other, its long arm stretching out to join the fuselage. They were smashed together with mud thick enough to hide the edges where steel ended and stone began.

"This is the gate of the past," Eslandaran said. "Thamari and I used to climb all over it when we were children, even inside the airplane. We called it the Mish-Mosh Gate, and everyone else stole our nickname. The parts were heaved up here centuries ago by giants we'd befriended. They had no sense of symmetry, but enough magic to know what would withstand time."

The Mish-Mosh Gate. Adya couldn't believe it. "There are dead people in that plane," Adya said. Through one of the 747's windows, the sun glinted off eyeglasses on a skeleton, still clutching a phone in its hand.

"Thamari and I discovered them long ago. He loved to pretend he could fly the machine, and I played the doomed flight attendant. We imagined that skeleton was trying to call their family before magic overcame technology and they crashed."

Adya followed Eslandaran through the Mish-Mosh Gate, past the Kapok Tower, a giant tree shooting up within the ruins of a concrete building, and on through the red doors of the palace. A fresh cadre of guards appeared to lead them. Ameer Thamari handed his sword over to one.

"We had word of the battle, Ameer." The soldier bowed to Thamari. "The queen awaits you in the Pale Hall."

Thamari turned to Adya for the first time since they'd met. "You will face Her Majesty now, girl. You cannot hide forever. The queen will know the truth."

"Then maybe she'll be smarter than you are," Adya said.

Thamari glared at her before spinning away.

Adya, along with Mohan, Imral, and the Hundred Finest, were herded into an immense chamber, where they were placed dead center, for all to see, with armed guards surrounding them. Copper spikes protruded from every wall. A tremendous amount of magical energy could be focused here to do to them whatever the Devas wanted.

A gray-haired woman wearing a long green sari sat on a low stool. A silver circlet rested on her head. Behind her were seated a cluster of elders. By her side stood the recorder, Sahas Towde.

"My rani, council members, we have returned," proclaimed Ameer Thamari, "but we left far too many behind."

The old woman bowed her head. "May they return to us in the next life." She looked up again and stood. "But amongst the sadness, our greatest singer returns."

Eslandaran stepped forward, and the queen took her in her arms. They exchanged hushed words Adya couldn't make out before the queen turned away, her brow creased with worry.

"Eslandaran brings hard news. We will soon face the full force of the British army—and the maharaja's troops as well."

The room erupted in shouts and groans before the queen silenced them with a sharp wave of her arm.

"We have much to learn and much to discuss. The maharaja gambles in the most dangerous of games to keep his power. Our lives are in play. But before we make any decision, we must listen." She nodded to the recorder. "Sahas, tell the members of my council what happened today, so we may all judge for ourselves."

CHAPTER THIRTY-TWO

I AM SAHAS TOWDE, RECORDER TO THE QUEEN IN MY TWELFTH
year of service. We recorders remain apart, for the shades of
truth are many.

"On sunrise of this day, word was brought that a small
British force approached the border of Svarga Lok. Never before
had the British ventured so close to our gates. It was thought to
be nothing more than an initial thrust into our lands to test our
strength. The queen sent forth a regiment of the home guard to
meet them, more than enough of our best troops to deal with
such a force. We thought Ameer Thamari far afield and had no
hope of his counsel or aid.

"Under command of Captain Mardir we marched to the
low hills. Archers were set in place, and the regiment was hidden to all but the keenest eye.

"The British appeared in the early morning, trying to hide
themselves amongst the trees as they came. With them were
the dwarves and some few elves, against whom we have had
success in past encounters. We attacked, and the British were
quickly surrounded. Captain Mardir led the assault, and the
outcome seemed certain. I forecast few losses and sent runners
to Svarga to report our success.

"Then, without warning, a foul mist covered the field,
obscuring my vision. Clods of earth erupted from the ground

and shot high above. I heard the screaming of Devas and the desperate blowing of horns. When I thought I could bear it no longer, a great howling commenced, along with a beating of drums that would not end. Those were my hardest moments, for the mist remained thick, and, try as I might, there was nothing to see. Nothing to hear but the screams of dying friends.

"When the mist cleared, I saw that disaster had befallen us. A second British force had appeared and had flanked our troops.

"In that wave were werewolves and trolls—and Vayu soldiers. The maharaja had betrayed us.

"They were led by an enormous wolf bearing a whip and chain. We had no silver with us. Our weapons were useless against him. Everywhere the great wolf cast his gaze, we fell.

"Mardir was soon surrounded. Worse, the werewolves had taken the high ground and leapt upon her archers. Only a third of the original regiment remained, and I could see no path for escape. I dispatched our last runner to foretell our defeat and drew my sword.

"Before I entered the fray, a new sight gave me pause. High on our borders, a strange group had gathered.

"The figure at their head rode a red-and-white machine that cast a blazing light before it. Her long hair streamed behind her. I know now it was the Atavi girl who stands before us.

"On the field, Mardir was beset. The largest of the trolls loomed over her. It was then that the Atavi fell upon the troll and cast it down. She pulled Captain Mardir from the fray and righted her. Then the new force washed over the British, their weapons glittering like stars."

• • •

The dismal patter of one man clapping echoed across the room. Thamari sat on the floor, his back against the wall. "Glittering like stars. Pure poetry. Bravo, recorder. You've spun a fine tale. I feel like I'm attending a child's reading of the *Hundred Finest* in school once more." Thamari stood and began to pace. He raised one finger. "But *we* are not children." He clearly hadn't changed his mind. Eslandaran had been right about him being a pompous ass.

The queen rose from her low stool. "Enough, Ameer Thamari. You are worn from your long journey. The sight of so much death has exhausted you."

Thamari opened his mouth to speak, but the queen silenced him with a hand. "You are ever angry away from your precious ocean—let calmer minds pass judgment while you recover. The account of the recorder cannot be doubted. I ask these people their forgiveness for our poor welcome. Bring them food and drink—they are our honored guests."

Soldiers hurried to obey as the queen continued. "But before you rest, I would hear Ameer Mardir's words. She who led the battle and sits on this council. Did you see as the recorder saw?"

Mardir stood. "I was in the midst of it, my rani. I watched my brethren die before me. What the recorder said was but the beginning of their valor. My debt to them is my life."

"Then a Deva name is yours to bestow," the queen said.

"No." Thamari slammed a fist against the council table.

Adya drew back. She had no idea why Thamari still hated her, but Mardir ignored him. She pulled Adya up and held her head in her hands. "You came to us unexpected, like a shadow cast over our enemies. I name you Shaya, the Dark Shadow, and call you a sister before us."

"And these Vayu?" The queen gestured to the Finest.

"We already have names, rani." It was Gudugu. "We're fine with them."

The queen didn't seem to know what to make of this. She gave the slightest of bows and offered a curious smile.

The queen turned to Adya. "You are exhausted, your . . . warriors battered. You will rest and be fed. Your weapons will be seen to. We will aid you as best we can. Only—who are you that comes as a sister to us in our time of need?"

Adya took a deep breath. She wanted to tell the truth. To say she was a simple girl who put together radios. A girl who only wanted to find her sister and go home. Someone who swore too much and hated being around so many people and wished she could be alone.

Gudugu answered the queen before she could. "She fights yakshas and gives life to machines," Gudugu declared, and the Finest nodded. Adya cringed. Mohan should never have told them those stories.

But Gudugu wasn't finished. "She dragged us from where we'd died and been long forgotten under the earth. She led us through the ghost wood. She inspired us to fight. We are the Hundred Finest. We're mentioned in a book that Mohan told us about, which he's going to show us one day, and we will be with her in her darkest hour."

It was the most she had ever spoken. Gudugu gave an

enormous bloody smile. Adya stared at the bedraggled farmer in amazement. The woman had just declared to everyone that they were the Hundred Finest, straight out of legend.

Silence filled the hall—a spell the Devas' magic could not break. Not even Thamari dared contradict her, for Gudugu clearly believed every word she had said. Her nose had stopped bleeding, but she still looked frightful—she probably had not had a bath in a decade, and her skin was the sunless color of death. The Finest looked and smelled like they had been pulled out as corpses from the deepest earth, stolen back from death itself, or perhaps ripped out of the pages of a story, just as Gudugu had proclaimed.

On her throne, the queen tried and failed to hide her bemusement. "Welcome, Finest" was all she managed.

"Does anyone believe this nonsense?" Thamari threw his hands in the air. "The Hundred Finest, come to us like this? This is some trick, designed to bring the enemy into our midst. Look at these creatures. Are they even men?"

"Many of us are women," Gudugu clarified.

The queen's eyes blazed. "Ameer Thamari, the decision has been made."

He ignored her. He raised an arm, and his soldiers drew their swords.

The queen pointed a finger at Thamari. "You go too far."

"To defend our home, I'll go a great deal farther. What we faced today was an initial thrust, a maneuver designed to test our strength, and it cost us many of our best. Eslandaran says we have little time before the entire British army arrives. Our greatest dilemma lies before us—will we stay to defend our home or flee from a battle which may destroy us? Whatever our choice, I will not let us be torn apart from within." He sang a deep note, and his guards echoed it back. Copper nails sparked with magic across the room. Adya felt herself driven back toward the wall with the other prisoners, held fast in a cage of sound.

"For all I've ever done, for any faith our queen and council have in me, listen to what I say. We've heard the recorder. By her own admission, a foul mist conjured by British wizards obscured her view. She knew not what happened beneath it, what trickery they used, how many of their own they were willing to sacrifice to place a spy amongst us.

"Amongst these prisoners is the maharaja's own daughter, who arrived as his soldiers attacked. Do you think this coincidence?"

Murmurs arose amongst the council. The queen remained silent. Thamari had resumed pacing the room.

"You sent me afield, far from Svarga, to see if our worst fear had come to pass, to see if our enemies had gained control of a creature we could not hope to stop. I have returned, and I tell you the naga lives again. The greatest of monsters is here, and it serves the enemy."

At this, shouts went up around the room. Adya tensed as Mohan grabbed her arm.

"I beheld the naga from a distance. It rises as tall as kapoks and crushes everything in its path—nothing can stand in the way of any army with the naga leading their soldiers. We have come to our final days."

"But there cannot be a naga," Adya whispered. "They left to sleep far beneath the sea." Adya looked beseechingly to the queen, hoping she would know the truth. That was what her father had told her. Had promised. "We risked our lives for all of you."

One of the soldiers tossed a sword in the air, and Thamari caught it. He spun the blade in his hand, aiming the tip at Adya's neck as his magic held her in place.

"Liar. I have looked into the eyes of the naga. I have seen her face, and it is yours."

CHAPTER THIRTY-THREE

A SWORD CLASHED AGAINST AMEER THAMARI'S WEAPON as Eslandaran dove between them. She'd lost her usual grin. "You'll have to take my neck too, Kian, and you're not good enough by half."

The ensuing crash of blade upon blade was too fast for Adya to follow. The Devas' movements were like raging water, like the silver flash of fish in a stream.

Eslandaran drove Thamari's sword wide and kicked him in the chest.

The general stumbled back. "You're more addled than usual, Es. Time in a dungeon has deepened your madness."

"This girl saved my life. You will not harm her." Eslandaran pointed her weapon at Thamari.

"Enough." The queen raised both hands and sang out a note so pure, Adya thought her ears would shatter. The copper spikes glowed bright enough to burn her eyes. Whatever magic was holding them in place vanished. Every weapon in sight clattered to the floor, and Ameer Thamari slid back to the far side of the room.

"Dev Kian Thamari, you try my patience. If you ever raise a blade to my chosen heir again, the consequences will be severe." The queen's voice stayed calm, but she gave him a look that didn't require further words. This was her hall; her magic reigned supreme. And she referred to Eslandaran as her heir? Adya had to swallow back her gasp. They had freed the heir to the throne from the maharaja's dungeons.

The queen pointed a finger at Thamari. "If you hadn't saved us a dozen times from disaster, if I didn't know of your long friendship with my niece, I might be cross. Instead, I will assume your thoughts are clouded by exhaustion. You claim the British are no more than a week away, yet this Atavi girl is our greatest danger? Explain yourself."

Thamari paced before the queen. "We saw the naga from a great distance, surrounded by an army. We were less than fifty soldiers, my bravest, my stealthiest, yet the British wizards detected our presence. We ran and they pursued.

"To survive, we had to cross the Kaveri River at its full strength. Crocodiles as long as boats were waiting for us. Their jaws and the crush of stone took a third of my men, and I could do nothing.

"When I reached the far bank, I looked back. The naga had reared to her full height, and I knew fear. Her serpent coils could crush elephants. In each hand she held a glowing spear. I tried to turn away, to flee, but she found my eyes and held them. I will never forget her face. I doubted myself before, because of Eslandaran, but I am not mistaken."

"You are." Eslandaran shook her head. "Adya has been with me for days."

Imral spoke for the first time. "She has a sister. A twin sister." Her voice was soft and hesitant.

Adya could not breathe. These people were mad. They were

wrong. Priya was out there somewhere, fighting the British.

But Imral wasn't finished. She turned to Adya and Mohan. "You saw what he did to Lalbag. The British demanded the naga. If your sister went to him. If she made the mistake of trusting him . . ."

"My sister is no monster," Adya snapped. "She's just lost. I'm bringing her home." But in her heart, she knew. The tears that streamed down Mohan's face told her he knew it as well. Adya's strength failed her. She remembered Lalbag, his eyes full of terror and madness. Priya, all goodness, trusting, hopeful. What had they done to deserve this?

The queen came to Adya and rested a hand on her shoulder. "If the maharaja has worked this sorcery, then it is only a false naga, a Vayu illusion, and not the real thing at all. We will reverse the spell. Our magics are every bit as strong as his."

Imral shook her head. "There's no way. I'm no good at any of it, but I've studied every bit of Vayu magic, every spell I could find. That spell sends their spirit away. What's left is beyond hope of repair."

The queen raised an eyebrow. "Sends them away? Where would he send a soul?"

"Into animals," Imral said.

Adya felt herself slipping. The world was spinning. She was falling endlessly.

Mohan grabbed Imral's arm. "He sent her soul into a snake?"

"No, no. Birds."

The world steadied again. Adya could barely breathe. She had no idea how she got the words out. "What kind of bird?"

Imral shook her head. "What difference does it make, Adya? I'm sorry. I'm so sorry."

"What kind of bird?"

"With those spells, it's always the same. They need a creature full of magic. A drongo. A black drongo."

Priya had been there all along, waiting for Adya to recognize her.

She had been too blind to see.

Black filled Adya's vision. She fell to the floor.

CHAPTER THIRTY-FOUR

TWO DAYS LATER, ADYA DROVE HER METAL FINGERS into a sheer cliff and pulled herself up as water poured around her. She'd forgone the stairs in favor of the climb on a rocky path toward the Lake in the Sky. Her clothes, her hair, her entire body was soaked with cold spray. She was starting to regret not choosing the easier way. She made the mistake of looking down, and her stomach churned—the waterfall above her poured into the river that ran through Svarga Lok. From this height, a slip would be certain death, with plenty of time to ponder her many mistakes as she fell.

The Devas had spent the time mourning the dead, but Adya had fled, riding the motorcycle over the mountain, exploring every inch of Svarga Lok, trying to clear her mind. Now the stronghold was in an uproar, some preparing for the coming assault while others argued that they should flee. Mohan and Imral had leapt into action, helping ready the defenses while Adya avoided everyone, plagued by the knowledge of what had happened to Priya, to Dsouza.

To get away from her own grief, she climbed.

The roar of the falls washed over her as wind struck the mountain, spraying water into her eyes. Handholds were few and the slick rock made it doubly treacherous, but there were advantages to steel fingers that could crack stone and an arm that wouldn't tire. The sheer physical exertion quieted her thoughts and let her forget for a while.

A flight of swallows fluttered overhead.

The birds circled her as she rose, forcing her to remember.

Priya had been ripped apart, her soul placed in a drongo, her body made monstrous. Adya clung to the crag and rested her head against it. It was a horrible place to cry. A gust blew over her again, and she shivered, reaching high to drag herself up onto a ledge. There was a long way to go.

Hand over hand she continued, thinking the entire time about what she should have done, what kind of twin she should have been. She'd driven Priya away with her unwillingness to listen, her inability to be the sister she'd needed.

A drongo always knew its way back home. Priya had been there, trying to send her a message. If only she'd had the imagination to see the truth.

Now she had no idea what to do. She wanted to run, fire up the bike and ride it to the ends of the earth until she and Mohan found somewhere safe. She'd dreamed of being a great technomancer, not a warrior. Another part of her wanted to crush the maharaja's hand in her steel fist until his bones crumbled. To make him pay for what he had done.

Twenty yards from the top, Adya reached the intricate dam the Devas had constructed to tame the falls and control its flow. It was a jumble of wood, metal, and magic forty yards high. Water poured from its mouth in a measured torrent down to the river below. Its gears had long since rusted into place, but the opening was wide enough to feed the river.

Adya found plenty of handholds amidst the jumble. She pulled herself over the final edge and collapsed, body spent. With her back against a giant cypress, she looked out onto the Lake in the Sky.

A silver disk stretched before her, reflecting the crescent moon in a cloudless sky. Storms of swallows spiraled skyward above the countless fires that floated on the water's surface. It took Adya a moment to realize that the drifting flames were candles set on paper disks. Three white-sailed boats strayed far from the shore while dozens of smaller crafts lingered closer. Upon their boats the Devas sang songs that sank her into oblivion.

She had never been on water. The first ship she'd ever seen was Huda's battleship, abandoned in its jungle graveyard. If only she could board one of those boats and sail far away.

Before she could dream further, there was a rustle in the trees. A figure dropped before her, clothed in black, wearing a long sword. She had no chance to defend herself.

Adya took in a breath to yell out to the boats.

The figure raised a finger to its lips. "Be quiet, for once. I've nearly fallen off this mountain three times trying to save you."

She shielded her eyes and blinked at a voice she couldn't mistake. She shot to her feet and surprised herself by crushing Dsouza in a hug.

"Don't break my ribs," he said. "I'll need them to get you out of here."

Adya stopped squeezing him but didn't let go. She held him at arm's length and studied him close to make sure he wasn't a ghost, that she wasn't dreaming. He'd found black clothes again somewhere, but these looked like he'd ripped bits of uniform off whatever dead British troops he could find and knotted them together into a disordered mess.

She finally released him. "What do you mean, get me out?" Before he could answer she poked him hard in the chest. "You were dead. Smashed under a troll. I actually cried." She realized she was doing it again and tried to blink away the tears.

"A damned big troll too," Dsouza agreed. "I covered myself in gore and slipped beneath the cursed thing to hide. I could barely stand after I crawled out. You cried?"

"Maybe a little."

Dsouza gave her his half smile and looked at her long and hard. "You're all wet, but you don't look like a carcass anymore."

Adya wiped a hand across her eyes. "Don't tell anybody about this."

"Never. The fearsome Mongoose can't be seen tearing up for criminals and scoundrels." His smile widened into a grin. "I've found out where Imral and your brother are being held. They're with the damned British. It won't be easy, but if we leave now, we'll have a chance to get out while the Devas are on their boats."

"You've come to rescue us?" The idea of it warmed her enough to banish the chill of the falls.

"It was hell getting past the gates. I had to wait more than a day until a bunch of them came by and sang one of their songs and I could sneak in after. I've been hiding, waiting for a chance. When I saw you start the climb, I followed."

"You climbed behind me?" She couldn't believe she hadn't noticed.

He laughed. "I took the stairs. I've been here for nearly an hour."

"We're not prisoners here," Adya explained. "They've given us as much freedom as we want. You're the only one who needs rescuing. You look like you haven't eaten in a week."

"Damn." He stared out at the boats. "All that sneaking around and going hungry for nothing." Dsouza grabbed her hand. She didn't pull away. "Your sister? Is she here?"

The relief at seeing Dsouza, the belief that things had taken a turn for the better vanished all at once. Dread and emptiness seized her once more.

She somehow told him what had happened to Priya, told him about how she'd wandered the mountain, daring the motor-cycle to go ever faster, not sure if she would drive it off a cliff or save herself. In a strange way, she felt like he might understand.

"I want to kill that man," Adya said.

Dsouza's eyes flashed black. "Get in line." His jaw grew tight. "Those racks we found with body parts in the dungeons. That was what he was doing all along. He's drawn too deeply on the magic of the well. He's lost his senses entirely."

"Whatever he did can't be undone. Imral's certain the magic can't be reversed. There's no way."

Dsouza squeezed her hand. "And Gouros told you your sister was dead, didn't he? And I told you to give up looking for her. Why do you believe other people's nonsense?" He pulled her closer. "You've spent your whole life fixing broken things, haven't you?"

Her body burned with Dsouza's touch. He was alive. She

329

remembered him wrapped in chains, springing to life in Huda's cells. Remembered her relief at finding out Imral was just his sister. It seemed a lifetime ago.

Adya pushed him away as a flame lit in her head.

"What is it?" Dsouza said. "Did I do something?"

"Imral said there was no way to reverse your father's spell, but—"

Dsouza waved a hand in the air. "They tell me that crap every time."

"A technomancer has to fix a machine before the magic will work. You have to know how to take it apart, the electronics, the mechanics, everything. Then, when the machine's soul awakens, it can find its way back. Find its way home. If I can get Mohan's help . . ."

"Your crazy brother's always dying to try out some idea. Let's go find him. I'm starved."

"I'll find you as much food as you can eat, but you can't run off. You have to stay with me when I explain my plan to everyone."

"On one condition."

She placed both hands on his chest and shoved him playfully. "Never something for nothing with you, Bad Day. What do you want?"

"We take the stairs."

CHAPTER THIRTY-FIVE

ADYA COULDN'T KEEP HER EYES OPEN MUCH LONGER. Four hours past midnight and the emergency meeting outside the Kapok Tower showed no sign of ending. Worse, she was no closer to winning Thamari's support than when it started.

The queen had placed him in charge of all defenses. She had left the city for refuge on the shores of the Lake in the Sky, where she could guard the children and everyone too old to fight. Her last words had been to her niece and heir, Eslandaran, whom she had embraced and commanded to survive.

Thamari flung his shiny helm on the ground. "That is the worst plan I've ever heard." He slammed a gauntlet against the concrete shell of the tower. "Why must we gamble our lives on this outsider's scheme?"

Eslandaran exited the main archway and set down a tray of silver cups. "Because death is on our doorstep, and it's the best idea we have, Kian. Despite your thousand battles, you can think of nothing better."

Adya stayed well away from the silver cups. She'd made the mistake of gulping the hard liquor, made from kapok trees' fruit, at the beginning of the meeting, and her head was still on fire. She leaned back against the tower and gathered her thoughts, staring up at the endless leaves.

On the surface, the Kapok Tower was a crumbling sky-scraper from the age before. But within the rusted steel-and-concrete frame sprang the most magnificent tree in the citadel. The tree had started as a seed within the tower's walls and burst through the shattered roof to thrust its limbs out every window. Over the centuries, the building and the living wood had melded together. The outer shell of thick concrete remained, glowing by lamplight, while the boughs, surrounded by staircases and elevator shafts, supported it all.

Adya tried again. "Unless we stop her, the naga will destroy the gates. Every defense you've created will be useless. Clive will take the city in days." She caught the copper tube her brother tossed her way. It reflected the light of the hundreds of candles surrounding them. "Mohan, explain."

Mohan was as animated as she'd ever seen him. It was like he was back in the cave, talking about one of his schemes. The Devas had outfitted him in gold-edged armor that shone like a coin, but they'd failed to find a helmet that could contain his thundercloud of hair.

"I got the idea from *The Hundred Finest against the World*," he explained. "You know, the part where the sorcerer makes that amazing pipe and blows a storm through it. I always thought there was something to that—the sorcerer didn't just clean the dirt out of the Hundred's ears, he found a way to make something permanent, something completely different. Some way to amplify a spell and create a path for new magic. We can do that too."

Thamari squeezed his hand into a fist. "This idiot is trying to steal magic out of a fairy tale to save us."

Mohan hesitated until Imral nodded at him to go on. "I know it sounds weird, but those old stories were full of mixed magic. I know it can work." Mohan gestured to the copper tube Adya was now holding. "We've inscribed it with Imral's healing spell. We're calling it a spell rod. The wiring will form a technomantic field that should reverse most any magic, and the copper's thin and light. Adya can hold it like a spear."

"Technomantic field?" Thamari shook his head. "He just made that up."

Mohan swallowed hard and continued. "Imral's healing spell will kick off when Adya flips this switch." The copper shaft was hollow, its point narrowing to a width of three fingers, its other end flared like a trumpet. Imral had inscribed Vayu spell runes that fused and melded with wires spiraling along its length.

Thamari pointed to the last line of Devas, marching up the mountain in the night to flee. "Look at those families," he said "They are depending on me. Am I supposed to rely on a length of copper two incompetent children pieced together? On a spell that can only be used once? On a girl whose sister is a demon come to destroy us? This is suicide."

Adya bristled. Priya was no demon.

Thamari scraped a hand through his hair. "Your plan relies on Eslandaran's magic to summon the drongo. But Eslandaran is more than our queen's heir. She is critical for our defense. Your plan robs me of my most useful tool. And look at your hundred idiots. What are they doing smashing our furniture?"

The Finest were gathered at the base of the Mish-Mosh Gate, where they'd been breaking off chair legs and readying makeshift weapons. Outfitted in the Devas' magical armor, they had been transformed into gleaming soldiers. The stink of death and dungeon was gone.

Adya sighed. "They do things their own way," she said. She had no idea what their way was, but they tried. Somehow, she had more faith in them than in most anyone she'd ever met. No matter how out of their element they were, without magic or great might, they worked together, and they tried to help. They had become her people.

Eslandaran thrust her hands into her sky-blue coat. "I'm touched, Kian. 'Useful tool' is the kindest thing you've ever called me. Now tell us your amazing idea. How do we stop an army of thousands led by a creature who can reduce our defenses to rubble? How do we survive?"

Before Thamari could answer, a messenger sprinted toward them. The woman's face was wet with tears. She spoke before she'd caught her breath. "The first soul arrows have struck. Erwas has fallen at the stone gate."

Thamari pressed his knuckles to his eyes. "May she be reborn amongst us." He raised his head and looked out toward where his soldier had fallen. "Wizards and soul arrows. The British hunt us from a distance." He pointed to the sky.

Blue streaks circled high in the night.

"All of you, come with me," Thamari commanded through gritted teeth. "You will understand what we fight and what we will give up before we commit ourselves to this girl's madness." He gestured to a group of archers to follow, and they hurried toward the seventh gate.

Thamari gazed up at the soul arrows, still circling over-head, then gave the order. "Take aim."

Twenty bows pointed skyward. Thamari spread his arms wide and screamed at the sky. "I'm right here, cowards. Strike me down. Claim your prize."

The swirling blue streaks responded to his challenge. The arrows coalesced into one line of force and streaked down like blue death. At the last instant, Thamari raised his hand and sang. His voice rang out deep and pure, and a silver shield of force spread wide twenty feet above them. The soul arrows struck the barrier and shattered.

Adya crashed to the ground as the impact washed over them. Nothing had penetrated the shield, but the echoes of magic floored her all the same. She wiped blood from her lip as she got to her knees.

Thamari remained standing as if nothing had happened. "To survive we must become hunters. Trace it, Es," he ordered.

Adya slapped her hands over her ears as Eslandaran sang three notes so piercing that the air itself tore apart. Beneath Thamari's silver shield pockets of darkness appeared, spinning ever wider. On the other side of these dark portals was a distant camp where fires burned. Three robed figures stood in front of one of the fires, their hands outstretched.

"Now." Thamari raised his arm, and his archers released. Arrows disappeared into the black spaces Eslandaran had conjured, followed shortly by screams from the other side. In another moment the pockets of darkness winked out of exis-tence, and the cries of alarm went silent.

Eslandaran looked exhausted. "Three British wizards are very unhappy," she said.

"Three assassins are dead." Thamari whirled to face Adya. "Look at what you're stealing from me, girl. With Eslandaran, I can destroy their wizards when they come for us. Her song is the only one strong enough to open spaces across such distance. With her, I can trace their magic and kill them where they stand. Without her, soul arrows will fill the sky unchallenged. Erwas was the guard you met at the stone gate four days ago. She was my friend. Will you tie our hands while they unsheathe their knives?"

Adya could see no other way.

"Even if you kill all their wizards, stop every soul arrow, the naga will still smash down your gates and destroy the city," Adya said. "Her eyes are liquid fire. Your homes will melt under her gaze, your ancient trees vanish into ash. Even the memory of the Devas will be burned to nothing. But if we stop the naga, we have a chance. My sister will know me. We can bring her back."

Thamari scoffed. "Your plan is one of mercy. Mercy for a monster that has come to kill us all. I need a greater promise from you." He raised his hand. "Awaz."

An aged Deva, his back bent, emerged from the shadows. Adya recognized the smith who'd befriended Mohan and worked with him on the copper spell rod. In his hands, he held the spear the maharaja had given Adya in jest.

"Awaz is our greatest smith. He claims this weapon is blessed by Kali and can kill any demon. I asked him to repair it, to endow it with the deadliest magic he knows, to make it ready for its purpose. I will agree to your plan on one condition: when it fails, use this spear. Forget mercy. Strike the naga down, or we all die." Thamari took the weapon from the smith and tested its weight. "Promise me that."

The general threw the spear, blacker than night, and Adya caught it. Darkness beat within its shaft. The weapon felt heavier than a mountain.

Killing the naga would be murdering her own sister. Adya swallowed the fear that threatened to overwhelm her. She was out of choices.

She slammed the point of the spear into the ground. "Agreed. Priya comes back to us, or the naga dies."

CHAPTER THIRTY-SIX

THE FOLLOWING NIGHT, THE BRITISH SURROUNDED the city. Soul arrows swirled high above, lighting the clouds with their eerie glow, making every glance at the sky a reminder of what was to come. The forests around Svarga Lok crackled with fire, for the naga burned everything as it came.

Adya leaned against the giant crane that made up half the seventh gate and choked on smoke billowing across the city. Overhead, the light of distant fires reflected off the windows of the 747. Eslandaran and Mardir stood nearby, arguing over final details. Mohan and Imral were at Adya's shoulder, furiously trying to explain something to her. She set aside her worries to listen.

"We made minor modifications to your bike," Mohan said. He tried to brush over this statement, but Adya grabbed him.

"How minor?" She was trying to have more faith in Mohan, but she knew what he and Imral were capable of together. Was this like the time he rearranged her bookshelf according to colors, or had they grabbed something out of a fairy tale and done real damage to the bike?

Imral rushed to defend Mohan. "Extremely minor. I promise we didn't break anything." She was wearing aluminum bracelets Mohan had fashioned for her, which he claimed would stabilize her magic. Adya didn't miss the Blue Wizard symbol Mohan had pressed into the ornaments.

"We kept things basic. The bike was cool with it," Mohan added.

Adya swallowed what she was about to say. These two had saved her life when no one else could have. The bike didn't look any different. Everything was probably all right.

Mohan handed Adya a final piece of equipment. "Try these goggles." The lenses and straps looked exactly like her old pair from the mine shaft.

Adya looked them over—they seemed normal enough. She slipped them on. "Do they shoot rays or something?" Her face didn't heat with the spark of an enchantment, but with these two you could never be sure. She felt something, though.

"I almost feel like myself again, back in the workshop. What kind of magic did you use for this?"

Mohan straightened the goggles on her face. "None. I just always picture you wearing them when you're working. I figured Priya would recognize you in them, that you should have them if . . . if . . ." He tried to get the words out but failed.

She hugged him tight. "They're perfect. You always need eye protection when you're doing the big stuff."

He squeezed back until his new armor nearly crushed her. "I need Priya back, but I can't lose the one sister who's still here."

Adya didn't let him go. She remembered the frightened child she'd held in her arms when their parents had died. When she'd been just as scared herself and had to pretend that a big sister could hold it together.

"Let's stay focused on fixing things." Part of her was always terrified to lose Mohan. But if she stayed afraid, they couldn't succeed.

She took Imral's hand and fought for something encouraging to say. She could do this. "You were really great that time with the werewolf, and that time in the forest . . . and—"

Imral laughed for the first time Adya remembered, and the strain left her face. "You're really not very good at this, are you? But that time in the forest, when you told me all we can ever do is have faith in ourselves and keep trying . . . that helped me more than you can imagine, and now these will help even more." She held up one of the bracelets Mohan had made for her. "But remember, Adya, the rod will only work once. When you activate the spell, it should shine bright as a torch. From that point on you won't have much time. You've got to be close."

Adya nodded. It was good to see Imral finally developing some confidence in her own power.

"I need to be ready," Imral said. "If my father is here, my brother will try to face him on his own." She spun a bracelet around her wrist, and her brief smile disappeared. "He's the last family I have left." She dashed off to make her final preparations.

Adya grabbed Mohan's shoulder. "Those bracelets—"

Mohan cut her off. "They'll work, Adya. You can count on Imral."

Before Adya could argue, the sky flashed, and a soul arrow seared down toward them. A Deva soldier launched a spell shield, and the missile shattered in a shower of magical energy. The strikes were becoming more frequent.

As the light of the magical assault faded, Josiah loped

A MAGIC FIERCE & BRIGHT

toward them, transforming from werewolf to human as he came. The entire shift took only a few seconds. Dsouza ran alongside him.

"They're camped two hundred yards from the stone gate, just out of bowshot," Josiah said. "Nearly ten thousand of them. The naga has taken refuge in the Krishna temple. We'll find no better time, Adya."

She could delay no longer. Priya was waiting.

Eslandaran nodded her agreement. "Raise the spell rod high when you're ready. I'll be watching from the wall. I'll bring the drongo in from wherever she flies."

Dsouza tugged Adya aside. "Listen, if anything goes wrong . . ."

Adya tried to brush him off. "Don't worry about me, Bad Day. Let's just get my sister back."

He grabbed her shoulders. "He's taken her soul, Adya. She may not have any idea who you are."

A crash of thunder drowned out Dsouza's words as a hail of soul arrows arced down around them. Twenty Devas sang out, and a blinding flash of silver shields banished the darkness, absorbing the rain of blue death. It was over in seconds, casting the world into black again. A single scream broke the silence.

"Gods." Eslandaran rushed toward a soldier sprawled on the ground at Adya's feet. An arrow white as bone protruded from her thigh.

Adya's heart crashed against her chest; it was Mardir, the captain she'd dragged from underneath a troll. Adya reached for the white shaft.

Eslandaran knocked Adya's hand aside as Mardir screamed again. "Leave it. Touch a soul arrow and you're dead." Eslandaran took Mardir's head in her lap. The captain's face was already pale, her breathing shallow. "Stay calm, Mardir. I have you."

Dsouza dragged Adya away. "A soul arrow draws out your life force in minutes. Anyone who touches it dies. You can't survive unless . . ."

Eslandaran's eyes shone wet silver. "Unless it's removed by someone whose love for you burns stronger than any magic. No other soul can touch it and survive. Otherwise, you both burn to death from the inside." She began to sing. The wounded soldier's shaking eased, though her eyes remained full of fear.

Dsouza planted himself between Adya and Mardir, trying to block her view. "I've watched brave fools die pulling out a soul arrow. Caring about someone isn't enough. Don't ever try it. It's the most horrible death I've ever seen."

Mardir spat blood and coughed without pause. In minutes, it was over.

Adya was paralyzed. She remembered the brave woman she'd dragged out from under the troll who immediately drew her sword and rallied her people around her. Mardir couldn't have died here, surrounded by allies. "We should have done something—anything," she said. She'd never felt so useless.

"The hardest decision," Eslandaran murmured, "is knowing who you can't save. Go now, Adya. If we don't meet again in this life, may we meet in the next."

CHAPTER THIRTY-SEVEN

THE LAST THING TEN THOUSAND BRITISH TROOPS would expect was an attack by a force of a few hundred in the middle of the night.

Adya was betting everything on that hope.

She and her Finest gathered at the second gate, eighty yards from the stone ring that surrounded Svarga Lok. Sheets of red silk twenty feet high brushed against Adya's face as she awaited Eslandaran's signal. Around her, Gudugu and the Hundred Finest adjusted their night glasses. Josiah and his turncoats hid amongst the swirling fabric. Three hundred against ten thousand. If her bet was wrong, she was leading the people she loved to their deaths.

The motorcycle would not put up with Adya's fear. It filled her mind with images of starter pistols and waving flags. The bike pulsed below her, eager to fly, eager to face the enemy and get her sister back.

She stroked the Yamaha's engine with her steel hand. *One more race and we win.*

Together. The bike sent her the word in a grating voice of gears and engine noise, but she understood it all the same.

A rail popped out of the left side of the bike as Dsouza approached. Adya had no idea what else her brother and the princess had made the motorcycle capable of. Dsouza stepped onto the rail, testing it.

"The bike's finally made space for me. It must not think I'm so bad, after all." He drew his blade.

"There's plenty of space right behind me this time," Adya said. She looked up into Dsouza's face and found him smiling at her.

He threw a leg over the bike's seat. "I'll take you up on that offer."

Imral stood nearby, tracing figures in the air, Mohan's Blue Wizard bracelets shining on her wrists. In the next moment the color drained from her face. "He's here, brother. The magic doesn't lie. Our father is beyond those walls."

Dsouza stared into the distance toward the army camped just outside the gates. "I don't need a spell to tell me that. I feel the monster in my bones."

They had hoped the maharaja would not lead his own troops, but there was no time now to change their plan.

Adya clutched her mother's pendant, keeping her focus on the first gate, where Eslandaran awaited atop the wall. Clamped to one side of the bike was the copper tube, its spell runes glowing. On the other side hung the spear. She ran a thumb along its blade, testing the edge. If everything failed, she would need it sharp enough to sever all the bonds she held dear.

"*Om Kali numaha.*" Adya spoke the final words of her prayer, and the motorcycle's engine rumbled. Inside the Krishna temple, just outside, her sister needed her.

The naga awaited.

Eslandaran sang a note pure as starlight, and a chorus of Devas took up the harmony. The stone gate creaked open, summoning Adya to a fate she could not forestall.

She raised her hand. "Hold on tight."

Dsouza slid his arms around her and squeezed. His head was almost on her shoulder. "I was hoping you would say that."

The bike rocketed forward. Adya's hair whipped in the wind as they shot down the hill. Josiah loped beside them, and the Hundred Finest charged behind.

Every Deva who could be spared sang atop the wall in a chorus of deafening song.

I'm here, Priya. I'm finally here. Adya shot out as copper spikes sparked across the barrier.

The mountain, covered in kapoks and lush vegetation only days before, was now a graveyard of dead trees, still smoldering. The force of the Devas' spell song swept across the burnt earth, and British soldiers collapsed in sleep as the wave struck. A hail of arrows followed, as Thamari's archers focused their fire, creating an open space around the Krishna temple, a circle fifty yards in diameter to give Adya the time she needed.

But not every enemy succumbed to the assault. A line of Vayu soldiers stood before the Krishna temple, untouched by spell or arrow, geometrical symbols glowing around them. Shimmering on each of their bright shields was the royal symbol of Mysore. The Vayu troops sprinted toward Adya, weapons drawn.

"Damn!" Dsouza shouted. "These fools should have stayed in Mysore."

He rolled off the moving bike, his sword in hand. Four of the maharaja's soldiers ran forward to meet him, and he dove into them like a whirlwind of destruction. He moved like a panther, too fast to touch.

Adya's shout of warning was lost in the clash of weapons as a broad man with a staff in each hand stepped out from amongst the maharaja's soldiers. He pointed his long staffs at Dsouza, and silver arcs of lethal magic erupted.

Dsouza never slowed, sliding under the blast and slicing both staffs in two. The sorcerer screamed as Josiah clamped his werewolf jaws upon him. The blasts of power vanished into nothing, and the soldiers broke. A space opened for Adya, and the motorcycle swerved, racing straight at the final group of guards blocking the path to the temple.

The bike told her what to do.

Before she crashed into the wall of shields, the sides of the motorcycle flew to pieces. Red-and-white metal spun around her in a tornado of slicing shards.

Vayu soldiers fell back in a panic. Adya arced the bike in a half circle as the steel swirled around her and slammed back into the bike, finding its rightful place once more. Mohan and Imral had definitely worked some improvements.

The Hundred Finest and Deva troops broke through the resistance and rushed the perimeter to hold the space. Gudugu and her crew descended upon their former Vayu jailers. The sight of the magically armored farmers was enough to make the Mysore troops run.

And then they were through.

Dsouza appeared at her side, blade wet with blood, a mad look in his eyes. "Looks like the kids tuned up your bike."

"Those two are good for each other." She caught Dsouza's chin, running a thumb along his jaw, their faces close.

He leaned in and spoke fast, all in a jumble. "When I fell into the well and was sure I was going to die, I couldn't bear it, not because I was afraid, but because I wanted, more than anything, to see you again."

She kissed him before he could move.

He broke away too soon. "You look good in those goggles."

The heat climbed up her chest into her face.

"Was that a compliment, from the Jackal?" She might not ever see him alive again. There was no time at all, but how she wanted to let this moment last.

In the distance, shouts rang out as the British encampment came alive. A side of the Krishna temple tumbled forward, and a block the size of a Volkswagen shot into the sky. The stone spun at its zenith and finally crashed down ten yards in front of them, spraying them with dirt. With the sound of an earthquake, the naga came.

Coil after coil of green-black serpent, thick as a tree, swept out, scattering stone in every direction. Above the coils rose the torso of a beautiful girl clad in silver-scaled armor, a girl with Adya's face and a glowing spear in each hand.

Adya stopped breathing. This was her twin sister, the person she'd been closest to her entire life, transformed into a monster. She felt something inside her break, felt she might never be able to move again.

"Get going if you want to help her." With a hand on her shoulder, Dsouza pushed her into action before sprinting toward the temple.

Troops scattered in every direction. Josiah reverted to

human form and rolled behind a boulder. A wave of fear swept over Adya. She desperately wanted to run, to send the motorcycle speeding away.

And the naga screamed.

Adya squeezed both hands over her ears as an unearthly sound tore the air. Her sister's eyes shone black and terrible. Priya gazed at the giant boulder where Josiah was crouched, and streams of fire shot forth from her eyes. Josiah leapt clear moments before the stone vaporized in a cascade of molten rock.

The line of flame swept up in an unending torrent, melting everything in its path. Devas screamed as the blast struck the stone gate's walls, tearing them to pieces and opening a hole wide enough for an elephant.

Adya bent her head over the handlebars, and the bike raced forward. The front wheel lifted, spinning over a boulder, and launched straight into the air. She flattened herself against the engine as the Yamaha took flight and the naga turned, aiming a spear in their direction.

Metal shards flew from the machine, whipping around Adya in a protective shield.

The naga roared as the bike's steel sliced into her. She threw her weapon, crackling with green fire, catching the bike through the spokes, sending it crashing onto the temple's roof.

Adya rolled free as they hit. She scrambled toward the bike to retrieve the spell rod, but her hand closed around her black spear instead. She spun just in time to block a thrust that would have gone through her chest.

And found herself at eye level with her sister.

The naga reared back, ready to strike. Her shining spear aimed at Adya's heart caught the moonlight and held it. The weapon froze in space as the naga's black eyes flickered, and she hesitated.

Adya had fought her way across South India for this moment, had turned it over in her head a thousand times, rehearsing what she might say when she finally found her sister.

"Come on, Priya—it's me, you dummy." This wasn't the deep emotional speech Adya had meant to give. She'd wanted to tell her sister how much she needed her back, how lost she felt without her. How she wished Priya would forgive her for always being so impatient, so grouchy, so stubborn. For not going with her when she left. For not being the sister she should have been.

Priya would have understood. She always did.

The naga leaned in, its giant snake body an arm's length away. Adya could feel the heat pouring off the scales as her sister peered into her eyes, searching.

"Is it you?" The words were half-human, half the hiss of a snake. "I have been lost. I have been far away. I'm no longer certain where I belong."

Adya threw both her arms wide. "Well, think a little harder, Priya. Remember, you and me against the world."

Priya's eyes flashed. "I'm afraid I shall never return."

Adya reached up toward her sister, still too far away. "When Baba told his stories, I'm the one who always got scared, not you. You're the brave one who's supposed to save me."

The naga lowered her spear. "You and me . . ." With each word the voice became more human, more Priya. Adya's heart ached with new hope.

A glowing figure, robed in white, his hands covered in flame, shot into the sky.

"Kill her." The command reverberated across the mountain as the maharaja of Mysore, supreme master of the naga, gave his order again. "Strike her down." Unfortunately, the maharaja had to ruin everything.

The naga's eyes glossed over once more, and Priya was gone. The spear drew back.

Before the maharaja's order could be carried out, another figure spiraled into the sky to meet him. "You'll answer to me first, Father." Imral stretched out her hands, and pulses of blazing energy screamed toward the maharaja.

The maharaja spread his fingers wide. *"Ajbalam."* The word escaped his lips, and a shining circle sprang up before him. Imral's bolts disappeared within it, but not before she conjured two more and threw up a shield of her own. The two combatants spun off, blasts arcing between them.

Leaving Adya and Priya alone once more.

"Don't listen to him, Priya. He is such a jerk." Adya's usual lack of eloquence took over. "Listen to me, for a change. You took the damn moped. You're going to have to be on cleanup duty for a month to make up for all this."

The naga hesitated, its spear trembling.

The words poured out of Adya in a torrent. "You know I never cared about the rest of it, Priya. About saving everyone and all the politics and being a hero. I just wanted to be back fixing radios with you, and you'd say that I'd done it all wrong, and I'd say whatever, and Mohan would have some crazy suggestion we'd shake our heads at. Your cat would try to steal a tool or something. You know what I mean. I never gave a damn about anything else. I only cared about you."

Adya prayed, hoping someone was listening. "Kali, I need her. She didn't deserve this." She lifted the copper tube and flipped the switch. Runes along its length lit up, and the smell of jasmine incense filled the air as Imral's magic activated. "Our crazy brother came up with this idea," she explained. "Stole it straight out of a fairy tale." Adya held the tube high, a glowing copper beacon visible from the stone gates.

At her signal, Eslandaran's voice rang out pure and clear. The air crackled as a hole two hands wide tore the space above them, and a black drongo teleported out of the darkness, its wings dusted with silver light. The bird shot through the portal and dropped to land on Adya's shoulder.

The naga opened her mouth, and Priya spoke with a voice all her own. "Of course it's you. Who else would call me dummy and not know what to say?" The bright fury faded from her eyes. "I'm the one who's sorry, Adya. Sorry I abandoned you."

"Whatever. I mean, you were kind of right there all along, anyways, so let's worry about that later. Now we fix all the mess. That's what we do." Adya held the copper tube level with Priya's heart.

"I knew you would come," Priya said. "No matter how terrible everything became, I knew you would come."

"Damn right. You can't get away from me that easy." Adya felt the magic vibrate through the spell rod. The drongo spread its wings, ready to fly.

"Adya!" Dsouza's warning came too late.

A gray mist seeped up through the stones, taking shape faster than Adya could move. A clawed hand seized the copper spell rod and tore it away from her as shining eyes, red as blood, met hers.

Cloaked in scarlet, a monster in the shape of a man loomed over her. A memory that seemed to be from a lifetime ago came back to her of the most dreaded of generals, lounging on Huda's ship.

The vampire dipped his head in the slightest bow, which was somehow more disturbing than if he'd growled. "The pleasure is mine, my dear. I am Lord General Clive, commander of Her Majesty's army, and I have had quite enough of you."

General Clive folded the copper tube in his hands like it was paper, the lights along its surface dimmed, and the spell path to her sister vanished. The world fell away beneath Adya.

The drongo launched itself into the air, spiraling high into the sky, and called out twice. It sounded almost human in its anguish—its last hope of returning home, gone.

CHAPTER THIRTY-EIGHT

THE DRONGO SOARED ABOVE THE BATTLEFIELD, screaming its grief to the world. It had been so close to being united with its true self, so close to being whole again. A drongo could always find its way back to where it came from, but now that was forever denied.

No one listened to the drongo's cries. Everything below was fire and destruction. A vast army was surging toward the walls of Svarga Lok. As the drongo watched, the ring of desperate defenders around the temple grew ever tighter. The people the bird cared about would soon be overrun. It would be lost and alone once more.

The drongo dipped in a tight circle. Amidst the chaos of the battle, the bird found the person responsible for all its torment—the sorcerer who had ripped its soul from its body and cast it out to wander the skies. The bird hovered, filled with anger and fear, watching as the maharaja of Mysore fought a girl in the sky.

The girl floated above the battle, her clothes flapping in the wind, energy crackling along her arms. She threw the magic forward at her father, at the twisted ruler who'd brought the naga back to India. How the drongo wished it were a great warrior or a tiger who could leap upon the enemy to aid her and tear him to pieces.

The maharaja's shield shattered, and he flipped through the air before righting himself. "Impressive. But you should be the last one fighting me. Return with me to Mysore instead." He held up the back of his right hand, displaying a spell mark in the shape of a king cobra. "With this spell, I control the naga. I will gift you the same mark, and you will rule at my side."

The drongo cried out in alarm. But the girl was not easily fooled.

"I've seen what you've done, Father. The people you've tortured, the creatures you've created. You've turned into a monster." Imral thrust her arms forward, and a tornado erupted, crushing her father in a storm.

The maharaja's face betrayed no emotion. His robes tore to pieces, but still, he did not move. "You've developed confidence, Imral. Where is your fear of heights? Your fear of failure?" Despite the winds besieging him, his voice was clear and sure.

Imral held up her arms, displaying the silver bands. "I am in control now. Fear has no hold on me."

"I see," the maharaja said. "The boy has fashioned trinkets for you. Trinkets that are nothing but illusion."

"This is no illusion." Imral's hands became fists above her head, and a steel cage appeared around the maharaja, the bars pressing tight. "Never again, Father. Never again."

The maharaja swirled a finger, and the bands around Imral's wrists unclasped. Mohan's silver bracelets spun away, floating in the air between them. "Your friend tricked you. These bands contain no magic. You are balanced on a platform of lies. Sense it, Imral. Sense the truth."

A look of confusion crossed the girl's face as she reached out, calling the bands back to her. Her flight spell faltered, and she fell through the air. The drongo's heart sank with her. The maharaja was too powerful. Nothing could withstand him. The drongo swooped down to bear witness. The bird could do nothing, but the brave girl would not die alone.

Moments before the girl hit the ground, the maharaja's laughter filled the air.

Ten feet before she crashed, the girl flung a spell at the ground. Wind surged around her, rocketing her back into the sky.

Imral righted herself, her hair streaming behind her, magic crackling along her forearms. "If the bands were not real, Father, then I've fought you on my own. I've always had what I needed. Mohan knew it; now I understand too."

The maharaja's calm expression vanished as Imral dropped behind him like a hawk. The iron cage slammed down again as the winds of her storm surrounded him.

The maharaja threw apart his arms, and her spell shattered like fine glass. "You don't understand, Imral. The Flame comes first. We must sacrifice everything for control of the infinity well." He closed his fist, and the winds died away. "The techno-mancers must serve us. The Devas must fall."

Imral froze in midair. "You betrayed the Devas to Clive. You set them up to be destroyed. I won't let it happen, Father. Not ever." She raised both arms and shouted, *"Brahmacharya."*

The ground below them erupted, and a forest of thin trees spiraled up, surrounding the maharaja.

"Trees?" The maharaja shook his head in disappointment.

"After everything I taught you, all you can manage in battle is a garden?" His hands filled with fire, and he pointed them at his daughter.

The drongo dove before him and spread its wings, blocking his vision.

The maharaja hesitated. "Which one were you, bird? Lalbag? Anand? Priya? There were so many I was forced to cast out. What have you come for now? Do you hope for revenge?"

He gestured, and a magical wind held the bird immobile in the sky.

But as he reached for the drongo, vines whipped around his arms, forcing them behind his back. His eyes went wide as they started squeezing. The drongo broke free and fled.

The maharaja glared at his daughter. "You cannot kill me, Imral. Clive possesses a spell mark. He will gain control of the naga if I die." He spoke a word of power, and Imral's spell began to unravel.

Imral thrust both hands toward the ground, and the tendrils held strong, dragging her father down. She dropped beside the tangle as a forest of branches sprang up around him.

Her father's eyes locked with hers. "You will understand one day. You need to create devils to fight demons." Flame erupted from his fingers, and the leaves began to burn. He would be free in moments.

Imral traced another pattern in the air. "Never again," she said. "Never again."

The plants surged with renewed vitality, wrapping tight around the maharaja.

356

"You cannot do this, Imral. You cannot." Leaves filled the maharaja's mouth as the vines pulled him deep into the earth.

"My real father died long ago." Imral reached out to the maharaja as the ground closed over him and he disappeared.

The drongo cried out as its tormentor died, hoping against hope that his death would free it, but in the end, it remained a bird. Exhausted, it landed on Imral's shoulder as she traced a spell and touched her fingers to her lips.

Imral's voice trumpeted across the battlefield. "Soldiers of Mysore, the maharaja is dead. I am Imral, your queen, your rani. Cease fighting and heed me."

CHAPTER THIRTY-NINE

GENERAL CLIVE TOSSED THE REMNANTS OF THE SPELL rod off the roof as if he was getting rid of garbage. "The best laid plans of fools often go astray."

Before he could say more, Imral's voice rang out in the night, triumphant.

"It would appear our maharaja is no more," Clive said. He held up his right hand, displaying a spell mark in the shape of a giant snake. As Adya watched, the mark began to glow red. "His death makes things far simpler—the naga is now mine to control, and Mysore will belong to us without a fight." Above him, the naga rose high, both spears ready, awaiting his command.

Adya struck at Clive's face with her steel fist.

Clive caught it in one hand. "You should have come with me in the jungle." He twisted his arm, and she crashed onto the roof. She crumpled when he kicked her in the gut. "There would have been no need to lose everyone you love. Look, my dear, look."

Below her, disaster was unfolding.

The Hundred Finest were pressed back in a shrinking circle. The British army had woken at last, and its strength seemed without limit. Adya watched in dismay as wave after wave of trolls and werewolves, dwarves and elves streamed toward the temple.

"You've delivered me quite the prize. The gates are open, the field won. I would have expected more from you, but—"

A body slammed into Clive, and he staggered back. Dsouza's blade flashed toward Clive's neck, but the vampire's own sword came up to meet it. Metal sparked faster than Adya could follow. With a roar, Dsouza threw himself forward, wrapped an arm around Clive, and they tumbled off the edge of the roof.

Adya lay on her back, the naga looming over her in the midst of the chaos. The ruined copper tube rested at her feet. The drongo circled overhead with nowhere to go.

The naga's coils lowered until Adya looked into her bright eyes wet with tears. She said no words, but Adya understood.

"No one rules you, Priya. You don't have to hurt me. You know that. You know me."

Priya picked up the black spear and pressed it into Adya's hands.

"He will force me to kill you." Priya gestured toward the stone gate and all those fighting below. "He'll make me destroy everything."

"No, Priya. It can't end like this." Tears stung Adya's eyes. Everything she'd ever done had been to bring Priya back, to save her. Not to murder her.

"Adya, you were always the one with the brightest fire. The one who saw sense when I was dreaming. Who could do the hard things. You can't let me be a destroyer of everything good. You have to set me free." Priya spread her arms wide, baring her chest.

Blue flashes shot through the sky, and a soul arrow struck

the roof. British troops flooded into the area around the temple. They'd gotten behind the Hundred Finest. No one would stand a chance if she didn't do this. The spear shook in Adya's hand. She lifted it above her shoulder, and it lit with flames, filling the night with fire. The weapon demanded the blood of a demon. Adya aimed it straight at her sister's chest.

"Strike, Adya, for god's sake. Strike." In the lull, as the armies below collided together, as Dsouza and Clive grappled, and it was just the two of them again, Priya's eyes were entirely her own.

Adya knew what had to be done, but the look in those eyes drained her strength away.

She wasn't a killer goddess sent from the sky to cleanse the earth. She was just a sister. She let the spear fall. The flame went out as the weapon clattered to the roof.

Priya threw back her head and screamed, and the naga's voice filled the night.

Adya cried out as a glowing spear pierced her side.

The naga rose up before her and struck again, its tail crashing down, cracking her ribs and sending her falling, crashing to the stones.

CHAPTER FORTY

ADYA OPENED HER EYES TO FIND HER MOTORCYCLE ON its side, smashed and bent amongst the temple's stones like a young warrior fallen to his grave.

General Clive looked down at her, his foot planted atop the Yamaha's ruined frame, in a stance that seemed almost nonchalant. "Your spine is severed, girl—a terrible way to die. Useless and limp, listening to the last cries of those you love." His hands glistened with fresh blood.

Priya lost. Dsouza most likely dead. Adya felt the motorcycle's fear as it struggled in vain to fire up its engine, to spin its shattered wheels and be free. Everywhere around her, people were falling—the Devas, the British, and her farmers. There was no space in the world for so much loss. No way she could face it alone.

She took a breath, and something stabbed her side. Priya's spear had pierced her lung, and a white arrow protruded from her calf. Her legs were beyond feeling. She knew what it all meant. At least she wouldn't have long to suffer.

Clive's red cape flapped in the wind. "There's not much left for me to do. The soul arrow will steal your life away soon. A pity, really, and a horrible way to go."

"Your cape looks really stupid," Adya said. She wished she could hit him, just once, but she didn't have the strength to lift her arm.

The vampire ran a tongue over his blood-wet fingers. "I didn't have time to savor your friend properly. No matter. Duty before pleasure. You've annoyed me terribly, Mongoose. You killed two of my favorite officers I sent after you in the jungle. I've looked forward to making you pay for it."

Faster than the eye could follow, Clive grabbed the motorcycle and cracked its frame in two. A scream ripped through Adya's mind as the vampire drove his hand into the Yamaha's gas tank.

"In the end, I am a merciful enemy," Clive said. "Your end shall be quick. You were attached to this contraption. At least you shall be joined in death."

In one movement, the vampire heaved five hundred pounds of metal over his head.

"Goodbye, Mongoose."

He smashed the bike down upon her.

Adya raised her metal hand to protect her face as red-and-white steel fell. That didn't stop the bike from absolutely crushing the rest of her body.

Her vision went black as she died.

She dreamed of finish lines and crowds cheering her madly on. Of rock music blaring and speed, such speed that nothing could ever catch her. She prayed that it would never end, and the racing wind would blow her paint clean.

You will be my friend always. I was never whole until I met you. The motorcycle's message was as clear as words spoken by a sister. *We will fly together. It cannot end until we triumph.*

She dragged in a breath as a jolt of energy surged through

every cell in her body, as the bike that loved her emptied every bit of its living soul into her.

No. No, don't do this, Adya begged, but the motorcycle didn't stop. This was a contest it intended to finish, and it would come in first, as always. The Yamaha flooded her body with the power of a thousand victories and the heat of a blazing sun. Adya felt the machine departing. Felt its soul receding, leaving her completely alone.

A voice rumbled in the back of her head. *Stop feeling sorry for yourself. There are races to be won. Pretenders to be vanquished. Turn on your radio and sing.*

The engine roared like a thousand monsoons.

Adya's eyes snapped open as the bike's magic flamed through her like jet fuel. The machine's soul had more power than any other, and it sent every bit of it into her. Rock music thundered in her ears. Her spine became liquid, her bones fusing together once more as magic tore through her nervous system, repairing shattered tissue. She opened her hand and screamed as the bike poured the final bit of its soul into her and her arm burned, her mind filled with the bike's memories, her heart overflowed with its desire.

Pull yourself together. I can't wait forever for you to get off the ground.

Adya seized the vampire by the neck with her steel hand as silver fire raced up her arm.

Clive's red eyes went wide. "You cannot be alive." He tried to pull away but couldn't break her grip.

Ha! You better believe she is. The race is not over, and you're slower than—

It was the motorcycle that whispered in her head, but Adya gave voice to the words. "The race is not over, asshole. And you're slower than a Kawasaki 750."

Her eyes filled with tears, and Clive became very hard to see, but she shook him hard and didn't let go.

Yet Clive was not the head of the British Southern Command for nothing. He raised a hand and took aim at Adya's head. Before he could move, he let out a terrible cry—as a chair leg pierced his thigh. The handle of a wooden hoe soon followed, thrusting through his chest as he spasmed. Then his body dropped to its knees, quite headless, as a black blade swept across his shoulders. Dsouza stood behind the vampire's twitching body, leaning heavily on Usually Sleeping.

Your pit crew has arrived. The voice of the motorcycle was fading. *The race is easier together. Finish strong.*

"Don't go!" Adya shouted, but the motorcycle went silent.

"We're not going anywhere, General." Gudugu left her hoe smoking in Clive's chest and pulled Adya off the ground. Her breath came out in a ragged wheeze. "It's the in-your-darkest-hour thing and all."

Adya struggled to her feet, the feeling coming back into her legs at long last. She looked down at the smashed frame of her Yamaha, her friend. "I'm tired of the darkest hour. I'm so tired of all the darkness."

Gudugu saw the soul arrow protruding from her leg and went silent.

"No." Dsouza reached out to her.

Adya drew away. "Stay away. I'm not losing anyone else."

The soul arrow glowed, white as bone, a sentence of death that couldn't be denied. Adya already felt the arrow draining what life her motorcycle had so recently bestowed. But the bike had given her what she needed. She would save her sister before she died.

The naga flung down the walls of the temple as it surged toward them. Rubble careened in every direction. Fire shot from its eyes, tearing the ground to pieces. The monster had become a force of pure chaos. No one controlled it now.

"Get back," Adya said. She couldn't contain the energy the bike had fed her any longer. She trembled with every step. The pattern of Mohan and Imral's spell still lingered in the air. The magic was hers to call.

Adya raised her arms, and the scraps of the bike floated into the air, red-and-white shards swirling before her. "*Om Kali numaba*," she shouted into the wind. She brought her hands together, and the metal shards formed a perfect tube aimed at the naga's chest. "Find your way home, Priya."

The black drongo swooped down and disappeared inside the maelstrom of steel. The naga's head rocked back, and Priya's mouth opened in a silent scream.

The sky flashed a blinding silver. The earth heaved and groaned in protest, flattening whatever remained of the battered temple and knocking Adya off her feet.

When the shaking finally stopped, Adya coughed, lying on her back, and spit out a mouthful of dirt. The soul arrow still burned, embedded in her calf. She rubbed at her eyes, the world around her a blurry mess of movement and shouting. As her vision returned, she made out the naga towering over her, a spear in each hand, and her heart fell to pieces.

The naga whipped both spears in great arcs around her, knocking away swords and sending figures tumbling. "Get away from her, Jackal. Take another step, and I'll shove that sword down your throat."

Adya knew that voice. Her vision cleared, and she made out two beautiful legs on either side of her body. Priya stood over her, warding off Dsouza and a host of the Hundred Finest who were trying to calm her down. Her long curls reached all the way down her back. Her face shone with moonlight.

Adya raised herself on her elbows. "They're with me, Priya, you goof. Put down the damn spears."

Priya turned in surprise, and Adya looked up into a face she'd seen all her life. The spears fell to the ground, and Priya caught Adya in an embrace tighter than the grip of the naga. Adya feared her ribs might break and still wanted it never to end. Her sister was back. Even if the soul arrow killed her, Priya was back.

Priya's eyes shone wet with tears. "Thank the gods you never know when to give up."

Adya held Priya as close as she could and said nothing. She didn't want to taint this moment, even if her sister was going to have to face the rest of it alone. Then her weakness betrayed her, and she slumped in Priya's arms. The drain of the soul arrow was unrelenting.

"Adya!" Dsouza ran toward her and hit the ground. He knew too well what was about to happen. He reached for the white shaft to seal his own death, but Gudugu tackled Dsouza and held him down. Adya gave a silent thanks. She wouldn't have to watch him die with her. There was no way to save her now. Gudugu had stopped the worst tragedy Adya could imagine.

But she couldn't stop Priya.

Adya screamed a guttural cry as her sister reached for the arrow. After everything, she was going to have to watch her sister's life force drain away, going to have to watch Priya die.

Priya pulled the arrow out with one smooth jerk and held it high. She stood shaking as the white-hot energy of the bolt washed over her. Adya didn't dare to breathe, as the blaze became as bright as a star and Priya's outline disappeared.

Then the magic of the soul arrow faded, and Priya drew in a shuddering breath. She wobbled, still holding the smoldering arrow, but she smiled. "You and me against the world. Right?"

"You and me," Adya said, and the feeling inside her burned stronger than any killing magic ever could.

"We have to go, General." Gudugu surveyed the approaching British army. "Before they realize we're just farmers."

Ten thousand invading troops were momentarily stunned by the disappearance of the naga, but they were disciplined and already organizing themselves. In the sky, a figure hovered over them momentarily, then hurtled down to land in their midst. Imral's hair was a wild mess, her face still wet with tears, but the look of doubt and fear that often plagued her was gone.

"They're coming fast," she announced.

Adya kept an arm around Priya as tight as she could. "Of course they are." She raised her other hand. "My Finest, to me."

They raced up the mountain as the British gathered behind them. They reached the Mish-Mosh Gate as the sun rose over the horizon.

"Where's Mohan?" Priya asked. She had a grip on Adya's arm she wouldn't let go.

Adya looked up and pointed to the mountain. The Deva troops had retreated to their refuges around the shores of the Lake in the Sky. A roaring deluge was pouring out of the dam toward them in a torrent of destruction. "Mohan's opened the floodgates to drown the city."

Priya's eyes stayed focused on the oncoming wave, sweeping away everything before it. "Do you have a plan to get us out of here, or is this going to be a glorious end?"

"You know I'm too self-centered for that." Adya estimated the distance between them and the oncoming British force. "We have five minutes."

"I'd give us three." Priya pointed out a large group of trolls charging ahead of the rest. A giant thudded along behind them.

"What do you need, Adya?" Imral asked.

"I need to get up there with the Hundred Finest." Adya pointed to the top of the Mish-Mosh Gate, where the old Boeing 747 rested, its nose aimed at the sky.

Imral traced a design in the air, and silver planks appeared along the arch. "This will work for everyone else," she said. She raised her hand, and the wind picked up around them. "You two fly with me."

Adya floated up to the plane alongside Imral and Priya, with Dsouza and the Hundred Finest just behind.

She slammed a hand onto the hull and felt its ancient soul, long asleep. The motorcycle's energy still surged beneath her skin.

"Imral, my sister and I are going to need a lot more power."

Imral raised her hands, and lines of radiant energy danced between them. "Sounds like a job for the Blue Wizard."

Stones fell away as the airplane took off, and the gate below them crumbled to pieces. The Hundred Finest fell into seats alongside centuries-old skeletons while Dsouza braced himself in the aisle. Adya and Priya each clutched one of Imral's hands as they steered up and away. Far below, water cascaded toward Svarga Lok, a veritable sea rushing toward the invading army to wash the citadel clean.

CHAPTER FORTY-ONE

A WEEK HAD NOT BEEN ENOUGH TIME TO CATCH UP— Priya and Adya spent hours and hours talking about everything, or else staring at the sky together and saying nothing at all.

The Kapok Tower still stood, and they were all once again gathered at its base. The city was a mess of small lakes, pools, and a river much too wide, swollen from the waterfall. The majority of the invading army had either been trapped in the gates or swept away, though some had escaped. Still, there were more survivors than Thamari knew what to do with. Josiah had put most of them to work cleaning up the mess.

But a week was all Thamari would allow before he ruined a perfectly good afternoon by publicly holding Adya responsible for the destruction of his city.

"It will take years to repair the damage you've caused. You drained the Lake in the Sky," he ranted, pacing before her.

Adya looked around at the mess and shrugged. "Whenever I left home, I used to take my time and clean up everything. I'd sweep the floor and put every last tool away." She tried to fit a red-and-white piece of metal over an old moped, searching for a spot that seemed right. "Lately, every time I leave a place, it seems to blow up. At least you still have a city to repair."

Dsouza stayed on his back with his hands folded under his

head, counting clouds. Mohan, Priya, and Imral didn't seem worried either. Imral had already sent the Vayu troops back to Mysore to secure her throne.

Thamari wouldn't stop complaining. "Those who escaped will tell the field marshal of the British army that our gates are destroyed. He will know all our weaknesses. We will have to strengthen our defenses, rebuild our garrisons, replenish our supplies. It can't be done in time."

Eslandaran had her sky-blue coat on and was leaning against an outcropping of black rock. "We are alive. The rest is details." She tried to shove a silver diadem into one of her many pockets, but it wouldn't fit. "Kian, if you stop being such a grouch and just keep silent for once, I might actually consider marrying you, but if you keep this yammering up, I swear I won't be able to bear it."

Thamari's cheeks went red. He opened his mouth to speak, then snapped it shut.

Eslandaran gave up trying to stuff the diadem in a pocket and slapped it on her head. "I hadn't expected my aunt to step down so soon, but if becoming queen forces Kian to listen to me, it might be worth it." She smiled at Thamari before she turned to Adya. "And now that you have your sister back, where will the Mongoose and her siblings go next?"

Priya was trying to help attach some of the old Yamaha parts to the moped and finally found one that fit the puzzle. "We're going back to the jungle. We have lots of junk that needs fixing."

"We've got to get the cat home," Adya added.

371

Useless, against all odds and rationality, was perched on the moped's seat. He twitched his tail and yowled in complaint.

"He says he wants to go home, but only if I promise not to leave him alone with Adya again," Priya translated. "Insists she has terrible taste in music and never fed him treats properly." Priya tapped the moped until the metal stuck firmly.

"How that beast got through the spell wall is beyond me," Dsouza said.

Priya reached up to stroke her cat on the head. "He says his entire coat caught fire, but he has at least five lives left. He also insists it was Adya's fault. She should have taken him along. I quite agree."

Eslandaran took Thamari's arm in hers and leaned forward to examine the cat. "An excellent cat and an excellent plan. We hope to visit you there some day."

Thamari didn't seem convinced. "The rest of us don't have as many lives as that cat. The British won't rest after this loss. They'll set a far greater army upon us."

Dsouza got to his feet. "They may not find it worth the bother now that my sister rules Mysore. I suspect she'll be able to strike an alliance with the Atavi queen in less than a month." He waved a hand in Adya's direction. "Especially with the support of the princess of rust and gears. All of us coming together may be enough of a threat to make a deal worthwhile. And I might know an accomplished trader with excellent negotiation skills."

"And you'd have to travel a great deal to accomplish those talks, wouldn't you?" Adya asked. She wasn't sure how much she liked the title the maharaja had given her. "Princess of rust and gears" had been intended as an insult, but it sounded somehow right. The promise of seeing Dsouza regularly was enough to put up with his teasing.

Dsouza took her face in his hands. He flashed his half smile. "Oh, I'd have to brave the jungle constantly. The travel would be endless. I'll be starved for food and conversation."

Adya put her forehead against Dsouza's and slid an arm around him. "Then I think you'd be excellent." She would finally get him all to herself and not have to worry about an ogre or troll crushing him.

"And when the British return for more than negotiations?" Thamari demanded. "When they come down upon us with the full force of their giants, what then?"

Adya had given this more thought than she'd admit. She reluctantly let go of Dsouza and walked to the edge of the mountain. "We'll have to fight together." She thought of the terrible jets she'd seen in Mysore and shivered. "And if we need reinforcements, if we need more power, I have an idea where we can find it."

Dsouza joined her, looking down on the forests and the ruins of the battlefield. "Things get dangerous when you have that look in your eye."

Eslandaran's smile faded as if the weight of being a queen was finally settling upon her. "Great danger often requires risk. Who are you planning on recruiting?"

Adya took a deep breath. Priya and Mohan were both safe. The stories her father had told her had turned out to be true.

Who said they couldn't recruit more allies? She thought back to a time long ago, when she and her mother had been alone in the jungle.

"The yakshas," she said. The word hung in the air like a thunderstorm.

Mohan shook his head in disbelief. "And you say *I* have the crazy plans?" He turned to stare off into the distance. "Somehow, though, I think you're right. The British are going to come after us. We're going to need a plan no one has ever tried before, something straight out of a storybook."

Adya ran a hand through Mohan's thick curls. "They may come, but before that, I've got one important thing planned."

Priya raised an eyebrow. "And what would that be?"

Adya wrapped her sister in a hug. Sparks and fire shot deep through her soul.

"Bad Day and I are cooking dinner together—for everyone."

ACKNOWLEDGMENTS

I've always wanted to have my own books on a library shelf that readers in need of a story could find and treasure. My sincere thanks to all those who made this, my first, possible.

To my truly wonderful agent, Jennifer Azantian, who took a chance on a new writer with a rough manuscript—may your inbox always be full of good news.

To Alyza Liu, my brilliant editor, who saw promise in the story and who has the patience of a saint—may you always have amazing stories to choose from and never lose your favorite stationery.

To all my writer friends who read the first draft of this and helped me along: Kimberly, Angie, Jen T., McKenzie, Jason W., Jason S., and Jason H. (all my male writer friends are named Jason for some reason).

A shout-out to my family, Veena, Malini, and Mohan, who always see me writing and think, *That goofball—we love him anyway!*

And a big thanks to the amazing team at Simon & Schuster: the people who worked on the magnificent cover, the eagle-eyed copyeditors, and the insightful marketers and publicists who fought to get this story into readers' hands.

To all of you—a deep bow of appreciation from me!